LOIS
LANE
and the
FRIENDSHIP
CHAL

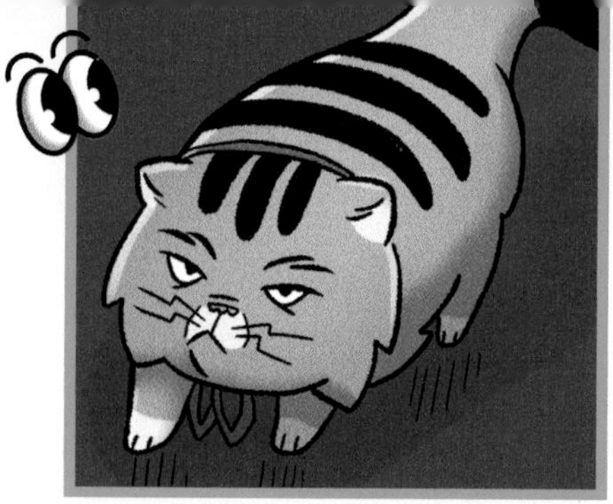

written by

GRACE ELLIS

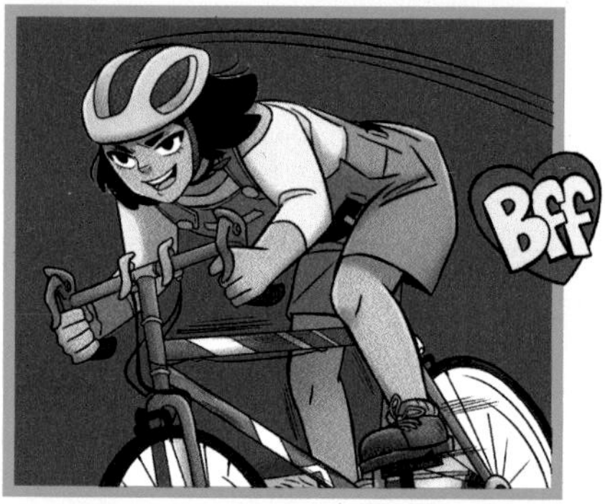
Bff

illustrated by

BRITTNEY WILLIAMS

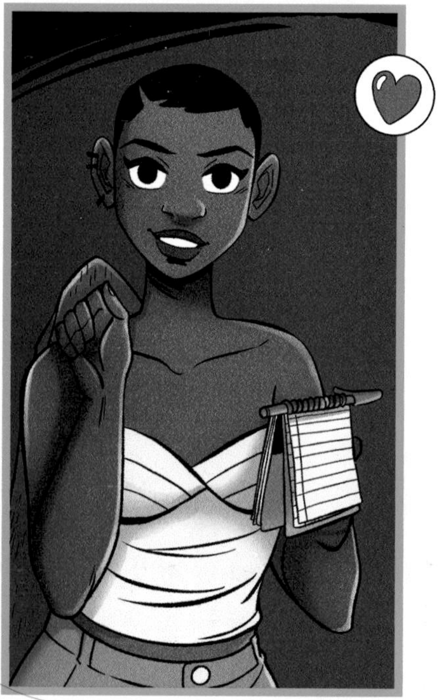

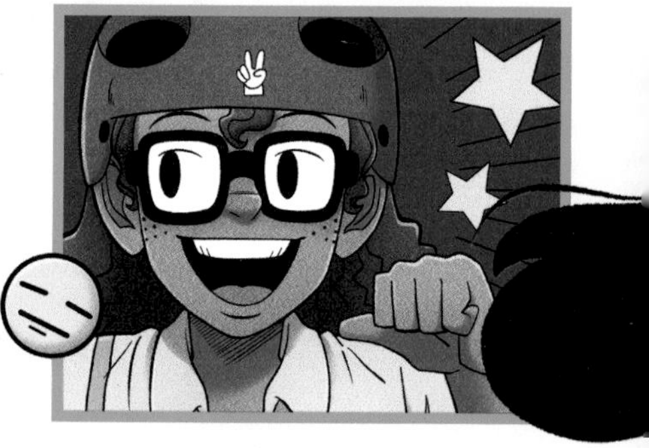

colored by

CAITLIN QUIRK

lettered by

ARIANA MAHER

LOIS LANE

and the FRIENDSHIP CHALLENGE

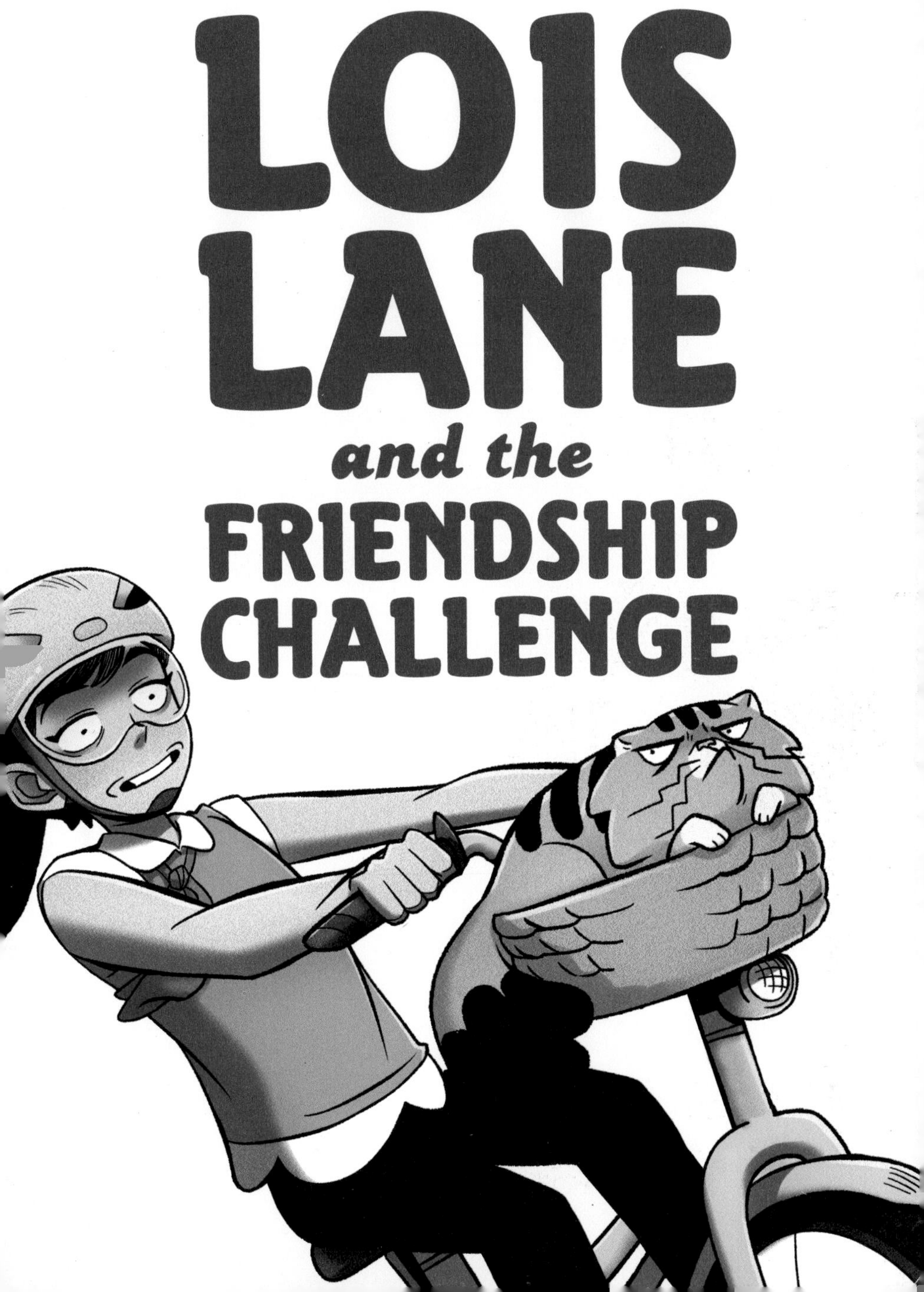

SARA MILLER Editor
STEVE COOK Design Director – Books
AMIE BROCKWAY-METCALF Publication Design

BOB HARRAS Senior VP – Editor-in-Chief, DC Comics
MICHELE R. WELLS VP & Executive Editor, Young Reader

DAN DiDIO Publisher
JIM LEE Publisher & Chief Creative Officer
BOBBIE CHASE VP – New Publishing Initiatives
DON FALLETTI VP – Manufacturing Operations & Workflow Management
LAWRENCE GANEM VP – Talent Services
ALISON GILL Senior VP – Manufacturing & Operations
HANK KANALZ Senior VP – Publishing Strategy & Support Services
DAN MIRON VP – Publishing Operations
NICK J. NAPOLITANO VP – Manufacturing Administration & Design
NANCY SPEARS VP – Sales
JONAH WEILAND VP – Marketing & Creative Services

LOIS LANE AND THE FRIENDSHIP CHALLENGE

Published by DC Comics. Copyright © 2020
DC Comics. All Rights Reserved. All characters,
their distinctive likenesses, and related elements
featured in this publication are trademarks
of DC Comics. The stories, characters, and
incidents featured in this publication are entirely
fictional. DC Comics does not read or accept
unsolicited submissions of ideas, stories, or
artwork. DC - a WarnerMedia Company.

DC Comics, 2900 West Alameda Ave.,
Burbank, CA 91505
Printed by LSC Communications,
Crawfordsville, IN, USA. 7/3/20.
First Printing.
ISBN: 978-1-4012-9637-7

PEFC Certified
This product is from
sustainably managed
forests and controlled
sources
PEFC
PEFC/29-31-337   www.pefc.org

Library of Congress Cataloging-in-Publication Data
Names: Ellis, Grace, author. | Williams, Brittney, 1989- illustrator. |
   Quirk, Caitlin, colourist. | Maher, Ariana, letterer.
Title: Lois Lane and the friendship challenge / Grace Ellis, author ;
   Brittney Williams, illustrator ; Caitlin Quirk, colorist ; Ariana Maher,
   letterer.
Description: Burbank, CA : DC Comics, [2020] | Audience: Ages 8-12 |
   Audience: Grades 4-6 | Summary: Lois Lane and her friend Kristen want to
   promote their friendship video channel at the big neighborhood barbecue
   and bike race but when the fireworks go missing and a new girl takes up
   all of Kristen's attention, Lois tries to face her challenges and still
   celebrate the summer.
Identifiers: LCCN 2020002168 | ISBN 9781401296377 (trade paperback)
Subjects: LCSH: Graphic novels. | CYAC: Graphic novels. | Internet
   videos--Fiction. | Friendship--Fiction.
Classification: LCC PZ7.7.E447 Lo 2020 | DDC 741.5/973--dc23

TABLE OF CONTENTS

CHAPTER 1
getting along famously 6

CHAPTER 2
thick as thieves 30

CHAPTER 3
nerds of a feather 52

CHAPTER 4
moving in the same circles 82

CHAPTER 5
all's well that friends well 106

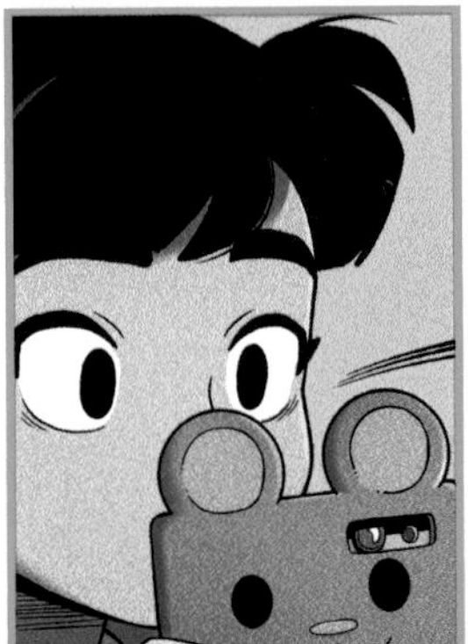

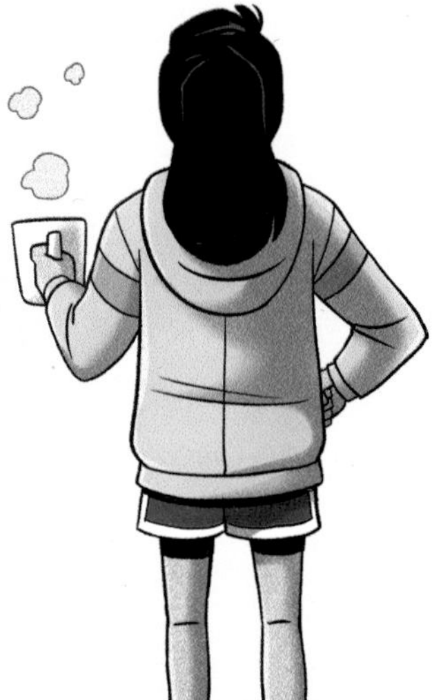

CHAPTER 1

getting along famously

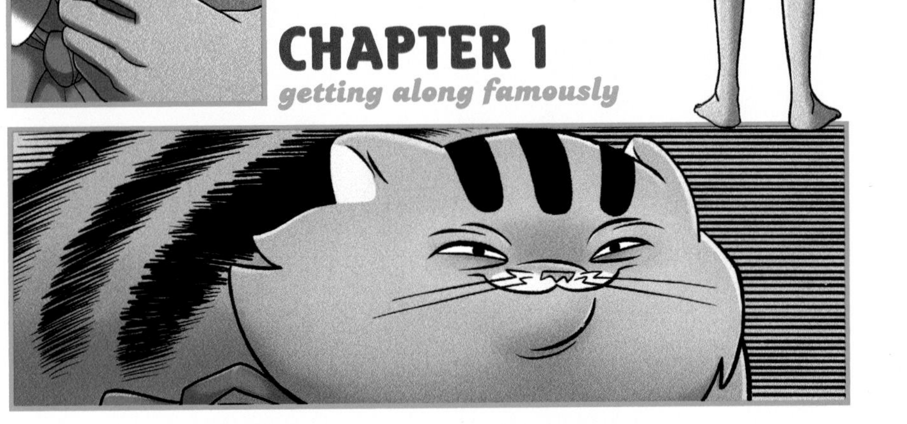

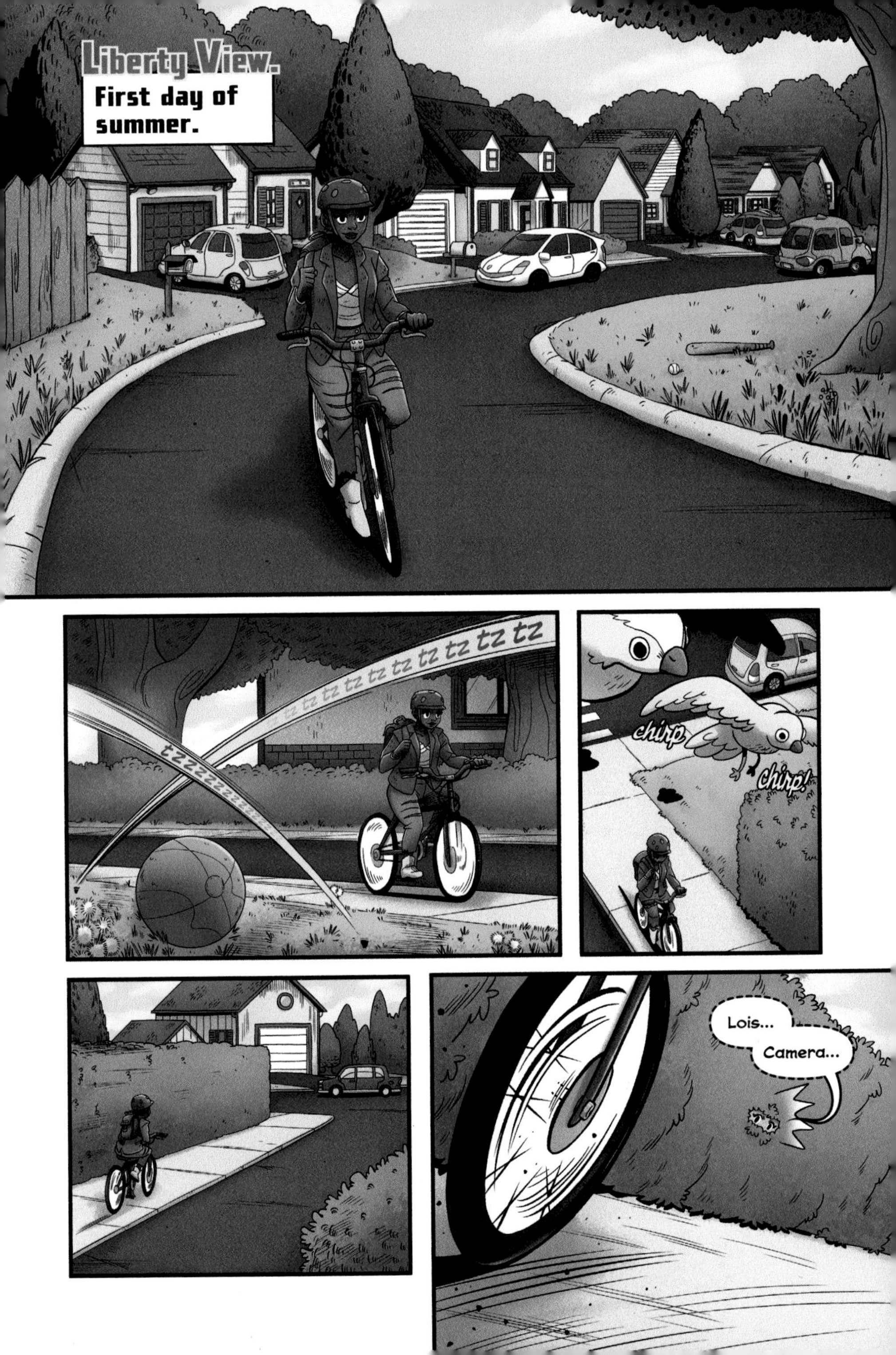
Liberty View.
First day of summer.
tz tz tz tz tz tz tz tz tz tz
tzzzzzzzzzz
chirp
chirp!
Lois...
Camera...

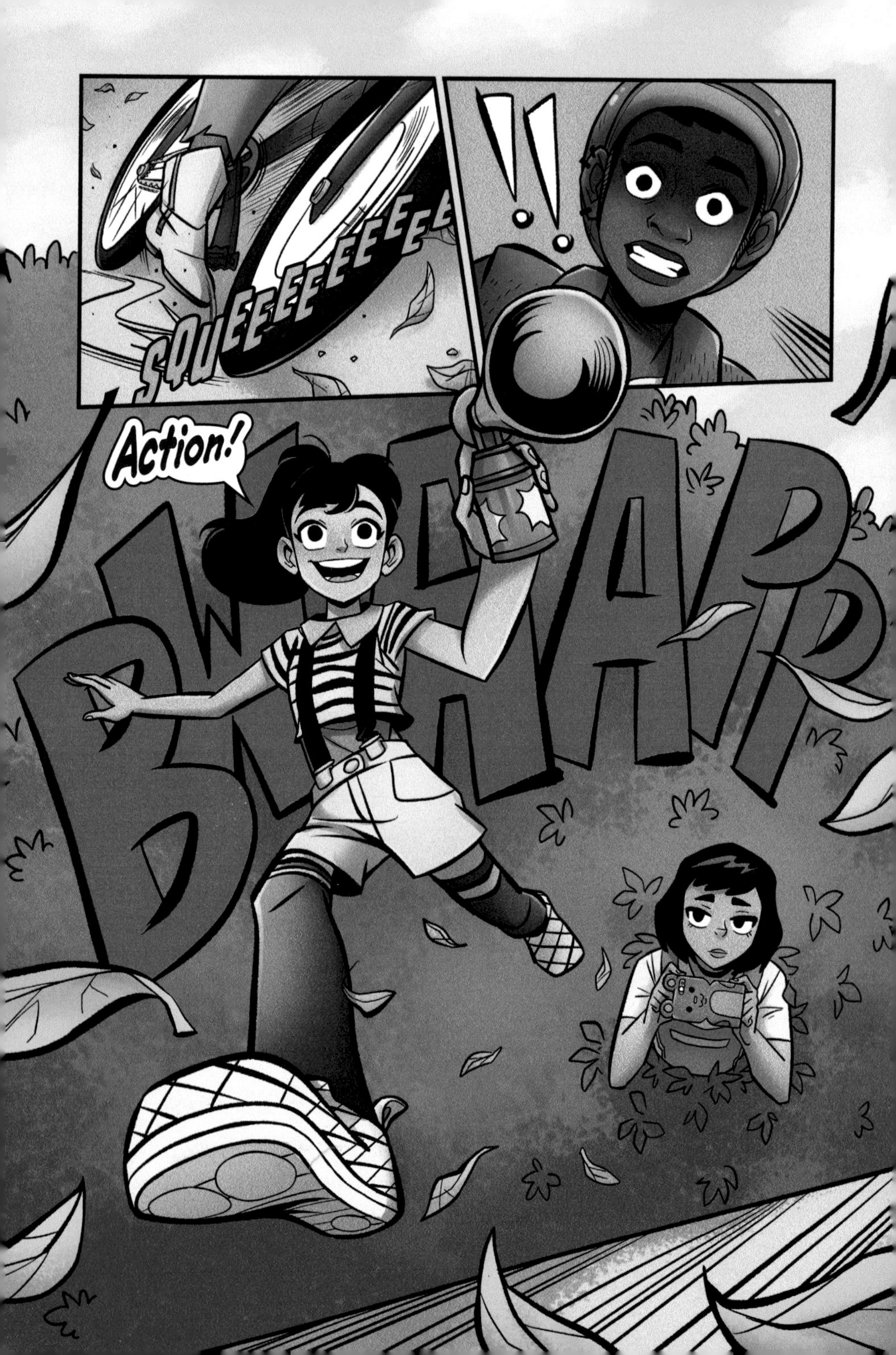
SQUEEEEEEEEEEEE
!!
Action!
BWAAR

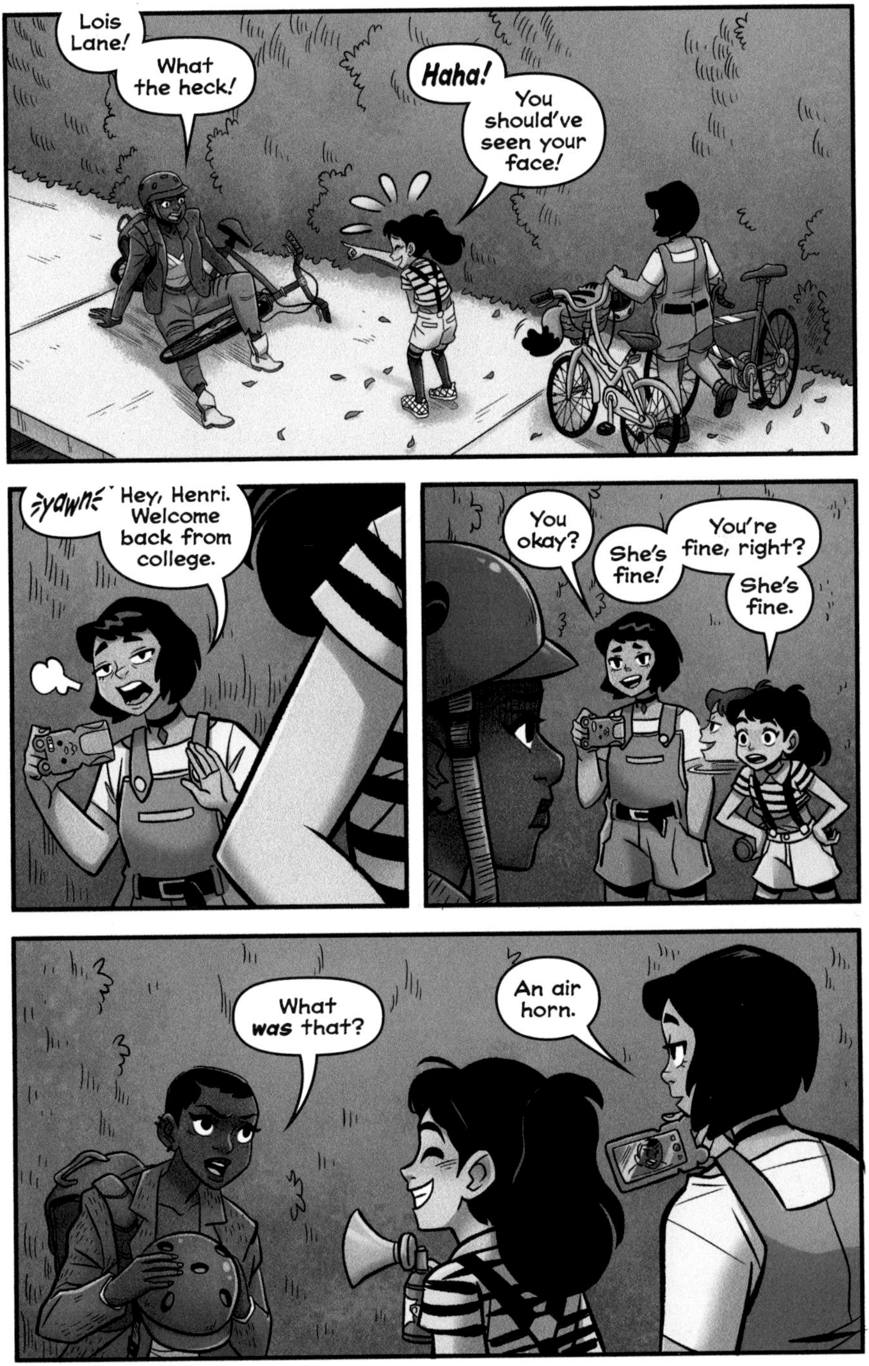
Lois Lane!
What the heck!
Haha!
You should've seen your face!
yawn Hey, Henri. Welcome back from college.
You okay?
She's fine!
You're fine, right?
She's fine.
What *was* that?
An air horn.

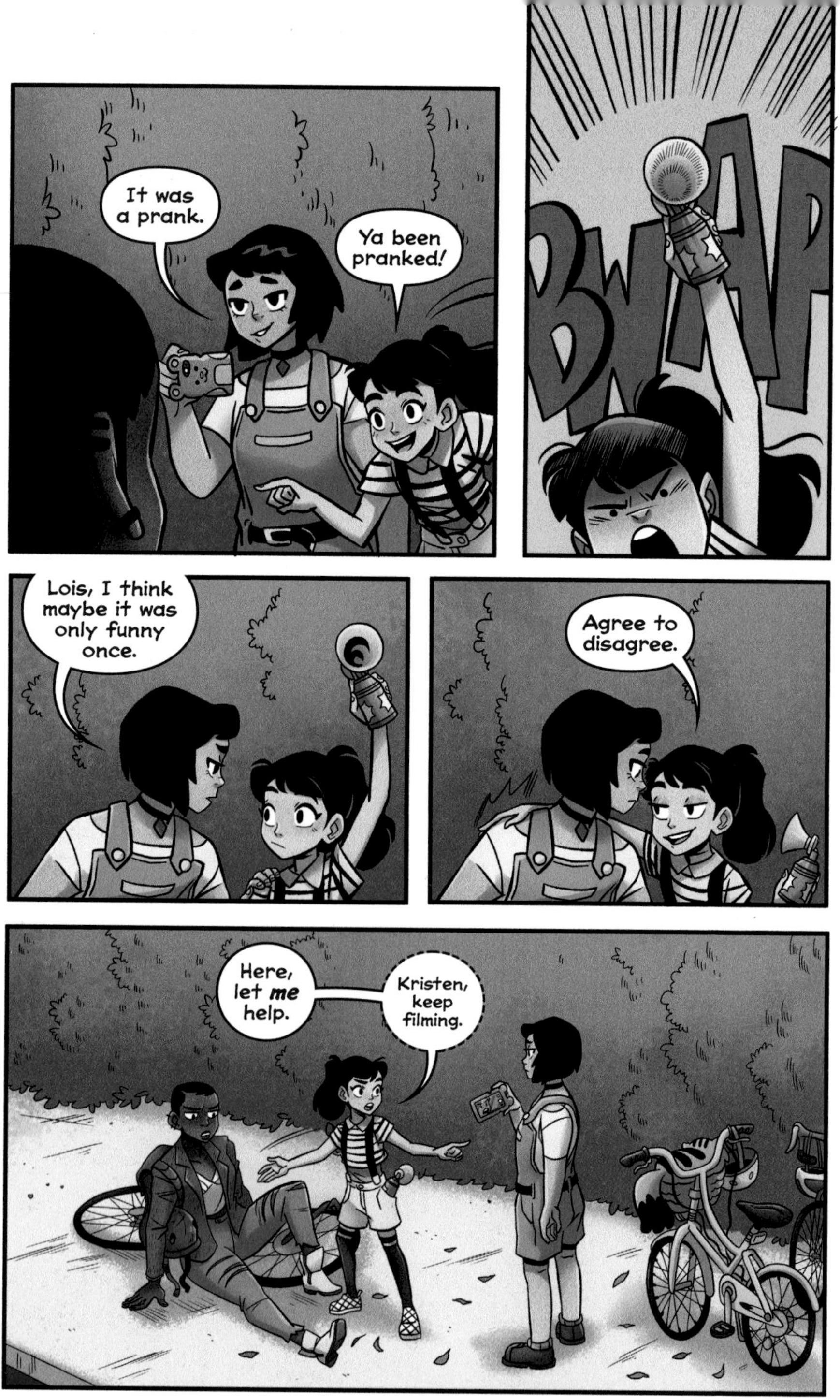

It was a prank.
Ya been pranked!
BWAP
Lois, I think maybe it was only funny once.
Agree to disagree.
Here, let *me* help.
Kristen, keep filming.

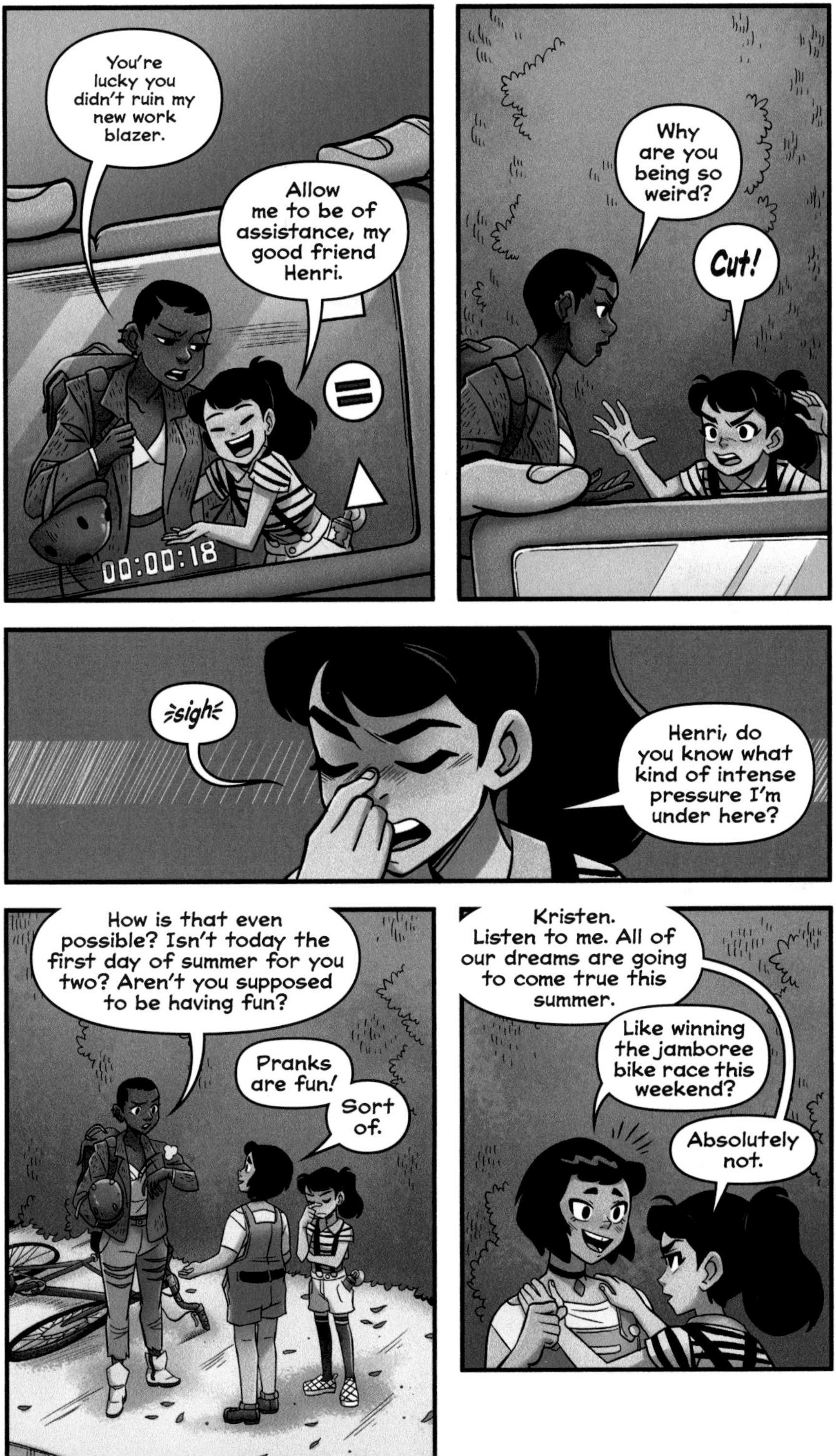
You're lucky you didn't ruin my new work blazer.
Allow me to be of assistance, my good friend Henri.
00:00:18
Why are you being so weird?
Cut!
sigh
Henri, do you know what kind of intense pressure I'm under here?
How is that even possible? Isn't today the first day of summer for you two? Aren't you supposed to be having fun?
Pranks are fun!
Sort of.
Kristen. Listen to me. All of our dreams are going to come true this summer.
Like winning the jamboree bike race this weekend?
Absolutely not.

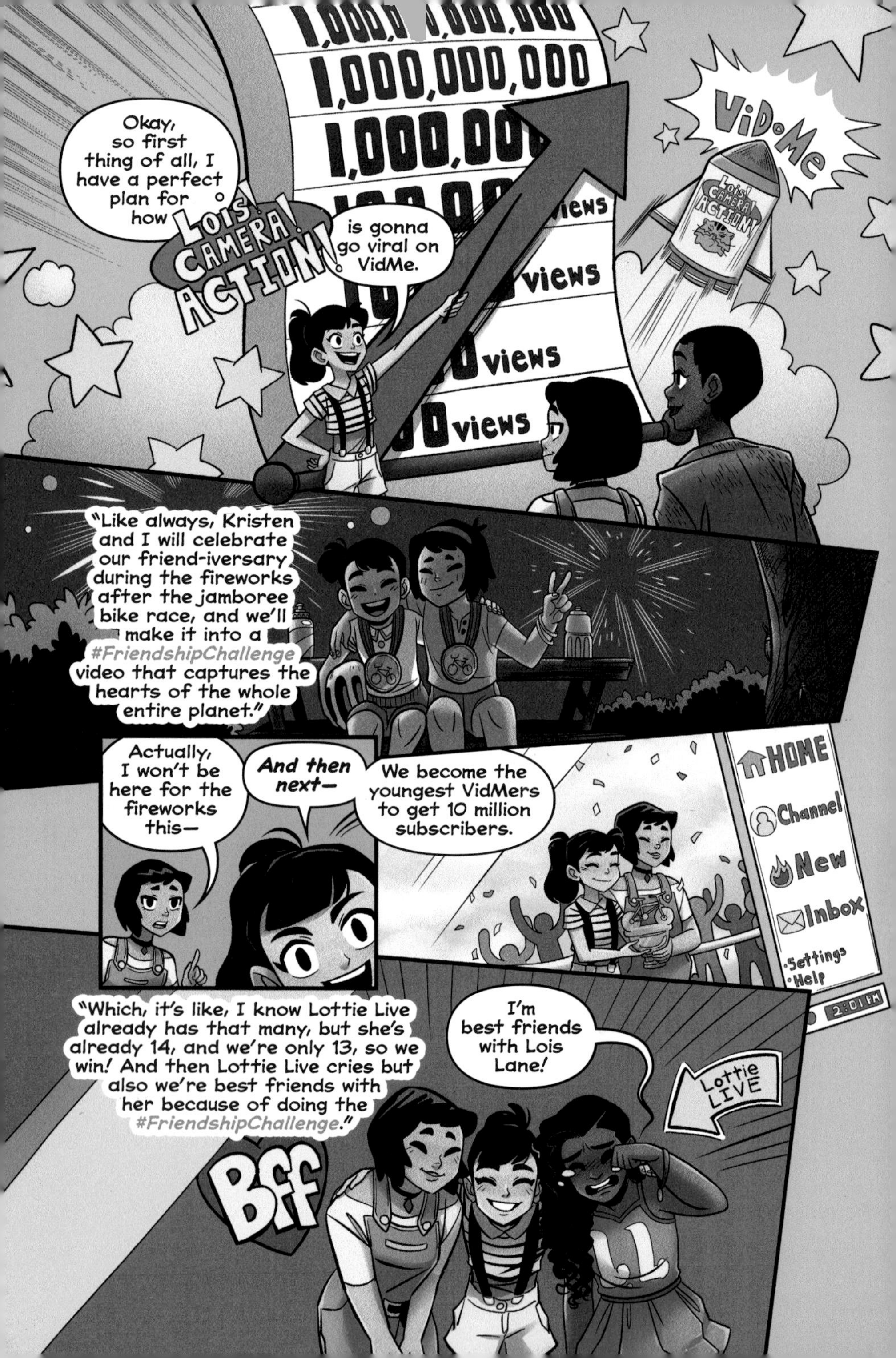
1,000,000,000
Okay, so first thing of all, I have a perfect plan for how
LOIS! CAMERA! ACTION!
is gonna go viral on VidMe.
views
views
views
views
VID•ME
Lois! CAMERA! ACTION!
"Like always, Kristen and I will celebrate our friend-iversary during the fireworks after the jamboree bike race, and we'll make it into a #FriendshipChallenge video that captures the hearts of the whole entire planet."
Actually, I won't be here for the fireworks this—
And then next—
We become the youngest VidMers to get 10 million subscribers.
HOME
Channel
New
Inbox
•Settings
•Help
2:01 PM
"Which, it's like, I know Lottie Live already has that many, but she's already 14, and we're only 13, so we win! And then Lottie Live cries but also we're best friends with her because of doing the #FriendshipChallenge."
I'm best friends with Lois Lane!
Lottie LIVE
BFF

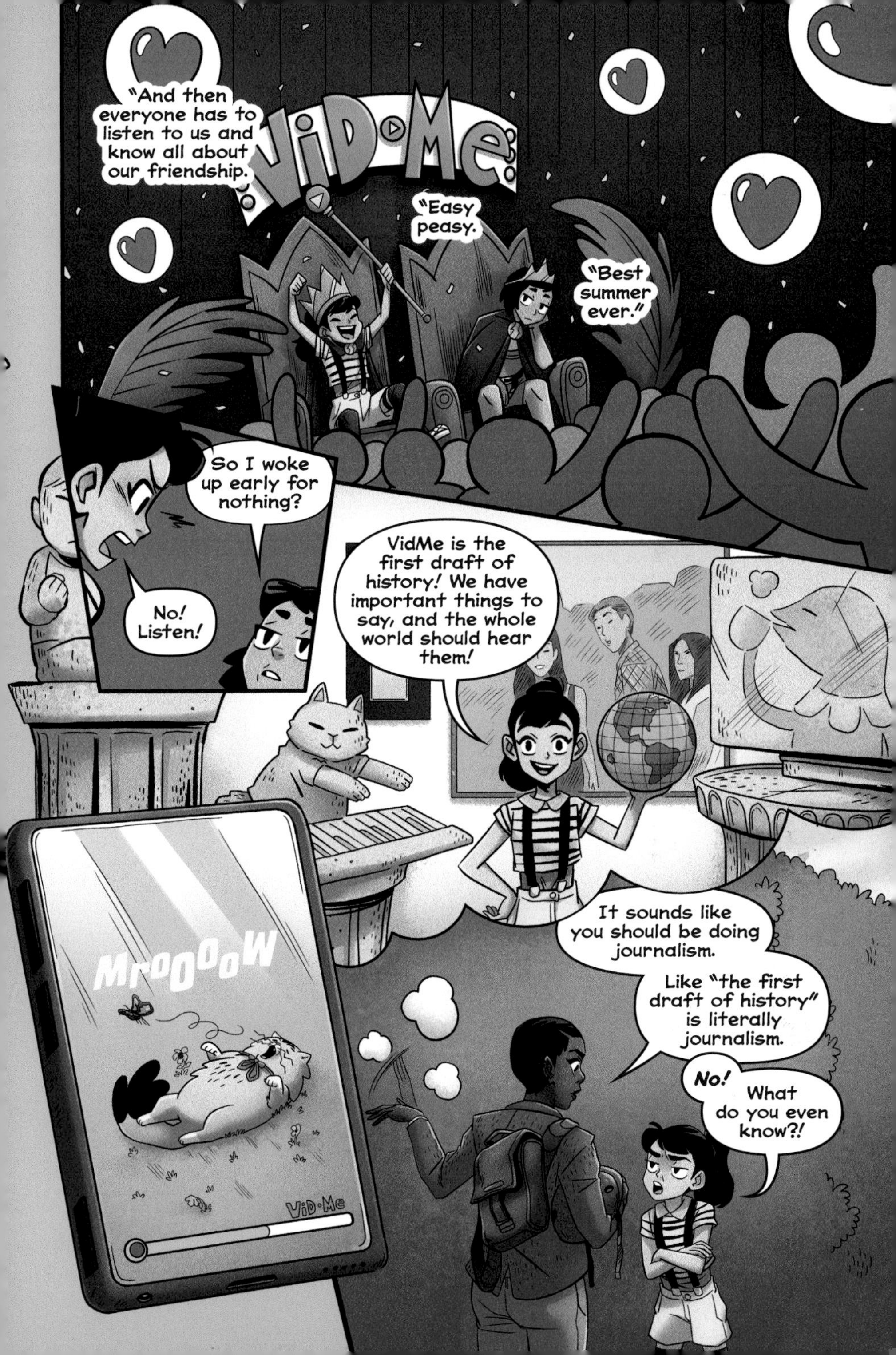
"And then everyone has to listen to us and know all about our friendship.
ViD·Me
"Easy peasy.
"Best summer ever."
So I woke up early for nothing?
No! Listen!
VidMe is the first draft of history! We have important things to say, and the whole world should hear them!
MrOOOoW
ViD·Me
It sounds like you should be doing journalism.
Like "the first draft of history" is literally journalism.
No! What do you even know?!

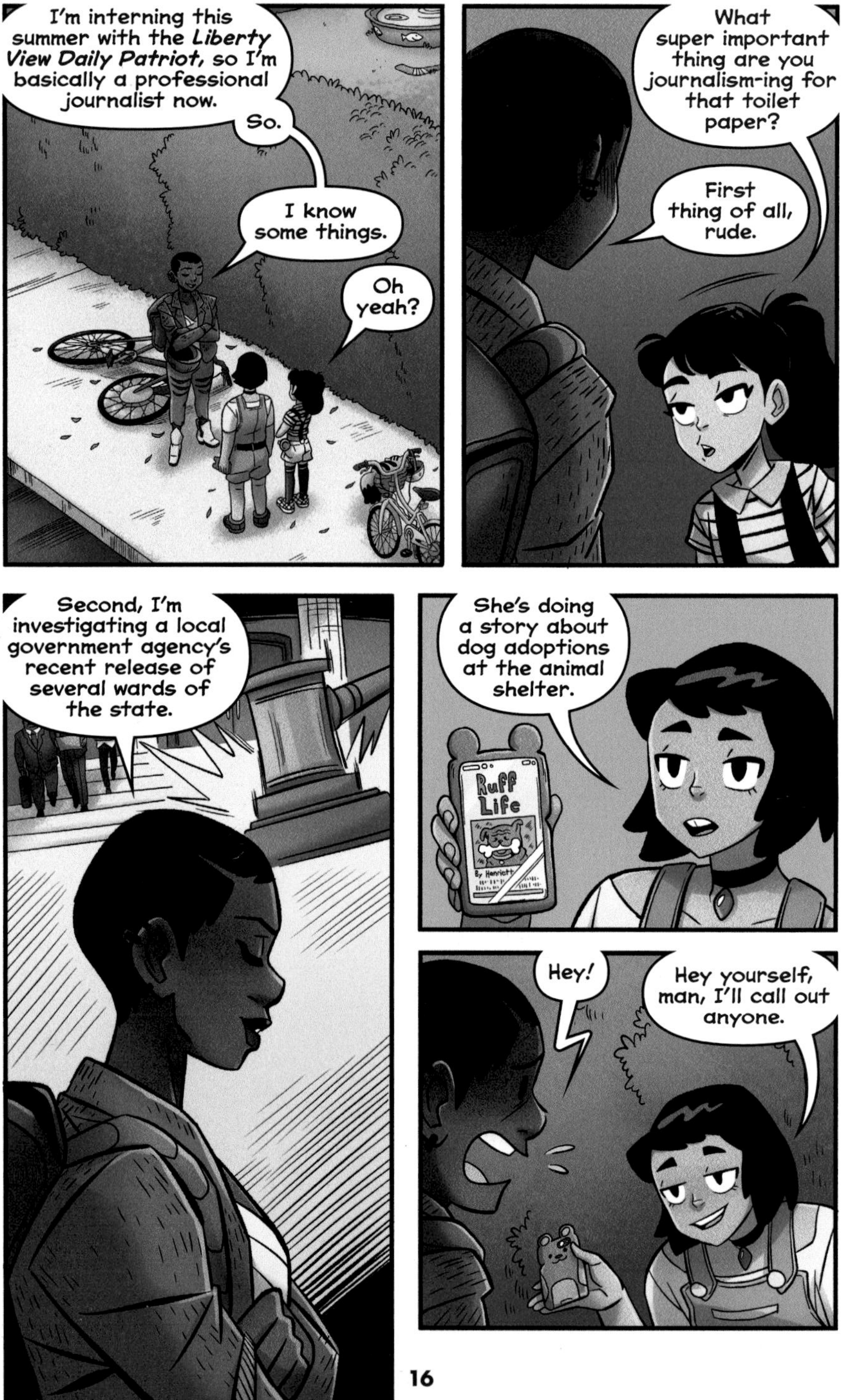
I'm interning this summer with the *Liberty View Daily Patriot,* so I'm basically a professional journalist now.
So.
I know some things.
Oh yeah?
What super important thing are you journalism-ing for that toilet paper?
First thing of all, rude.
Second, I'm investigating a local government agency's recent release of several wards of the state.
She's doing a story about dog adoptions at the animal shelter.
Ruff Life
Hey!
Hey yourself, man, I'll call out anyone.

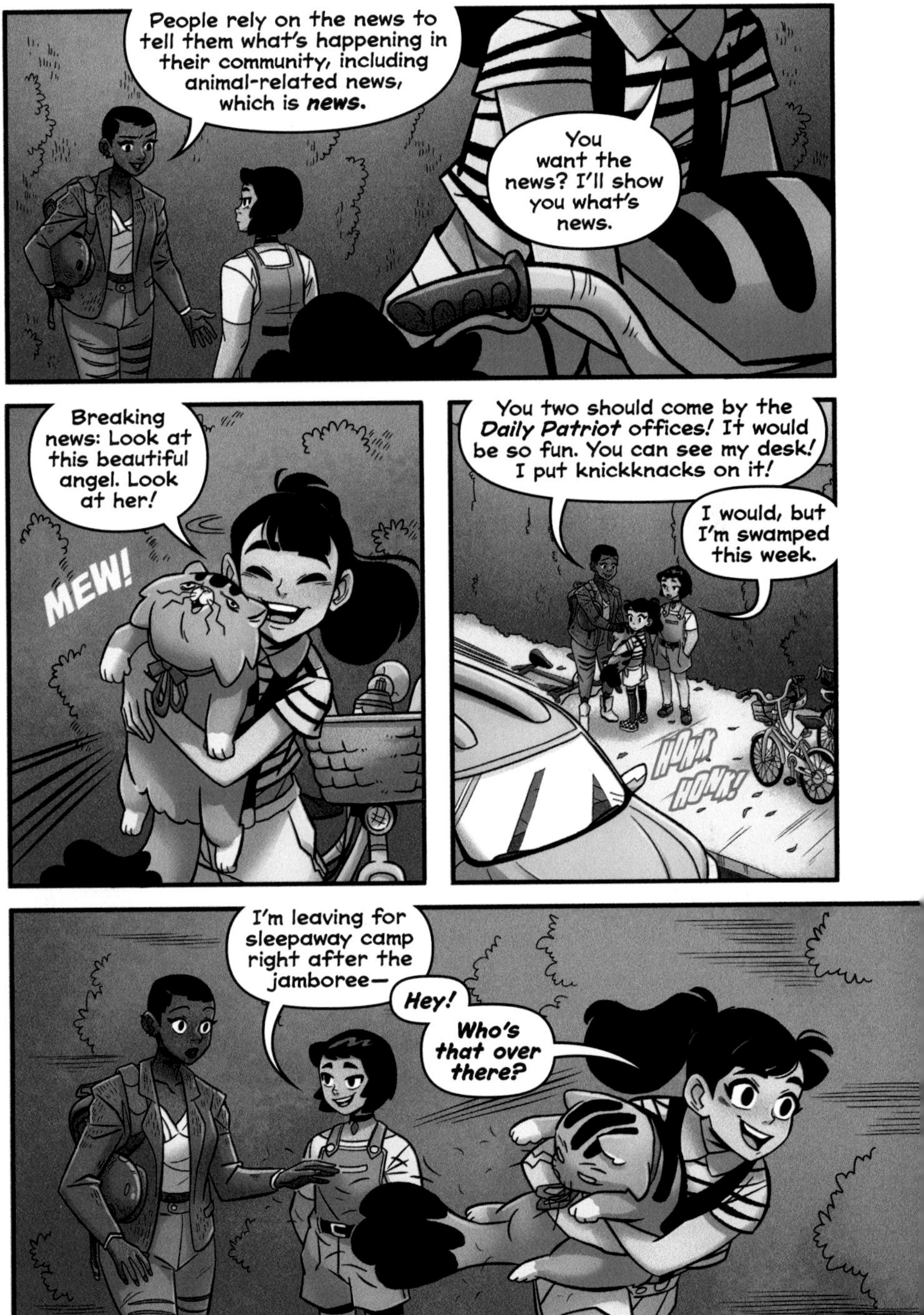

People rely on the news to tell them what's happening in their community, including animal-related news, which is *news.*
You want the news? I'll show you what's news.
Breaking news: Look at this beautiful angel. Look at her!
MEW!
You two should come by the *Daily Patriot* offices! It would be so fun. You can see my desk! I put knickknacks on it!
I would, but I'm swamped this week.
HONK HONK!
I'm leaving for sleepaway camp right after the jamboree—
Hey!
Who's that over there?

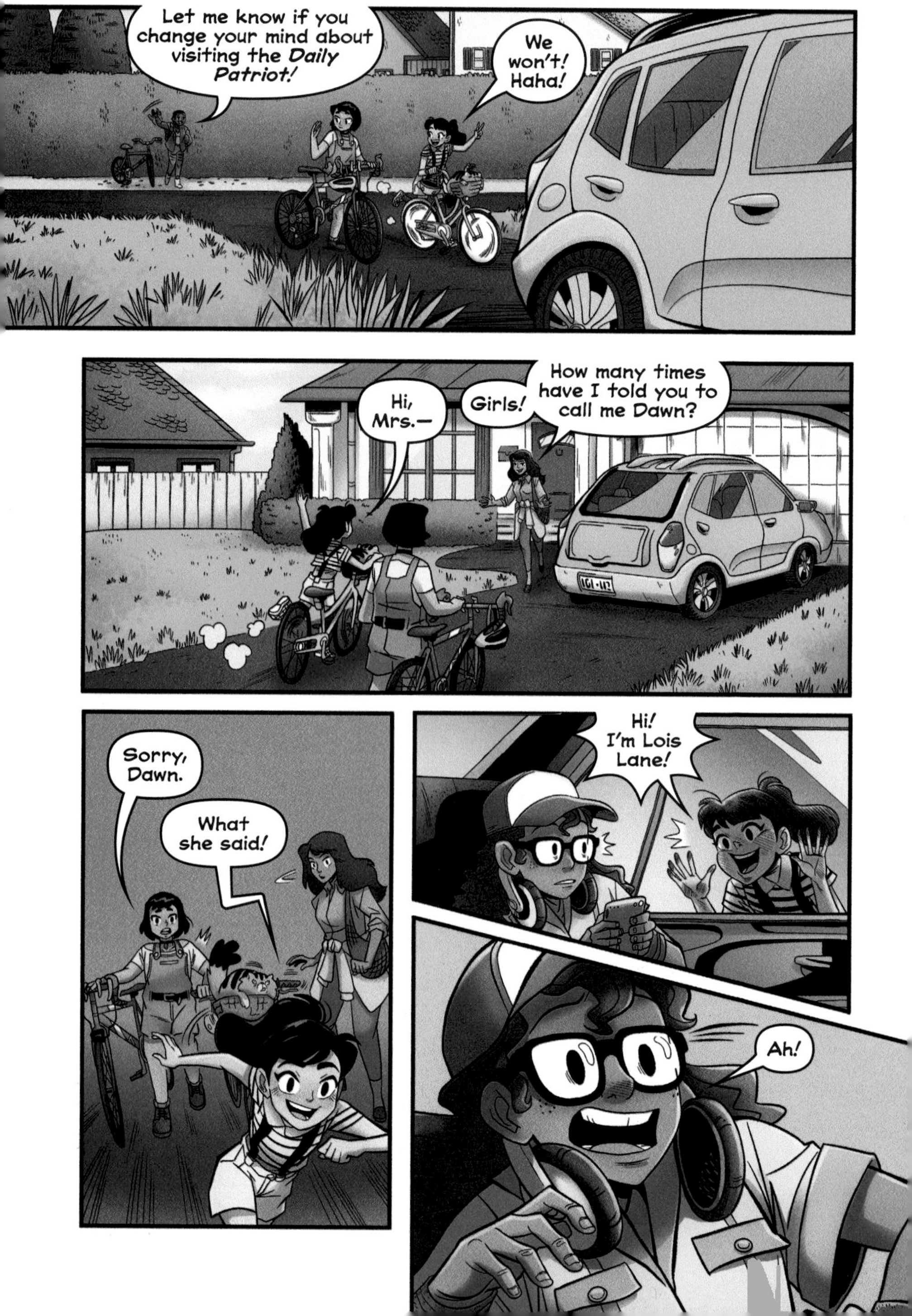
Let me know if you change your mind about visiting the *Daily Patriot!*
We won't! Haha!
Hi, Mrs.—
Girls!
How many times have I told you to call me Dawn?
Sorry, Dawn.
What she said!
Hi! I'm Lois Lane!
Ah!

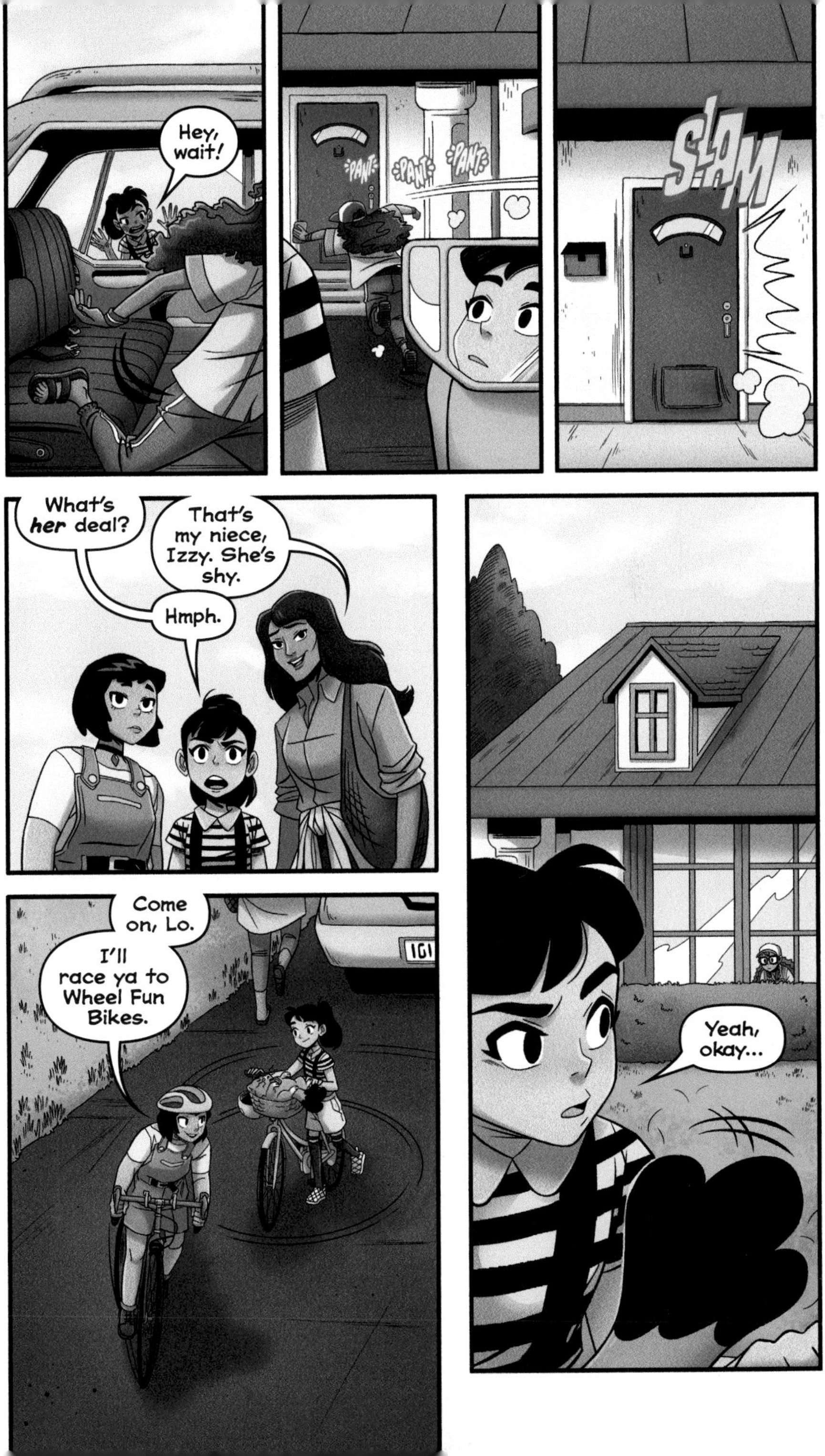

Hey, wait!
PANT
PANT
PANT
SLAM
What's *her* deal?
That's my niece, Izzy. She's shy.
Hmph.
Yeah, okay...
Come on, Lo.
I'll race ya to Wheel Fun Bikes.

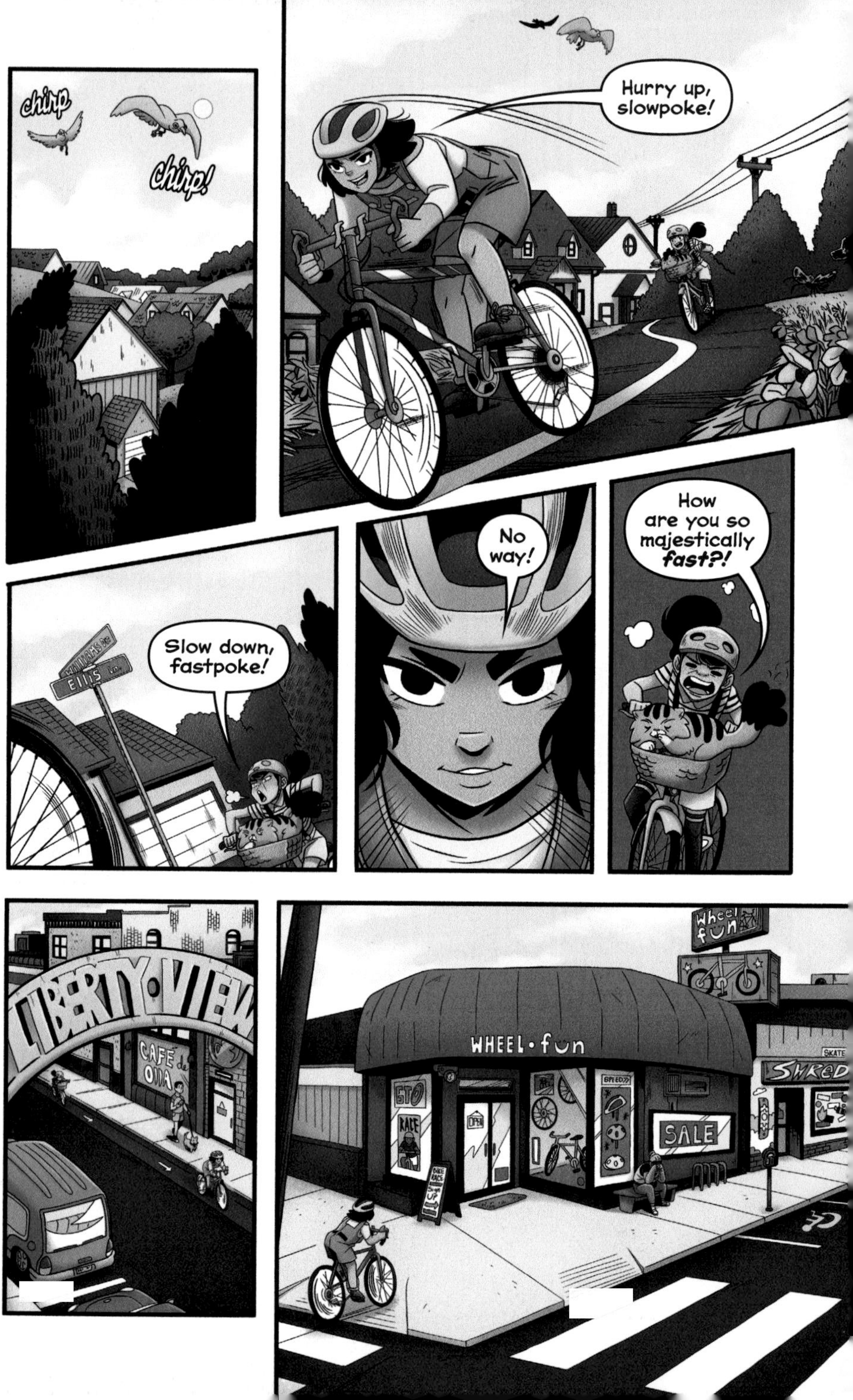
chirp
chirp!
Hurry up, slowpoke!
Ellis Ln.
Slow down, fastpoke!
No way!
How are you so majestically fast?!
LIBERTY VIEW
WHEEL • fun
SALE
SKATE
SHRED

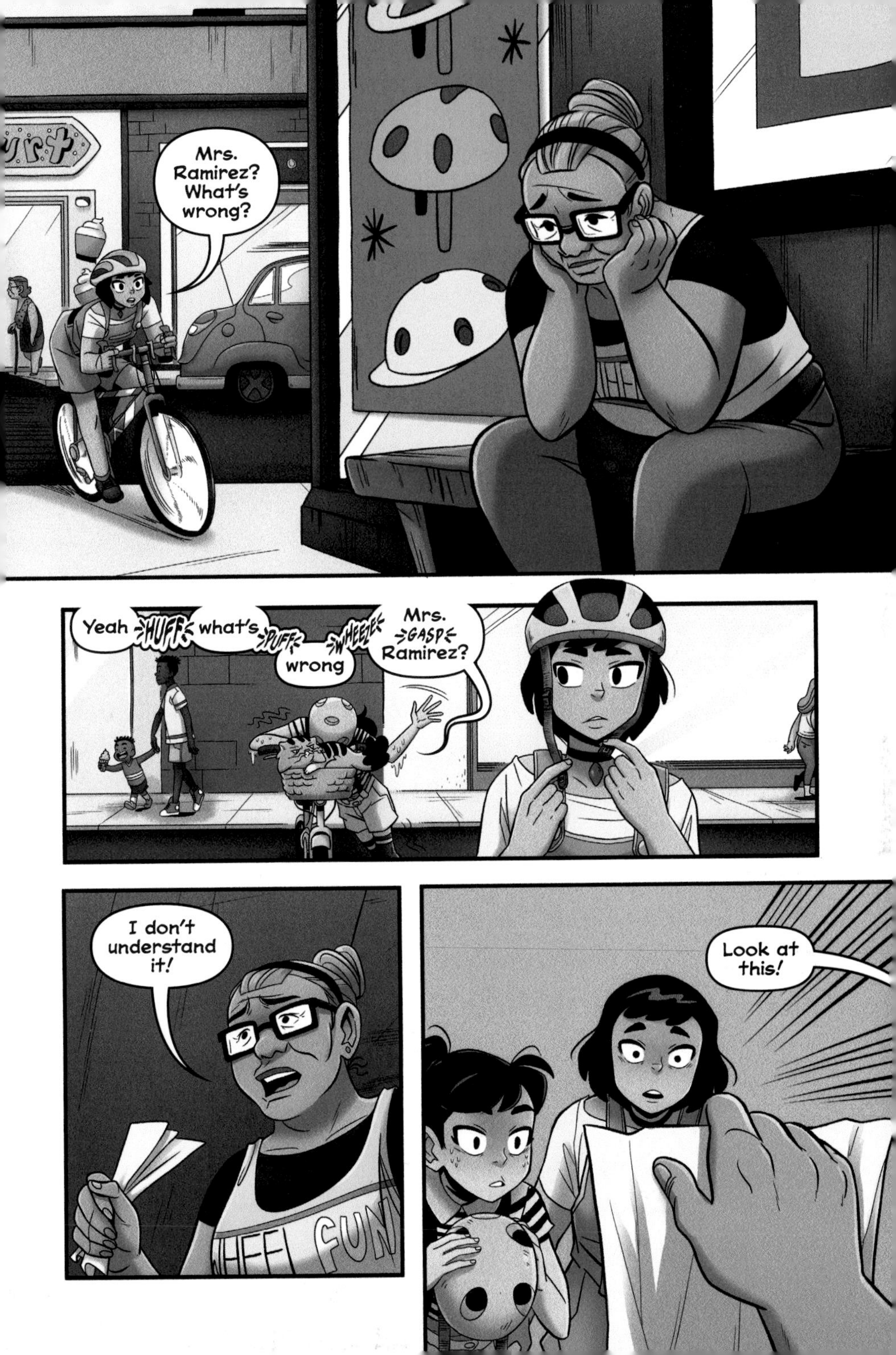
Mrs. Ramirez? What's wrong?
Yeah
HUFF
what's
PUFF
wrong
WHEEZE
Mrs.
GASP
Ramirez?
I don't understand it!
WHEEL FUN
Look at this!

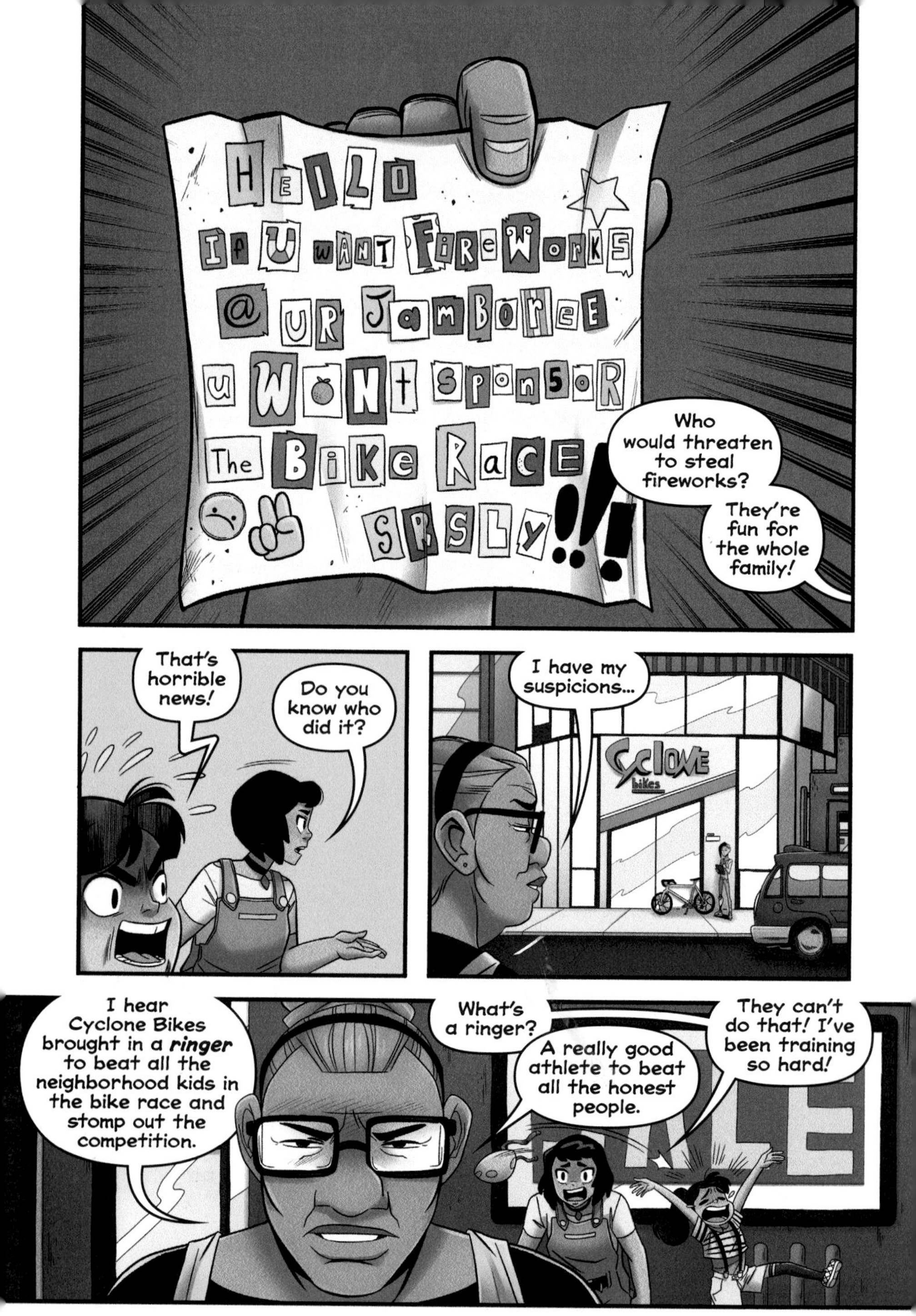
HELLO
IF U WANT FIREWORKS
@ UR JAMBOREE
U WONT SPON5OR
THE BIKE RACE
SRSLY!!!
Who would threaten to steal fireworks?
They're fun for the whole family!
That's horrible news!
Do you know who did it?
I have my suspicions...
CYCLONE bikes
I hear Cyclone Bikes brought in a *ringer* to beat all the neighborhood kids in the bike race and stomp out the competition.
What's a ringer?
A really good athlete to beat all the honest people.
They can't do that! I've been training so hard!

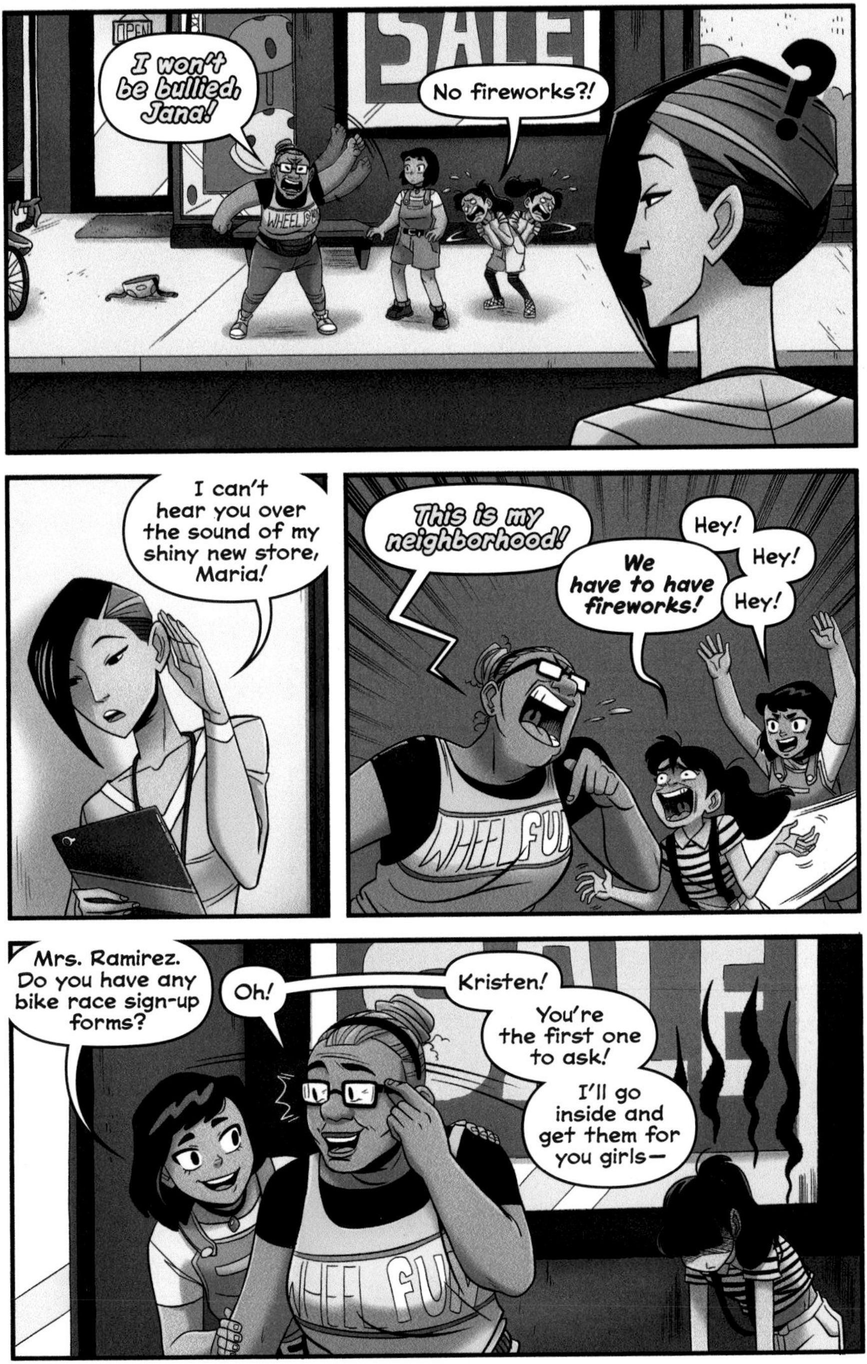
I won't be bullied, Jana!
No fireworks?!
?
OPEN
SALE
I can't hear you over the sound of my shiny new store, Maria!
This is my neighborhood!
We have to have fireworks!
Hey!
Hey!
Hey!
WHEEL FUN
Mrs. Ramirez. Do you have any bike race sign-up forms?
Oh!
Kristen!
You're the first one to ask!
I'll go inside and get them for you girls—

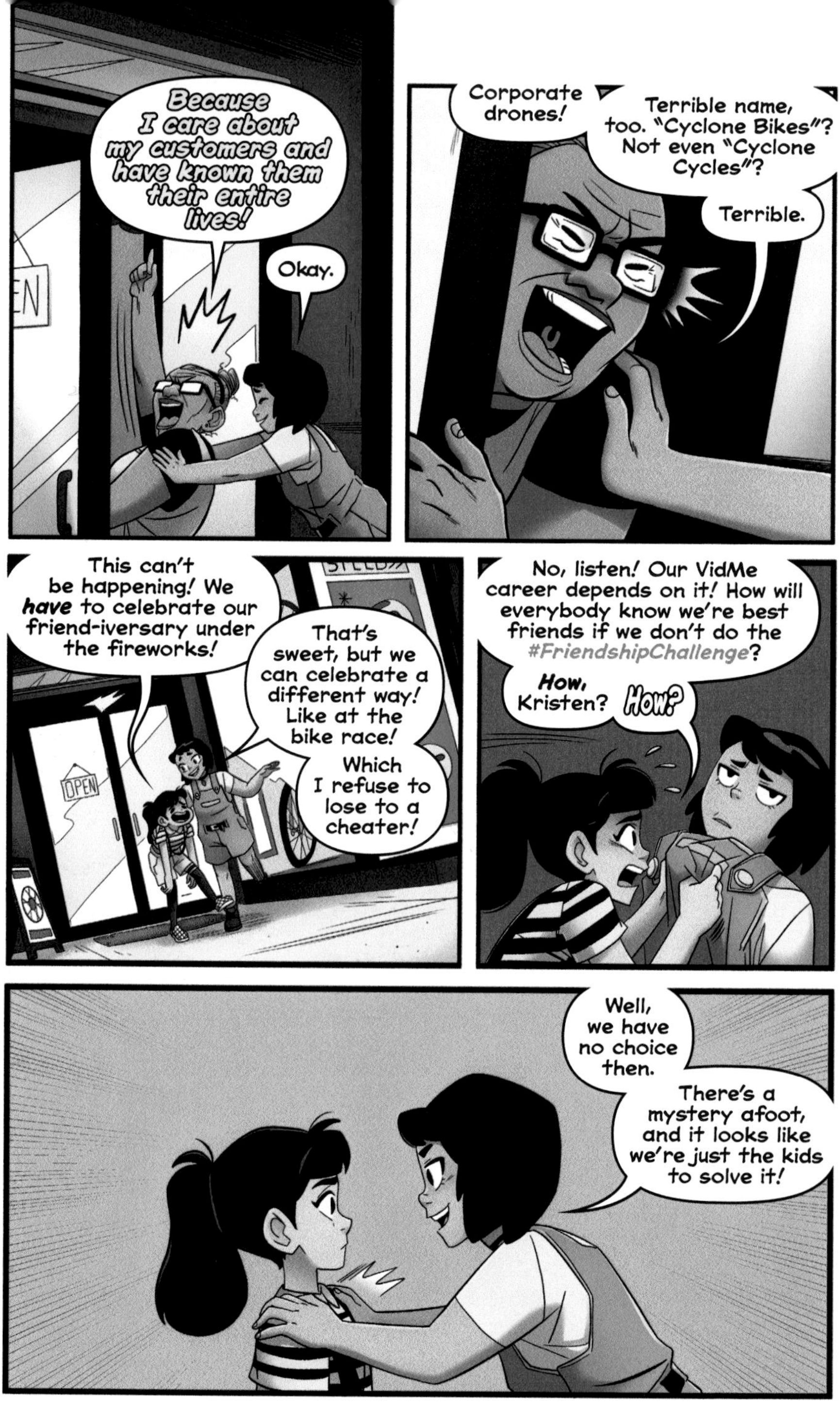

Because I care about my customers and have known them their entire lives!
Okay.
Corporate drones!
Terrible name, too. "Cyclone Bikes"? Not even "Cyclone Cycles"?
Terrible.
This can't be happening! We have to celebrate our friend-iversary under the fireworks!
That's sweet, but we can celebrate a different way! Like at the bike race!
Which I refuse to lose to a cheater!
OPEN
No, listen! Our VidMe career depends on it! How will everybody know we're best friends if we don't do the #FriendshipChallenge?
How, Kristen?
How?
Well, we have no choice then.
There's a mystery afoot, and it looks like we're just the kids to solve it!

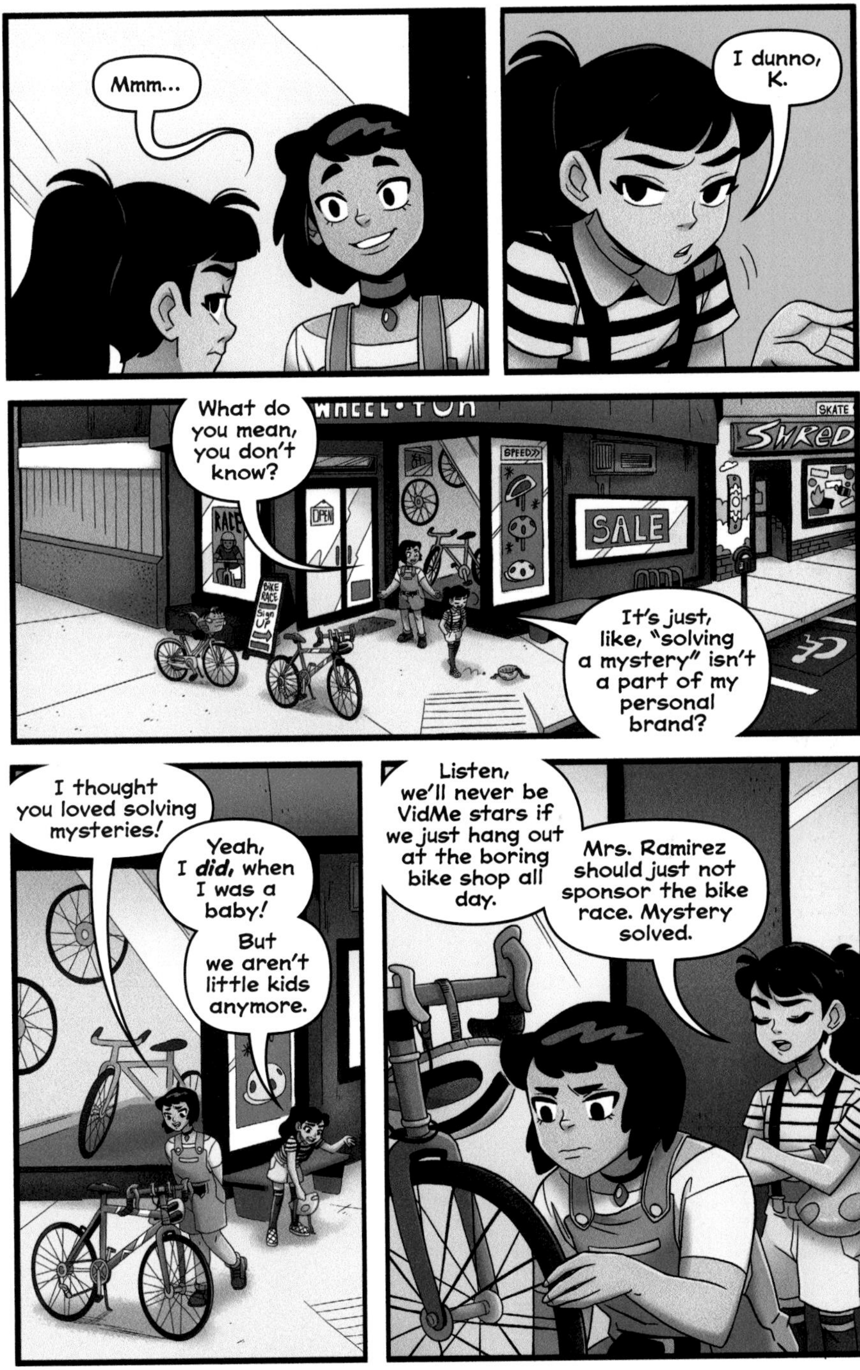
Mmm...
I dunno, K.
What do you mean, you don't know?
WHEEL•FUN
SKATE
SHRED
SPEED
OPEN
RACE
SALE
BIKE RACE Sign UP
It's just, like, "solving a mystery" isn't a part of my personal brand?
I thought you loved solving mysteries!
Yeah, I *did*, when I was a baby!
But we aren't little kids anymore.
Listen, we'll never be VidMe stars if we just hang out at the boring bike shop all day.
Mrs. Ramirez should just not sponsor the bike race. Mystery solved.

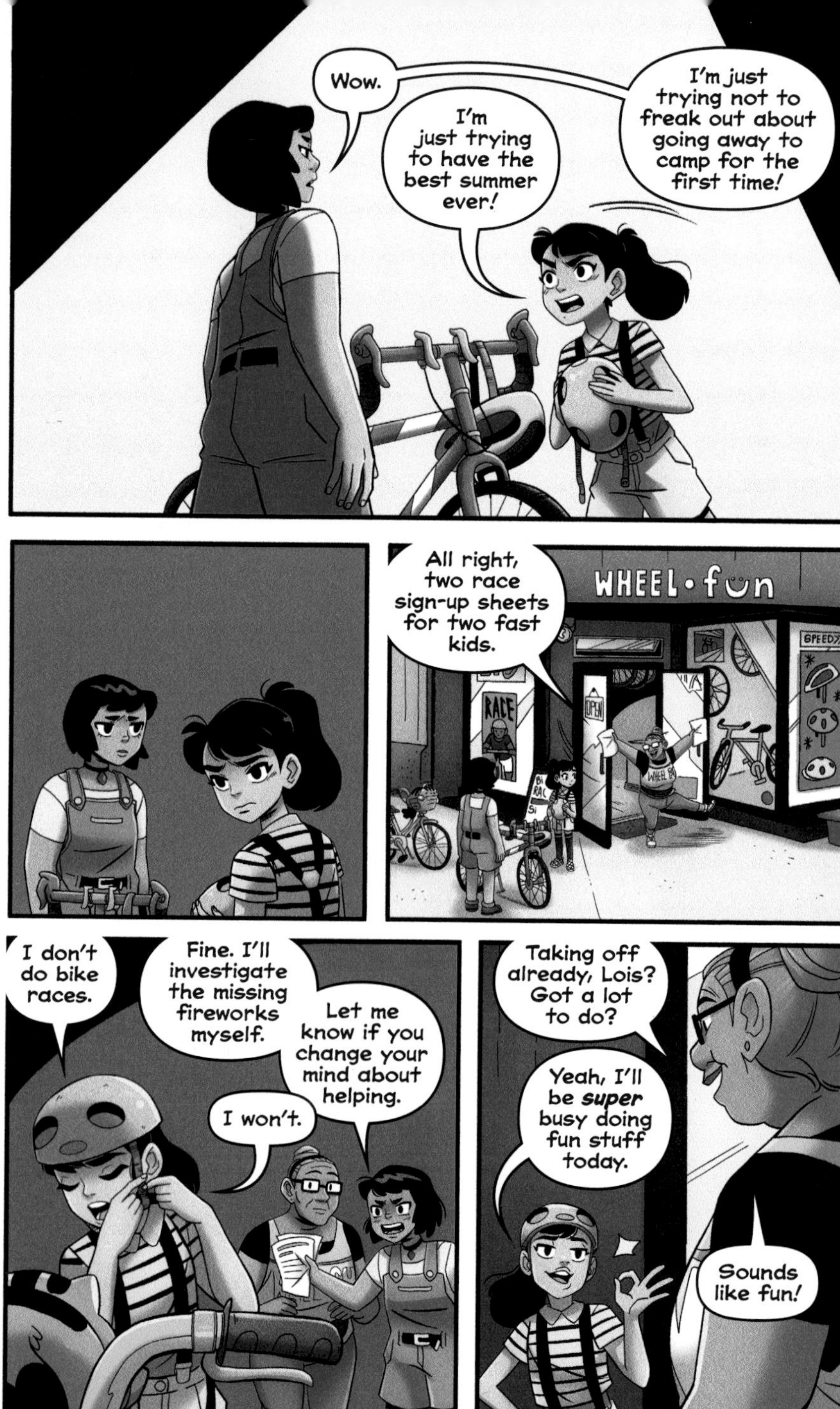

Wow.
I'm just trying not to freak out about going away to camp for the first time!
I'm just trying to have the best summer ever!
All right, two race sign-up sheets for two fast kids.
WHEEL • fun
RACE
OPEN
SPEED
I don't do bike races.
Fine. I'll investigate the missing fireworks myself.
Let me know if you change your mind about helping.
I won't.
Taking off already, Lois? Got a lot to do?
Yeah, I'll be *super* busy doing fun stuff today.
Sounds like fun!

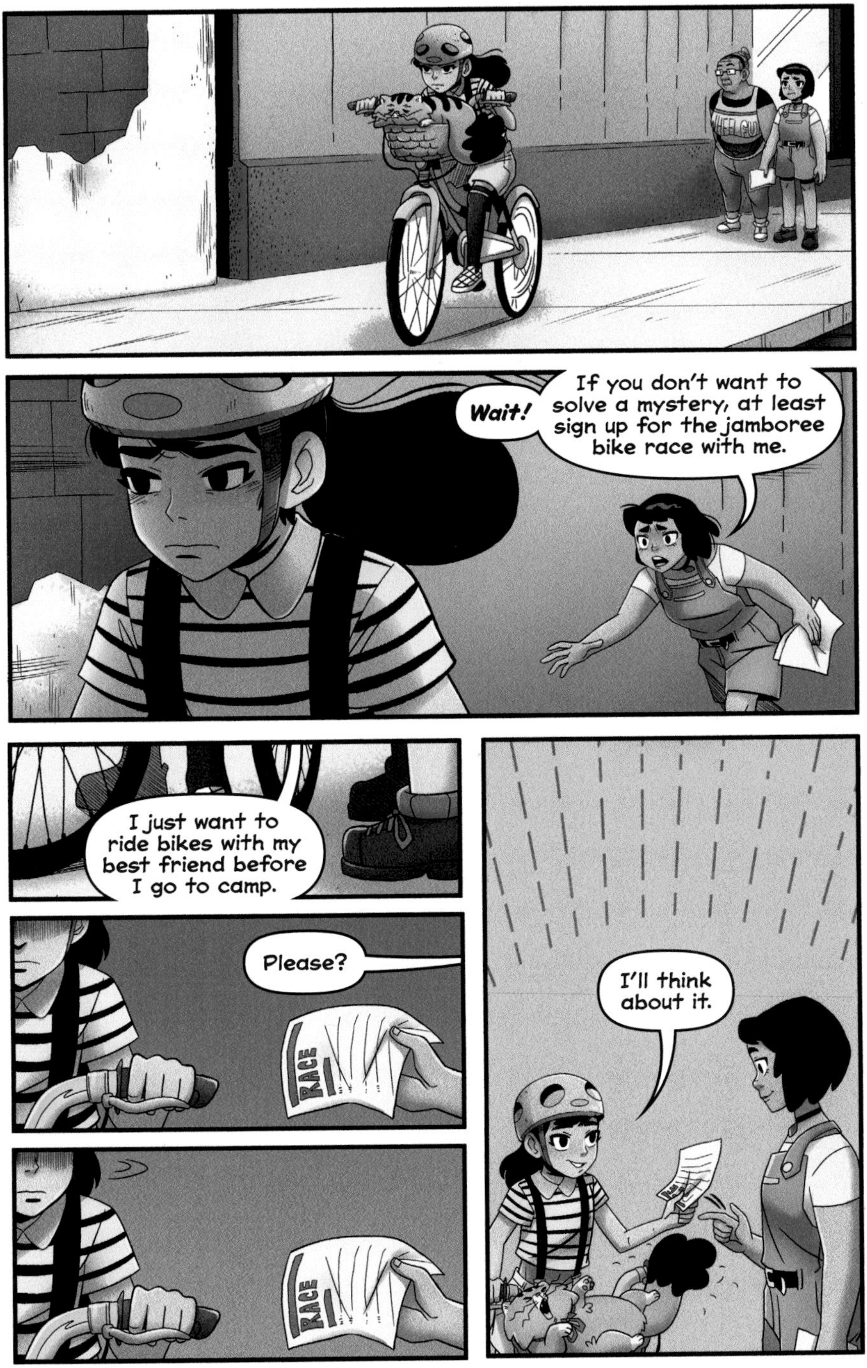
WHEEL GU
Wait!
If you don't want to solve a mystery, at least sign up for the jamboree bike race with me.
I just want to ride bikes with my best friend before I go to camp.
Please?
RACE
RACE
I'll think about it.

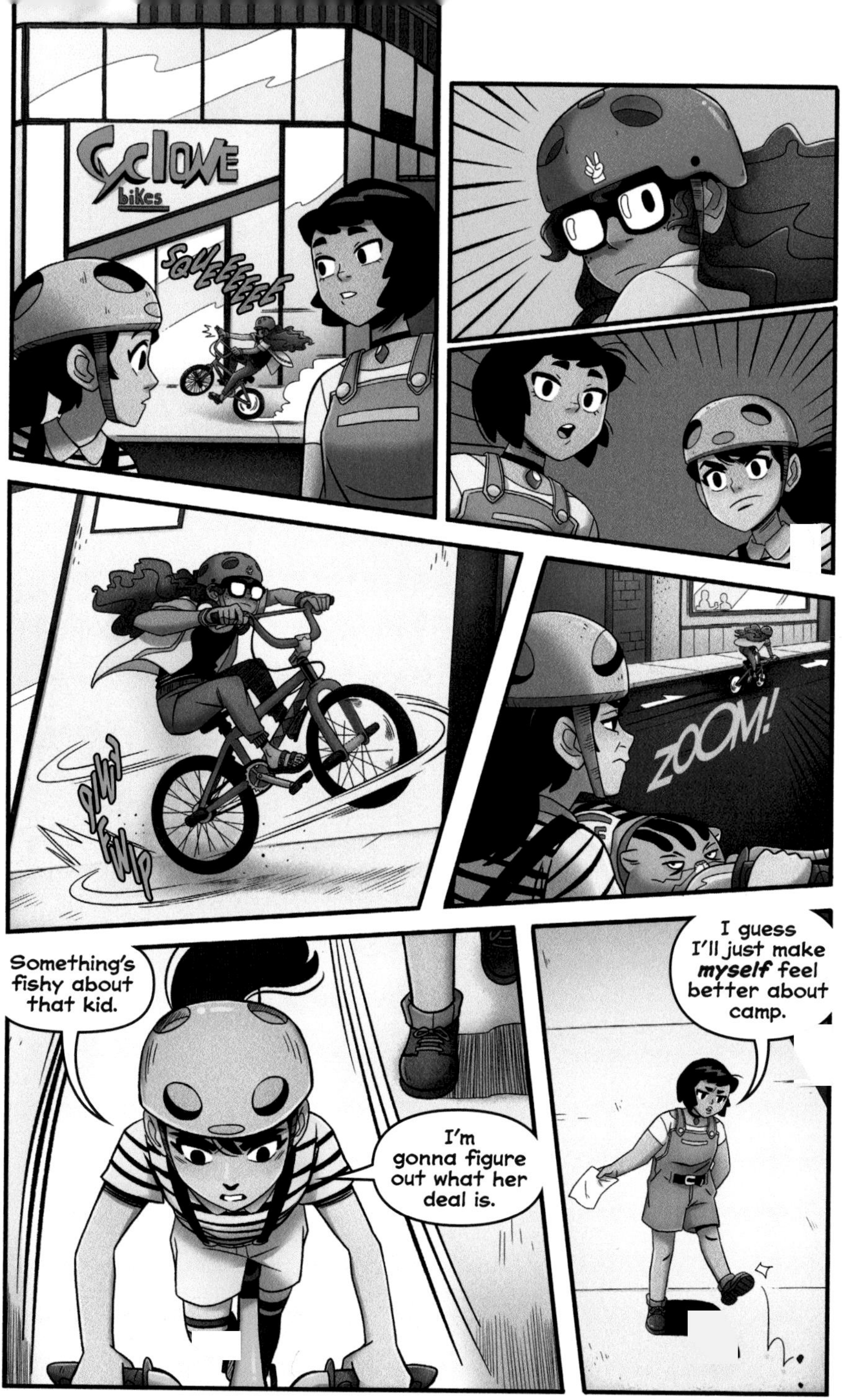
Cyclone bikes
SQUEEEEEEE
FWIP FWIP
ZOOM!
Something's fishy about that kid.
I'm gonna figure out what her deal is.
I guess I'll just make *myself* feel better about camp.

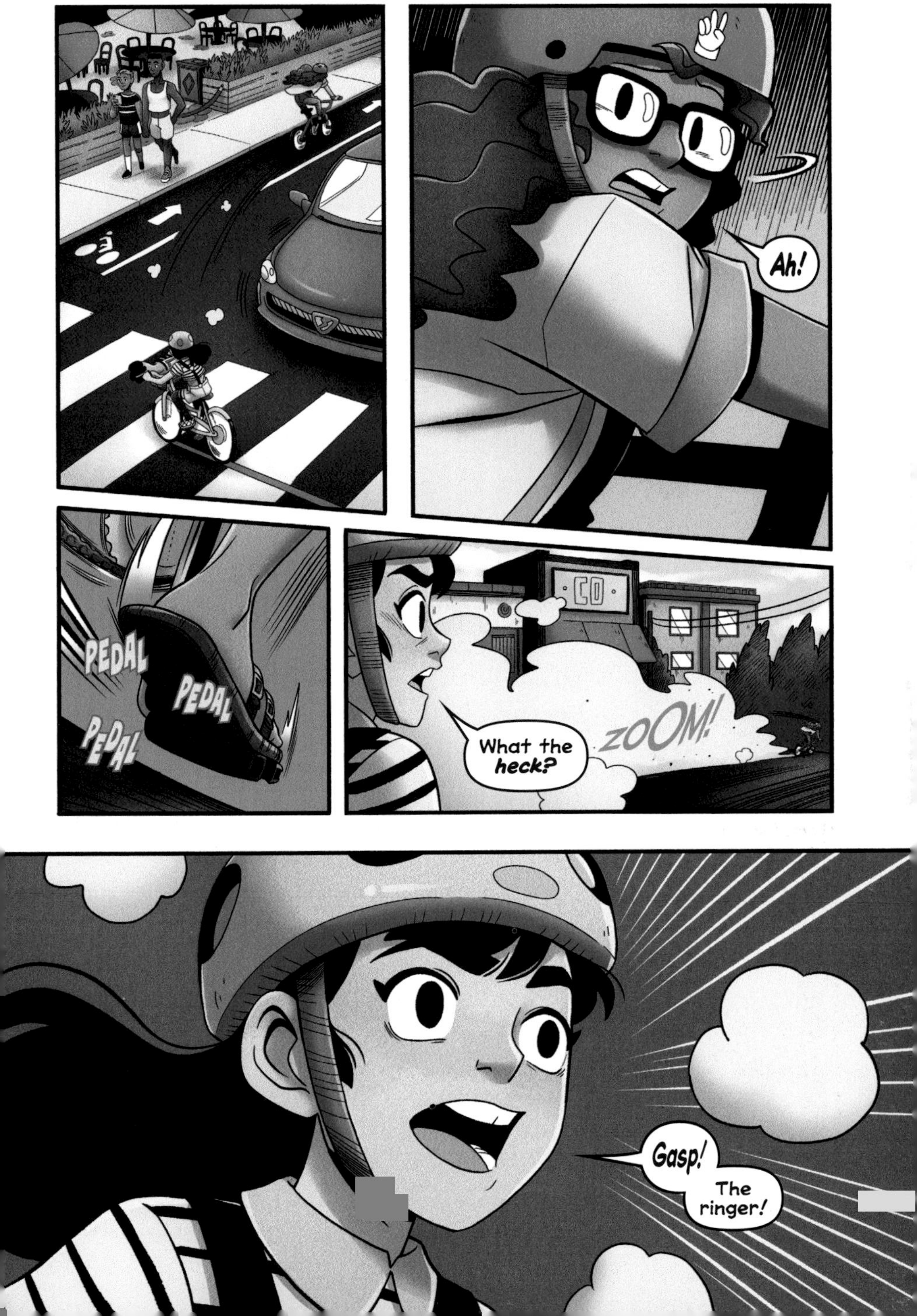
Ah!
PEDAL
PEDAL
PEDAL
CO
What the heck?
ZOOM!
Gasp!
The ringer!

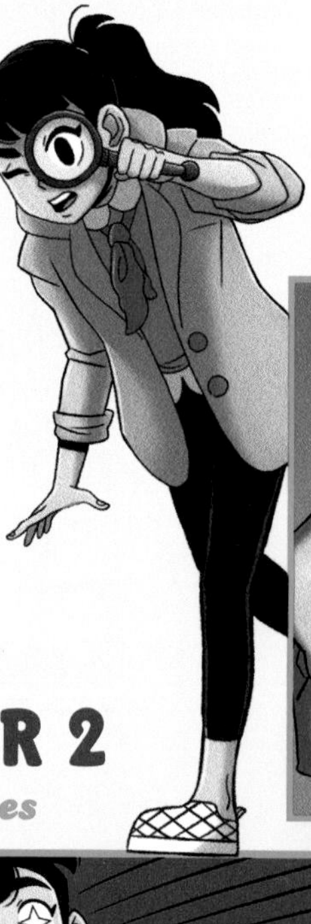

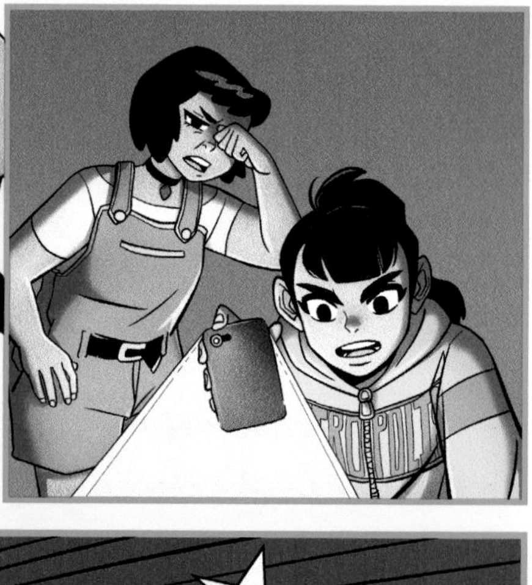

CHAPTER 2

thick as thieves

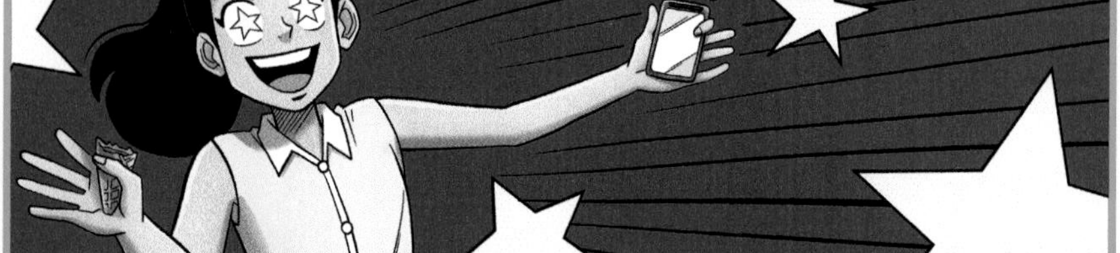

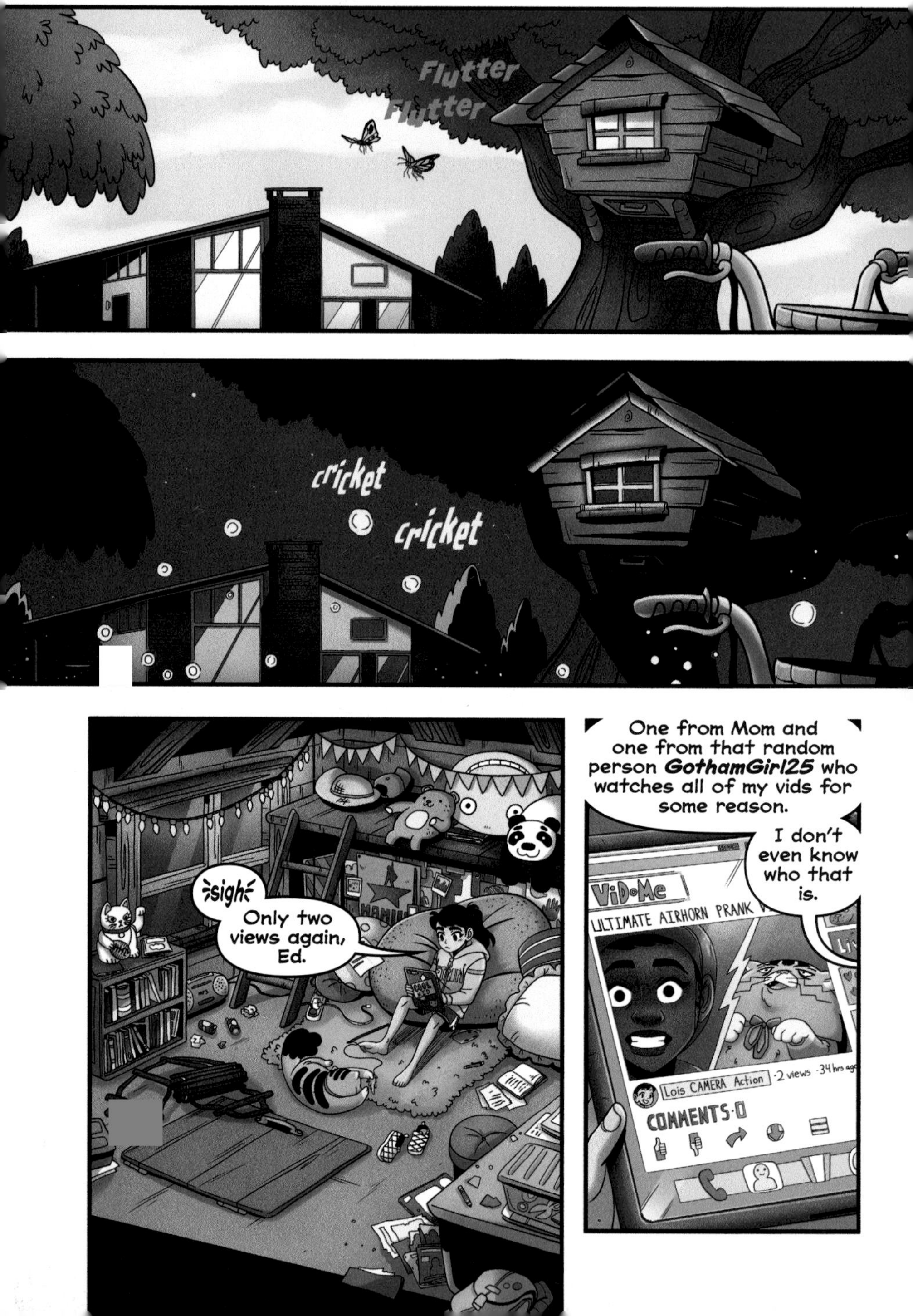
Flutter
Flutter
cricket
cricket
sigh
Only two views again, Ed.
One from Mom and one from that random person GothamGirl25 who watches all of my vids for some reason.
I don't even know who that is.
ViD-Me
ULTIMATE AIRHORN PRANK
Lois CAMERA Action · 2 views · 34 hrs
COMMENTS · 0

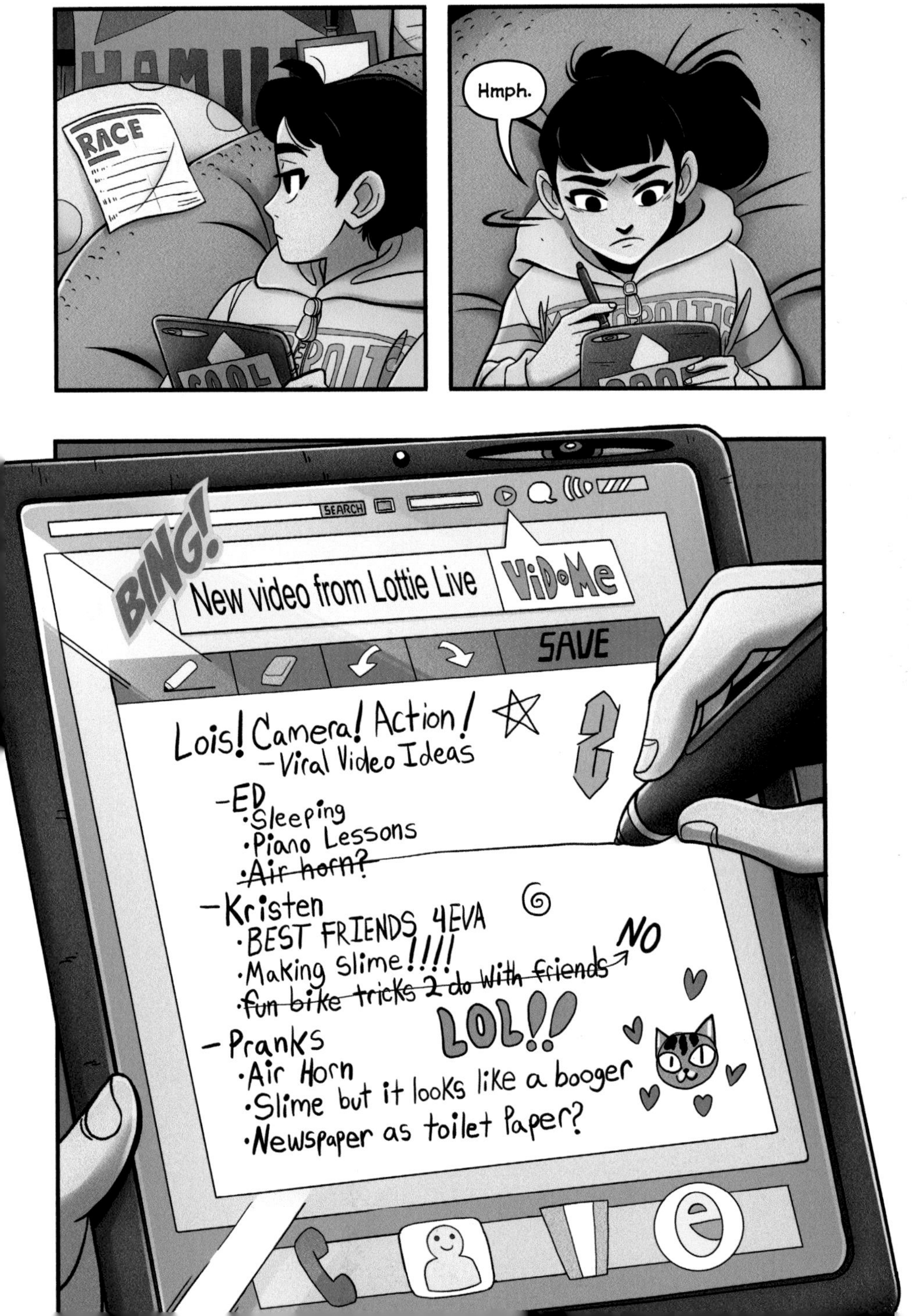
RACE
Hmph.
SEARCH
BING!
New video from Lottie Live
ViDoMe
SAVE
Lois! Camera! Action!
—Viral Video Ideas
—ED
·Sleeping
·Piano Lessons
·~~Air horn?~~
—Kristen
·BEST FRIENDS 4EVA
·Making Slime!!!!
·~~fun bike tricks 2 do with friends~~ NO
—Pranks
·Air Horn
·Slime but it looks like a booger
·Newspaper as toilet Paper?
LOL!!

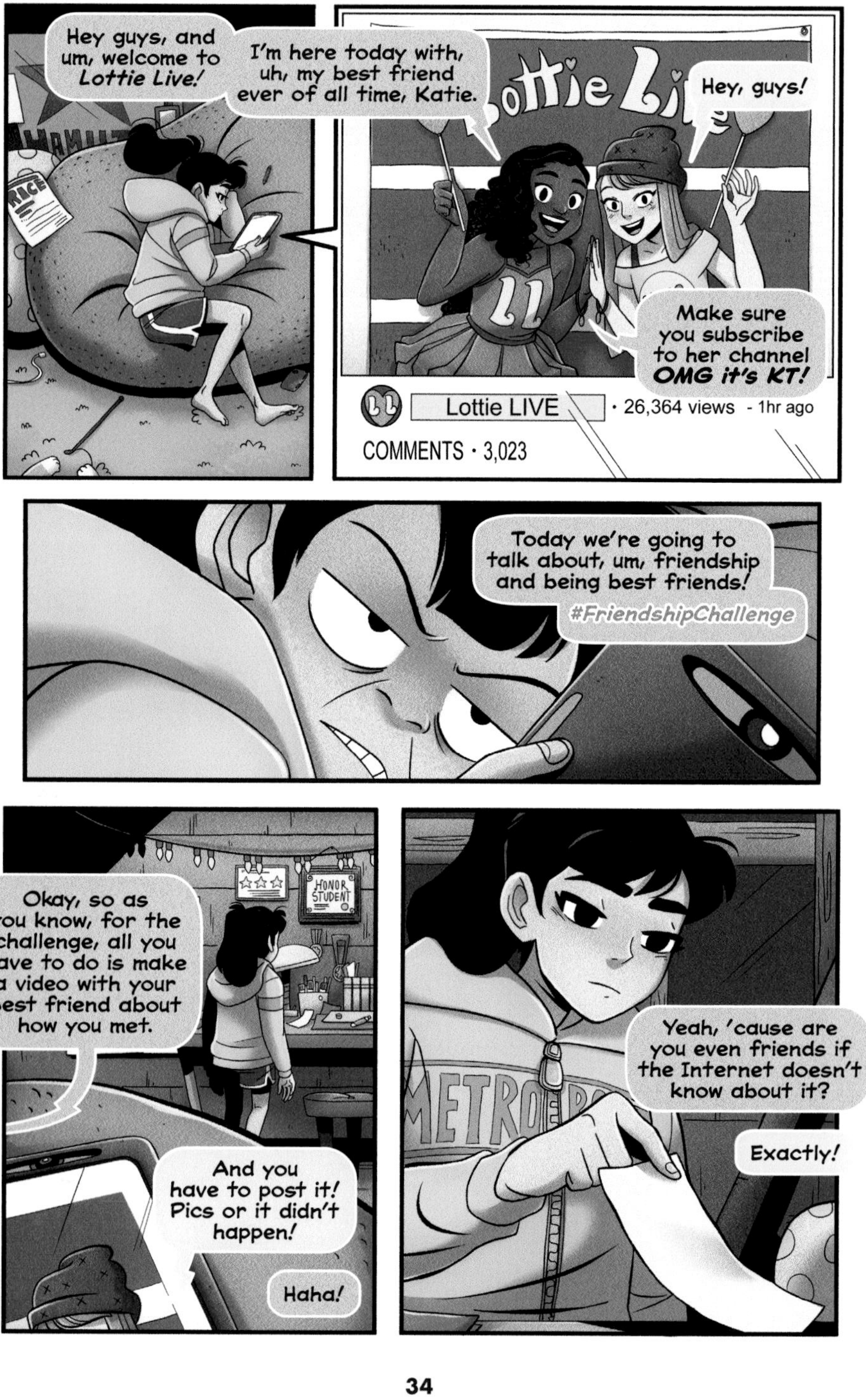
Hey guys, and um, welcome to Lottie Live!
I'm here today with, uh, my best friend ever of all time, Katie.
Hey, guys!
Make sure you subscribe to her channel OMG it's KT!
Lottie LIVE
• 26,364 views - 1hr ago
COMMENTS • 3,023
Today we're going to talk about, um, friendship and being best friends!
#FriendshipChallenge
HONOR STUDENT
Okay, so as you know, for the challenge, all you have to do is make a video with your best friend about how you met.
And you have to post it! Pics or it didn't happen!
Haha!
Yeah, 'cause are you even friends if the Internet doesn't know about it?
Exactly!

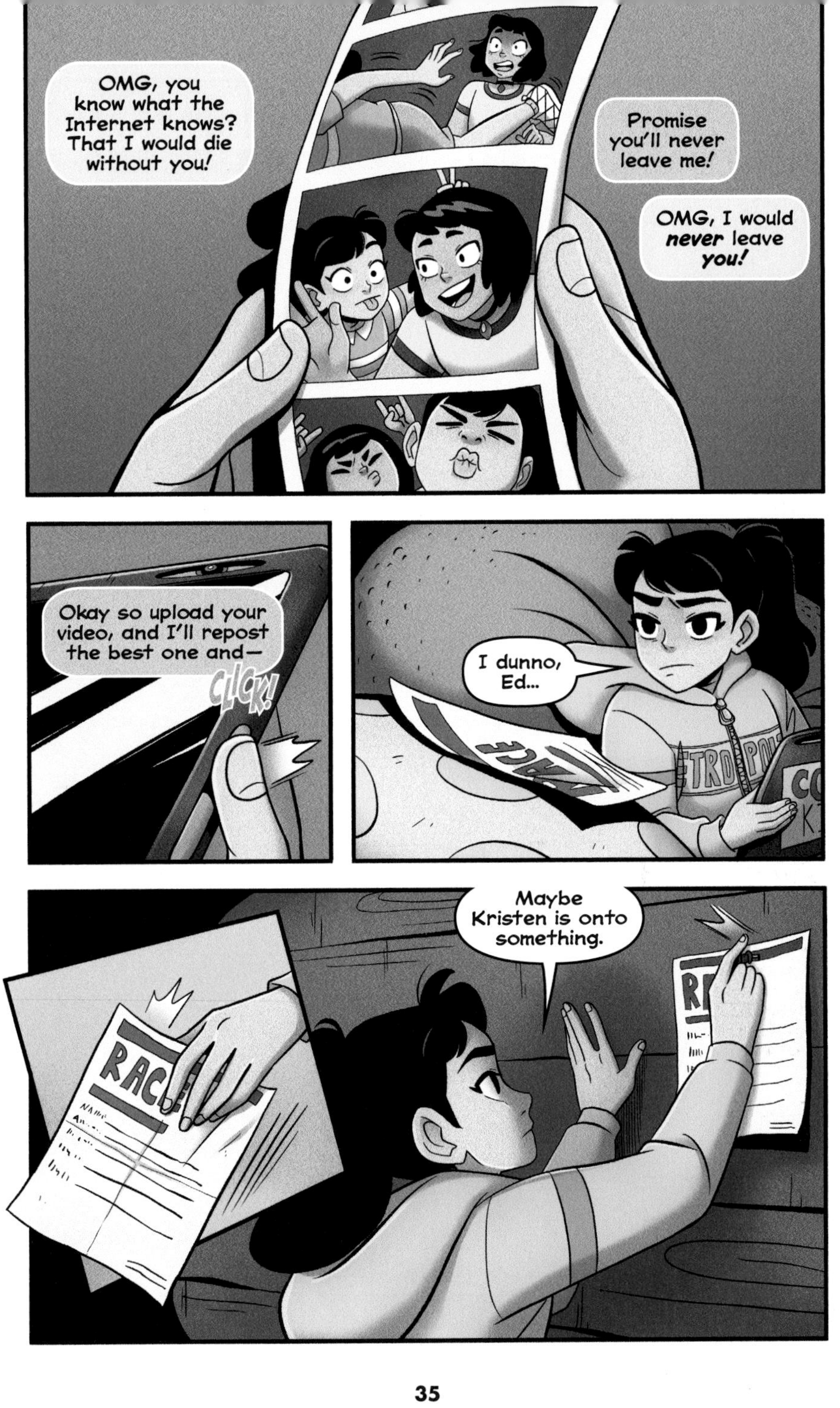
OMG, you know what the Internet knows? That I would die without you!
Promise you'll never leave me!
OMG, I would ***never*** leave ***you!***
Okay so upload your video, and I'll repost the best one and—
CLICK!
I dunno, Ed...
Maybe Kristen is onto something.

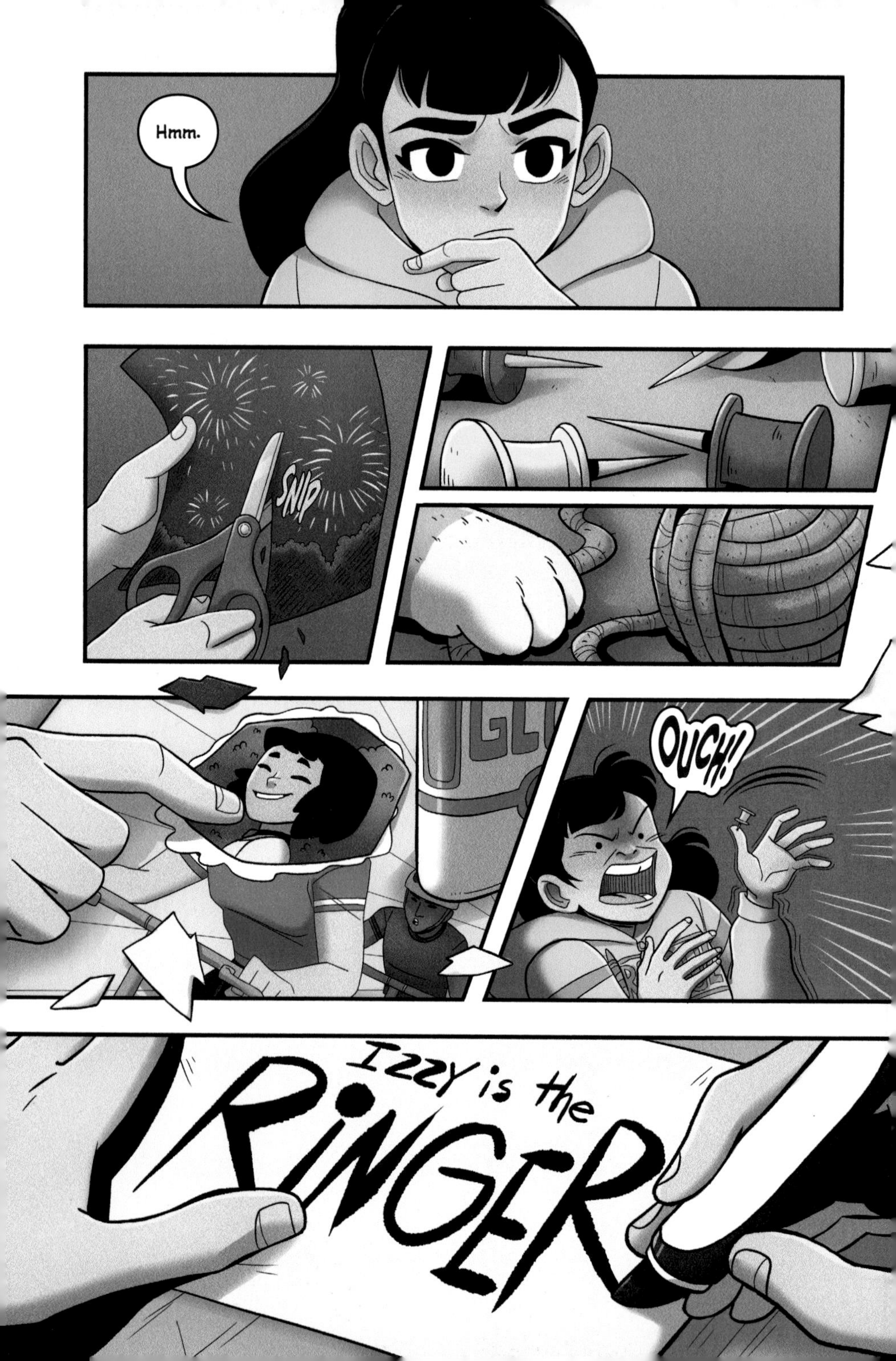
Hmm.
SNIP
OUCH!
IZZY is the
RINGER

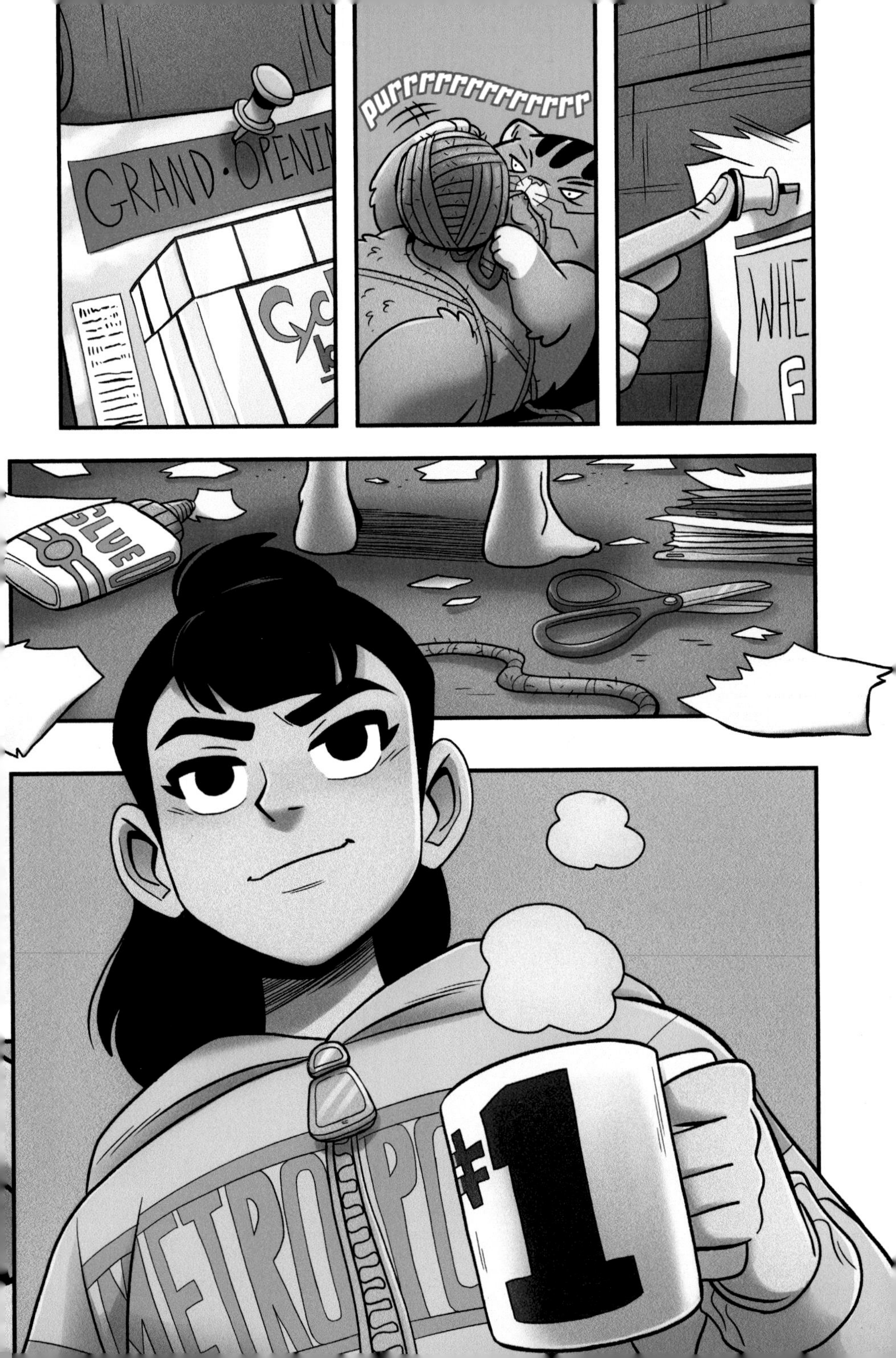
GRAND·OPENIN
purrrrrrrrrrrr
WHE
GLUE
METROPO
#1

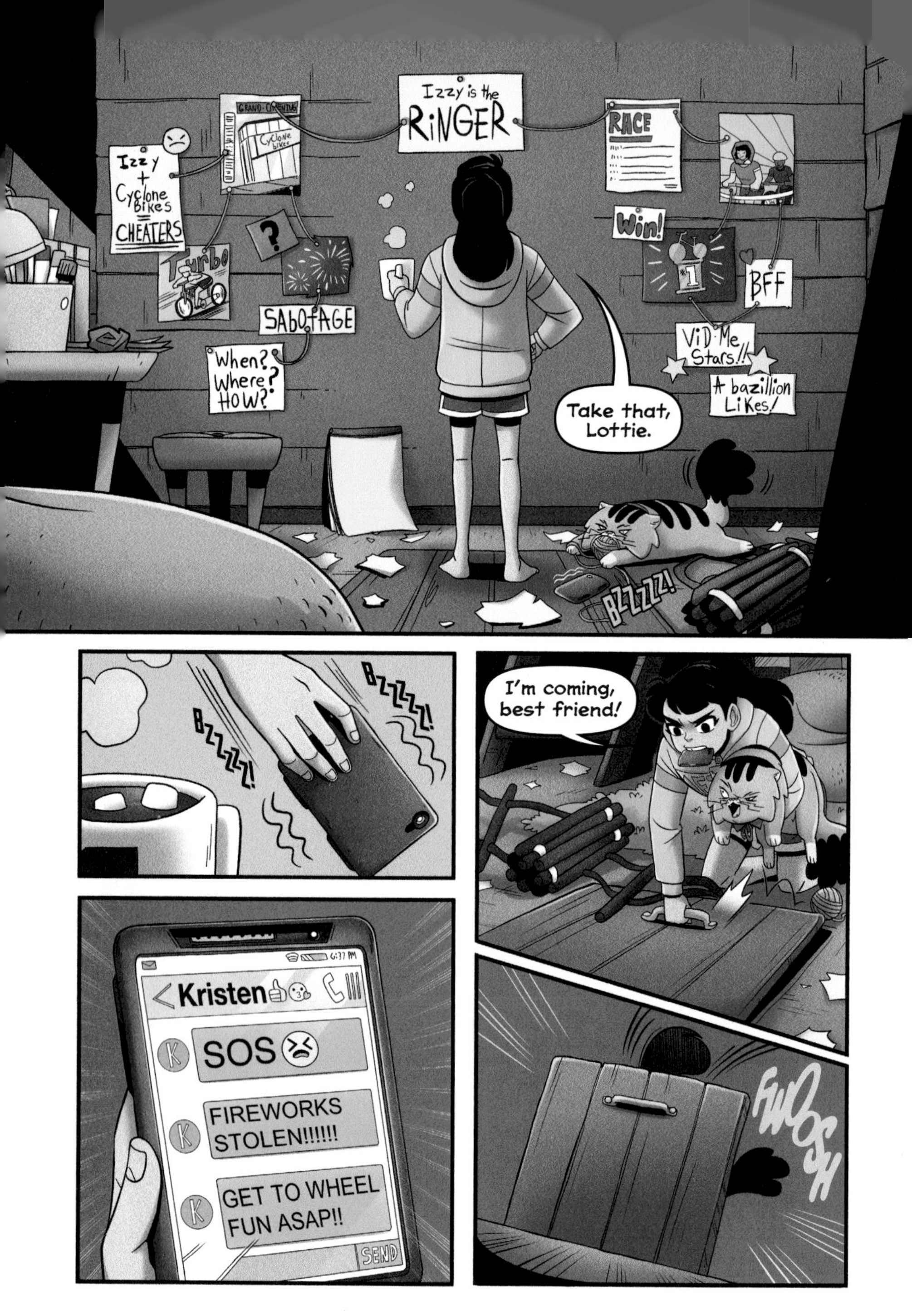
Izzy is the RiNGER
Izzy + Cyclone Bikes = CHEATERS
Cyclone bikes
Turbo
?
SABOTAGE
When? Where? HOW?
RACE
Win!
#1
BFF
ViD Me Stars!!
A bazillion Likes!
Take that, Lottie.
BZZZZZ!
BZZZZZ!
BZZZZZ!
I'm coming, best friend!
6:37 PM
Kristen
SOS
FIREWORKS STOLEN!!!!!!
GET TO WHEEL FUN ASAP!!
SEND
FWOOSH

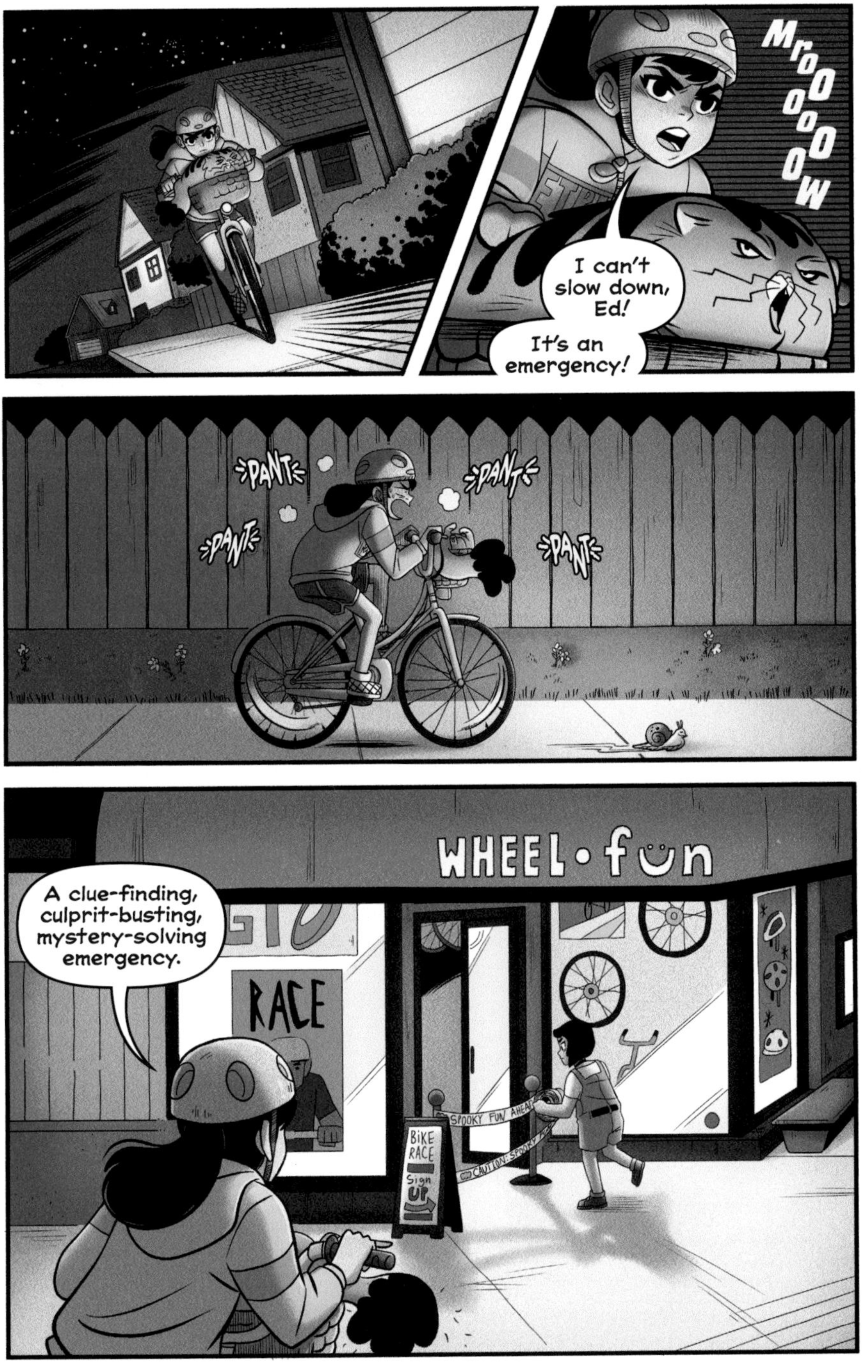
Mroooooow
I can't slow down, Ed!
It's an emergency!
PANT
PANT
PANT
PANT
WHEEL • fun
A clue-finding, culprit-busting, mystery-solving emergency.
RACE
BIKE RACE Sign UP
SPOOKY FUN AHEAD
CAUTION: SPOOKY

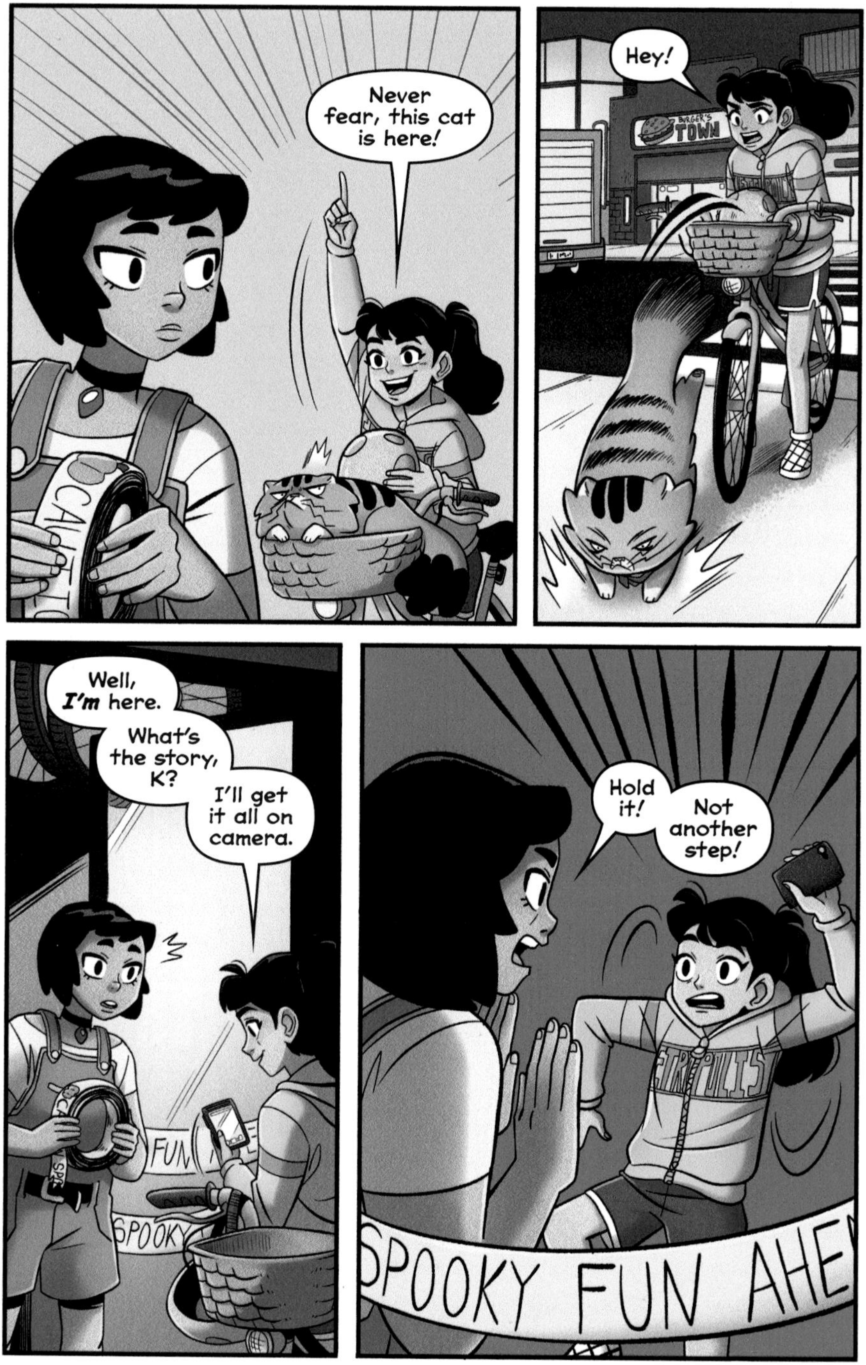

Never fear, this cat is here!
Hey!
BURGER'S TOWN
Well, *I'm* here.
What's the story, K?
I'll get it all on camera.
FUN
SPOOKY
Hold it!
Not another step!
SPOOKY FUN AHE

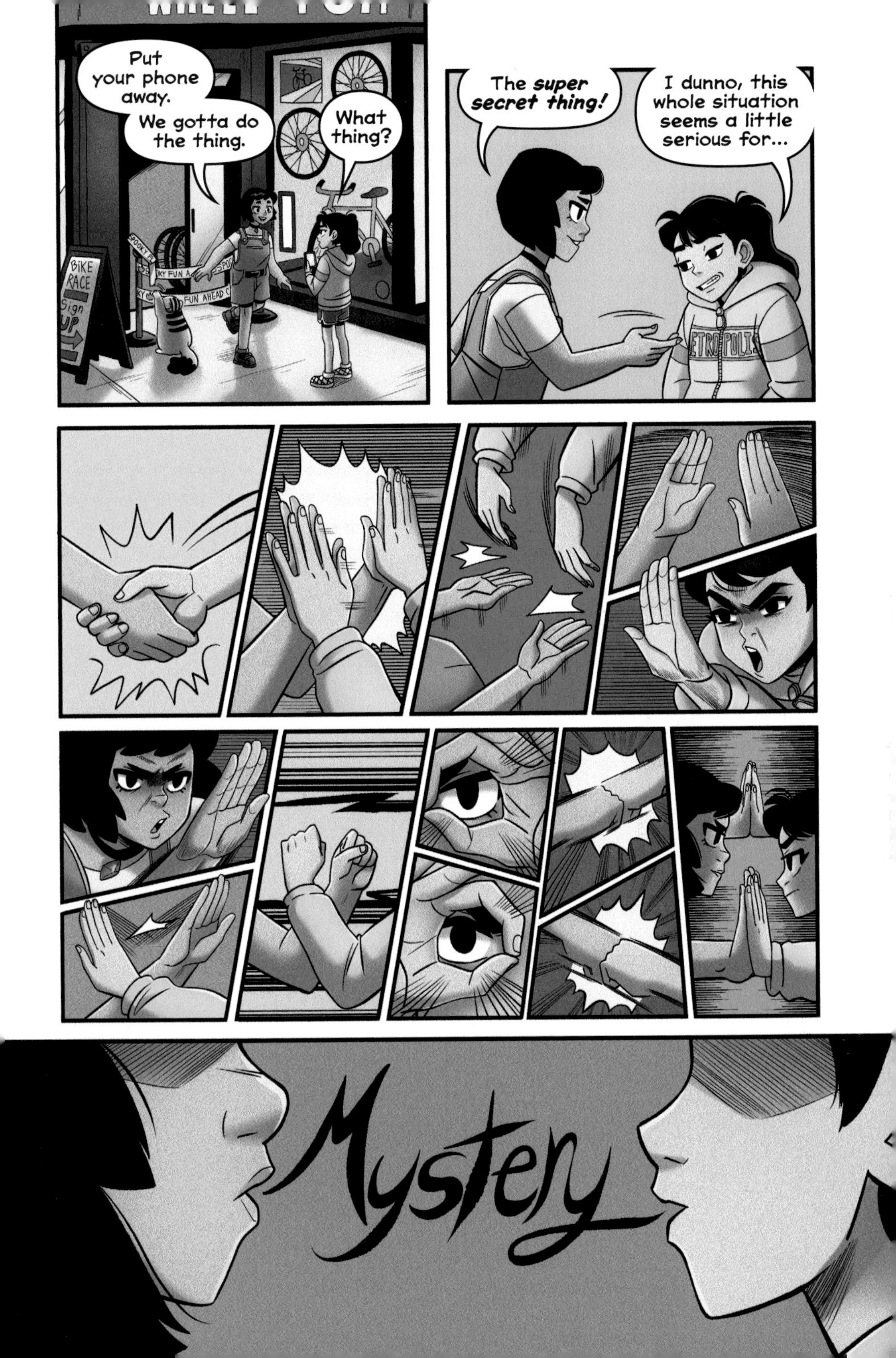
Put your phone away.
We gotta do the thing.
What thing?
BIKE RACE Sign UP
FUN AHEAD
The *super secret thing!*
I dunno, this whole situation seems a little serious for...
Mystery

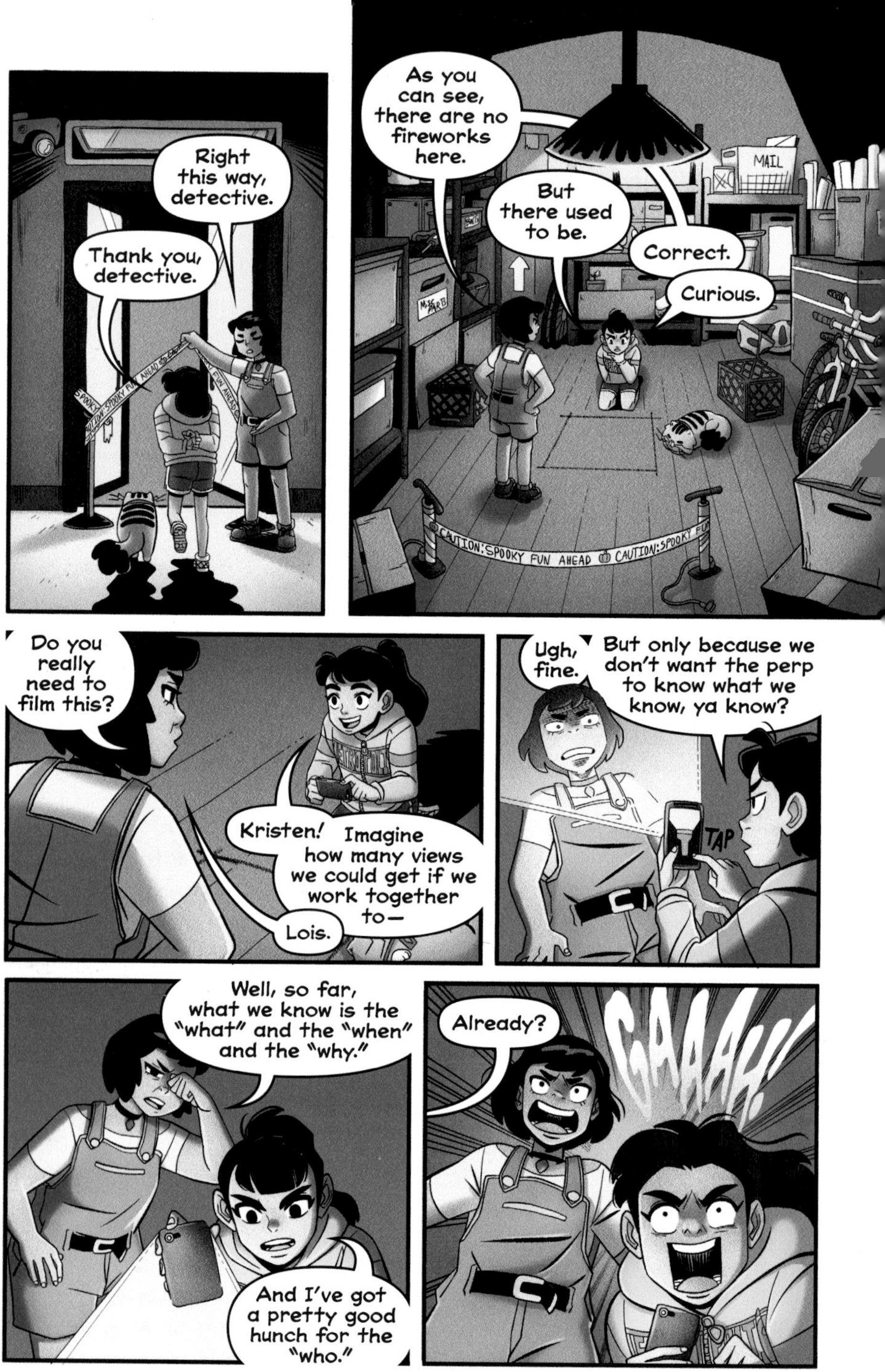

Right this way, detective.
Thank you, detective.
SPOOKY FUN AHEAD
As you can see, there are no fireworks here.
But there used to be.
Correct.
Curious.
MAIL
CAUTION: SPOOKY FUN AHEAD CAUTION: SPOOKY FUN
Do you really need to film this?
Kristen!
Imagine how many views we could get if we work together to—
Lois.
Ugh, fine.
But only because we don't want the perp to know what we know, ya know?
TAP
Well, so far, what we know is the "what" and the "when" and the "why."
And I've got a pretty good hunch for the "who."
Already?
GAAAH!

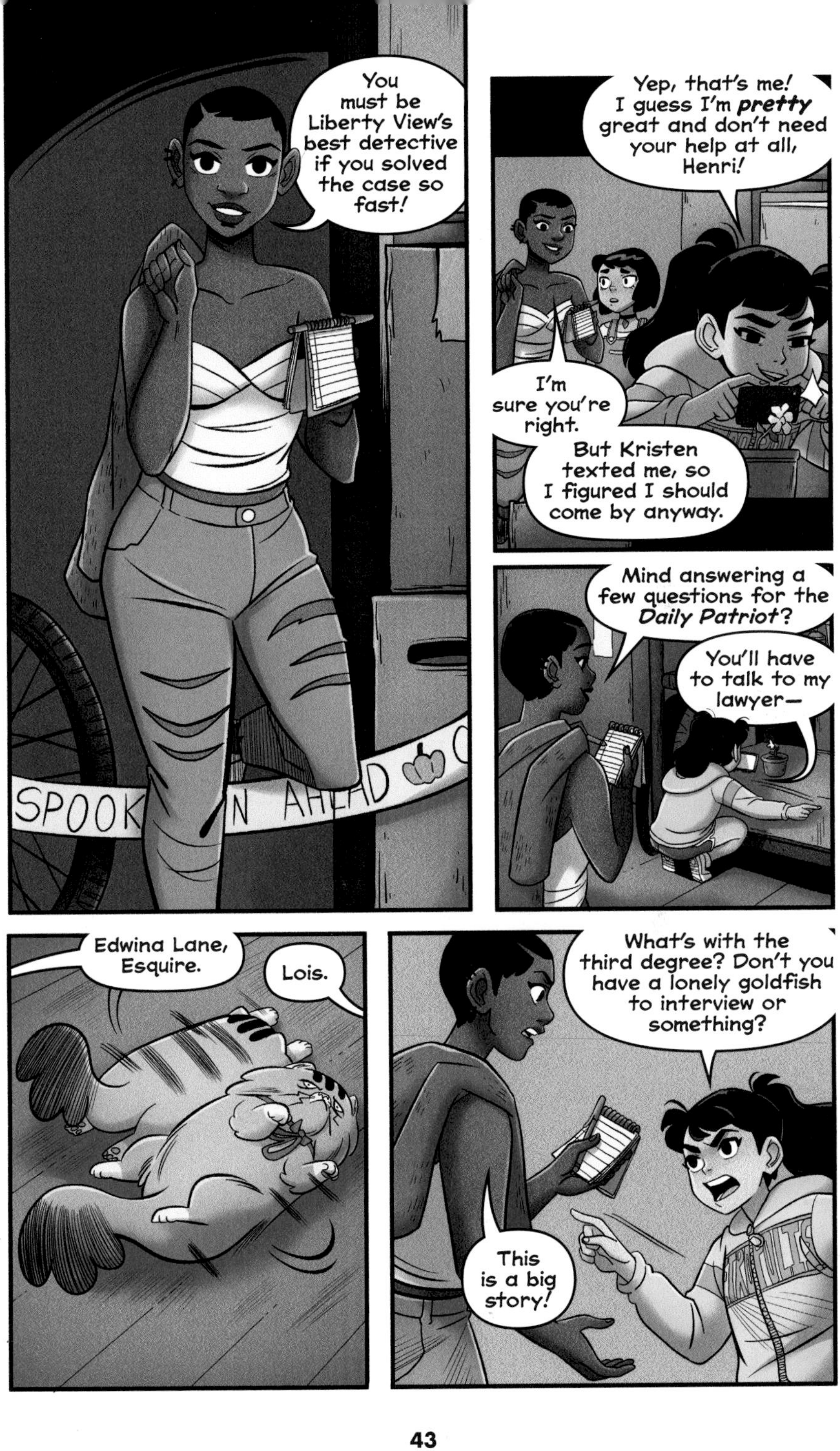

You must be Liberty View's best detective if you solved the case so fast!
Yep, that's me! I guess I'm ***pretty*** great and don't need your help at all, Henri!
I'm sure you're right.
But Kristen texted me, so I figured I should come by anyway.
Mind answering a few questions for the *Daily Patriot*?
You'll have to talk to my lawyer—
Edwina Lane, Esquire.
Lois.
What's with the third degree? Don't you have a lonely goldfish to interview or something?
This is a big story!

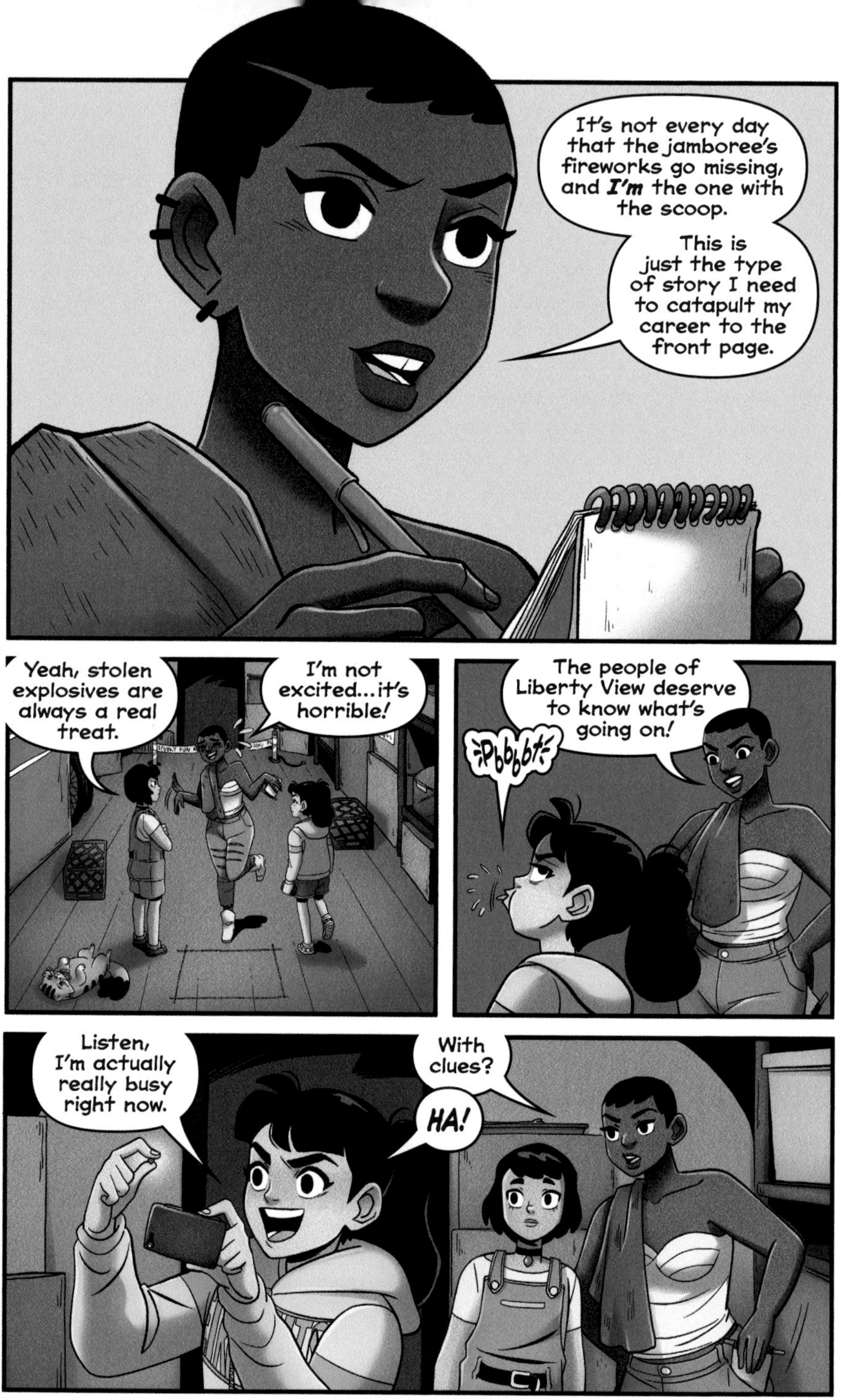
It's not every day that the jamboree's fireworks go missing, and *I'm* the one with the scoop.
This is just the type of story I need to catapult my career to the front page.
Yeah, stolen explosives are always a real treat.
I'm not excited...it's horrible!
The people of Liberty View deserve to know what's going on!
Pbbbbt!
Listen, I'm actually really busy right now.
With clues?
HA!

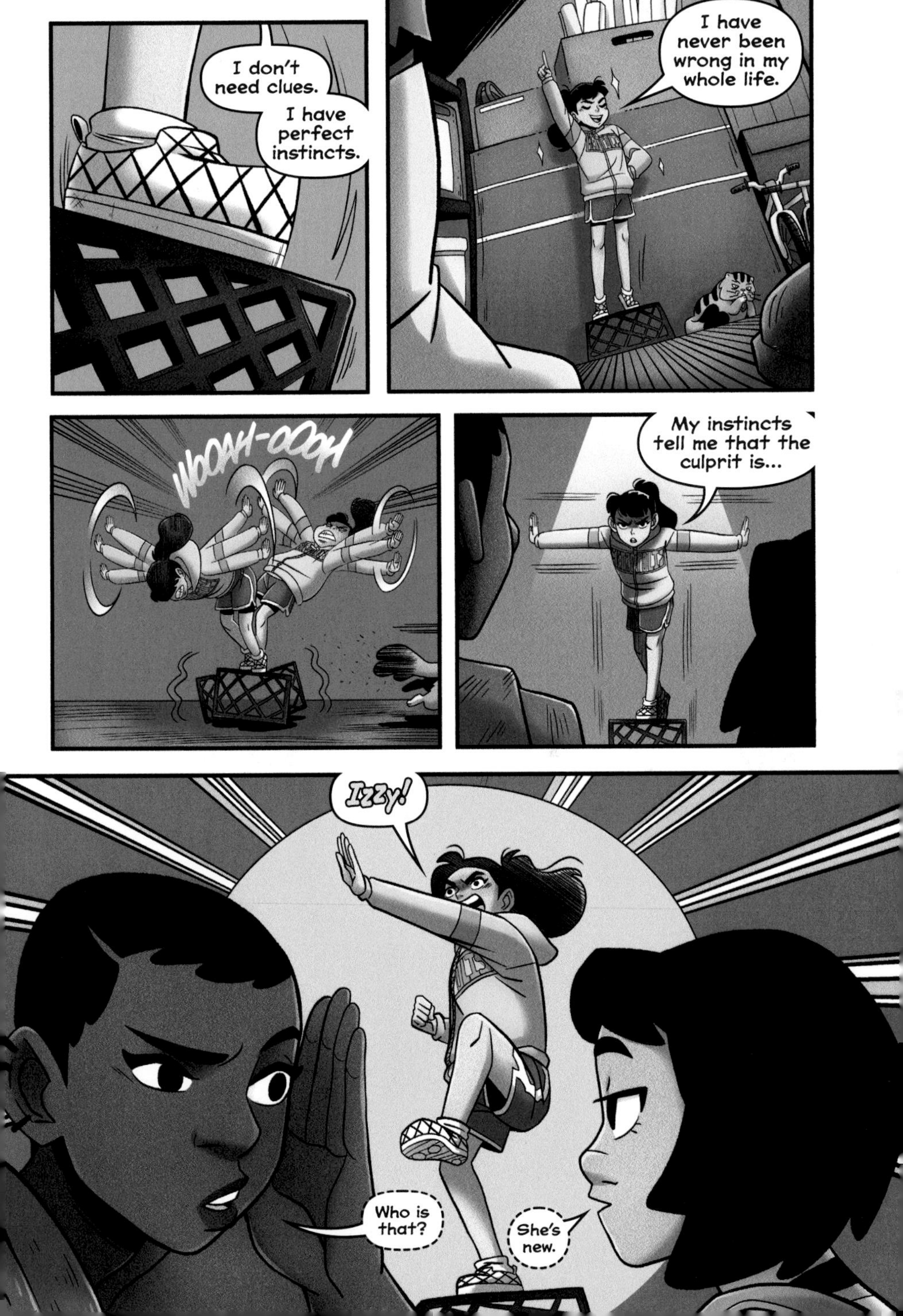
I don't need clues.
I have perfect instincts.
I have never been wrong in my whole life.
WOOAH-OOOH
My instincts tell me that the culprit is...
Izzy!
Who is that?
She's new.

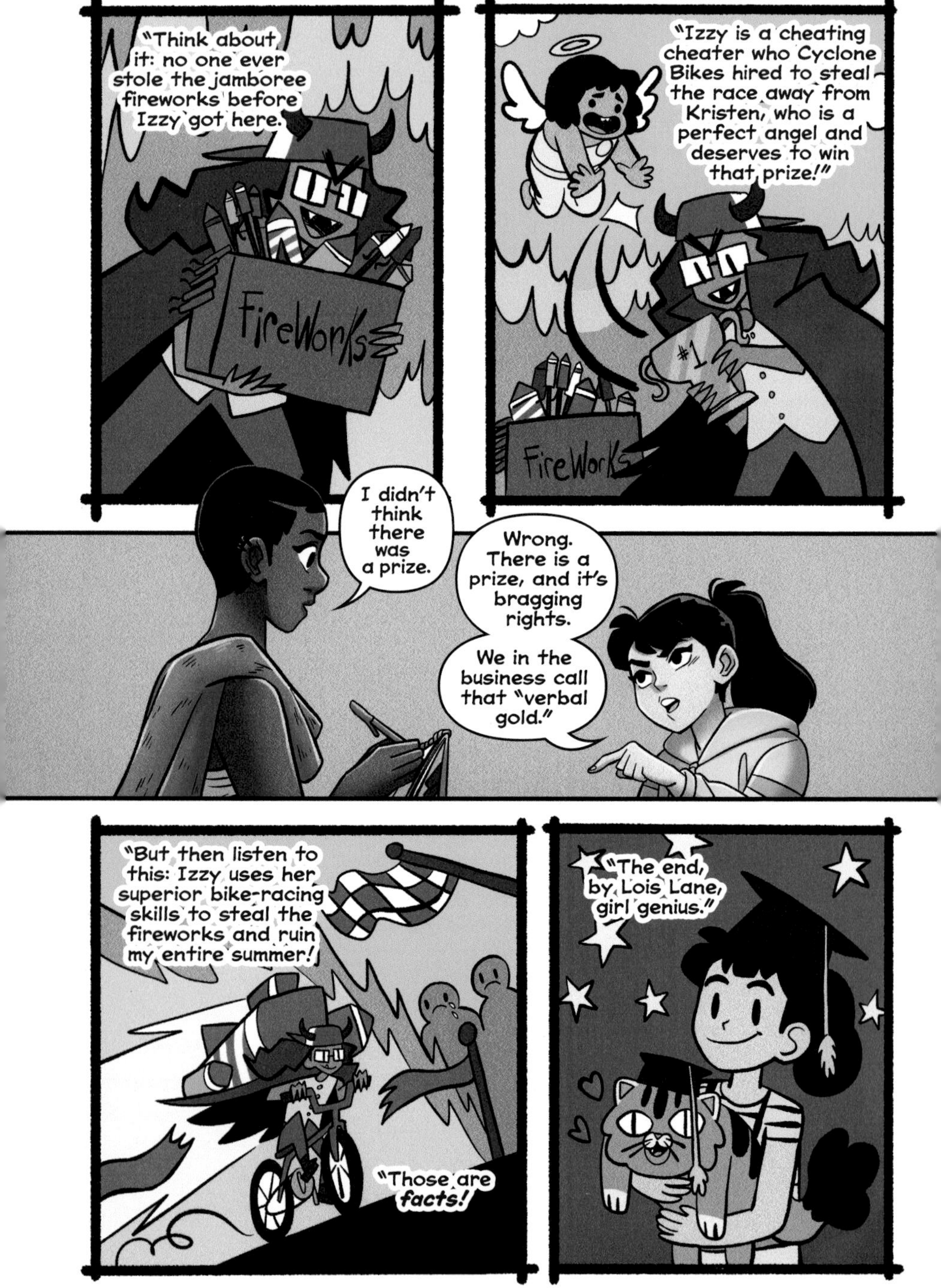
"Think about it: no one ever stole the jamboree fireworks before Izzy got here.
FireWorks
"Izzy is a cheating cheater who Cyclone Bikes hired to steal the race away from Kristen, who is a perfect angel and deserves to win that prize!"
#1
FireWorks
I didn't think there was a prize.
Wrong. There is a prize, and it's bragging rights.
We in the business call that "verbal gold."
"But then listen to this: Izzy uses her superior bike-racing skills to steal the fireworks and ruin my entire summer!
"Those are *facts!*
"The end, by Lois Lane, girl genius."

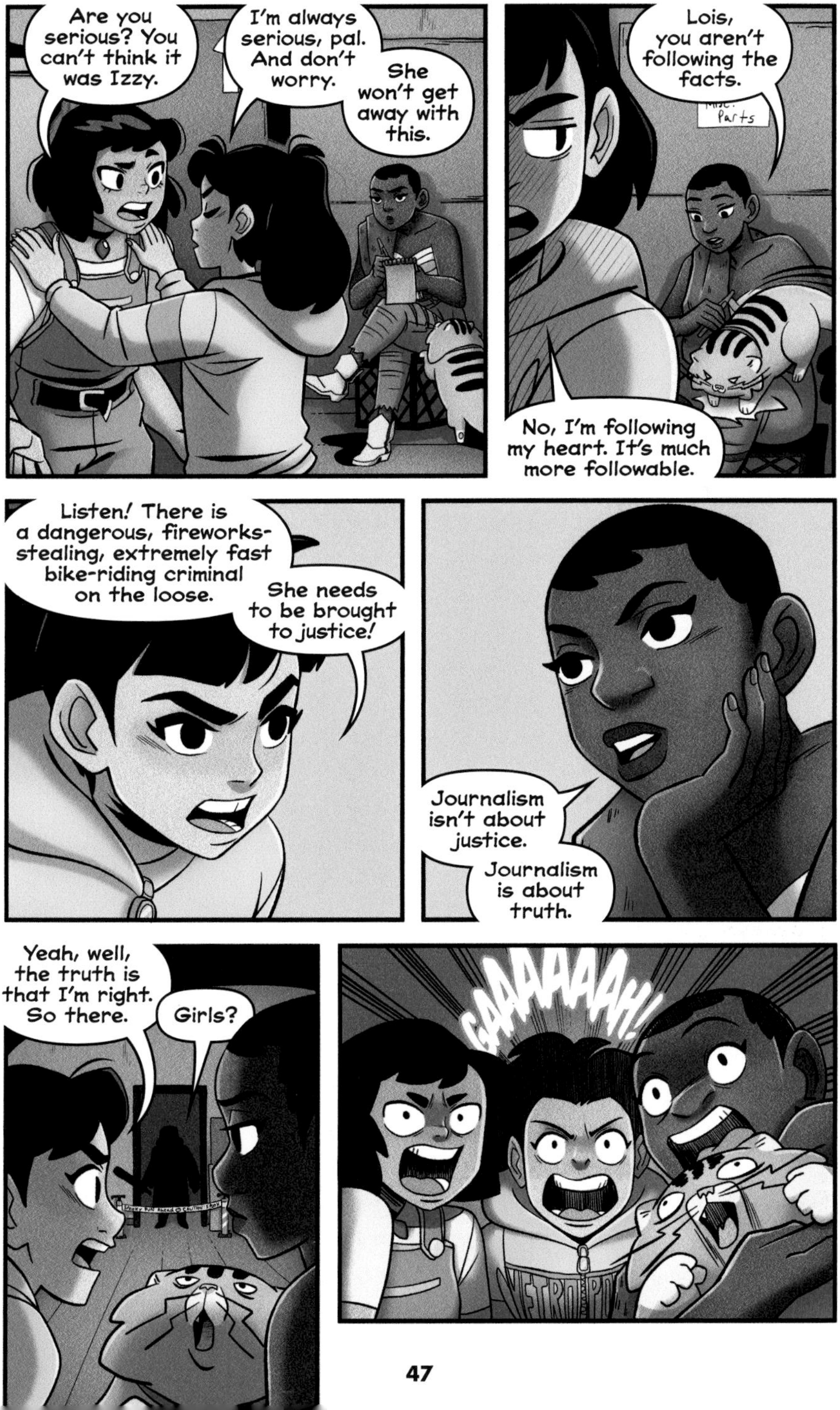
Are you serious? You can't think it was Izzy.
I'm always serious, pal. And don't worry.
She won't get away with this.
Lois, you aren't following the facts.
Parts
No, I'm following my heart. It's much more followable.
Listen! There is a dangerous, fireworks-stealing, extremely fast bike-riding criminal on the loose.
She needs to be brought to justice!
Journalism isn't about justice.
Journalism is about truth.
Yeah, well, the truth is that I'm right. So there.
Girls?
GAAAAAH!
METROPOLIS

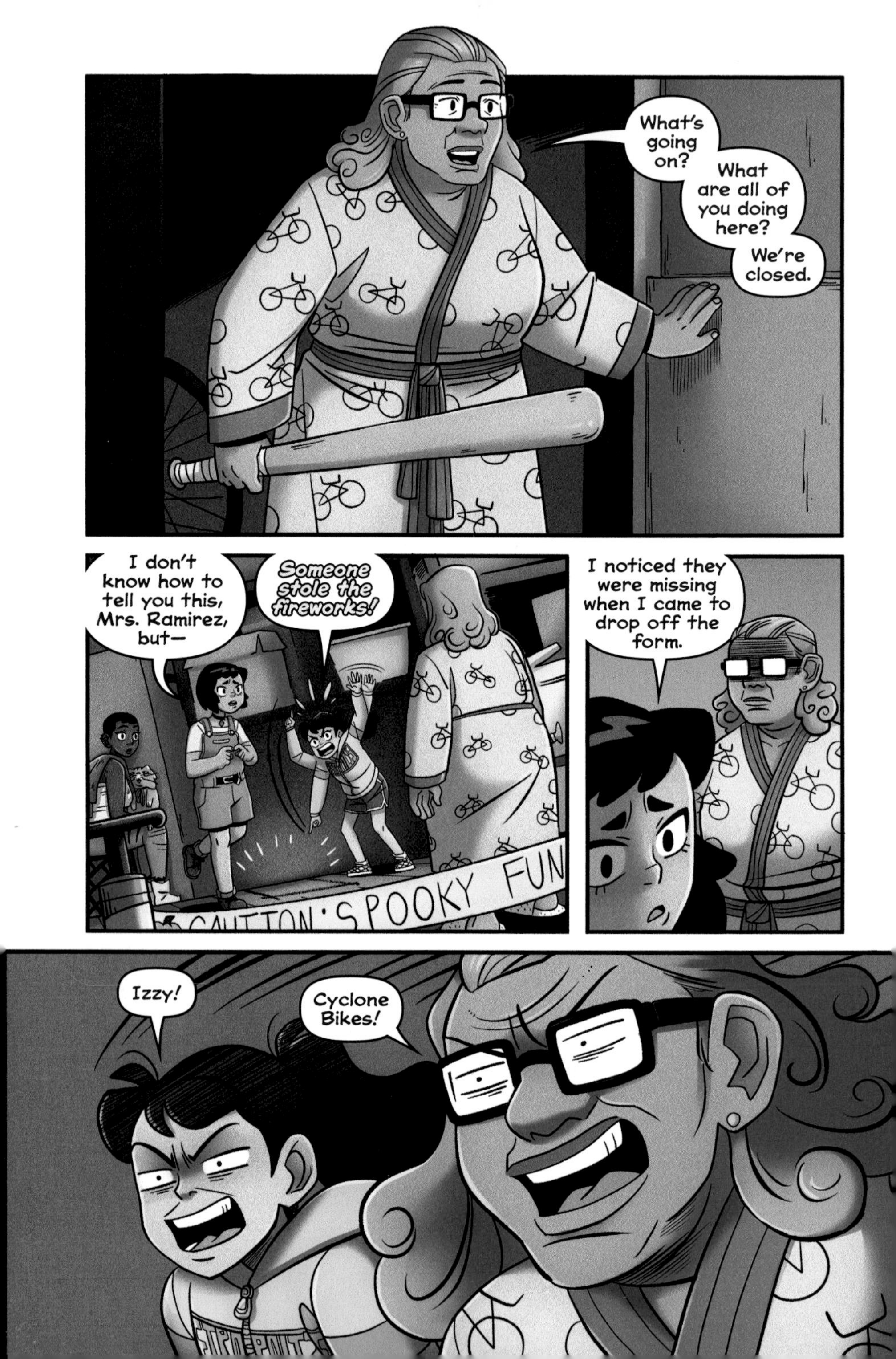
What's going on?
What are all of you doing here?
We're closed.
I don't know how to tell you this, Mrs. Ramirez, but—
Someone stole the fireworks!
I noticed they were missing when I came to drop off the form.
CAUTION · SPOOKY FUN
Izzy!
Cyclone Bikes!

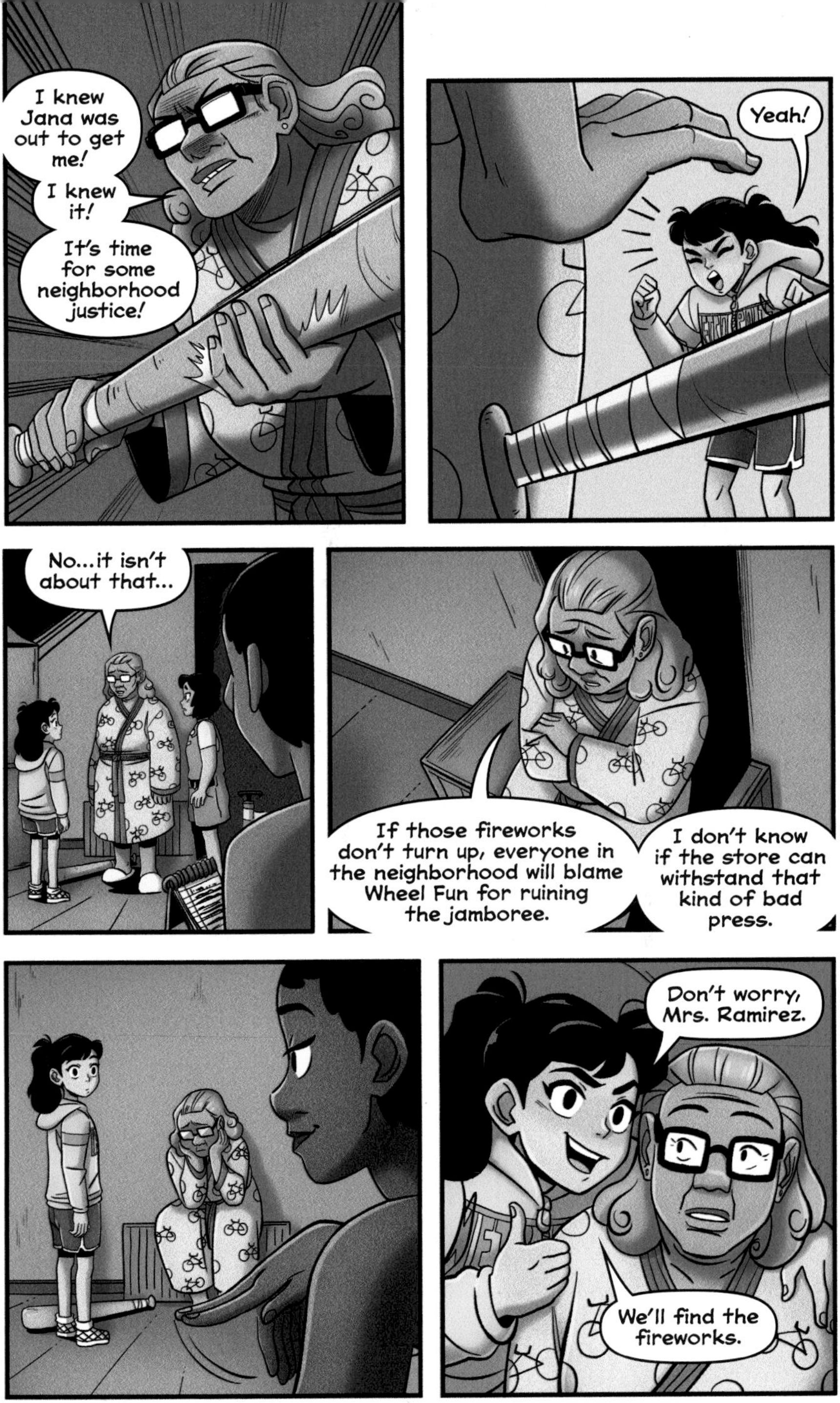
I knew Jana was out to get me!
I knew it!
It's time for some neighborhood justice!
Yeah!
No...it isn't about that...
If those fireworks don't turn up, everyone in the neighborhood will blame Wheel Fun for ruining the jamboree.
I don't know if the store can withstand that kind of bad press.
Don't worry, Mrs. Ramirez.
We'll find the fireworks.

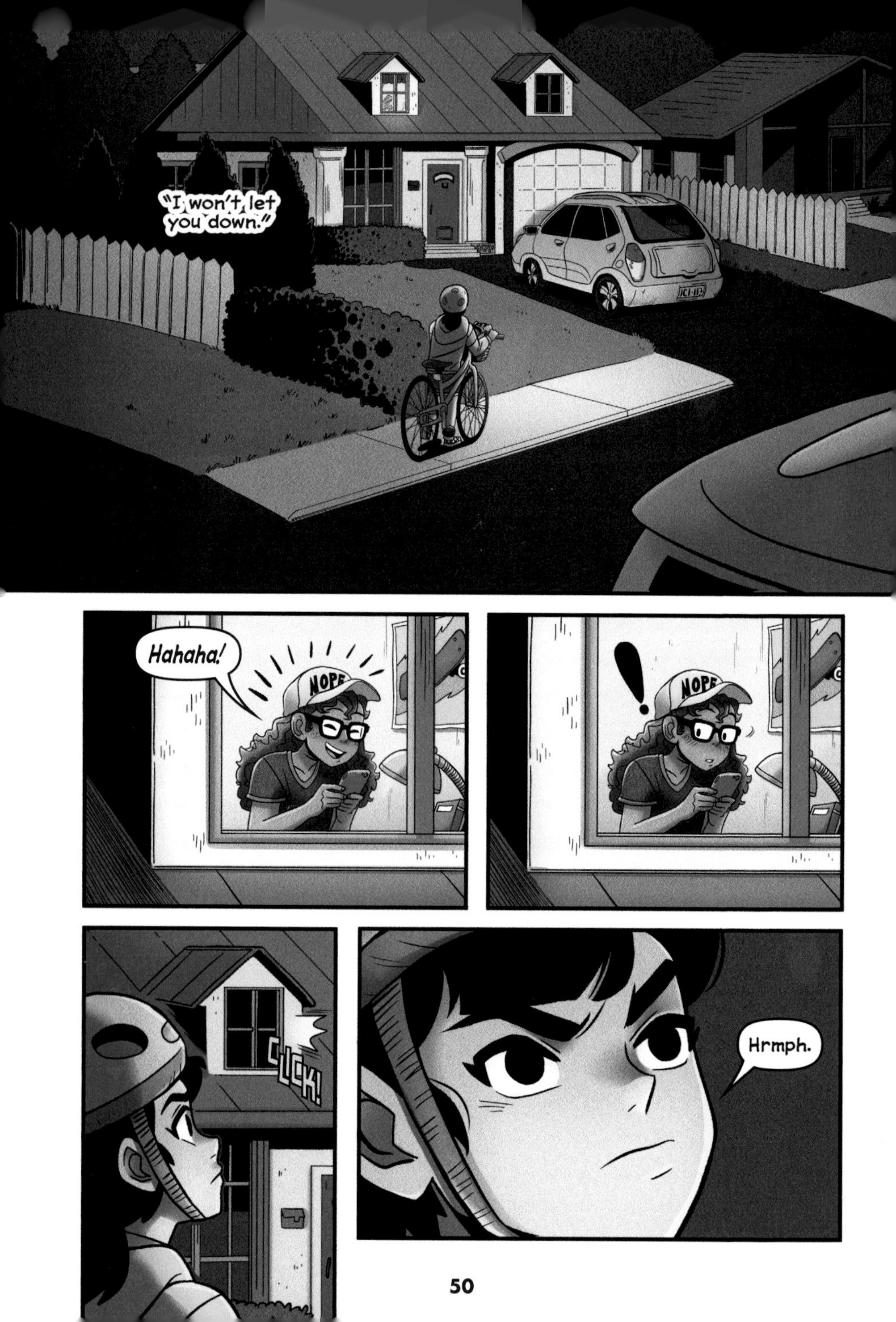
"I won't let you down."
Hahaha!
NOPE
NOPE
!
CLICK!
Hrmph.

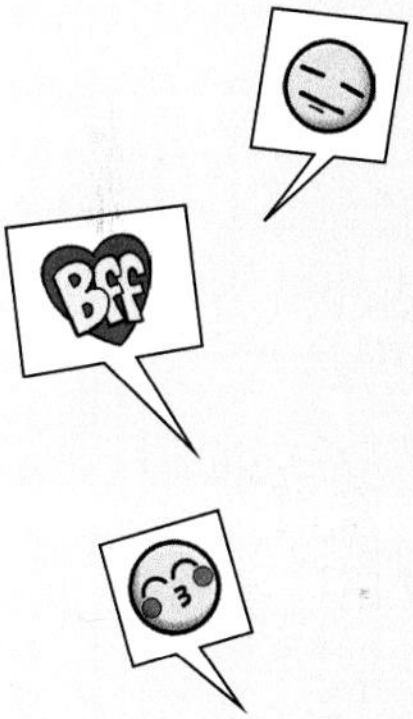
Bff

CHAPTER 3

nerds of a feather

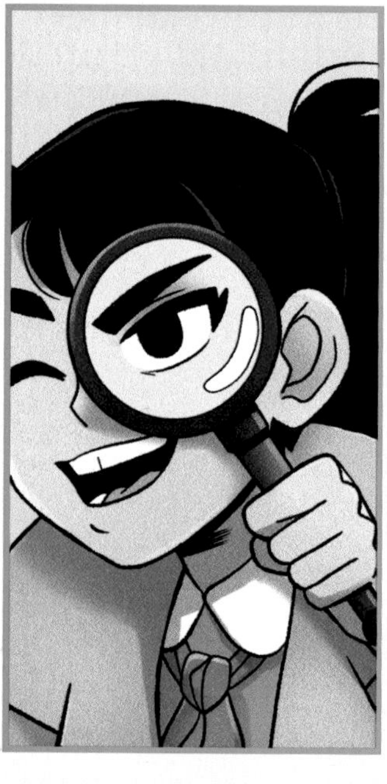

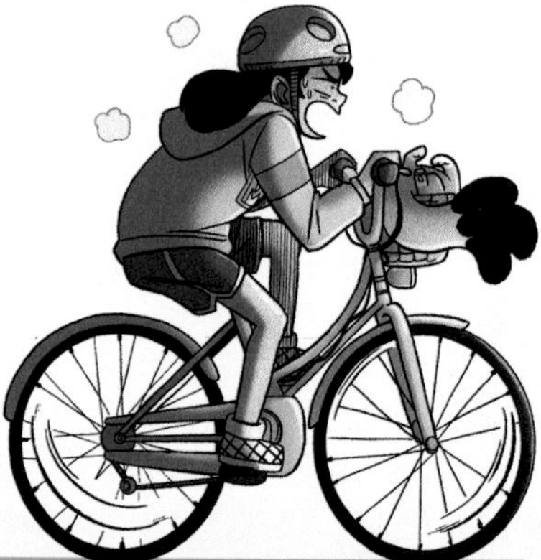

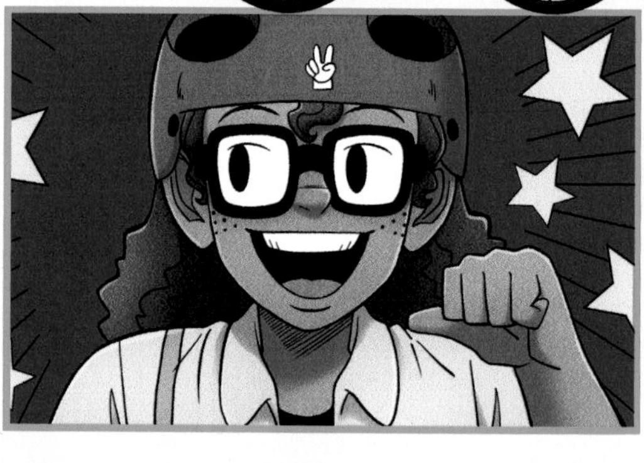

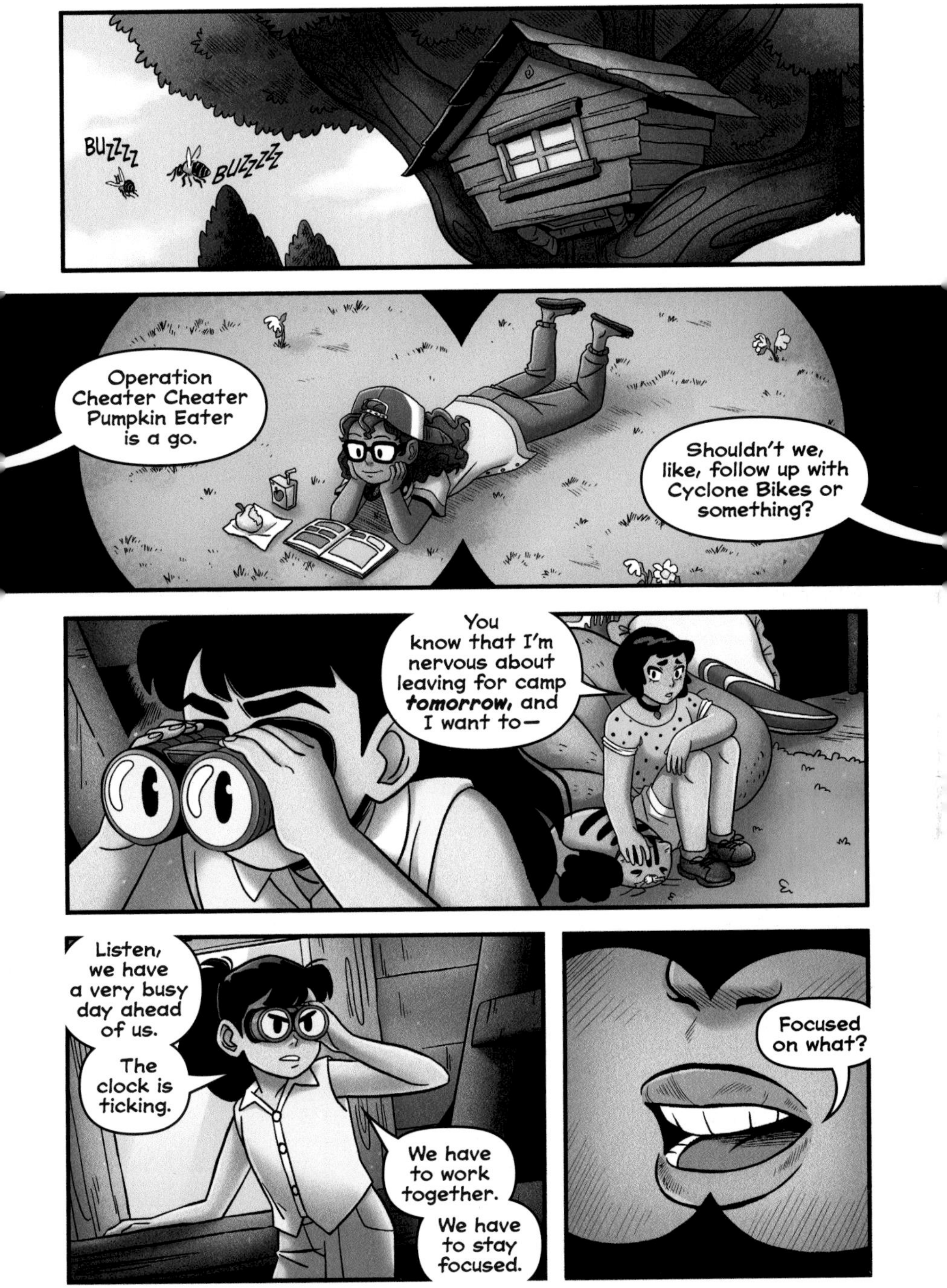
BUZZZZ
BUZZZZZ
Operation Cheater Cheater Pumpkin Eater is a go.
Shouldn't we, like, follow up with Cyclone Bikes or something?
You know that I'm nervous about leaving for camp *tomorrow,* and I want to—
Listen, we have a very busy day ahead of us.
The clock is ticking.
We have to work together.
We have to stay focused.
Focused on what?

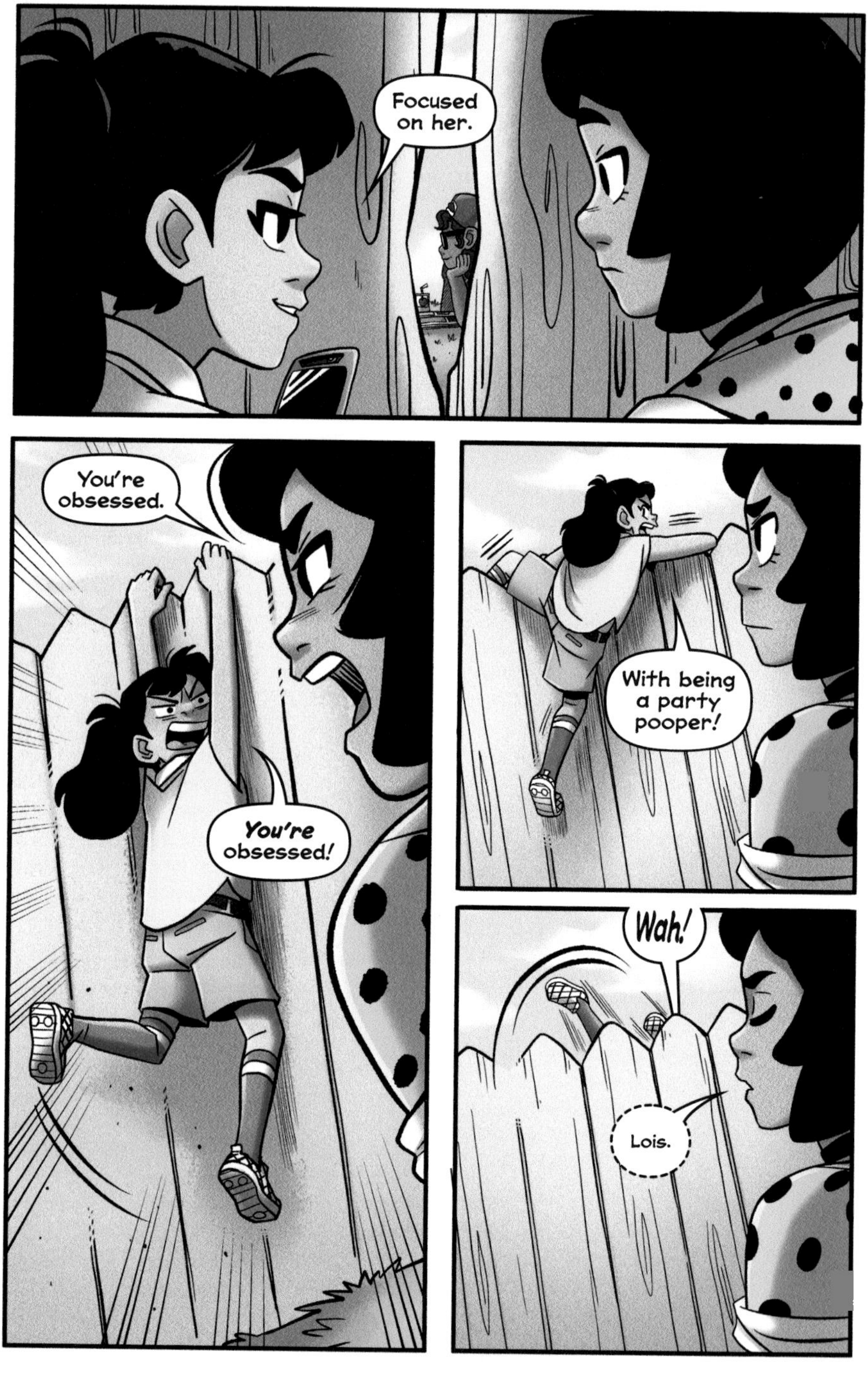
Focused on her.
You're obsessed.
You're obsessed!
With being a party pooper!
Wah!
Lois.

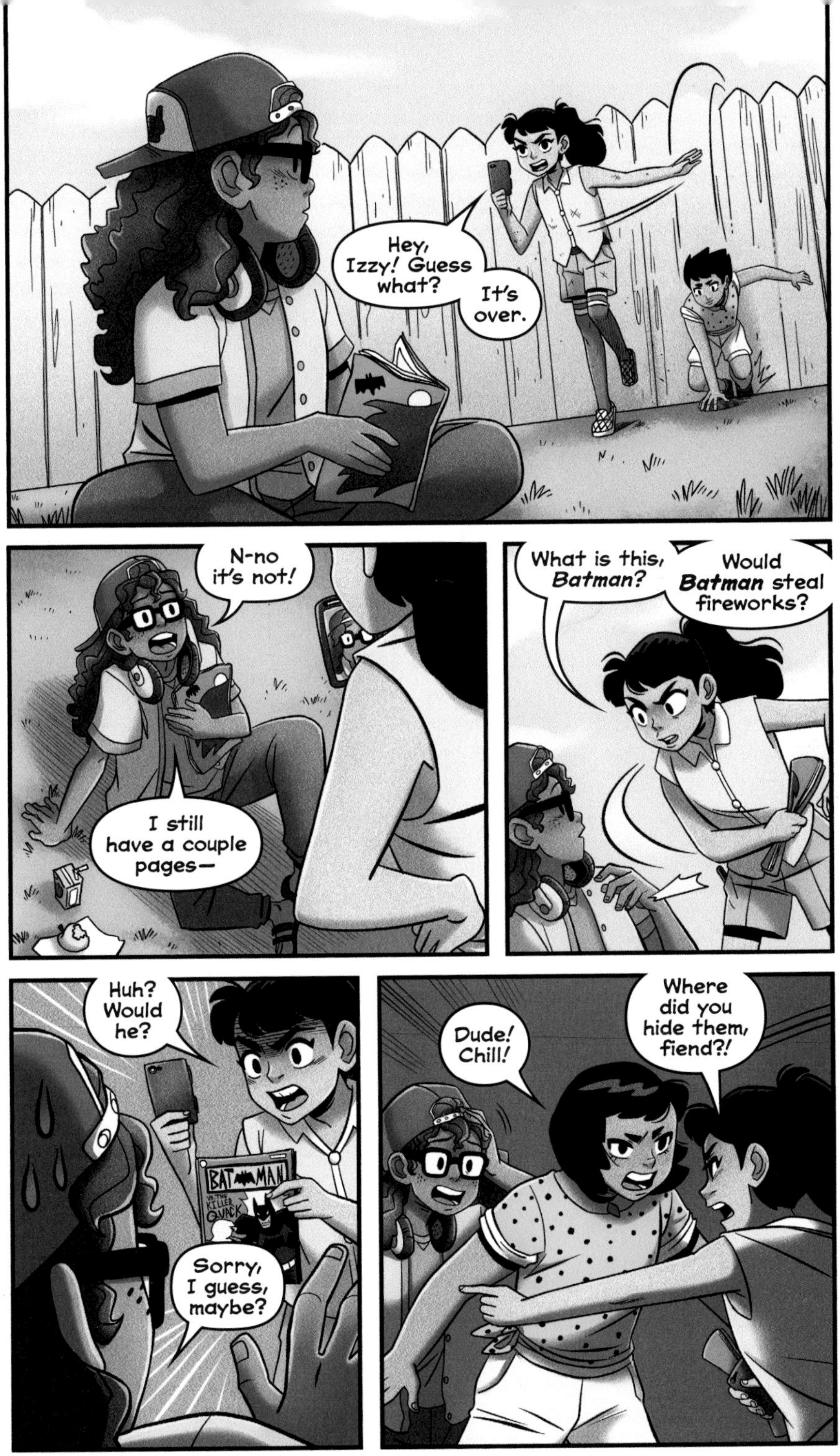
Hey, Izzy! Guess what?
It's over.
N-no it's not!
I still have a couple pages—
What is this, Batman?
Would Batman steal fireworks?
Huh? Would he?
BATMAN
Sorry, I guess, maybe?
Dude! Chill!
Where did you hide them, fiend?!

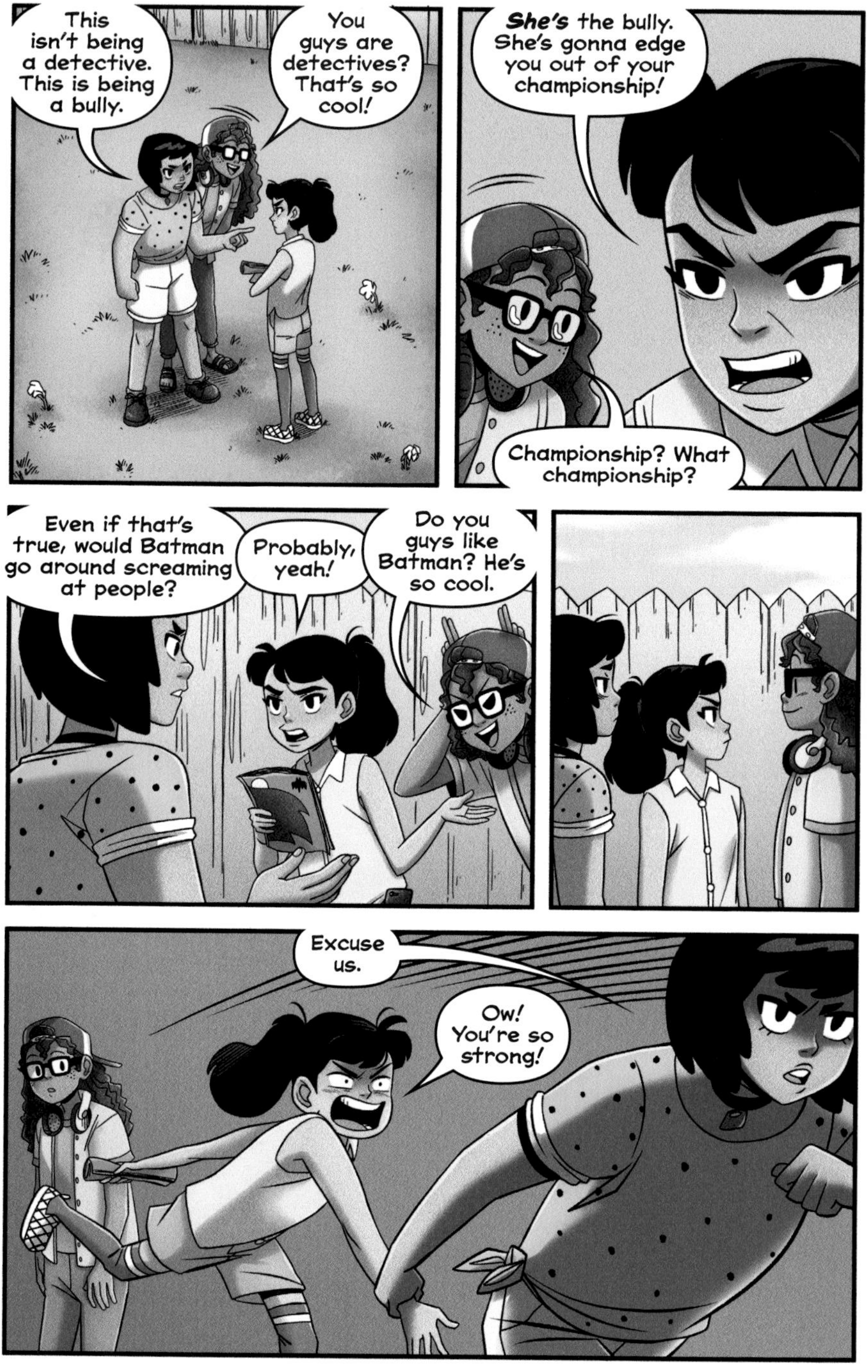
This isn't being a detective. This is being a bully.
You guys are detectives? That's so cool!
She's the bully. She's gonna edge you out of your championship!
Championship? What championship?
Even if that's true, would Batman go around screaming at people?
Probably, yeah!
Do you guys like Batman? He's so cool.
Excuse us.
Ow! You're so strong!

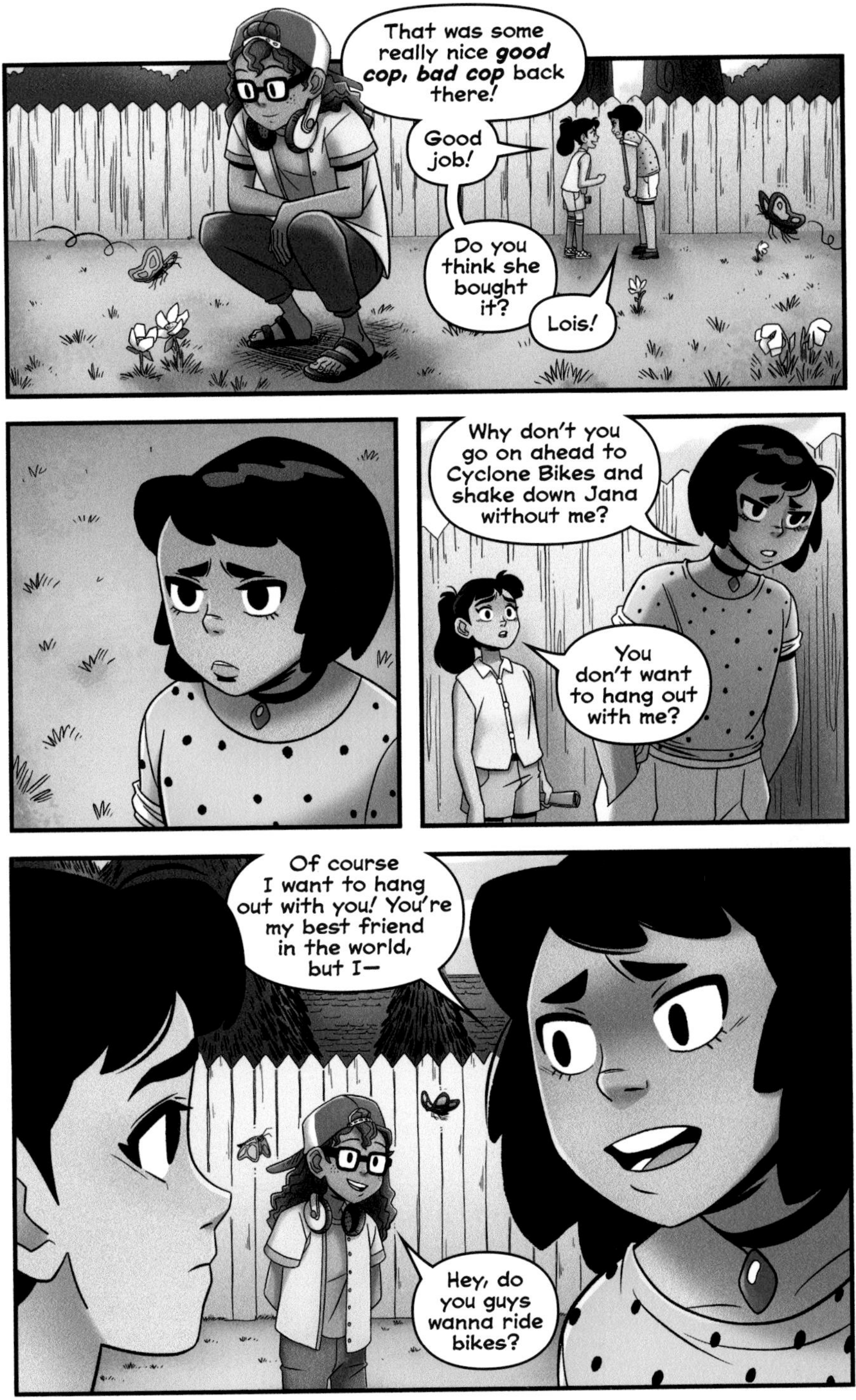
That was some really nice **good cop, bad cop** back there!
Good job!
Do you think she bought it?
Lois!
Why don't you go on ahead to Cyclone Bikes and shake down Jana without me?
You don't want to hang out with me?
Of course I want to hang out with you! You're my best friend in the world, but I—
Hey, do you guys wanna ride bikes?

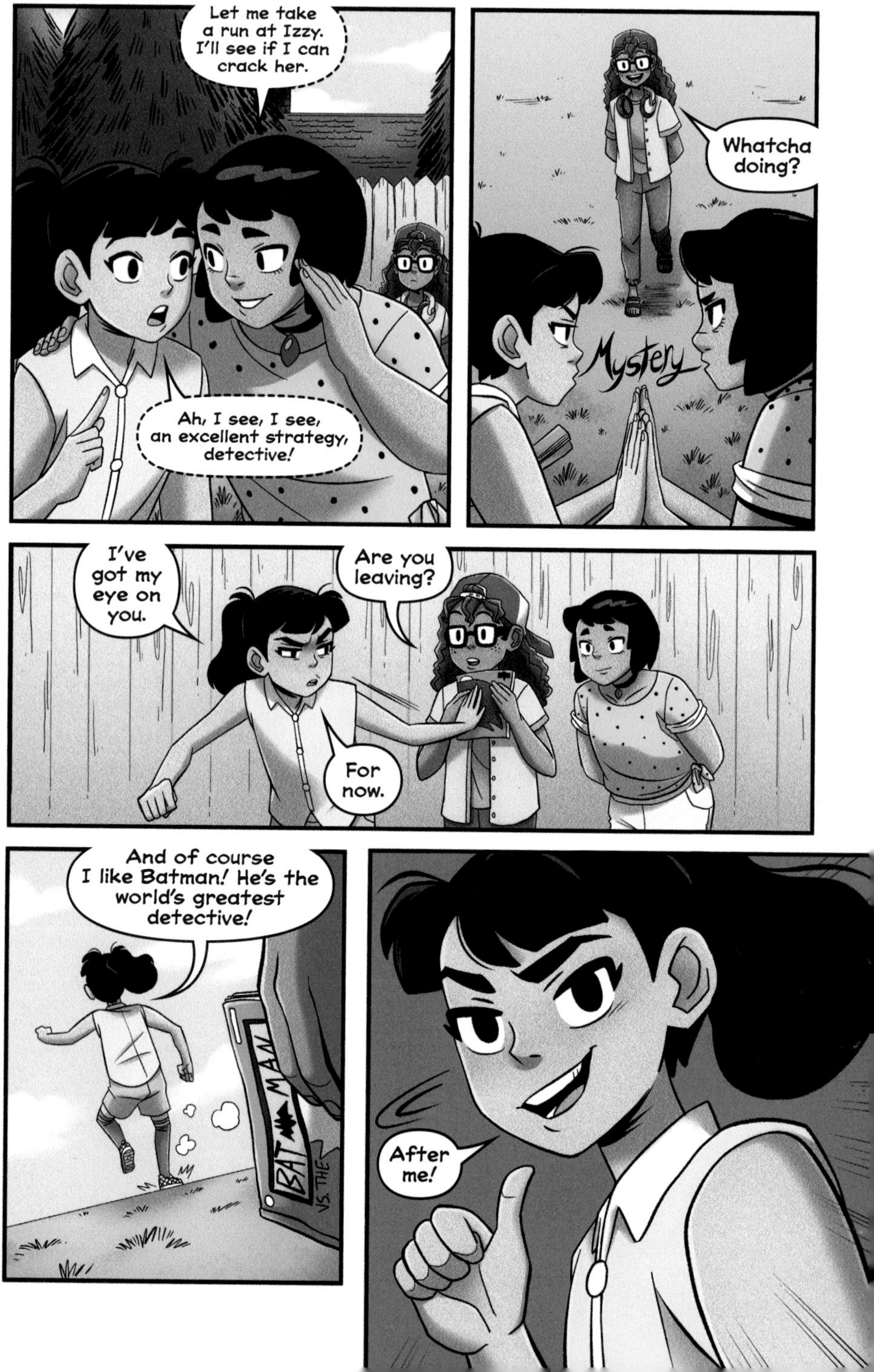
Let me take a run at Izzy. I'll see if I can crack her.
Ah, I see, I see, an excellent strategy, detective!
Whatcha doing?
Mystery
I've got my eye on you.
Are you leaving?
For now.
And of course I like Batman! He's the world's greatest detective!
BATMAN
VS. THE
After me!

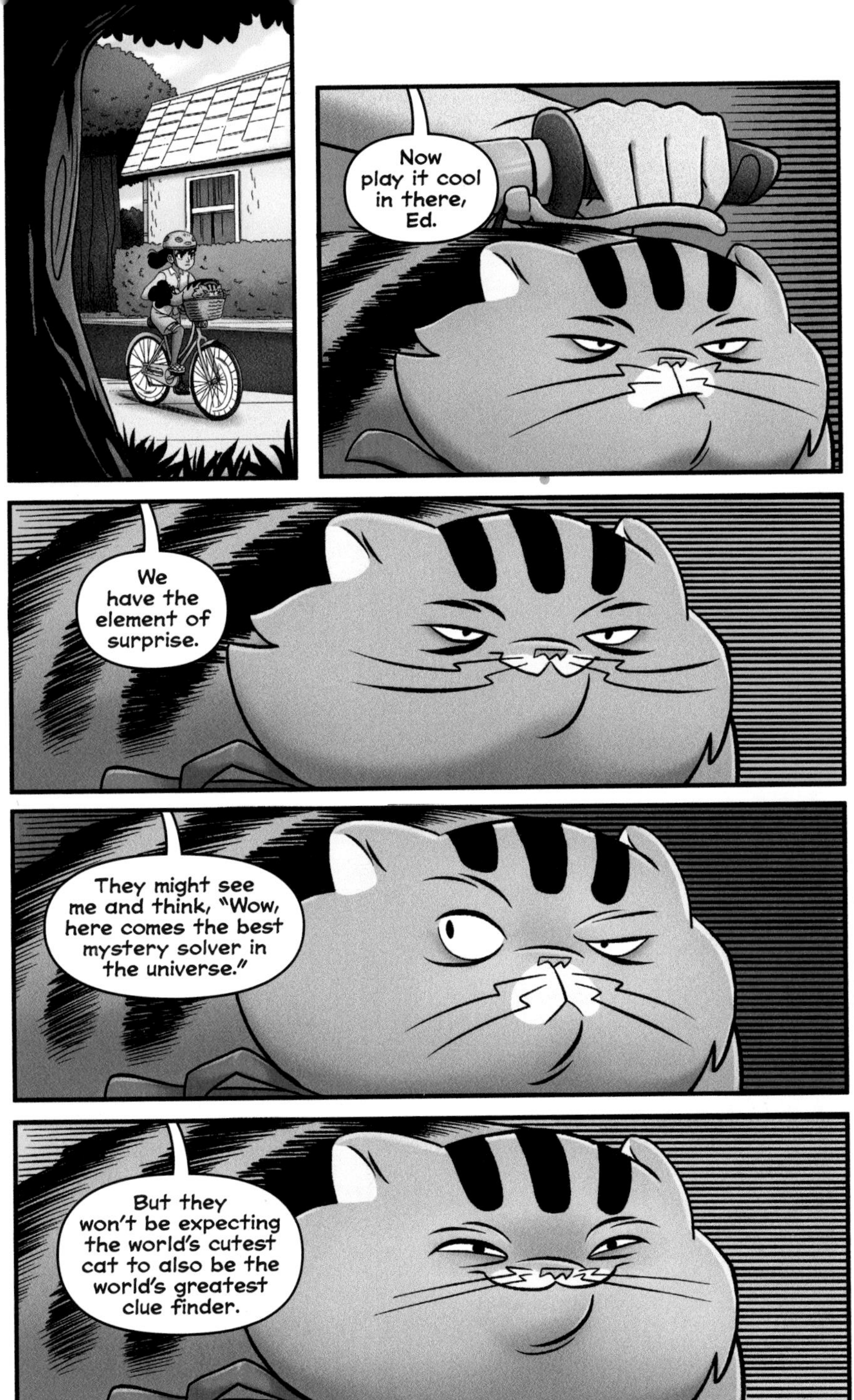
Now play it cool in there, Ed.
We have the element of surprise.
They might see me and think, "Wow, here comes the best mystery solver in the universe."
But they won't be expecting the world's cutest cat to also be the world's greatest clue finder.

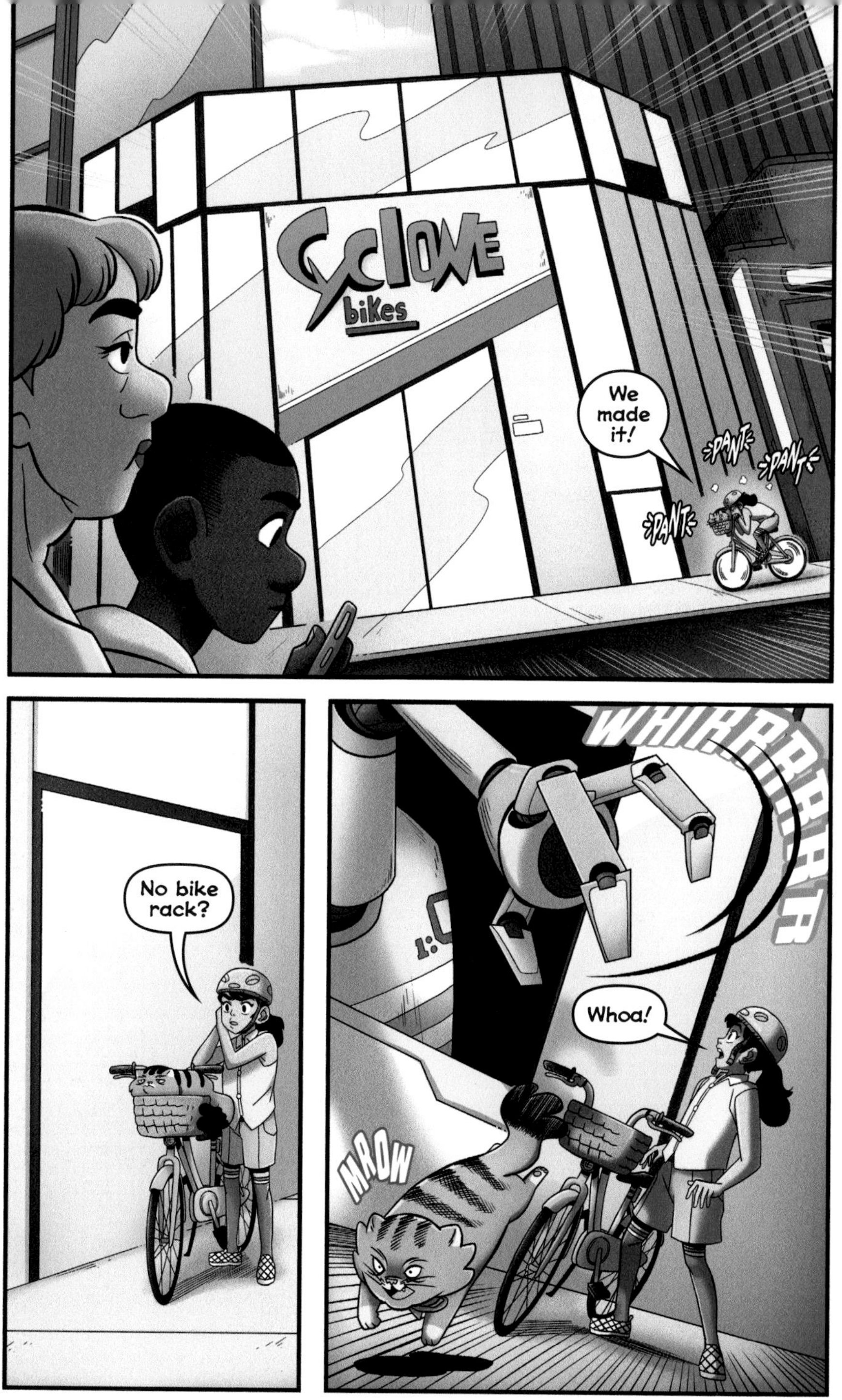
CYCLONE
bikes
We made it!
PANT
PANT
PANT
No bike rack?
WHIRRRRRRR
1:
Whoa!
MROW

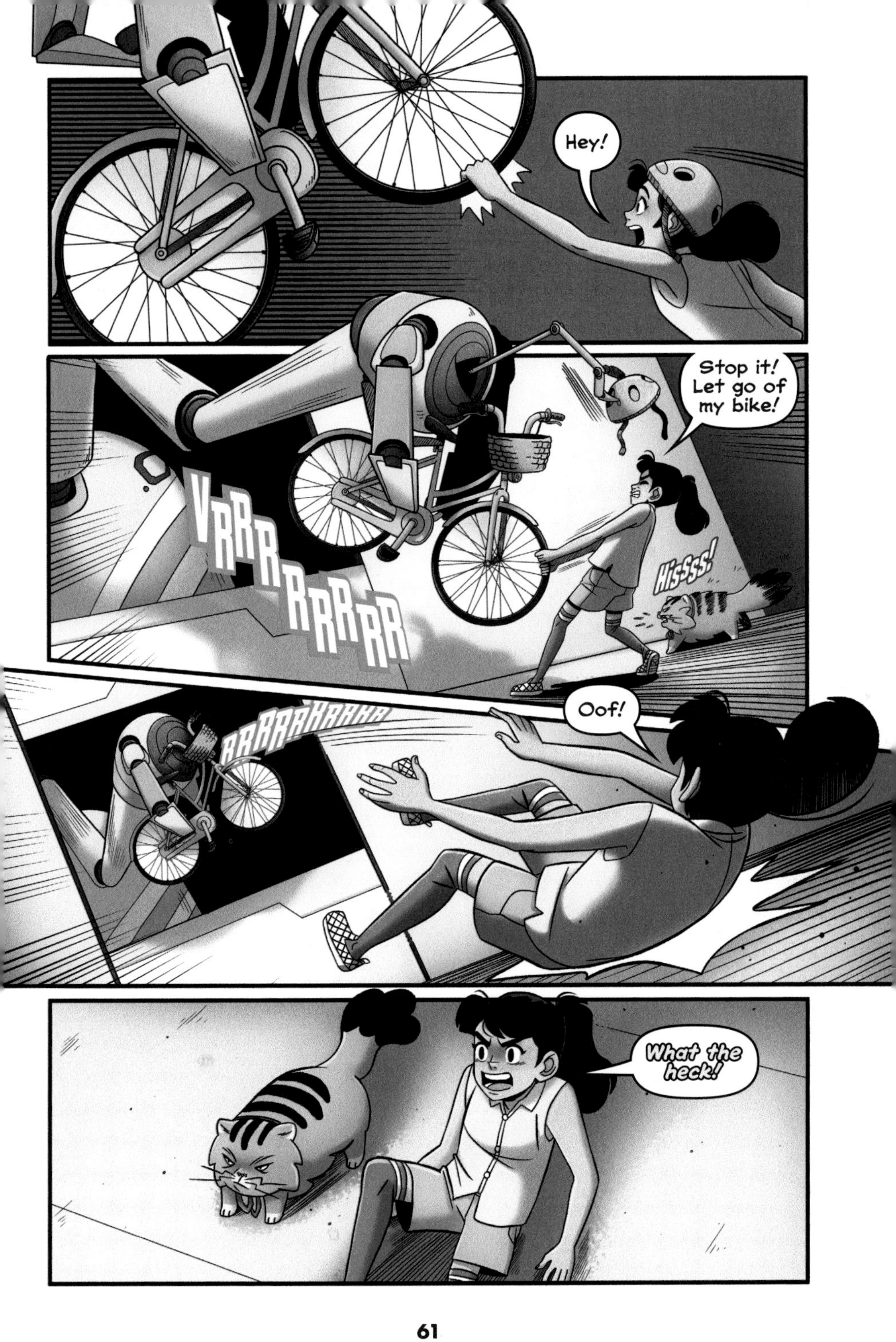
Hey!
Stop it! Let go of my bike!
VRRRRRRRRR
HISSSS!
RRRRRRRRR
Oof!
What the heck!

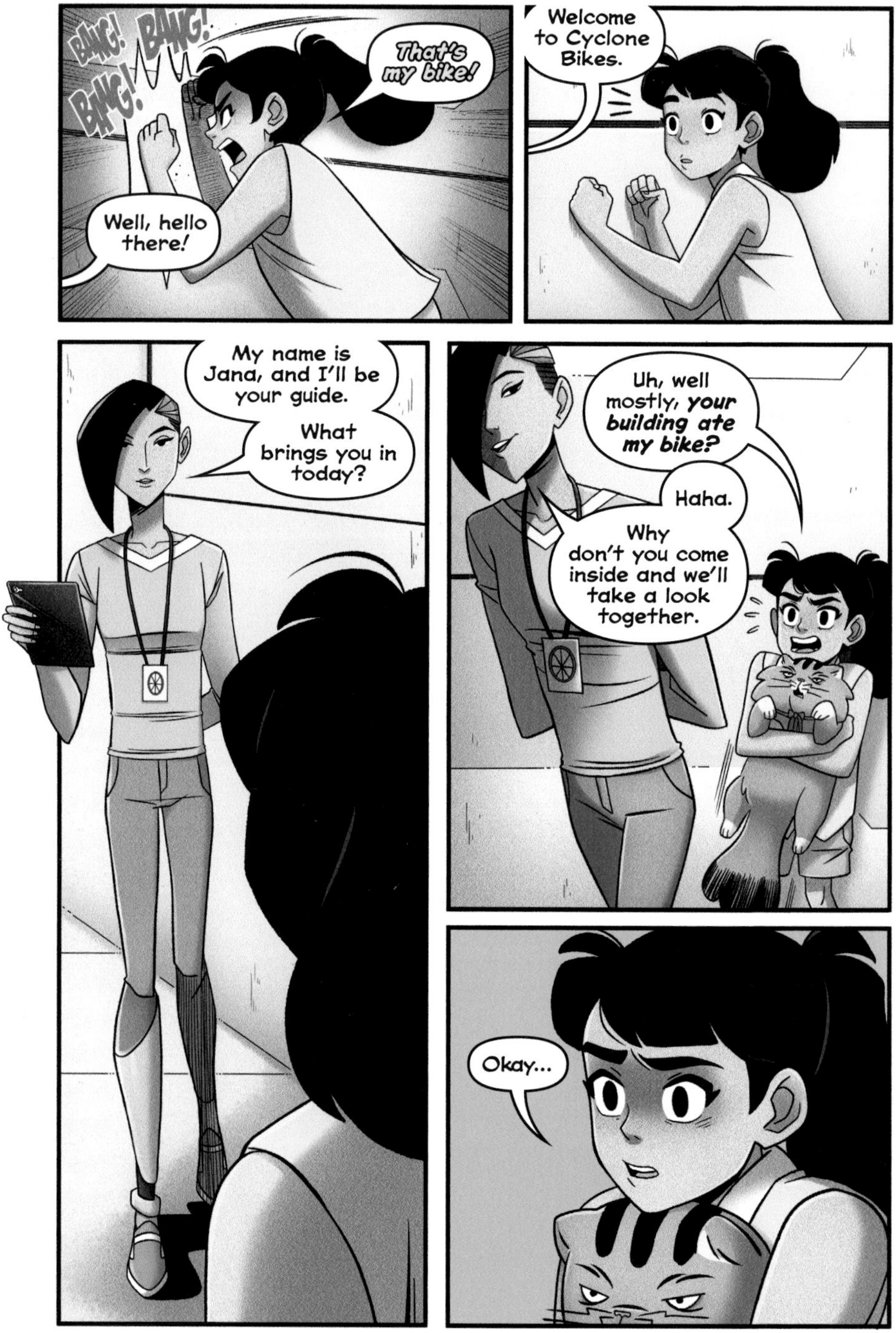
BANG! BANG! BANG! BANG!
That's my bike!
Well, hello there!
Welcome to Cyclone Bikes.
My name is Jana, and I'll be your guide.
What brings you in today?
Uh, well mostly, *your building ate my bike?*
Haha.
Why don't you come inside and we'll take a look together.
Okay...

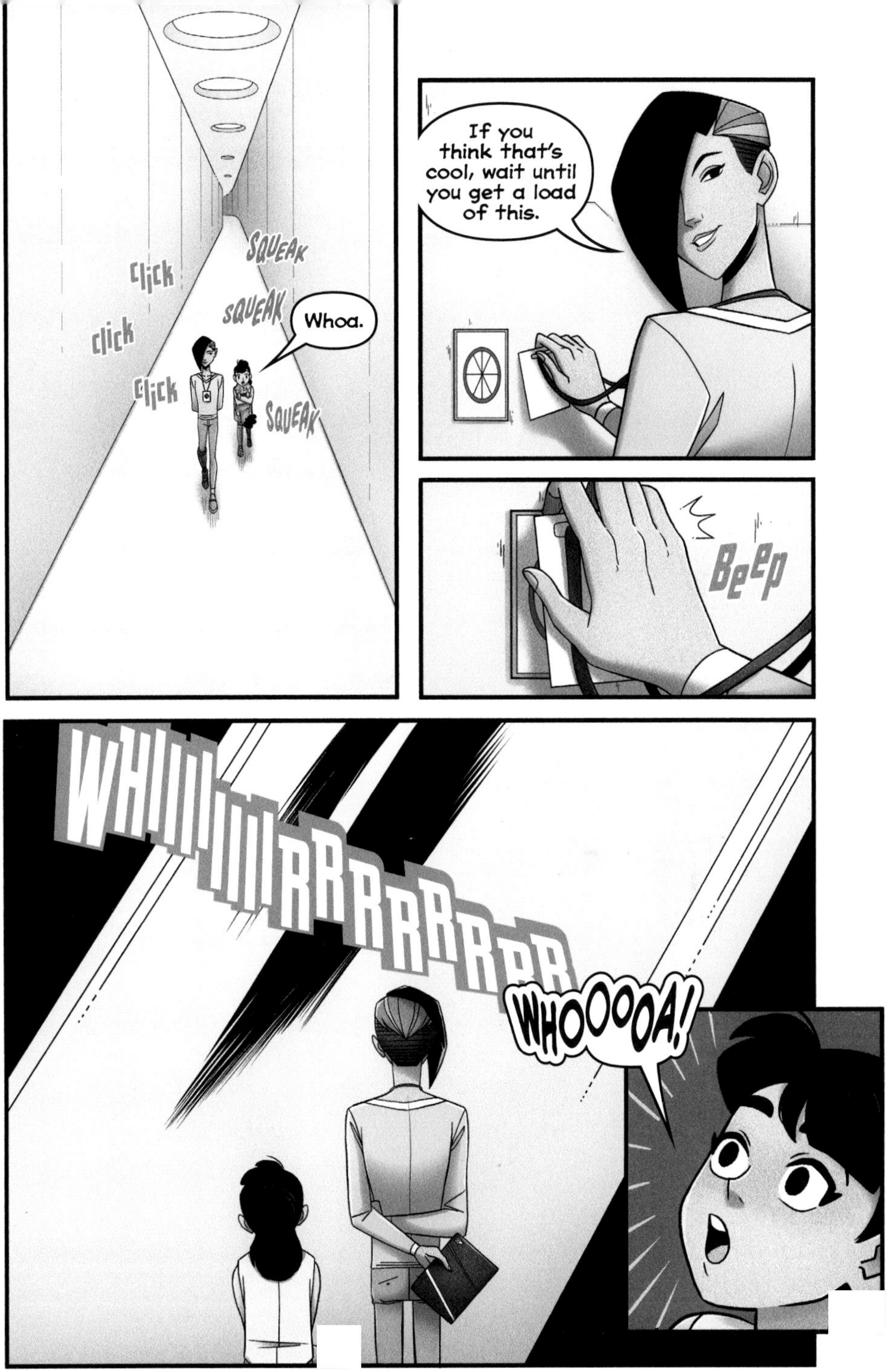
SQUEAK
click
SQUEAK
click
Whoa.
click
SQUEAK
If you think that's cool, wait until you get a load of this.
Beep
WHIIIIIIIRRRRRRRRR
WHOOOOA!

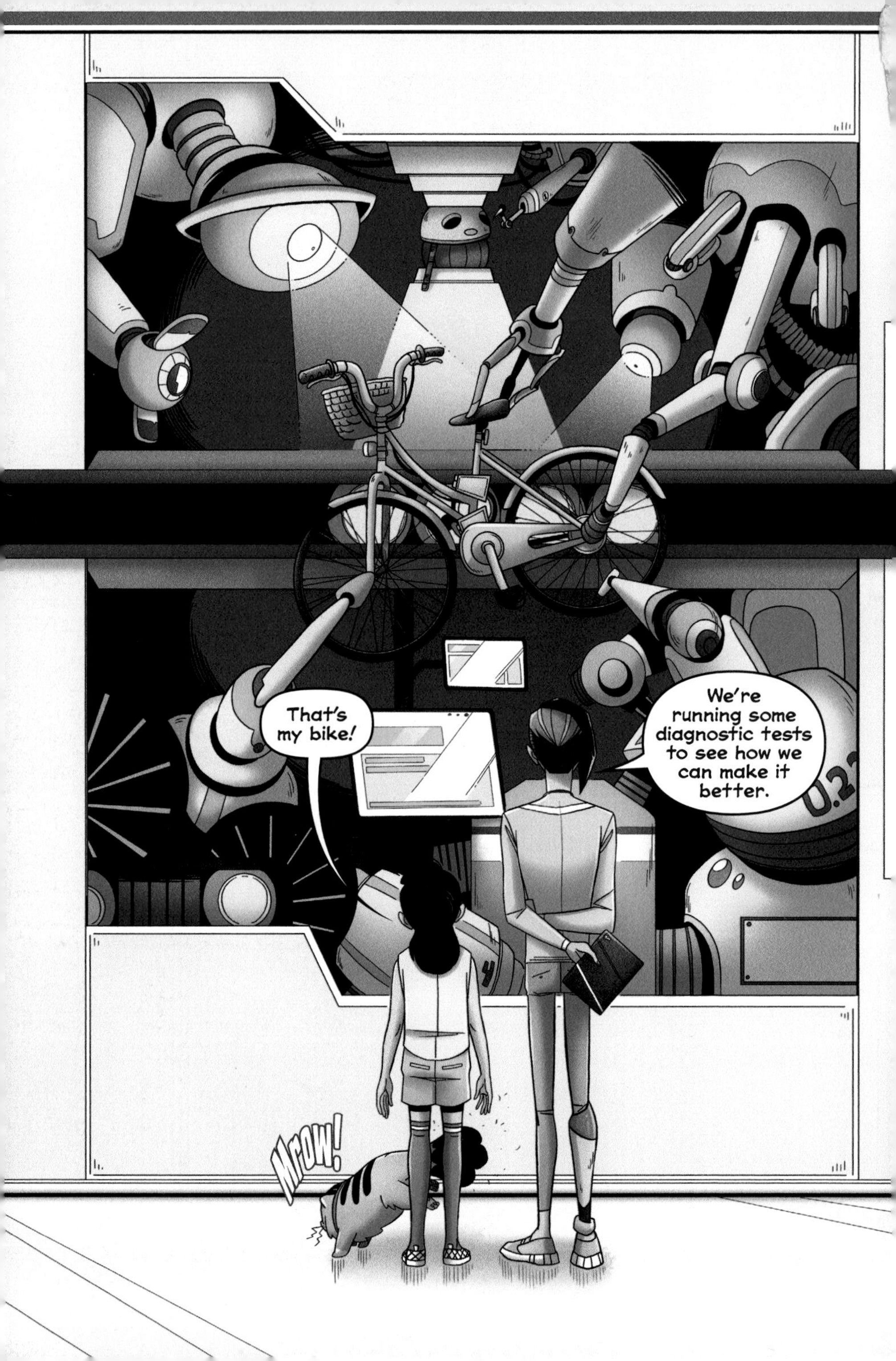
That's my bike!
We're running some diagnostic tests to see how we can make it better.
Mrow!

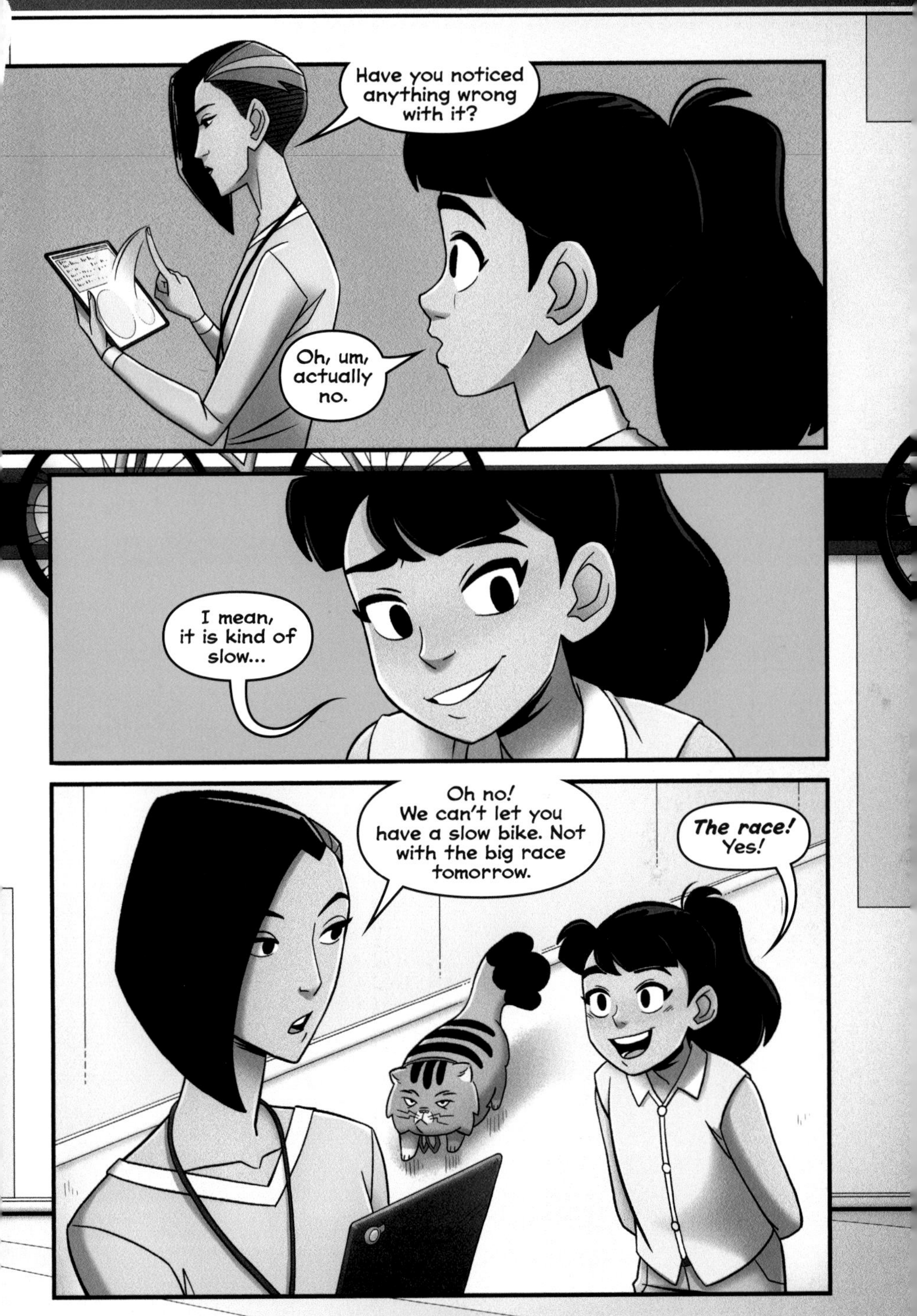
Have you noticed anything wrong with it?
Oh, um, actually no.
I mean, it is kind of slow...
Oh no! We can't let you have a slow bike. Not with the big race tomorrow.
The race! Yes!

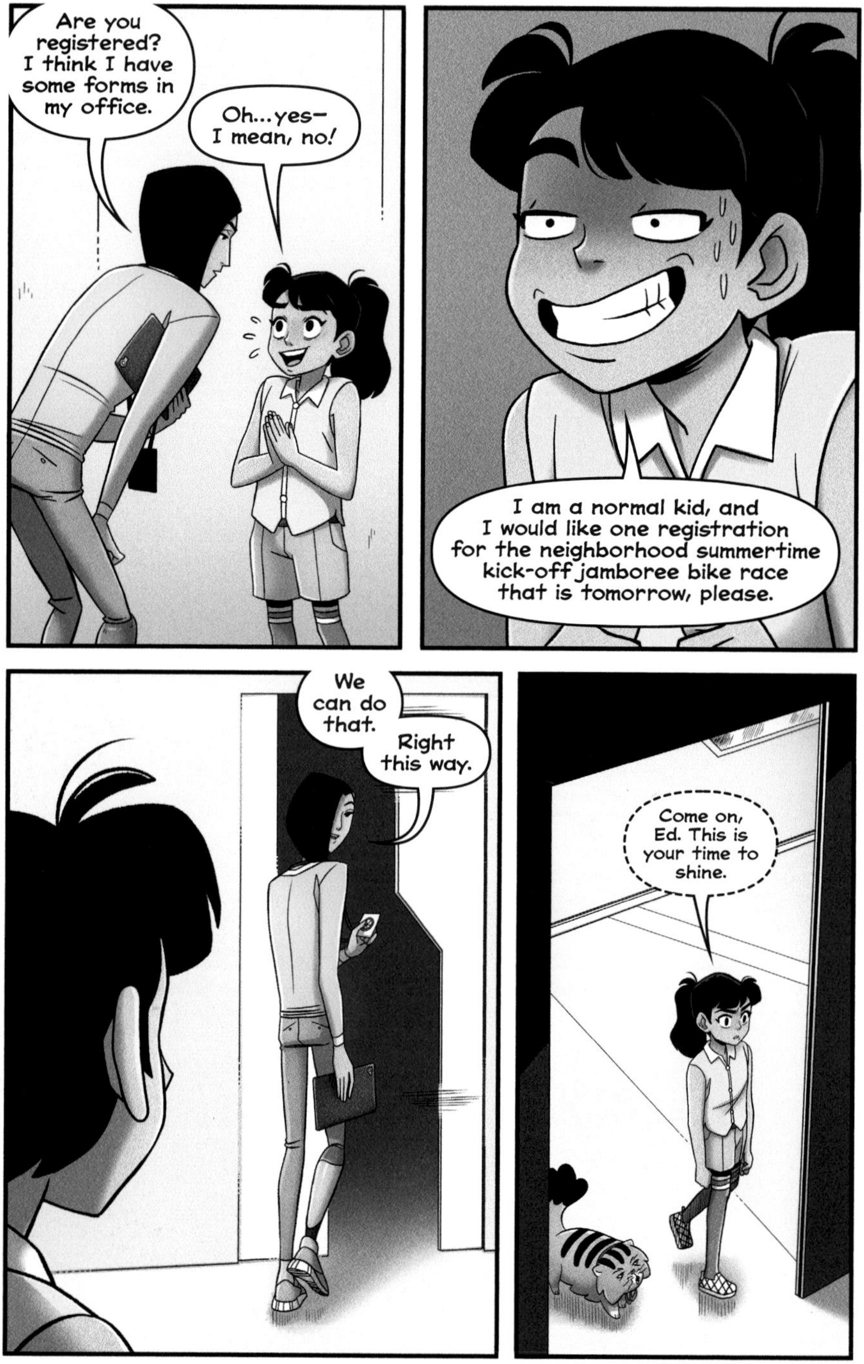
Are you registered? I think I have some forms in my office.
Oh...yes— I mean, no!
I am a normal kid, and I would like one registration for the neighborhood summertime kick-off jamboree bike race that is tomorrow, please.
We can do that.
Right this way.
Come on, Ed. This is your time to shine.

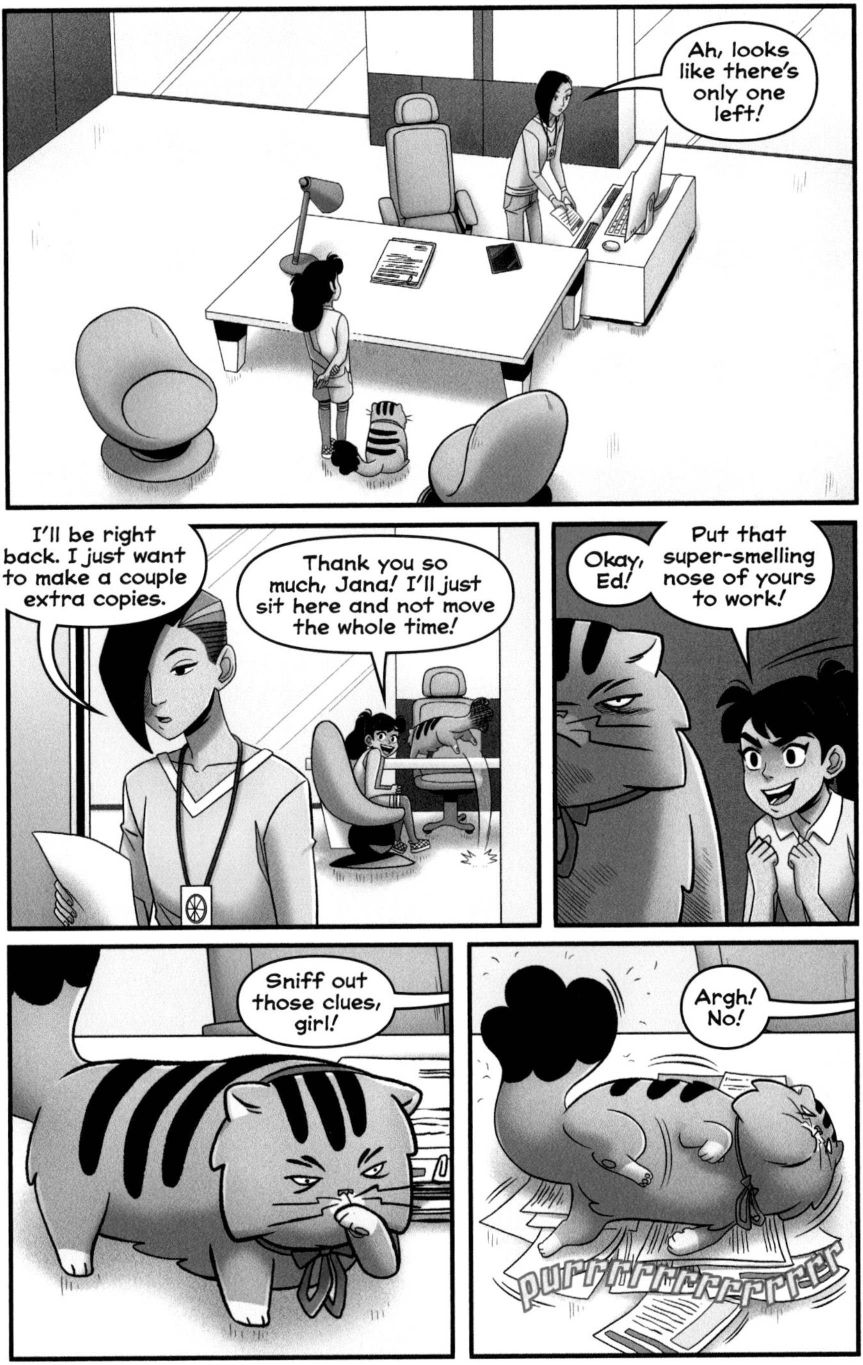
Ah, looks like there's only one left!
I'll be right back. I just want to make a couple extra copies.
Thank you so much, Jana! I'll just sit here and not move the whole time!
Okay, Ed!
Put that super-smelling nose of yours to work!
Sniff out those clues, girl!
Argh! No!
purrrrrrrrrrrrrrr

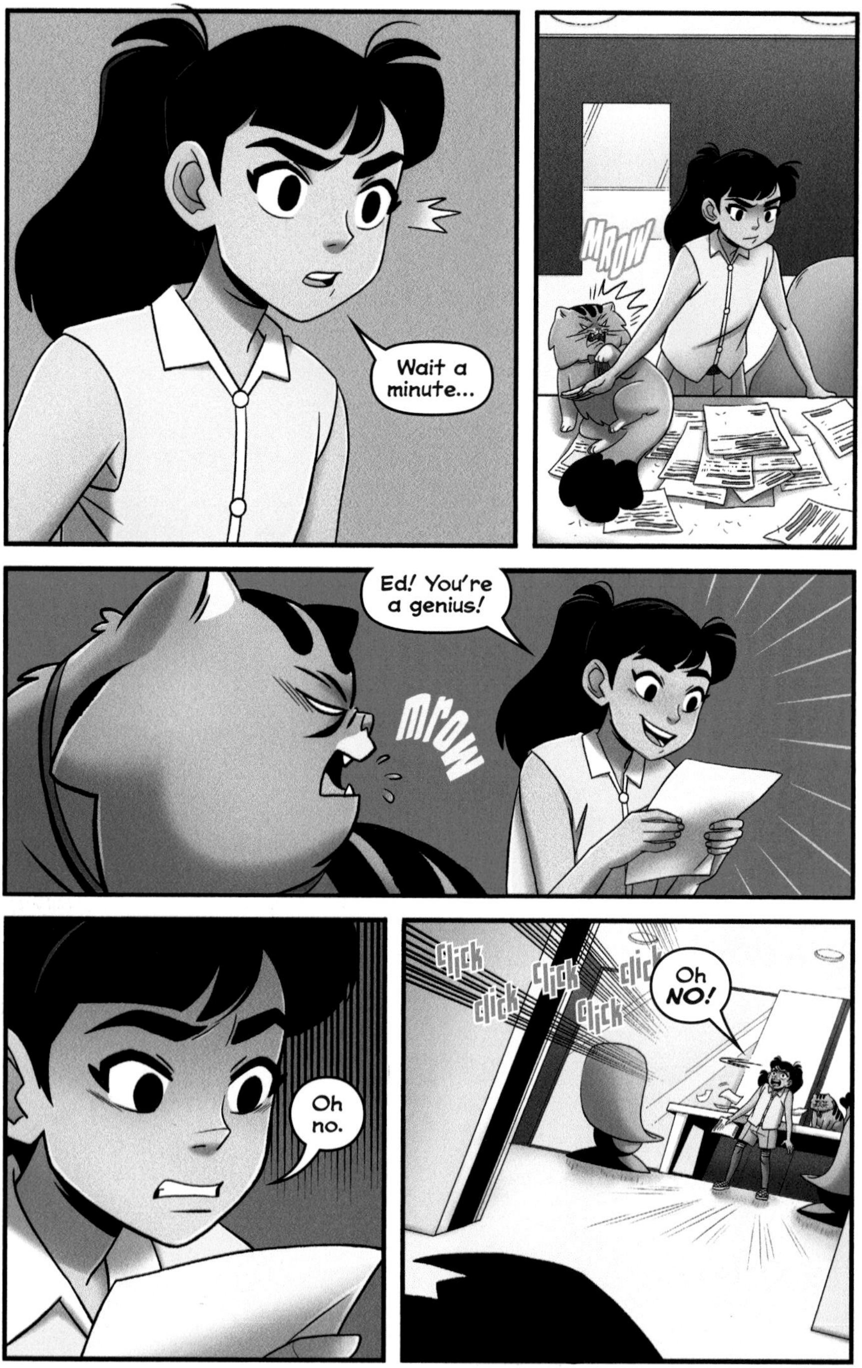
Wait a minute...
MROW
Ed! You're a genius!
MROW
Oh no.
click
click
click
click
click
Oh NO!

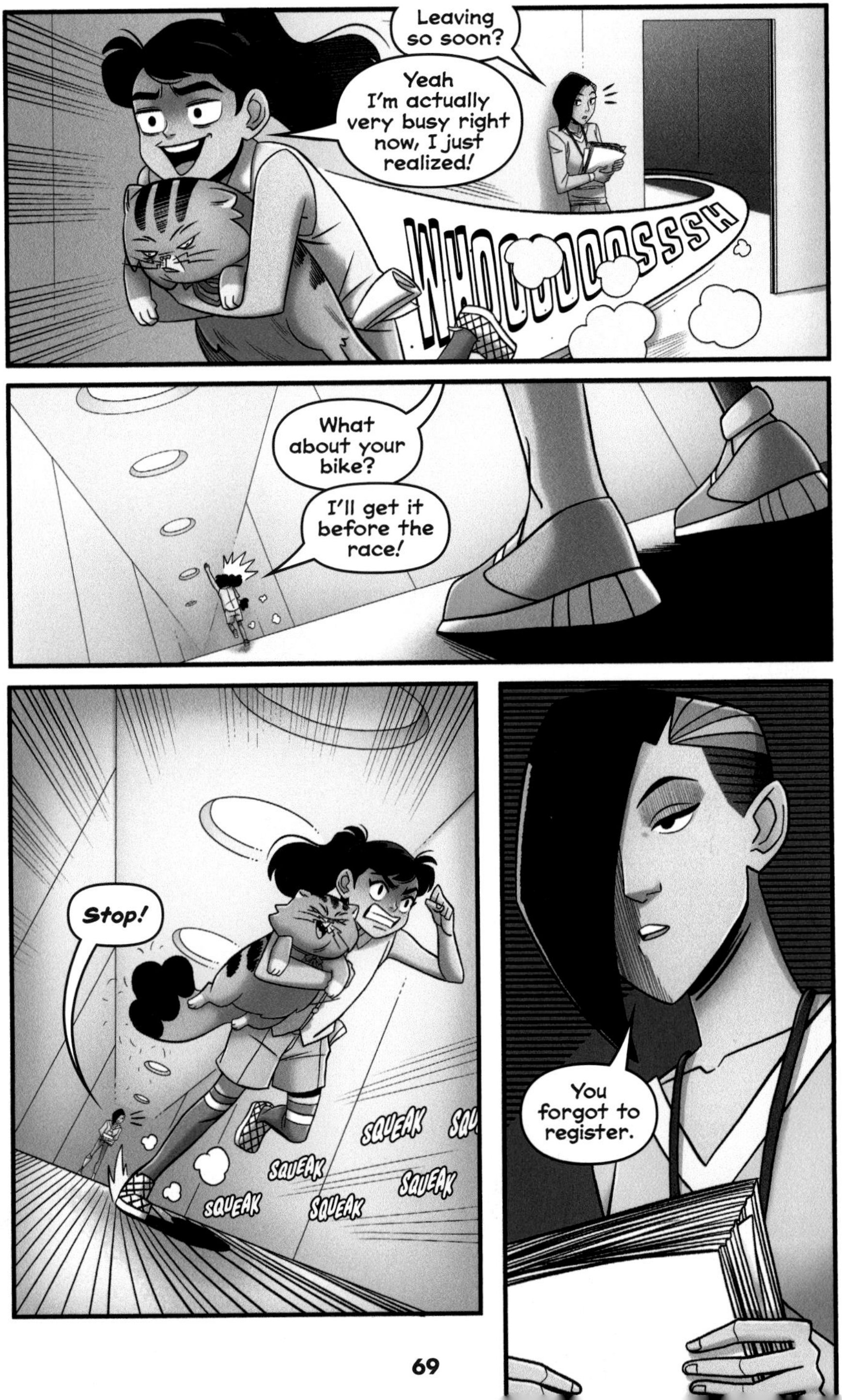
Leaving so soon?
Yeah I'm actually very busy right now, I just realized!
WHOOOOOOOSSSSH
What about your bike?
I'll get it before the race!
Stop!
SQUEAK
SQUEAK
SQUEAK
SQUEAK
SQUEAK
You forgot to register.

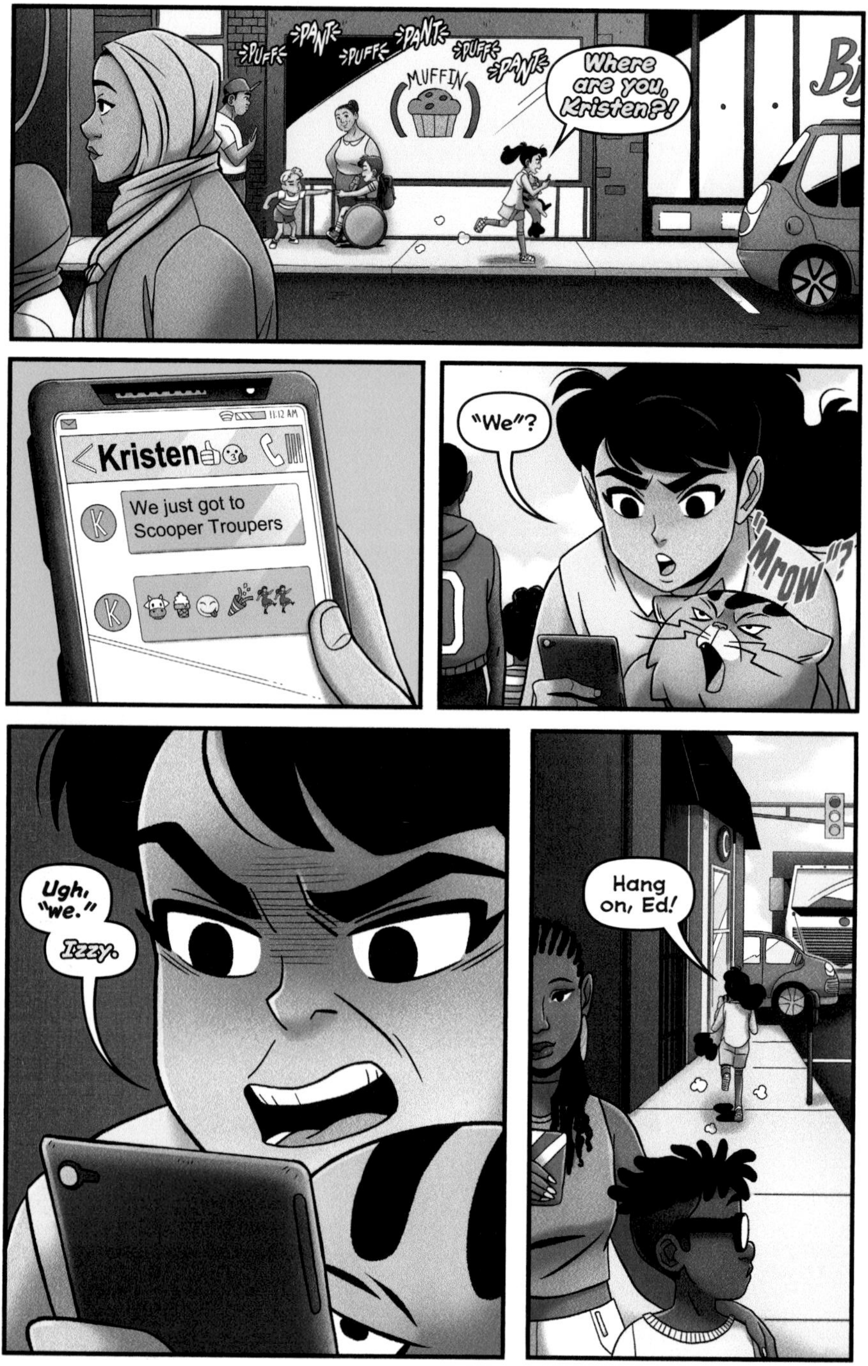

PUFF
PANT
PUFF
PANT
PUFF
PANT
MUFFIN
Where are you, Kristen?!
11:12 AM
Kristen
We just got to Scooper Troupers
"We"?
"Mrow"?
Ugh, "we."
Izzy.
Hang on, Ed!

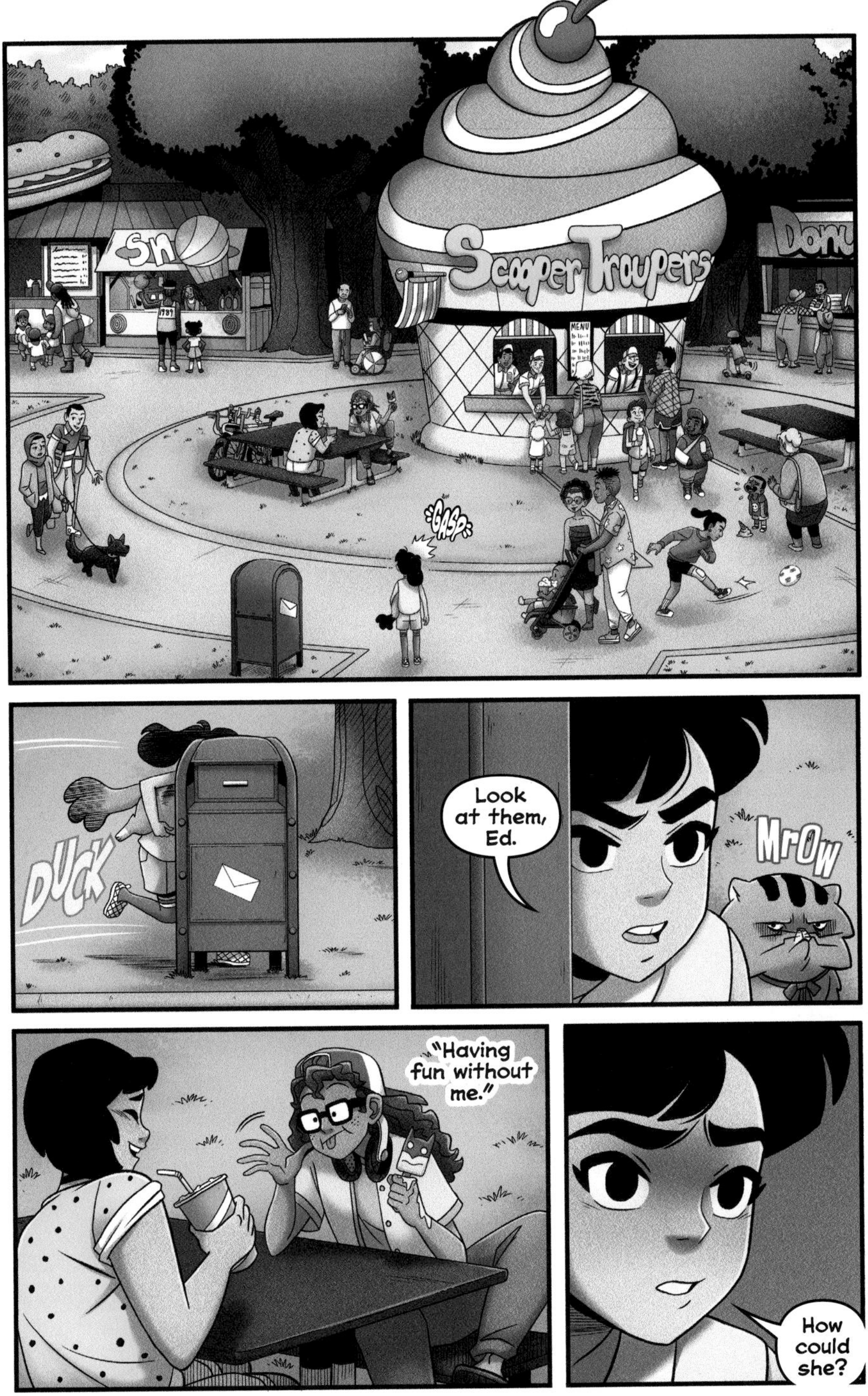
Sn
Scooper Troupers
MENU
Don
GASP
DUCK
Look at them, Ed.
MrOw
"Having fun without me."
How could she?

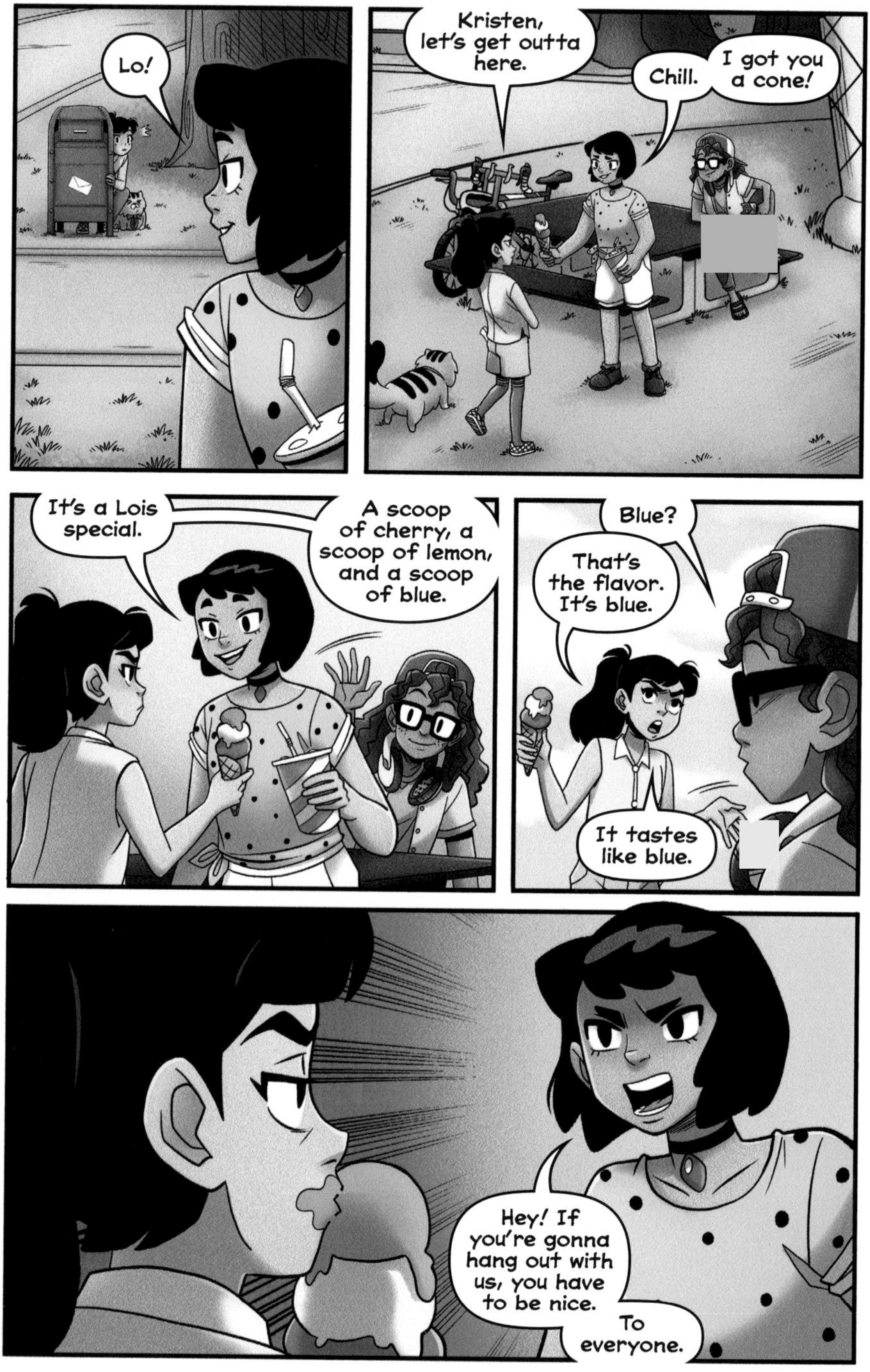
Lo!
Kristen, let's get outta here.
Chill.
I got you a cone!
It's a Lois special.
A scoop of cherry, a scoop of lemon, and a scoop of blue.
Blue?
That's the flavor. It's blue.
It tastes like blue.
Hey! If you're gonna hang out with us, you have to be nice.
To everyone.

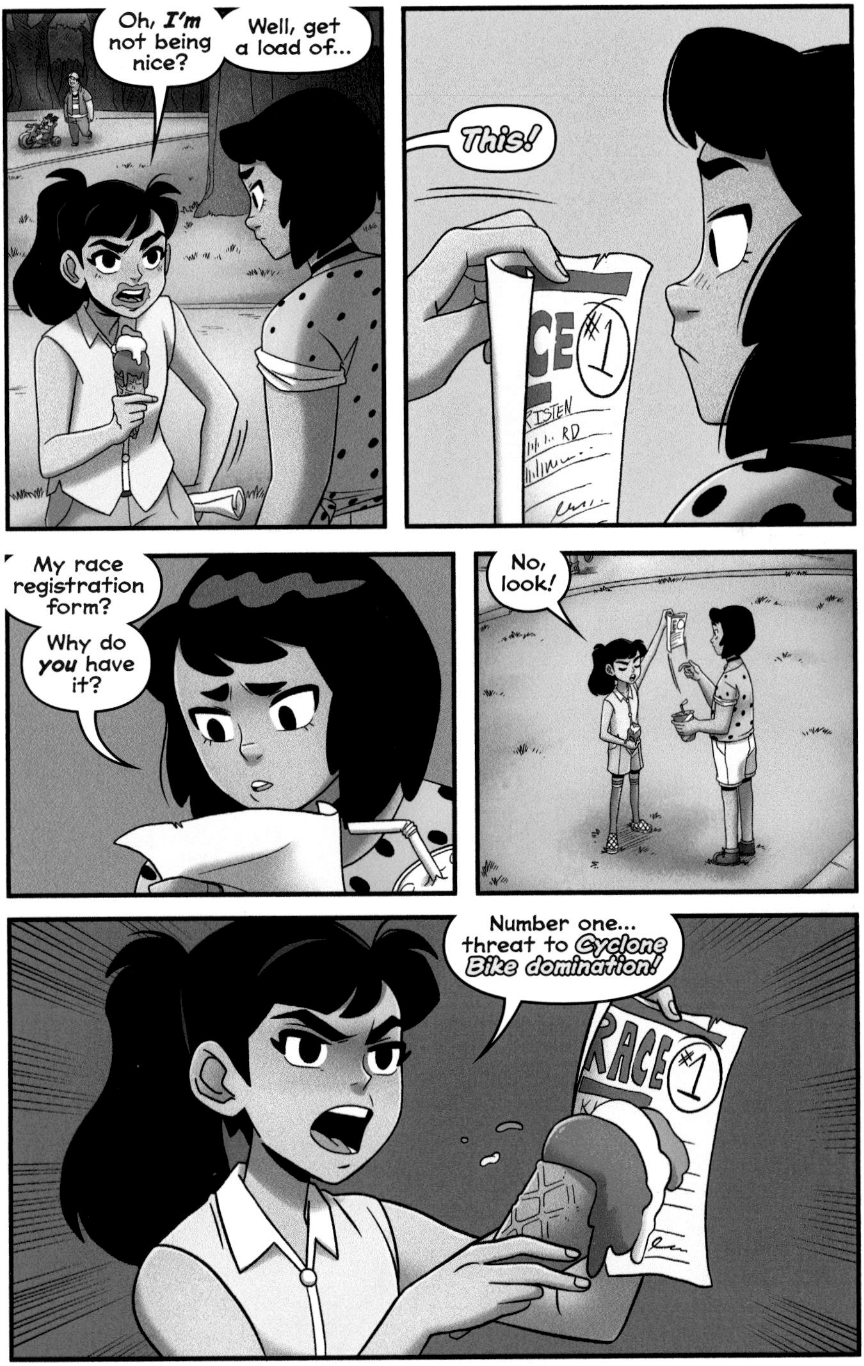
Oh, *I'm* not being nice?
Well, get a load of...
This!
My race registration form?
Why do *you* have it?
No, look!
Number one... threat to Cyclone Bike domination!

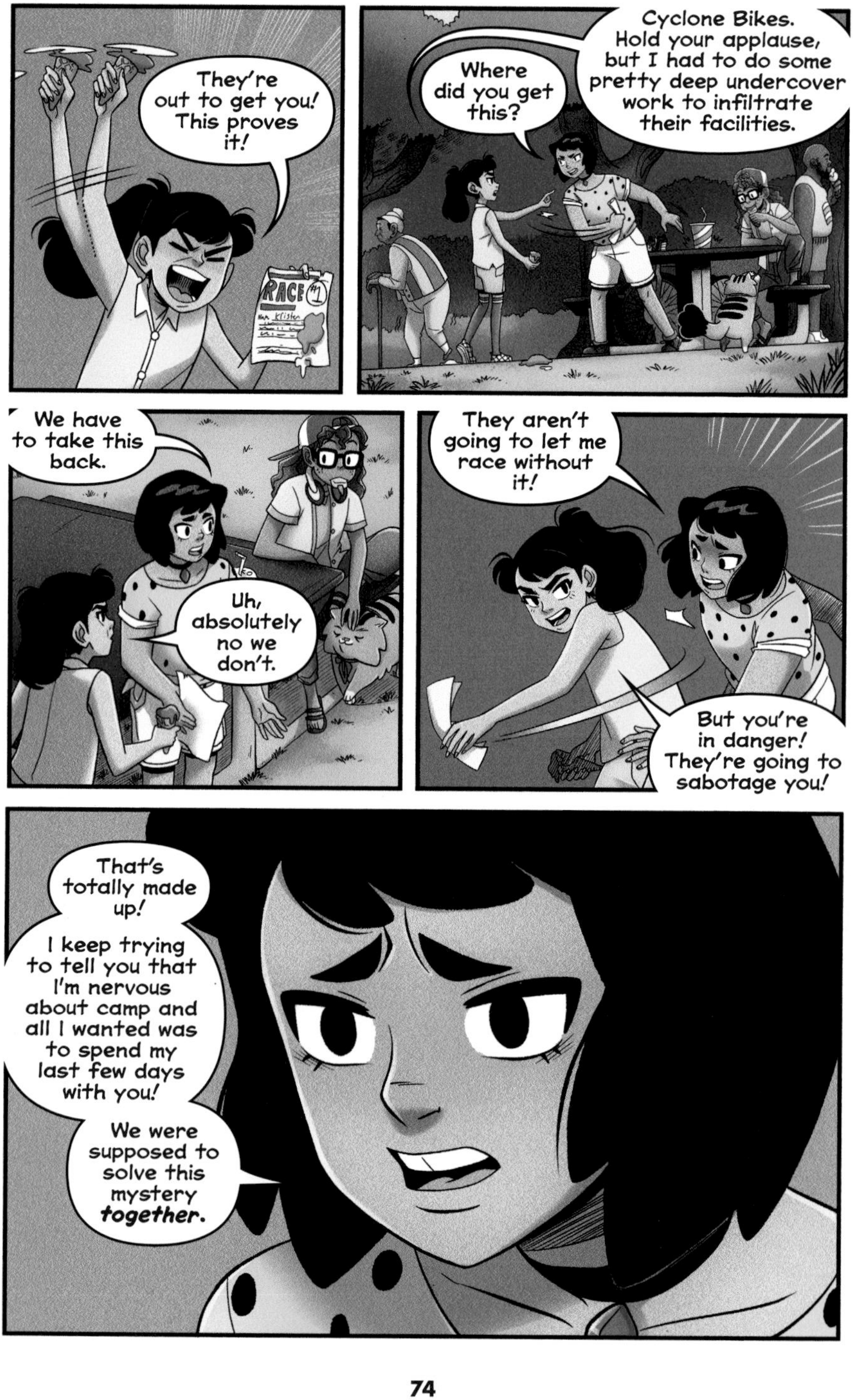
They're out to get you! This proves it!
RACE #1
Where did you get this?
Cyclone Bikes. Hold your applause, but I had to do some pretty deep undercover work to infiltrate their facilities.
We have to take this back.
Uh, absolutely no we don't.
They aren't going to let me race without it!
But you're in danger! They're going to sabotage you!
That's totally made up!
I keep trying to tell you that I'm nervous about camp and all I wanted was to spend my last few days with you!
We were supposed to solve this mystery ***together***.

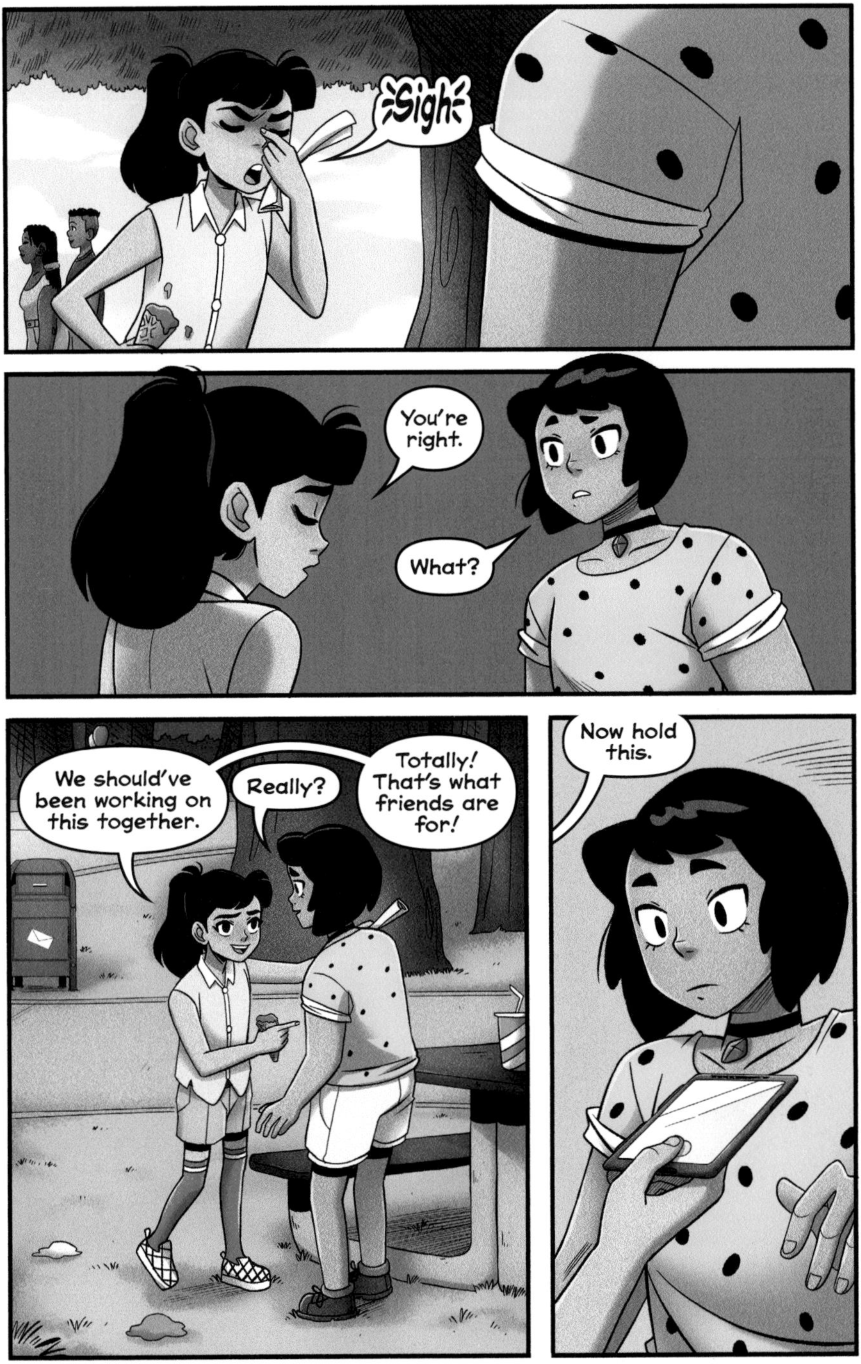
Sigh
You're right.
What?
We should've been working on this together.
Really?
Totally! That's what friends are for!
Now hold this.

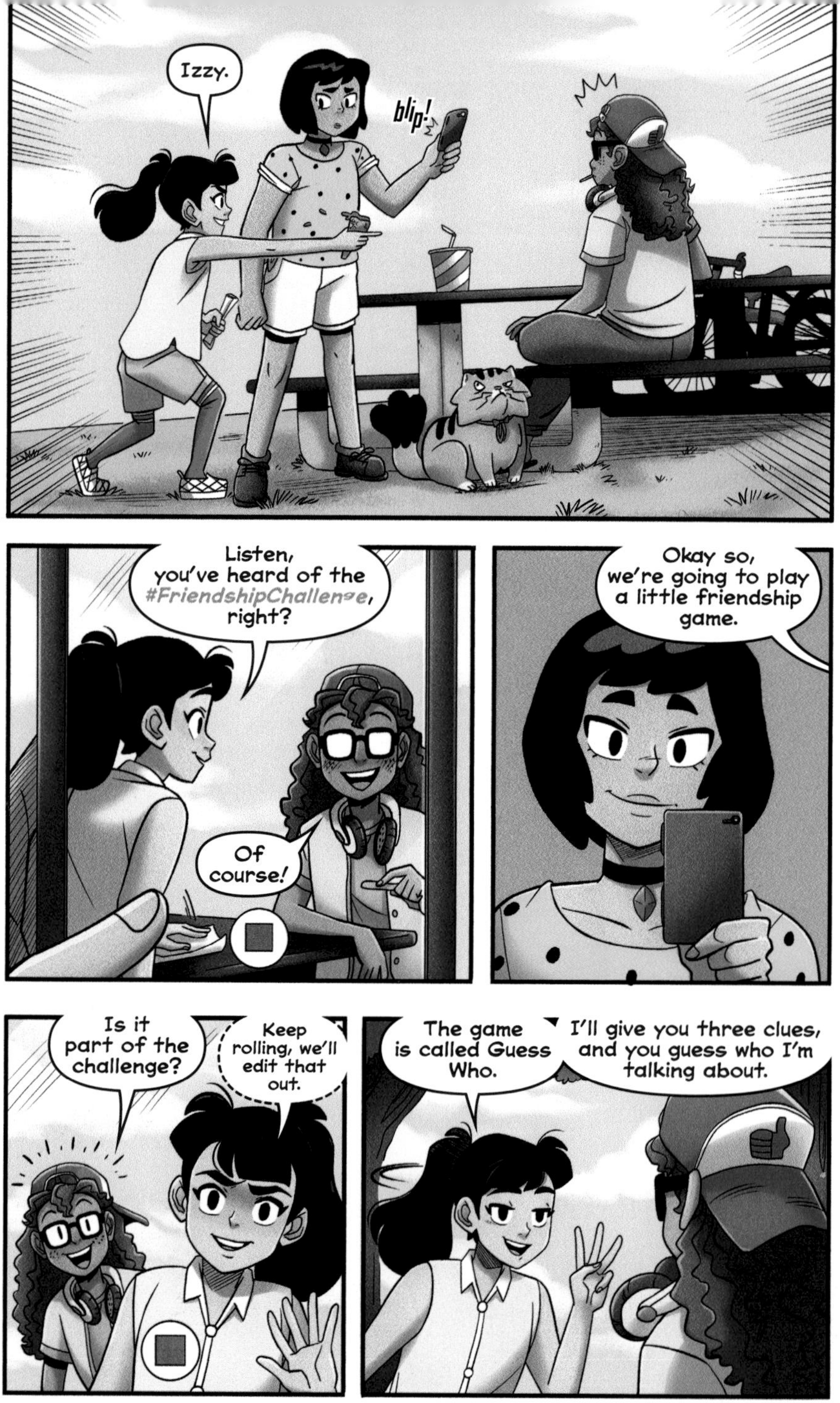
Izzy.
blip!
Listen, you've heard of the #FriendshipChallenge, right?
Of course!
Okay so, we're going to play a little friendship game.
Is it part of the challenge?
Keep rolling, we'll edit that out.
The game is called Guess Who.
I'll give you three clues, and you guess who I'm talking about.

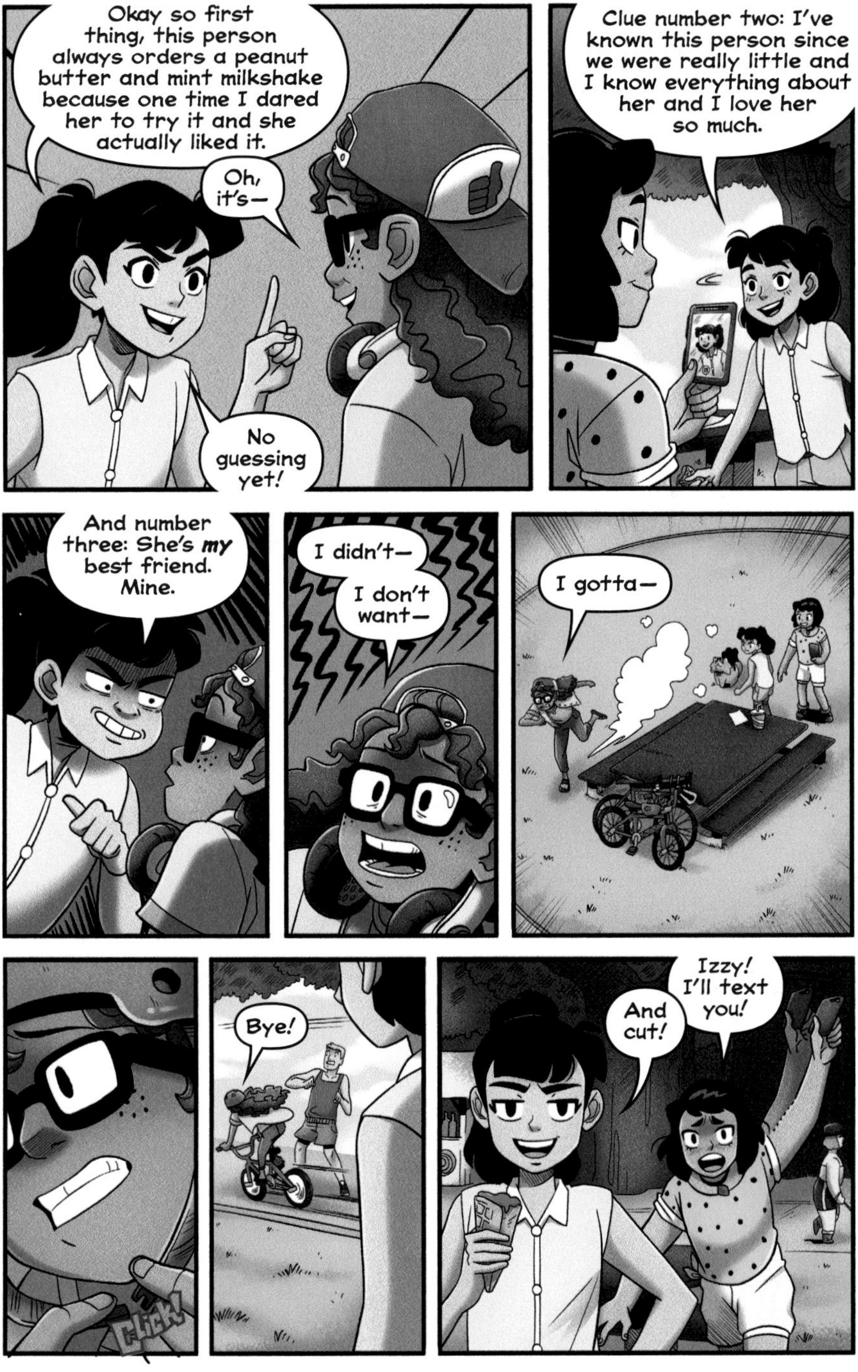
Okay so first thing, this person always orders a peanut butter and mint milkshake because one time I dared her to try it and she actually liked it.
Oh, it's—
No guessing yet!
Clue number two: I've known this person since we were really little and I know everything about her and I love her so much.
And number three: She's *my* best friend. Mine.
I didn't—
I don't want—
I gotta—
CLICK!
Bye!
And cut!
Izzy! I'll text you!

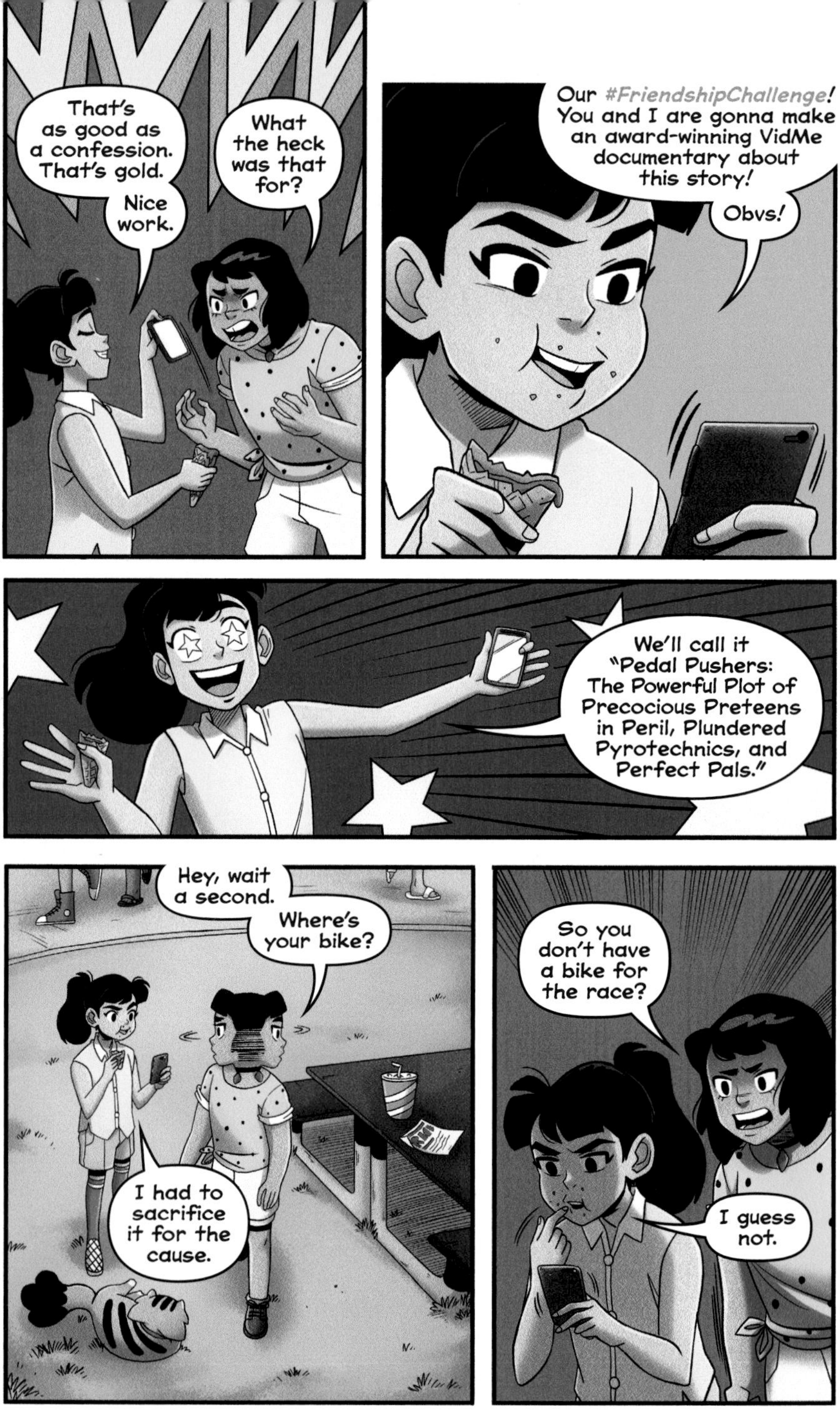

That's as good as a confession. That's gold.
Nice work.
What the heck was that for?
Our #FriendshipChallenge! You and I are gonna make an award-winning VidMe documentary about this story!
Obvs!
We'll call it "Pedal Pushers: The Powerful Plot of Precocious Preteens in Peril, Plundered Pyrotechnics, and Perfect Pals."
Hey, wait a second.
Where's your bike?
I had to sacrifice it for the cause.
So you don't have a bike for the race?
I guess not.

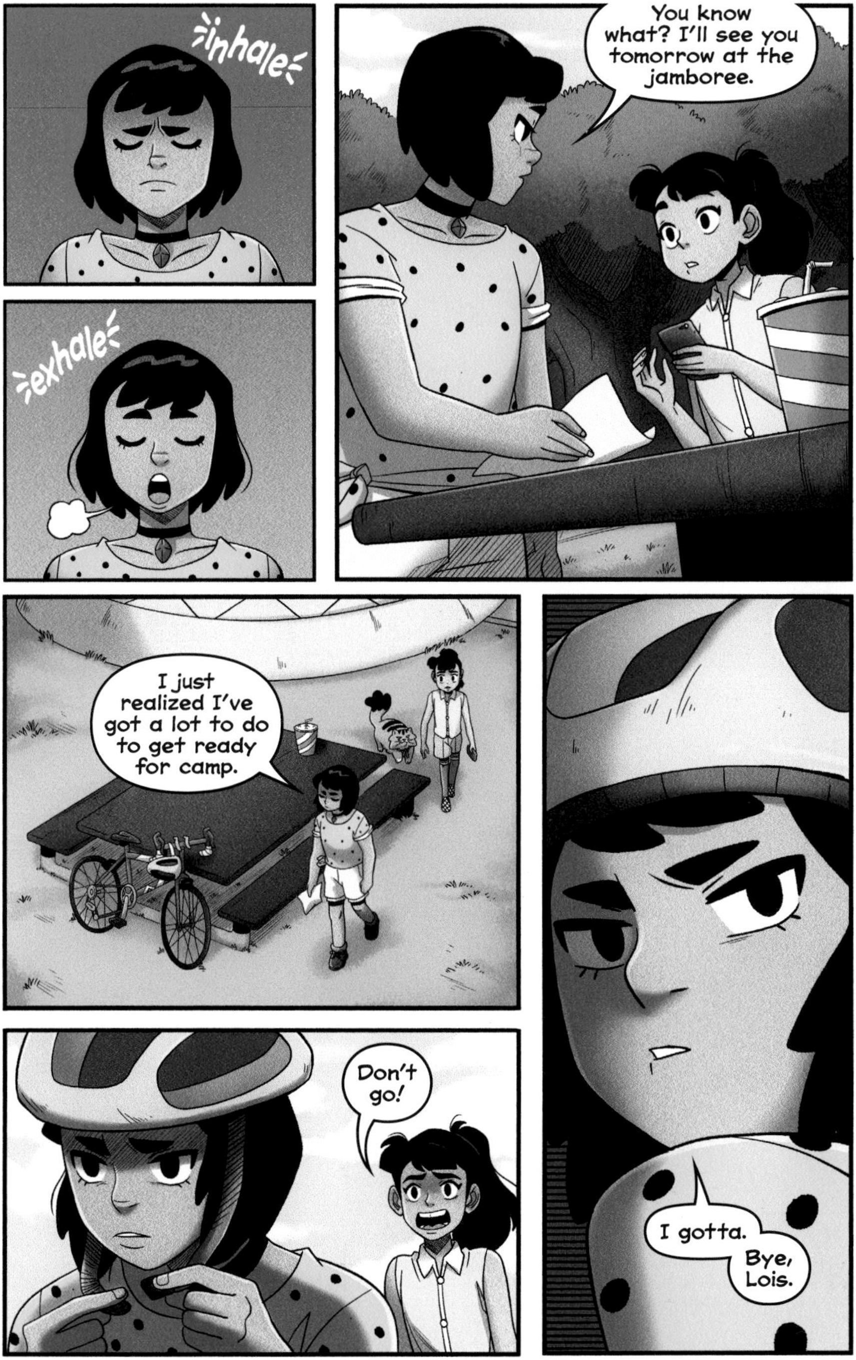
inhale
exhale
You know what? I'll see you tomorrow at the jamboree.
I just realized I've got a lot to do to get ready for camp.
I gotta. Bye, Lois.
Don't go!

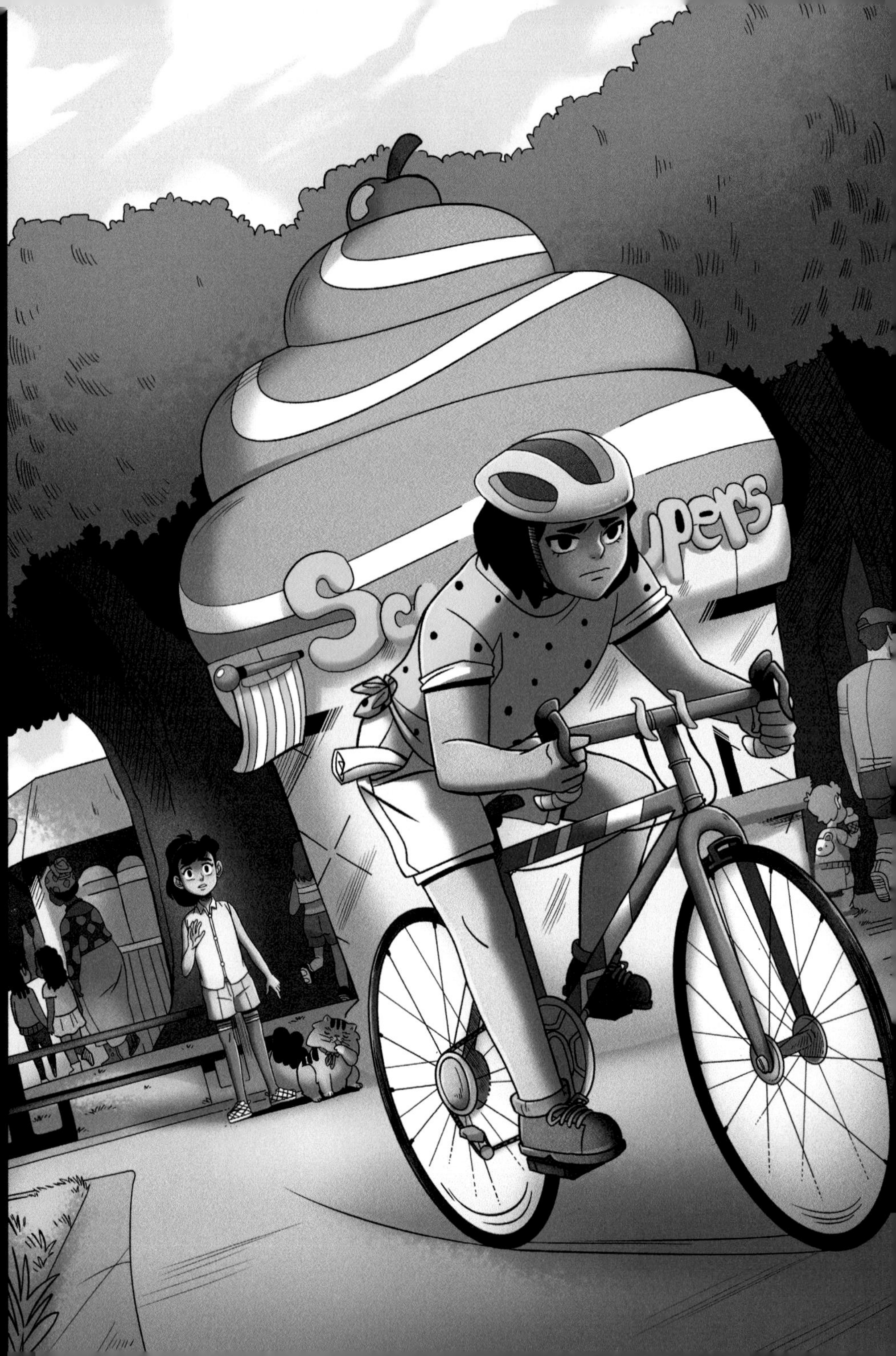
Sc
upers

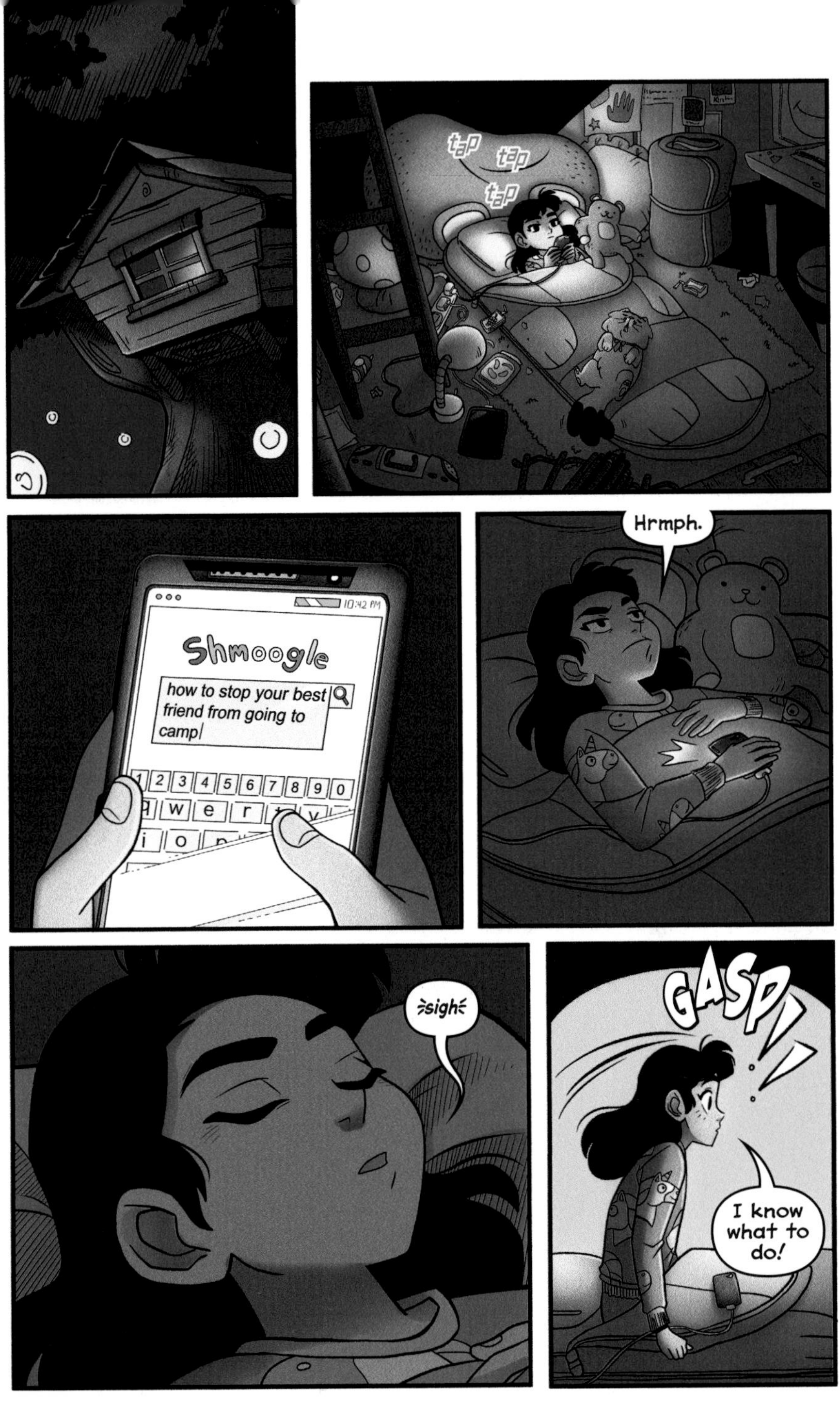
tap
tap
tap
Shmoogle
how to stop your best friend from going to camp
Hrmph.
sigh
GASP!
!
I know what to do!

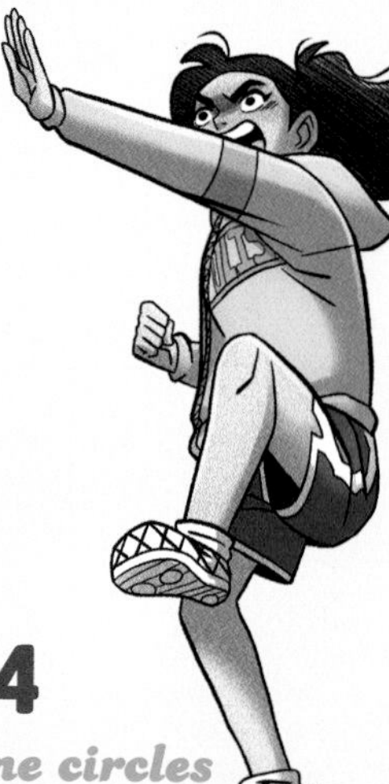

CHAPTER 4

moving in the same circles

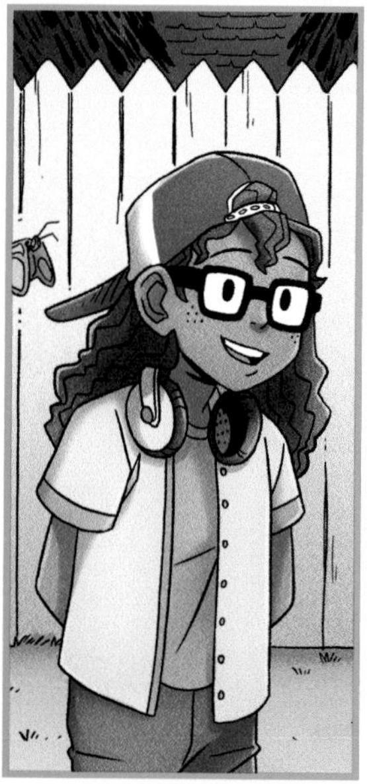

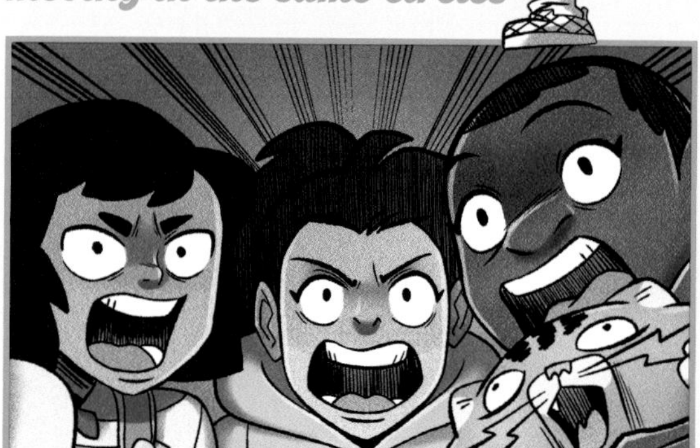

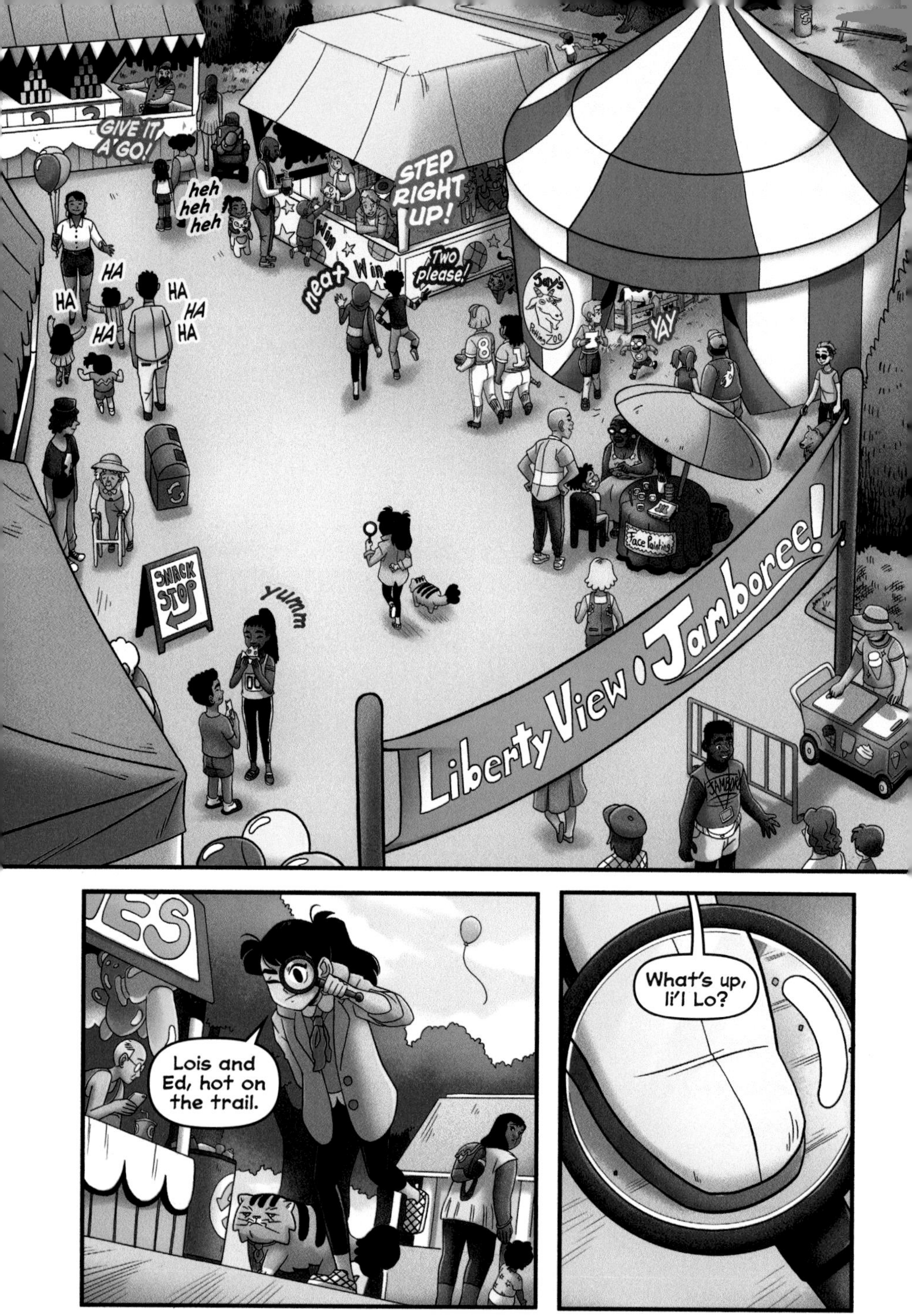
GIVE IT A'GO!
heh heh heh
STEP RIGHT UP!
Win
neat Win
Two please!
HA HA HA
HA HA HA
Say's Petting Zoo
YAY
Face Painting
SNACK STOP
yumm
Liberty View Jamboree!
JAMBOREE
Lois and Ed, hot on the trail.
What's up, li'l Lo?

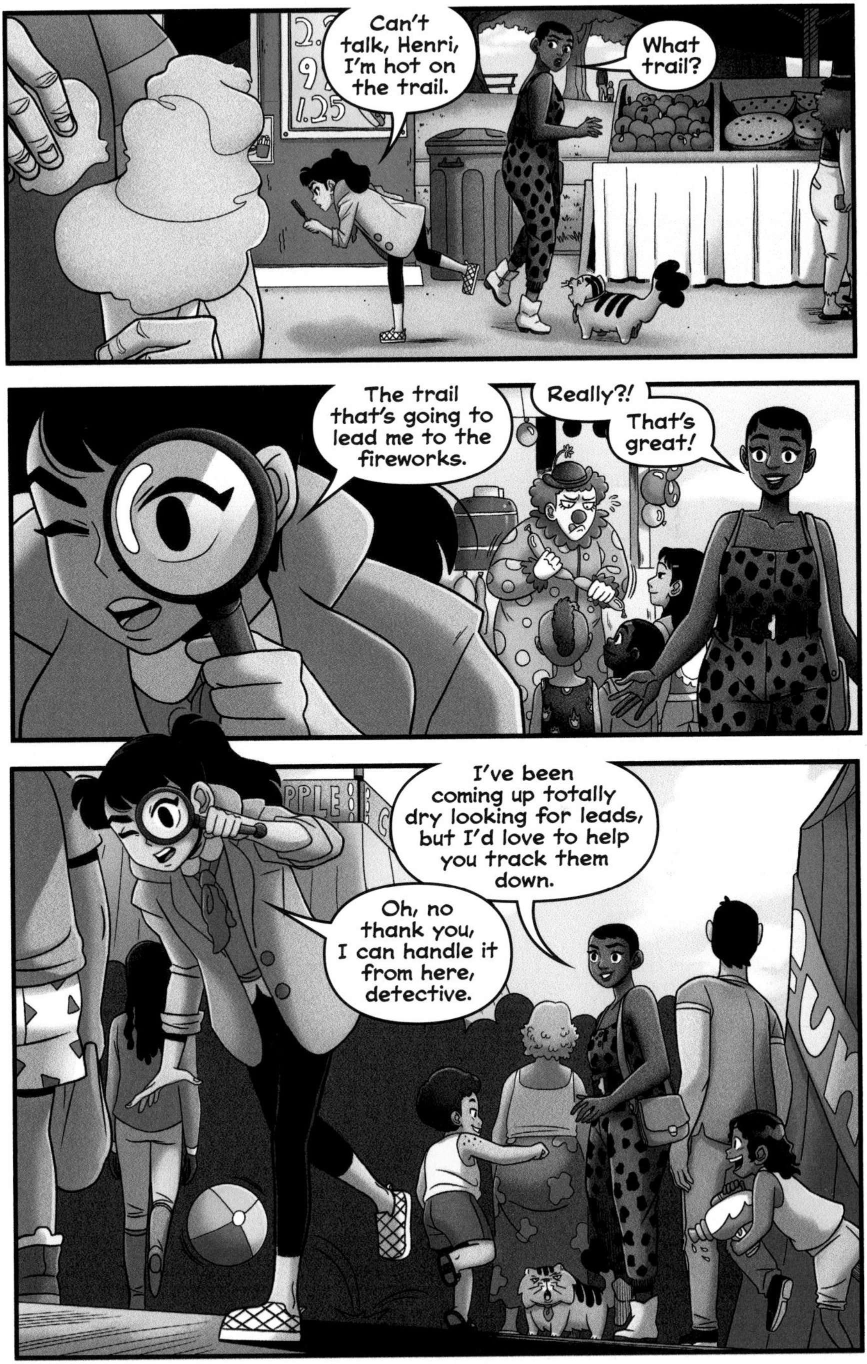
Can't talk, Henri, I'm hot on the trail.
What trail?
The trail that's going to lead me to the fireworks.
Really?!
That's great!
I've been coming up totally dry looking for leads, but I'd love to help you track them down.
Oh, no thank you, I can handle it from here, detective.

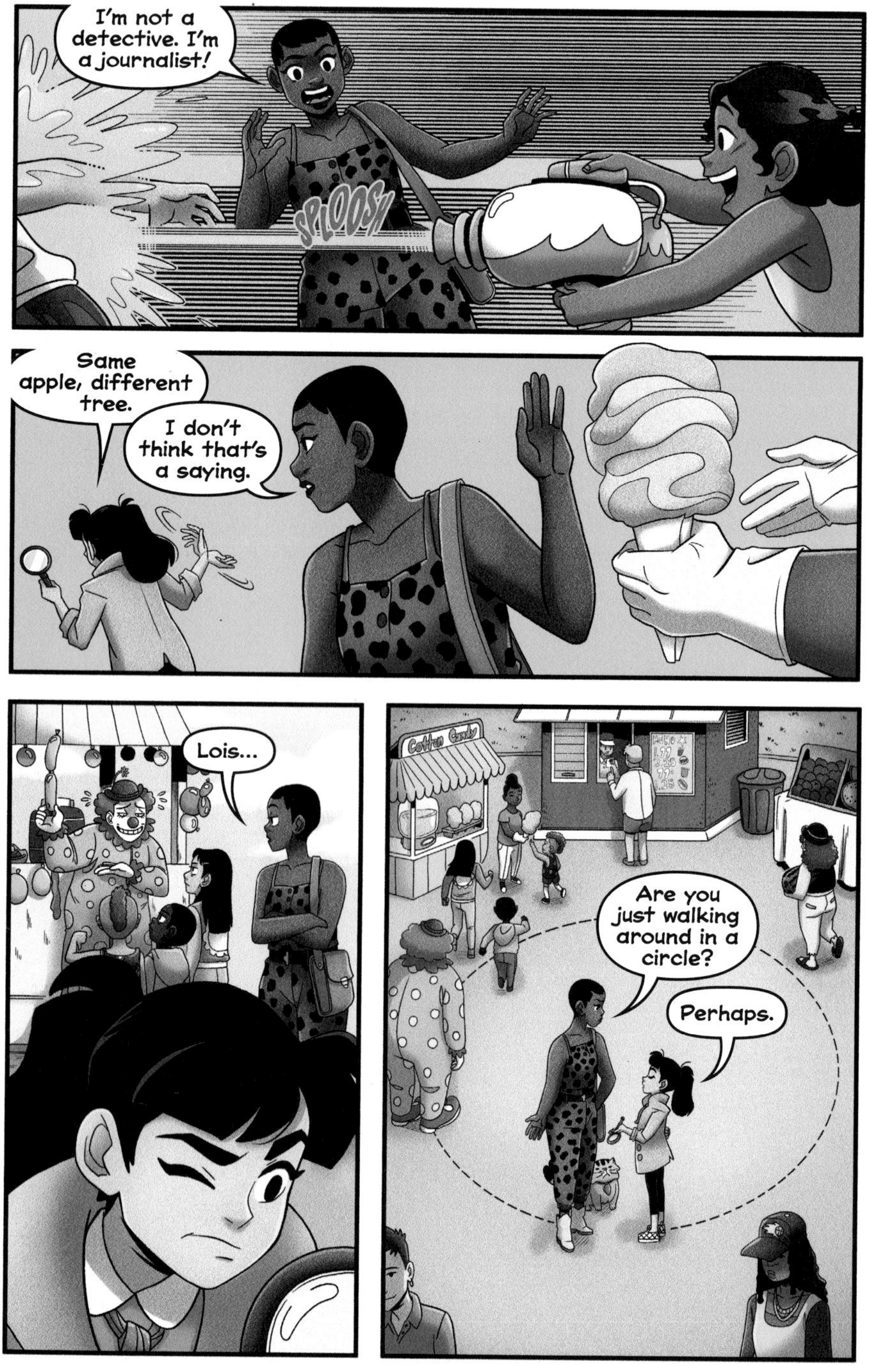
I'm not a detective. I'm a journalist!
SPLOOSH
Same apple, different tree.
I don't think that's a saying.
Lois...
Cotton Candy
Are you just walking around in a circle?
Perhaps.

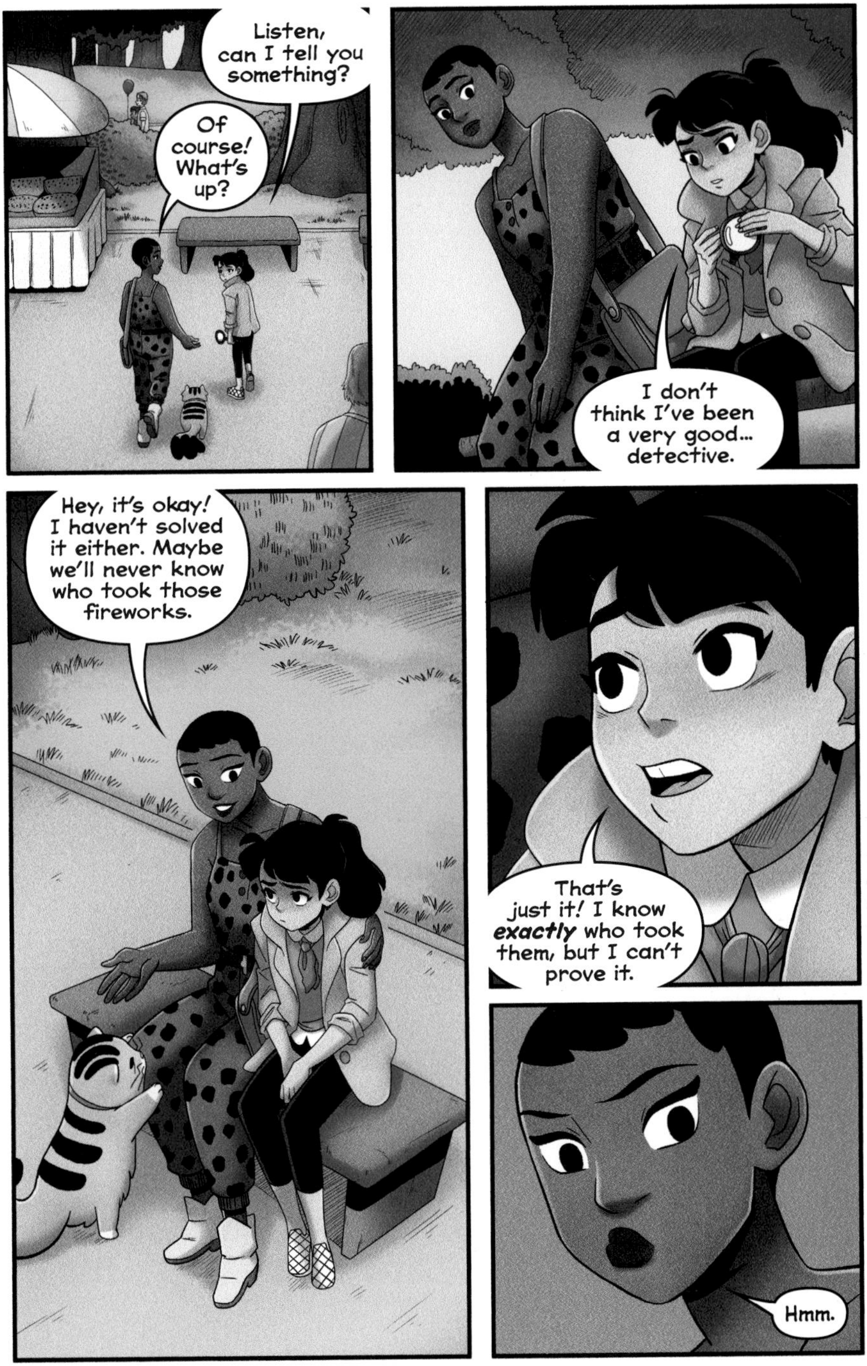
Listen, can I tell you something?
Of course! What's up?
I don't think I've been a very good... detective.
Hey, it's okay! I haven't solved it either. Maybe we'll never know who took those fireworks.
That's just it! I know *exactly* who took them, but I can't prove it.
Hmm.

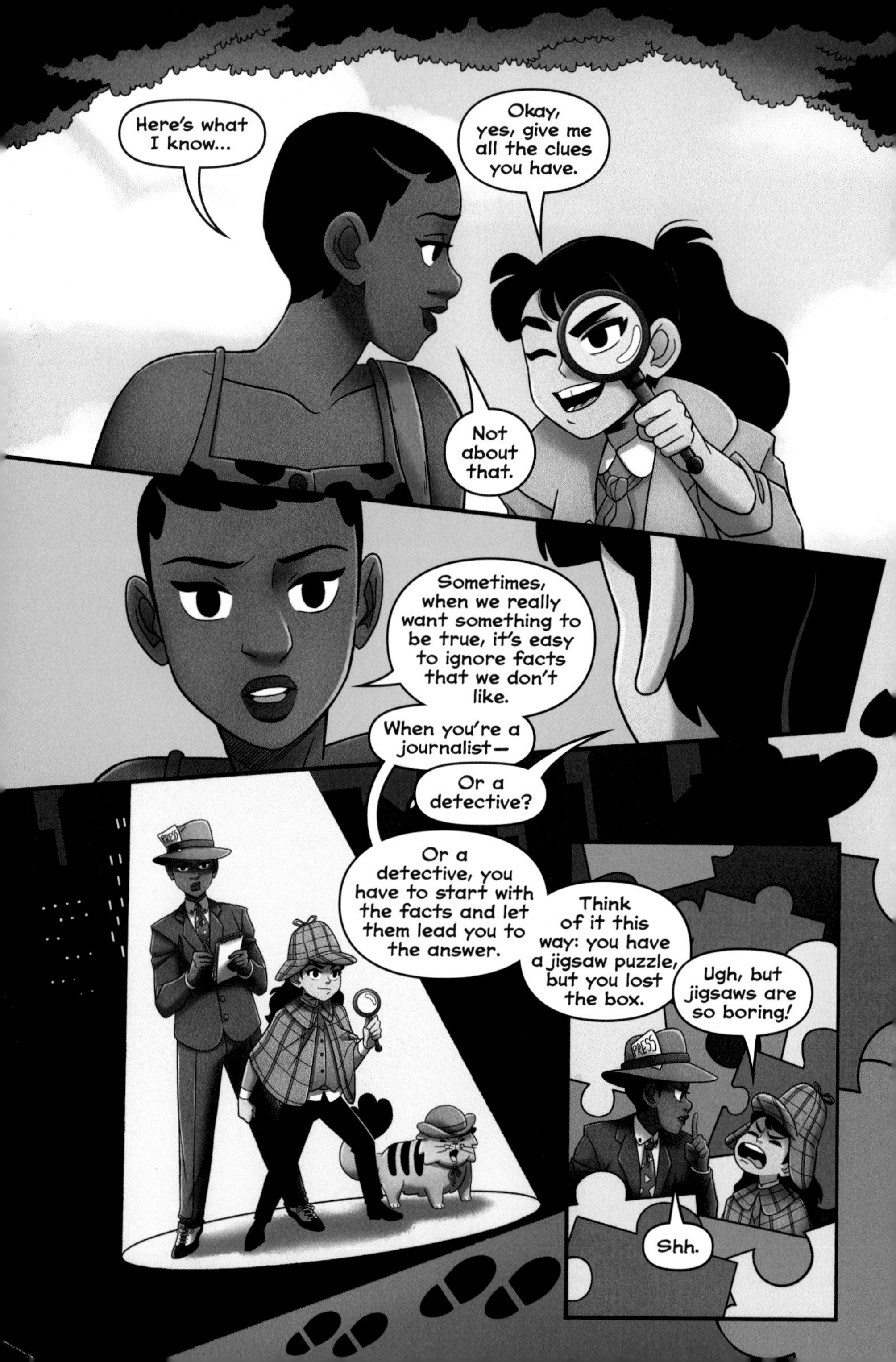
Here's what I know...
Okay, yes, give me all the clues you have.
Not about that.
Sometimes, when we really want something to be true, it's easy to ignore facts that we don't like.
When you're a journalist—
Or a detective?
Or a detective, you have to start with the facts and let them lead you to the answer.
PRESS
Think of it this way: you have a jigsaw puzzle, but you lost the box.
Ugh, but jigsaws are so boring!
PRESS
Shh.

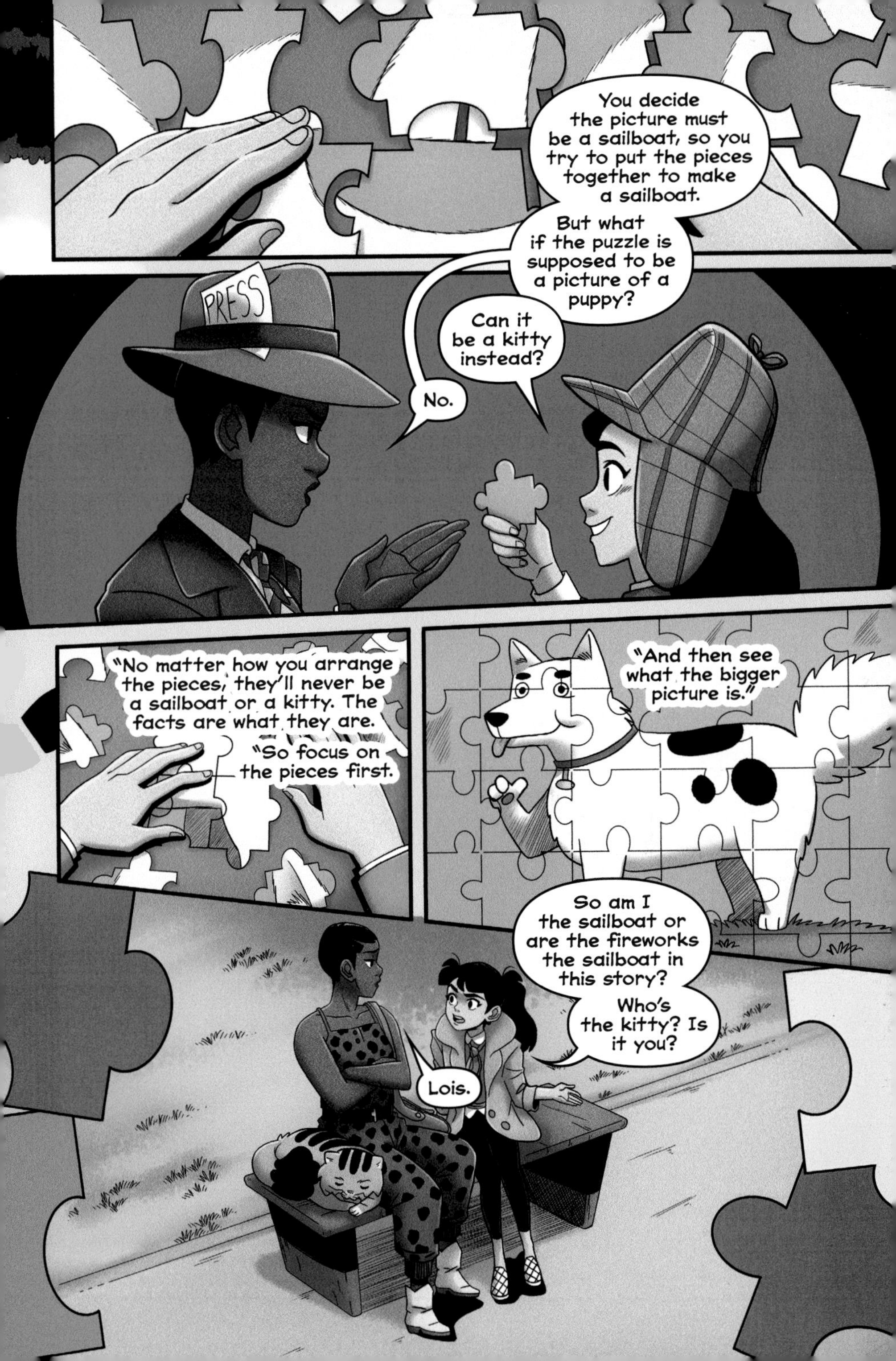
You decide the picture must be a sailboat, so you try to put the pieces together to make a sailboat.
But what if the puzzle is supposed to be a picture of a puppy?
PRESS
Can it be a kitty instead?
No.
"No matter how you arrange the pieces, they'll never be a sailboat or a kitty. The facts are what they are.
"So focus on the pieces first.
"And then see what the bigger picture is."
So am I the sailboat or are the fireworks the sailboat in this story?
Who's the kitty? Is it you?
Lois.

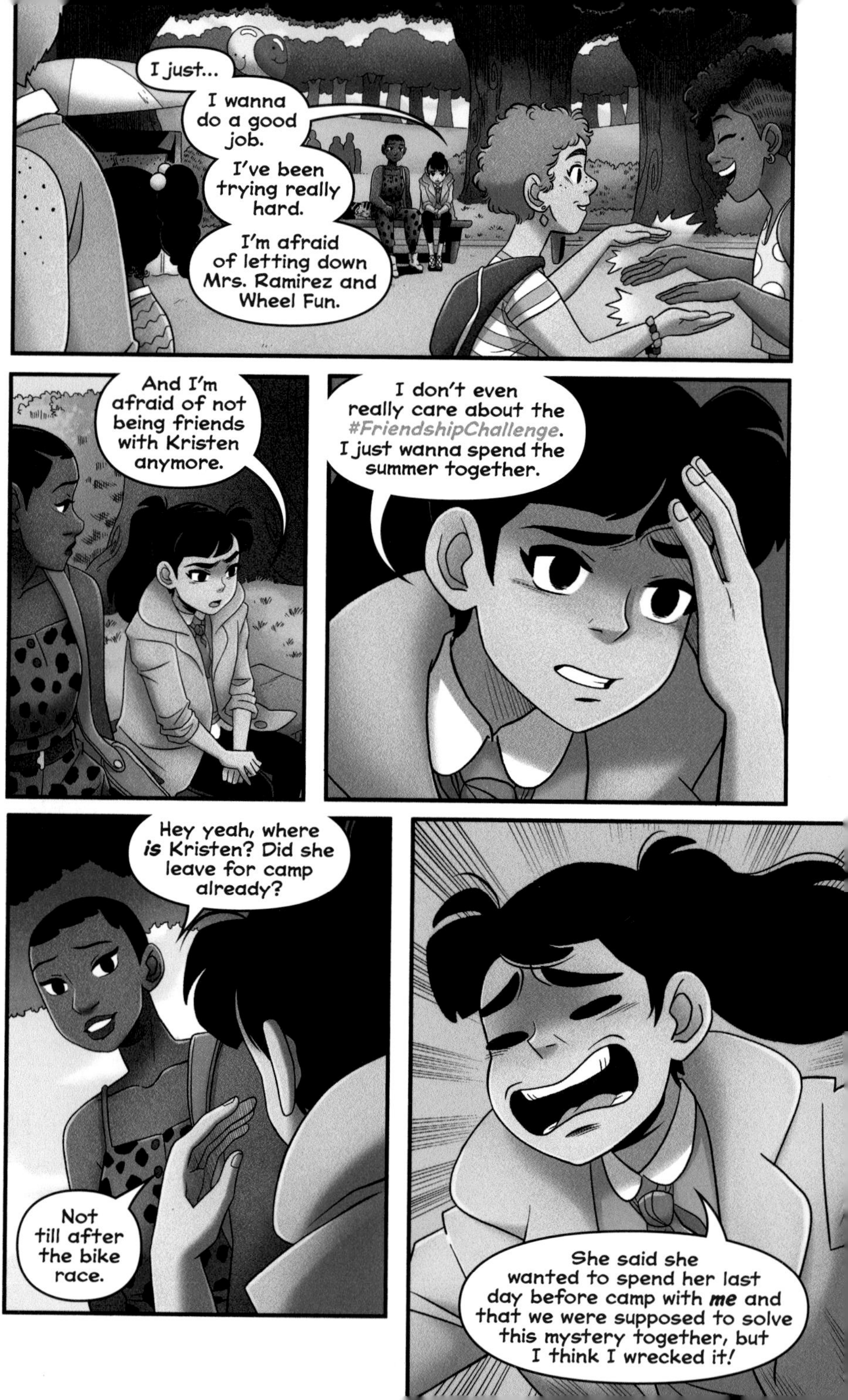
I just...
I wanna do a good job.
I've been trying really hard.
I'm afraid of letting down Mrs. Ramirez and Wheel Fun.
And I'm afraid of not being friends with Kristen anymore.
I don't even really care about the #FriendshipChallenge. I just wanna spend the summer together.
Hey yeah, where *is* Kristen? Did she leave for camp already?
Not till after the bike race.
She said she wanted to spend her last day before camp with *me* and that we were supposed to solve this mystery together, but I think I wrecked it!

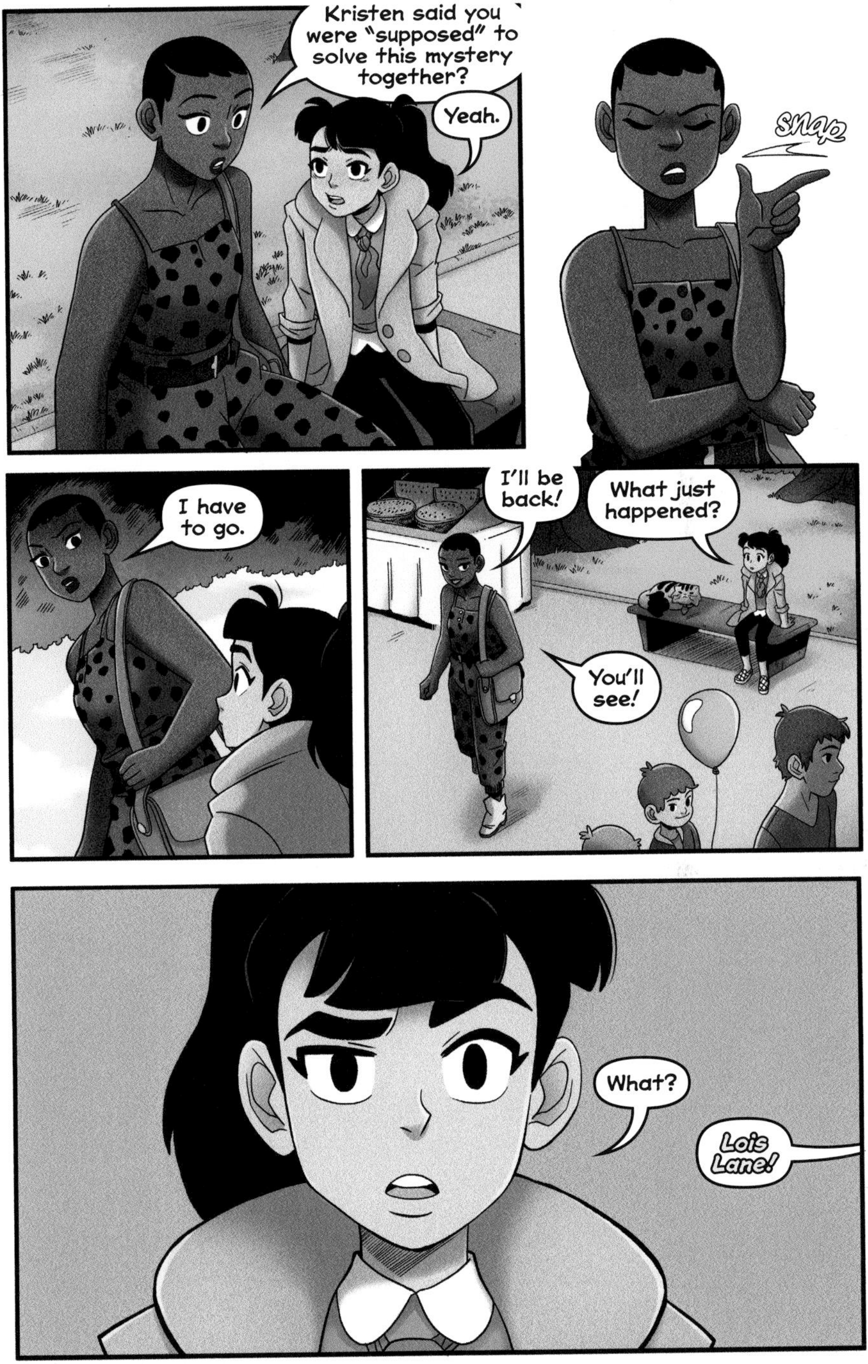

Kristen said you were "supposed" to solve this mystery together?
Yeah.
SNAP
I have to go.
I'll be back!
What just happened?
You'll see!
What?
Lois Lane!

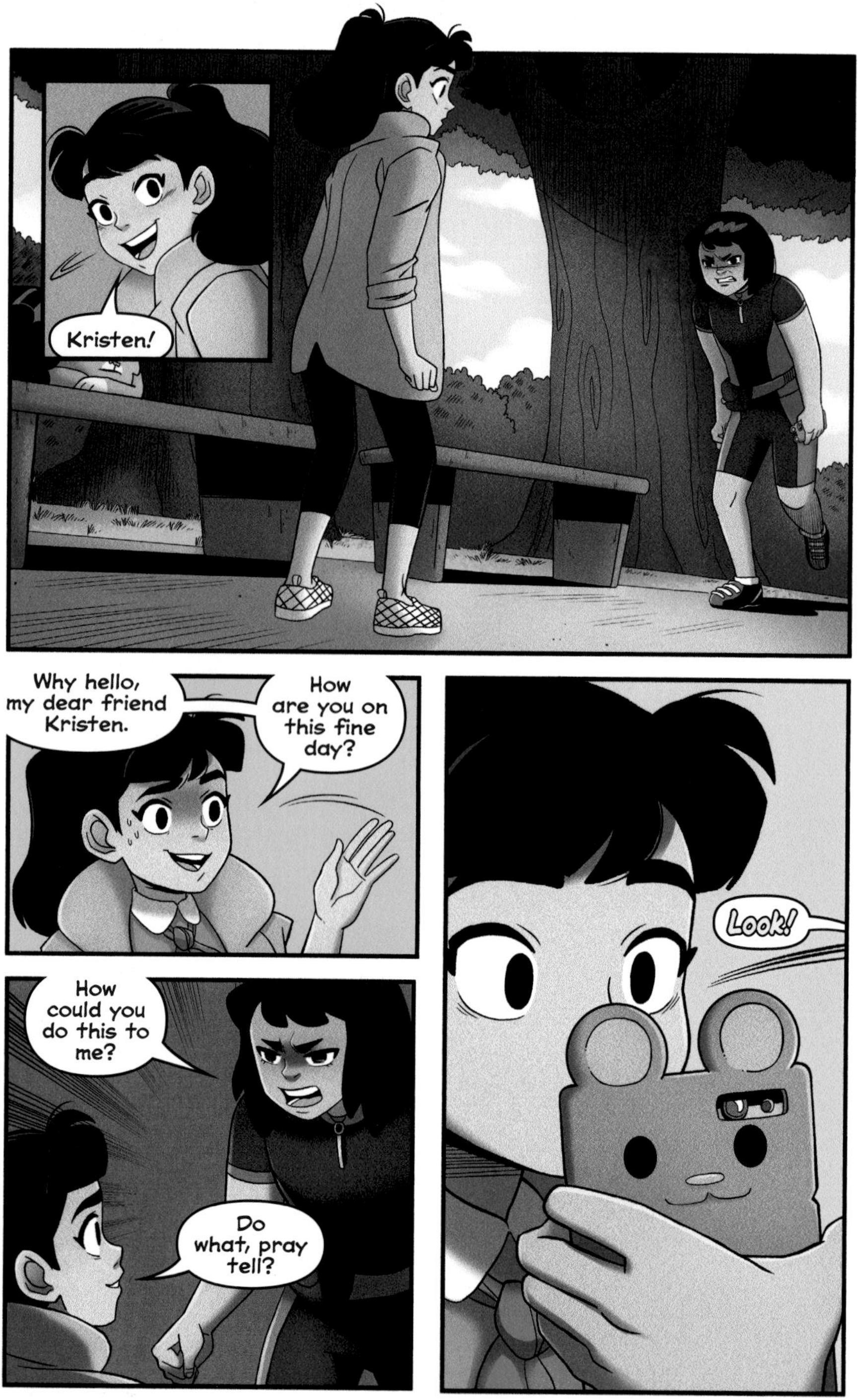
Kristen!
Why hello, my dear friend Kristen.
How are you on this fine day?
How could you do this to me?
Do what, pray tell?
Look!

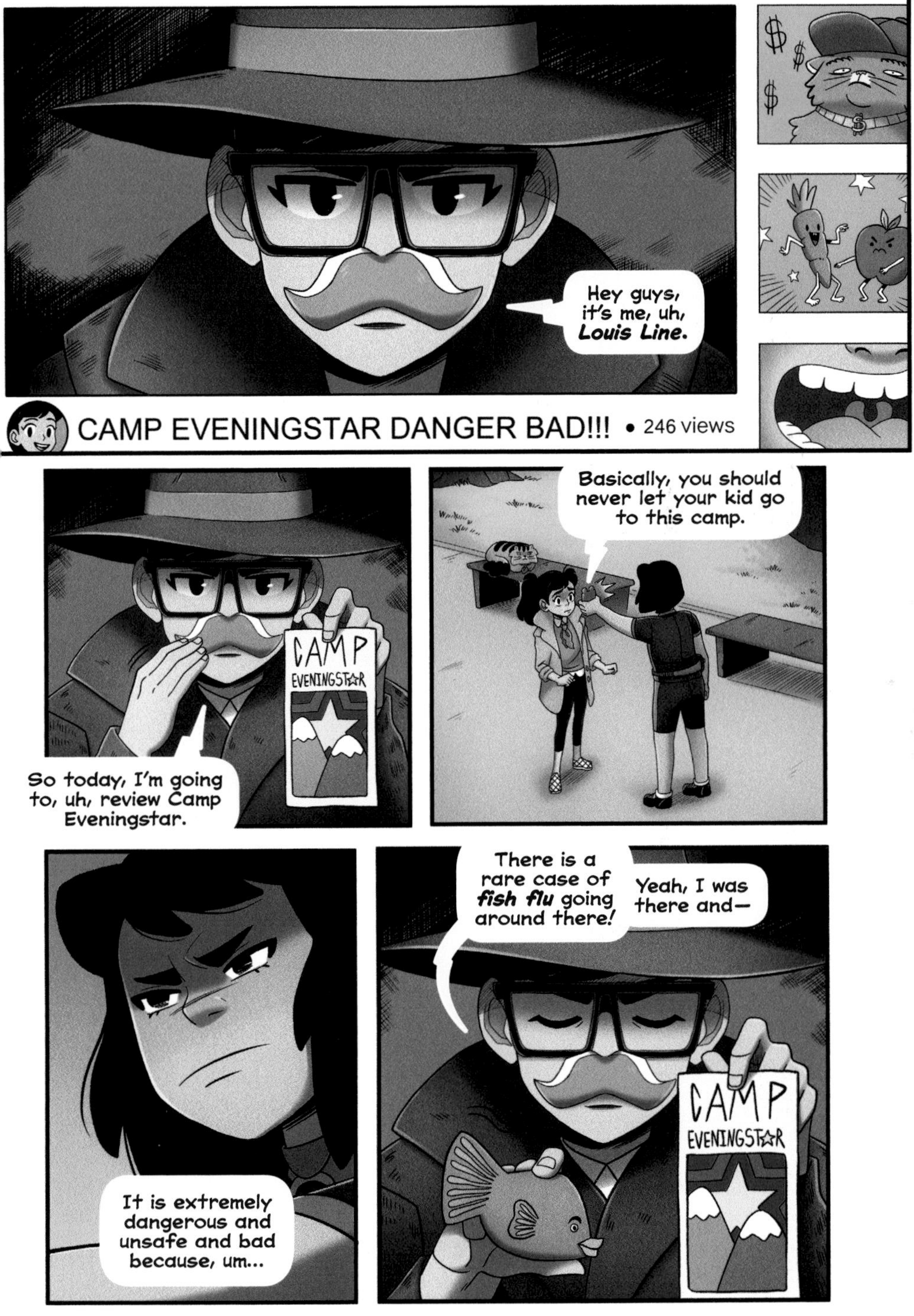
Hey guys, it's me, uh, ***Louis Line.***
CAMP EVENINGSTAR DANGER BAD!!! • 246 views
So today, I'm going to, uh, review Camp Eveningstar.
CAMP EVENINGSTAR
Basically, you should never let your kid go to this camp.
It is extremely dangerous and unsafe and bad because, um...
There is a rare case of ***fish flu*** going around there!
Yeah, I was there and—
CAMP EVENINGSTAR

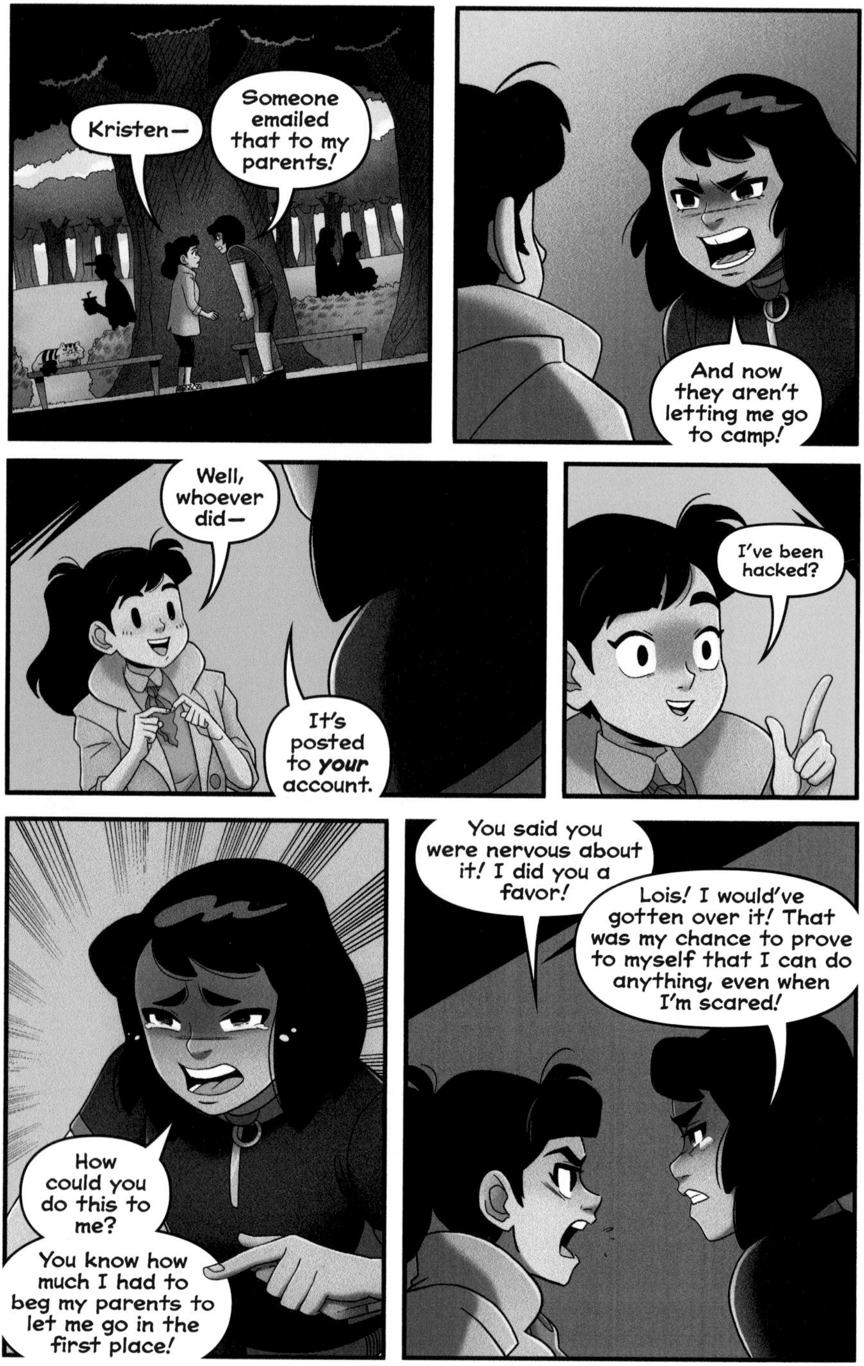
Kristen—
Someone emailed that to my parents!
And now they aren't letting me go to camp!
Well, whoever did—
It's posted to **your** account.
I've been hacked?
How could you do this to me?
You know how much I had to beg my parents to let me go in the first place!
You said you were nervous about it! I did you a favor!
Lois! I would've gotten over it! That was my chance to prove to myself that I can do anything, even when I'm scared!

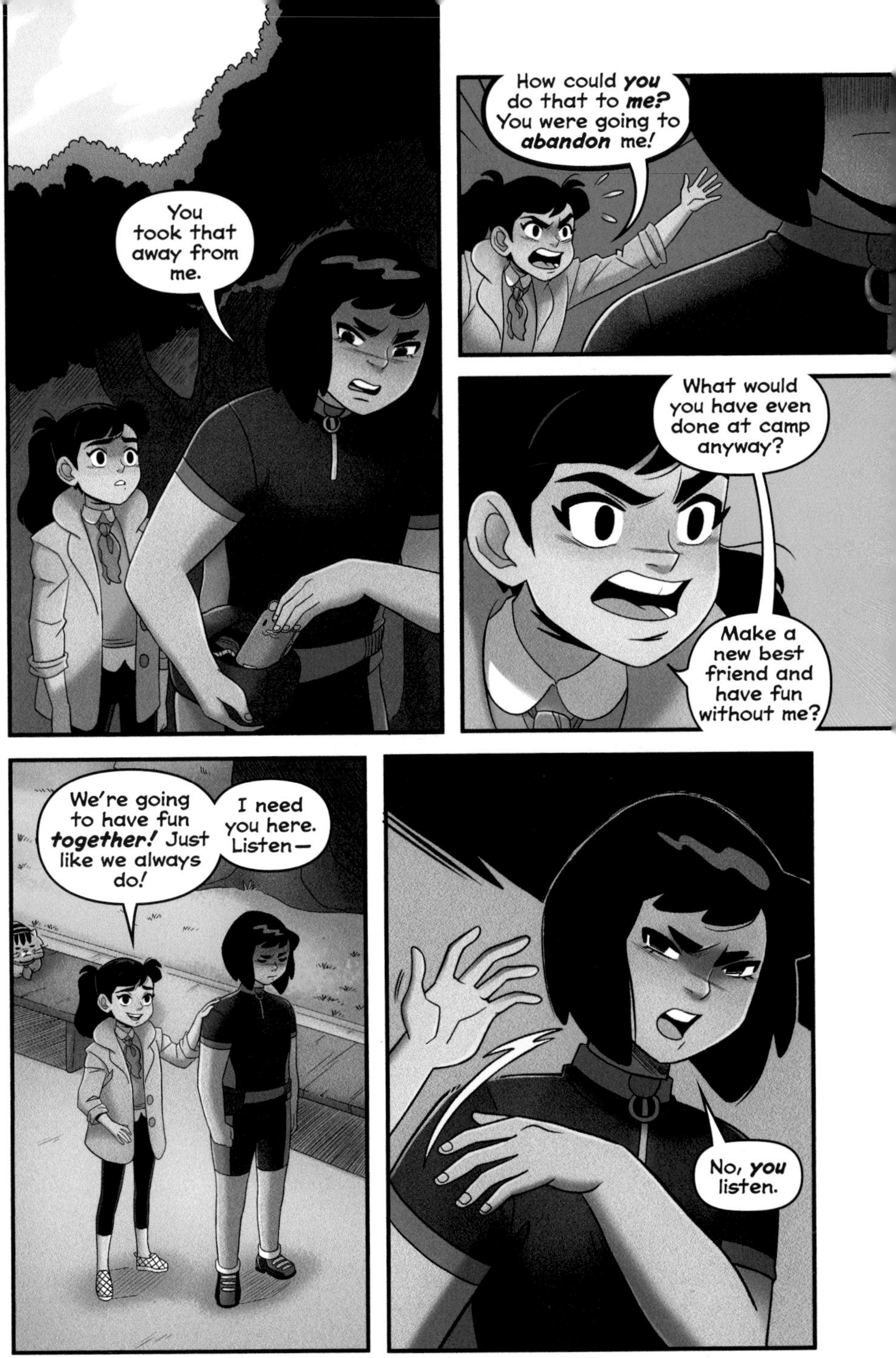
You took that away from me.
How could *you* do that to *me?* You were going to *abandon* me!
What would you have even done at camp anyway?
Make a new best friend and have fun without me?
We're going to have fun *together!* Just like we always do!
I need you here. Listen—
No, *you* listen.

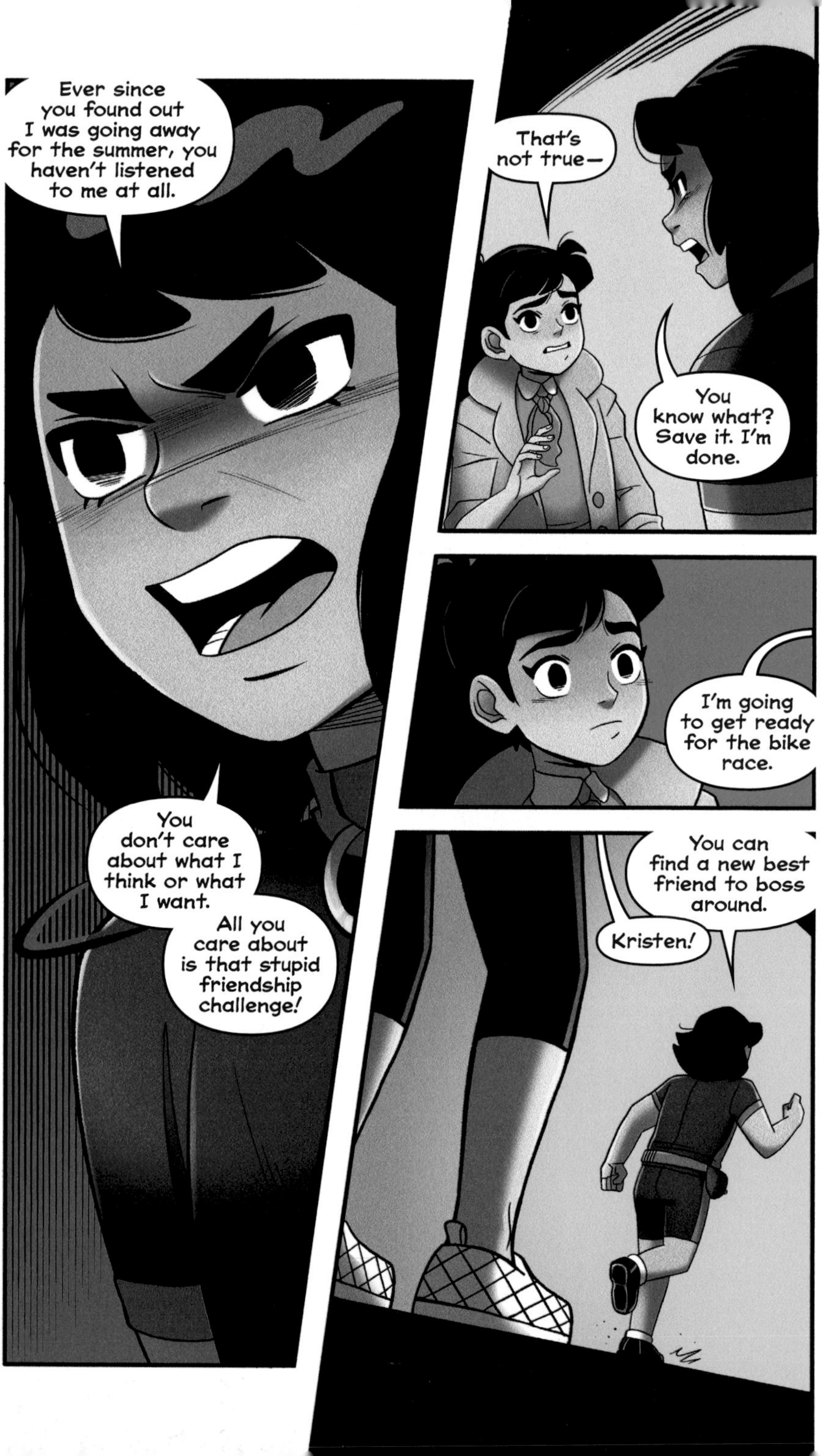
Ever since you found out I was going away for the summer, you haven't listened to me at all.
That's not true—
You know what? Save it. I'm done.
You don't care about what I think or what I want.
All you care about is that stupid friendship challenge!
I'm going to get ready for the bike race.
You can find a new best friend to boss around.
Kristen!

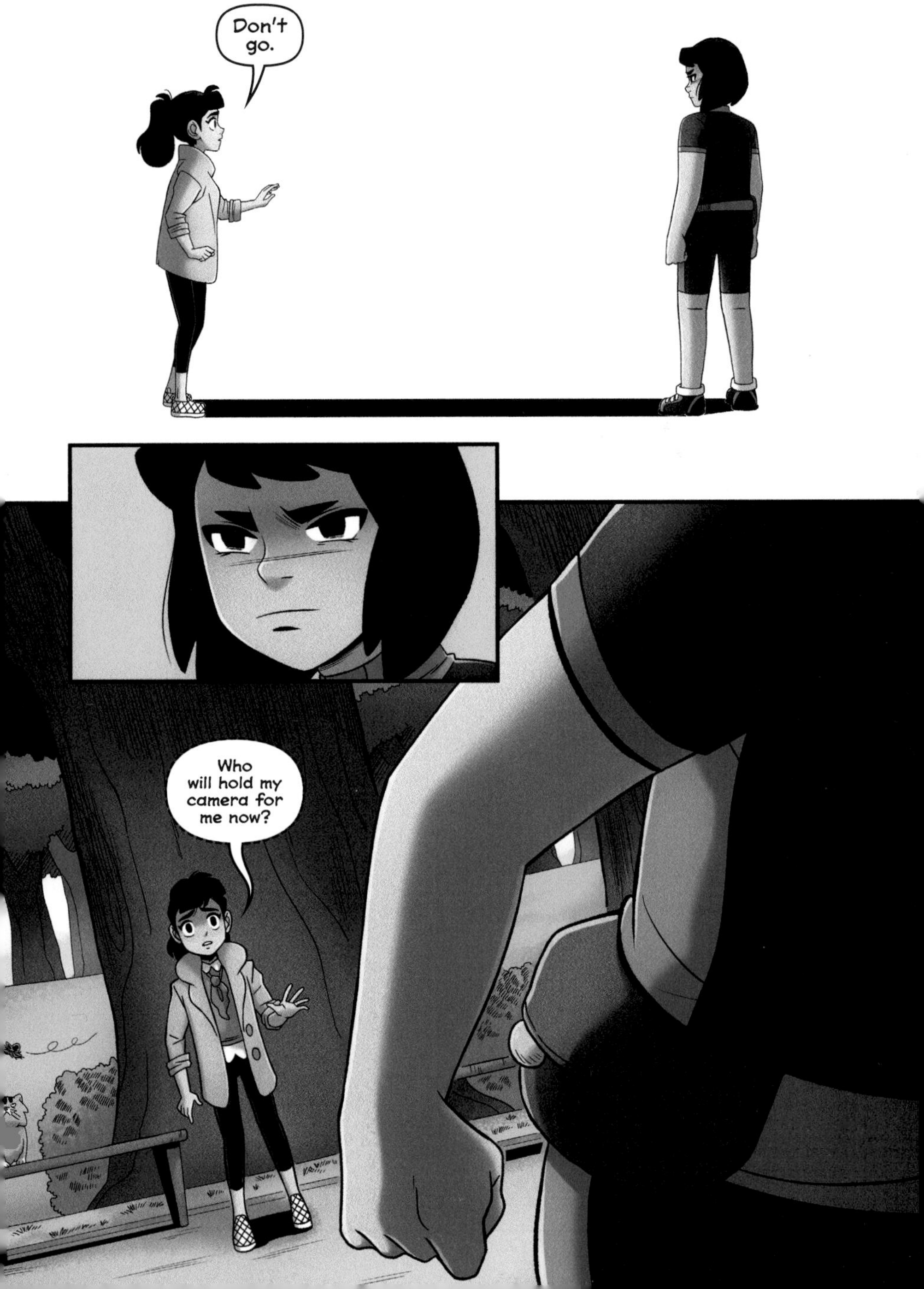
Don't go.
Who will hold my camera for me now?

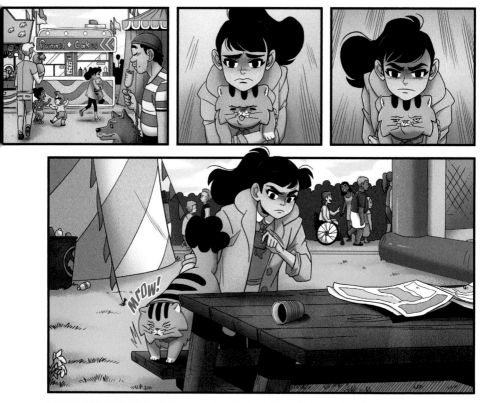

MrOw!

mutter *mutter* do it myself *mutter* mutter

PBBBt

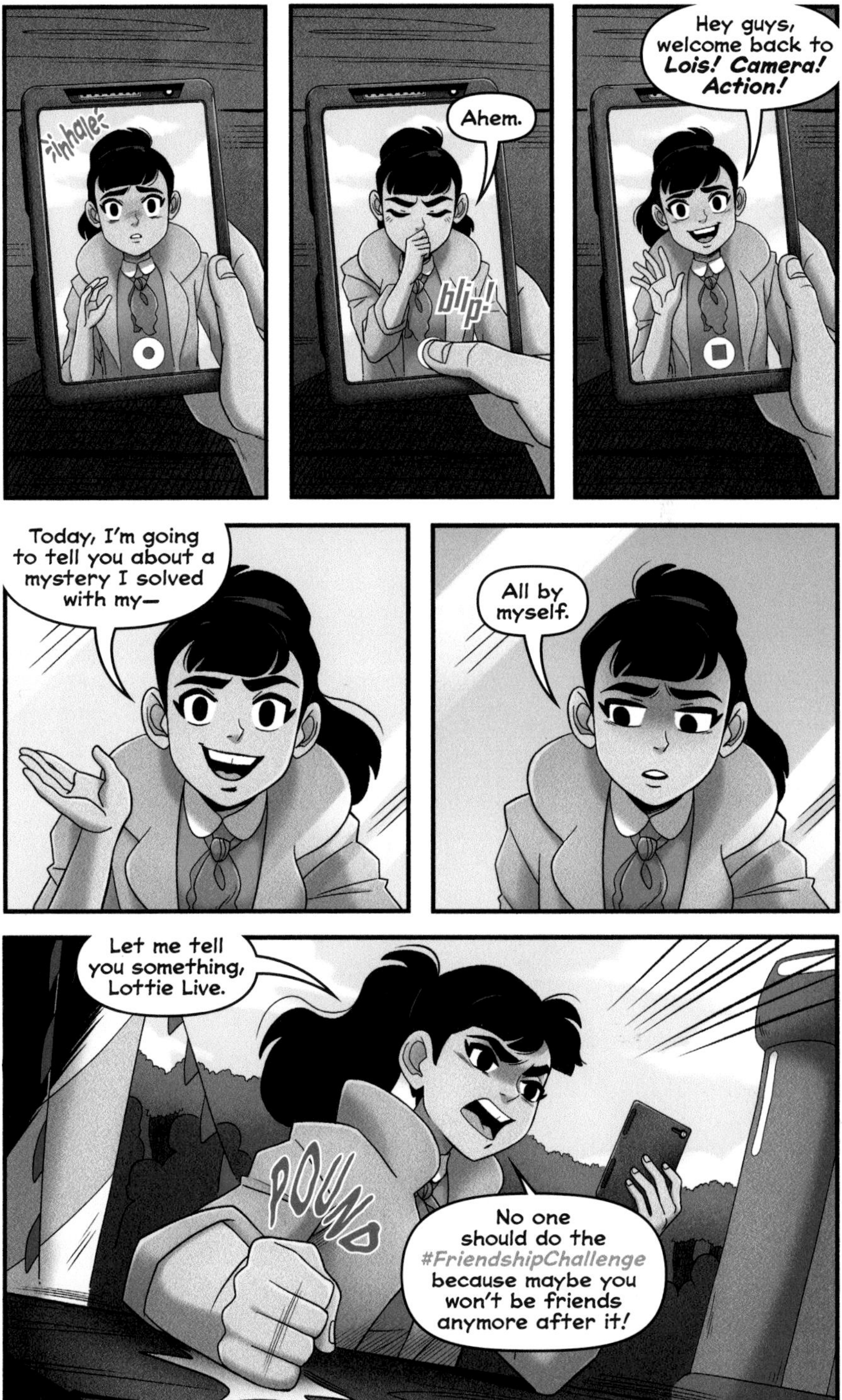
inhale
Ahem.
blip!
Hey guys, welcome back to Lois! Camera! Action!
Today, I'm going to tell you about a mystery I solved with my—
All by myself.
Let me tell you something, Lottie Live.
POUND
No one should do the #FriendshipChallenge because maybe you won't be friends anymore after it!

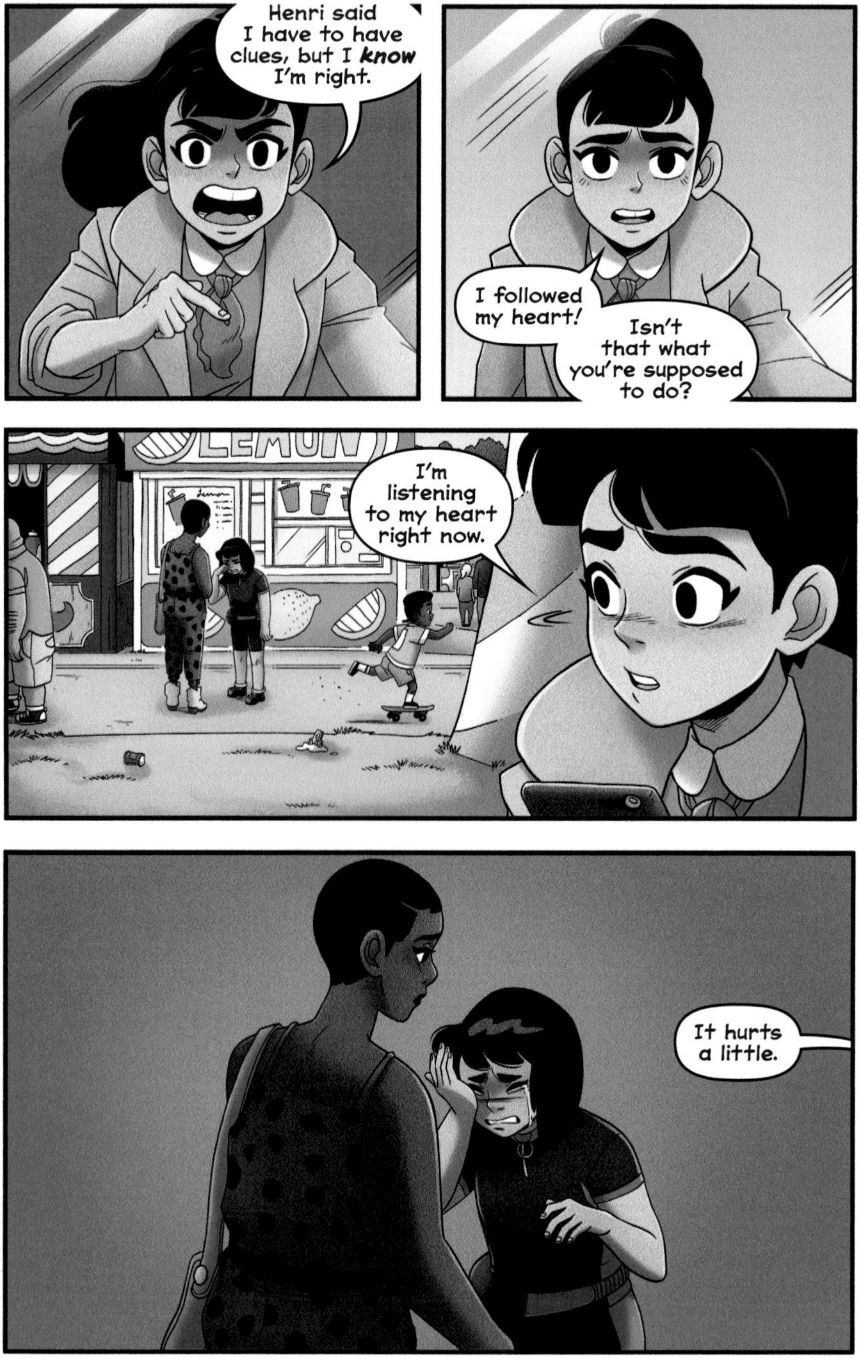
Henri said I have to have clues, but I **know** I'm right.
I followed my heart!
Isn't that what you're supposed to do?
I'm listening to my heart right now.
It hurts a little.

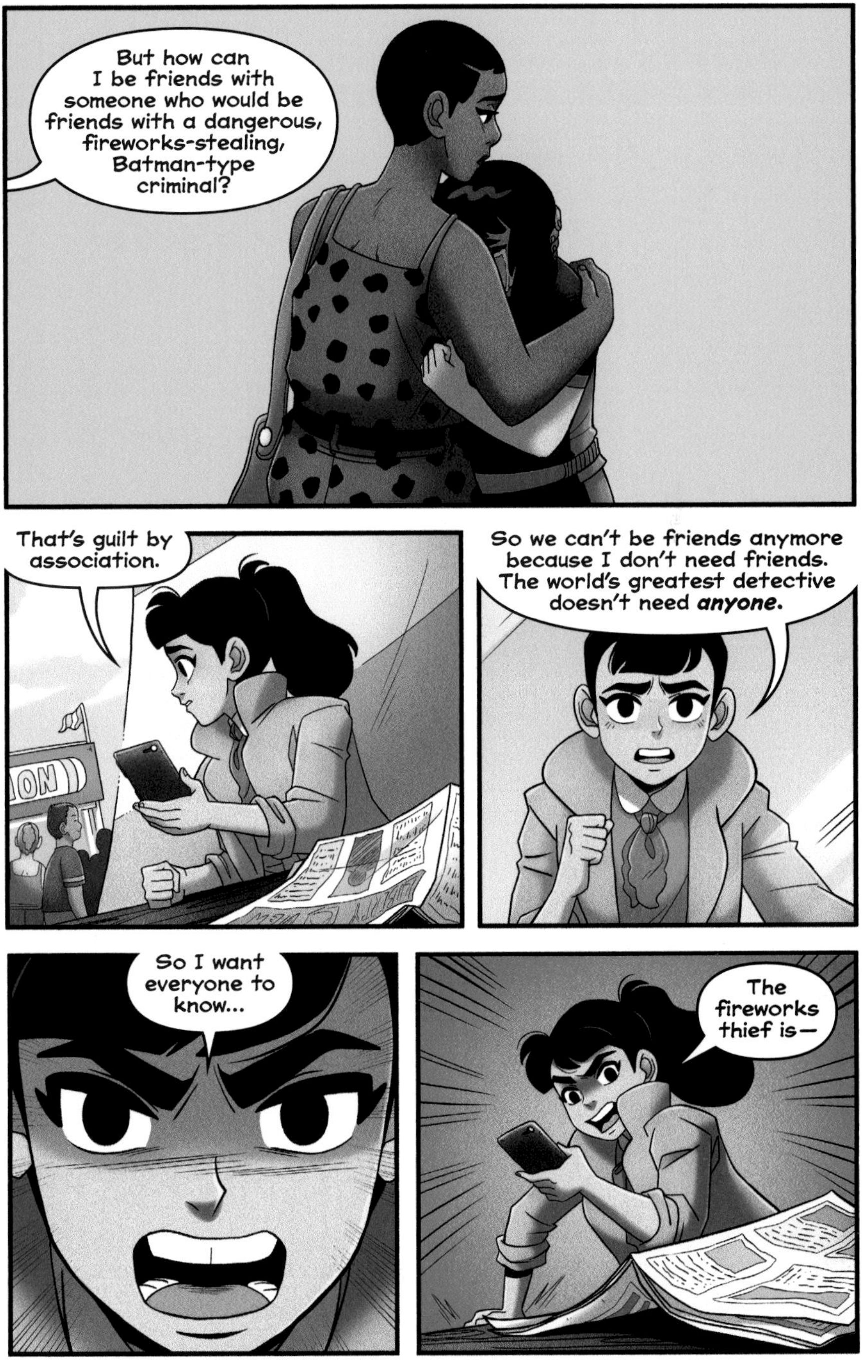
But how can I be friends with someone who would be friends with a dangerous, fireworks-stealing, Batman-type criminal?
That's guilt by association.
So we can't be friends anymore because I don't need friends. The world's greatest detective doesn't need *anyone*.
So I want everyone to know...
The fireworks thief is—

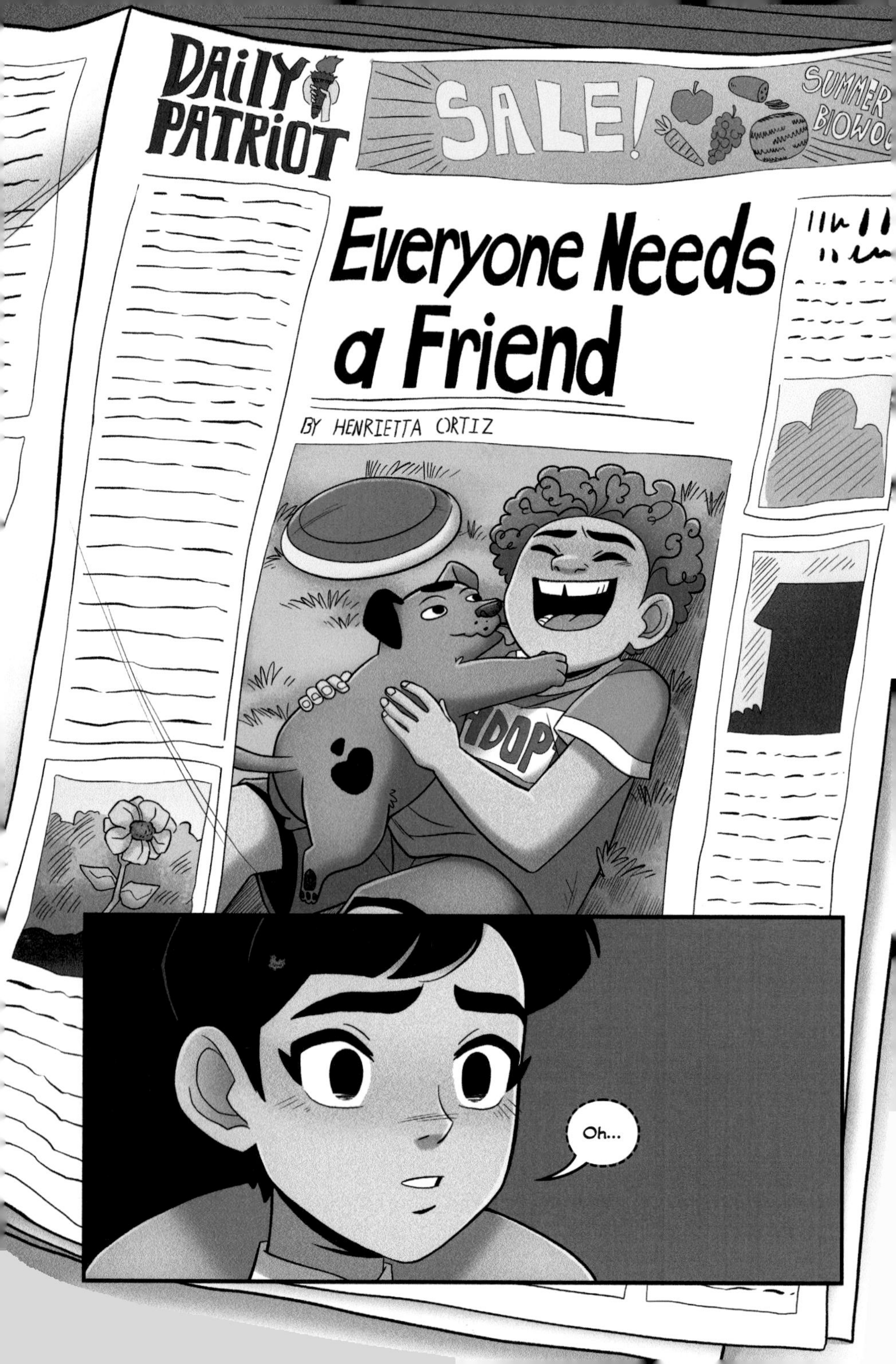
DAILY PATRIOT
SALE!
Everyone Needs a Friend
BY HENRIETTA ORTIZ
Oh...

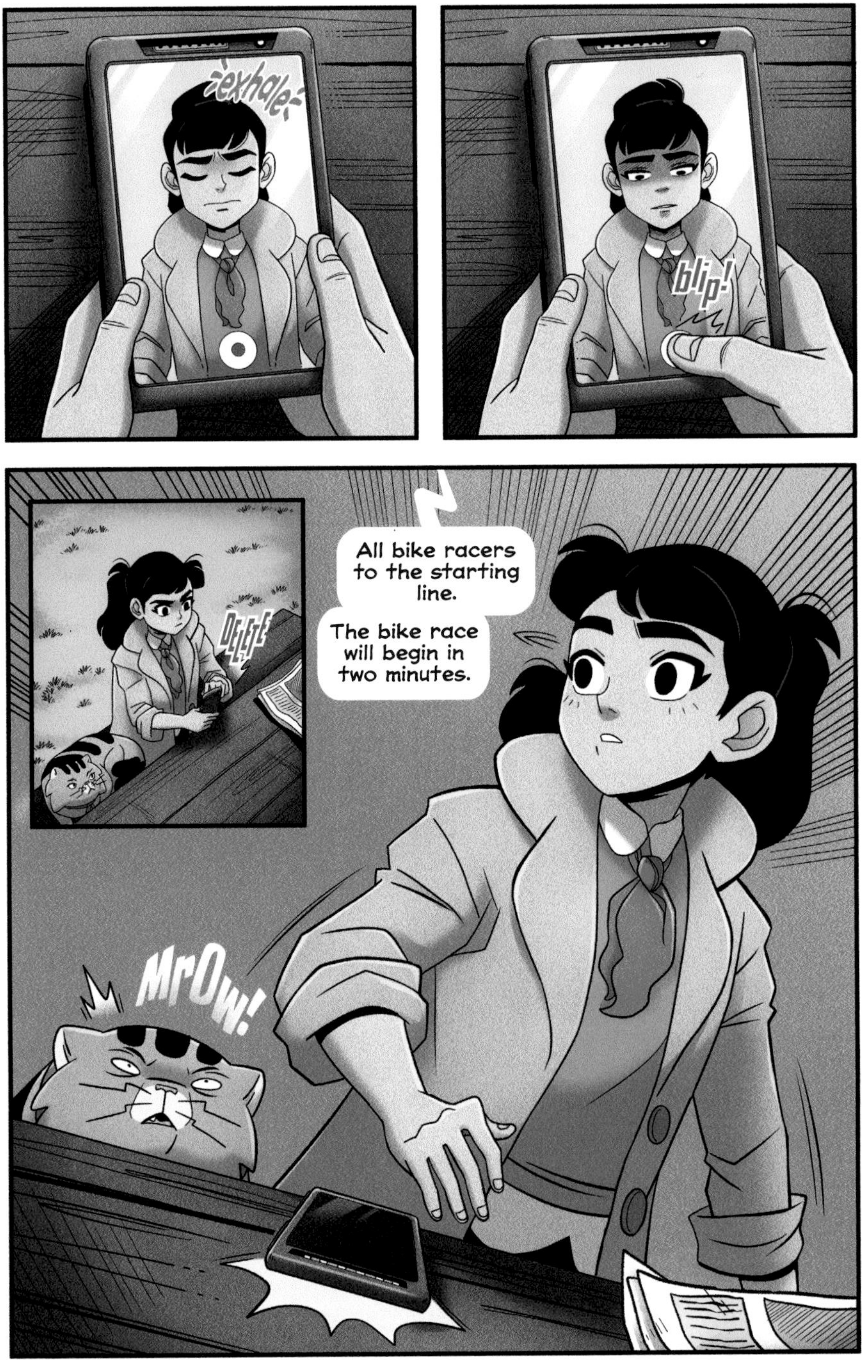
exhale
blip!
DELETE
All bike racers to the starting line.
The bike race will begin in two minutes.
MrOw!

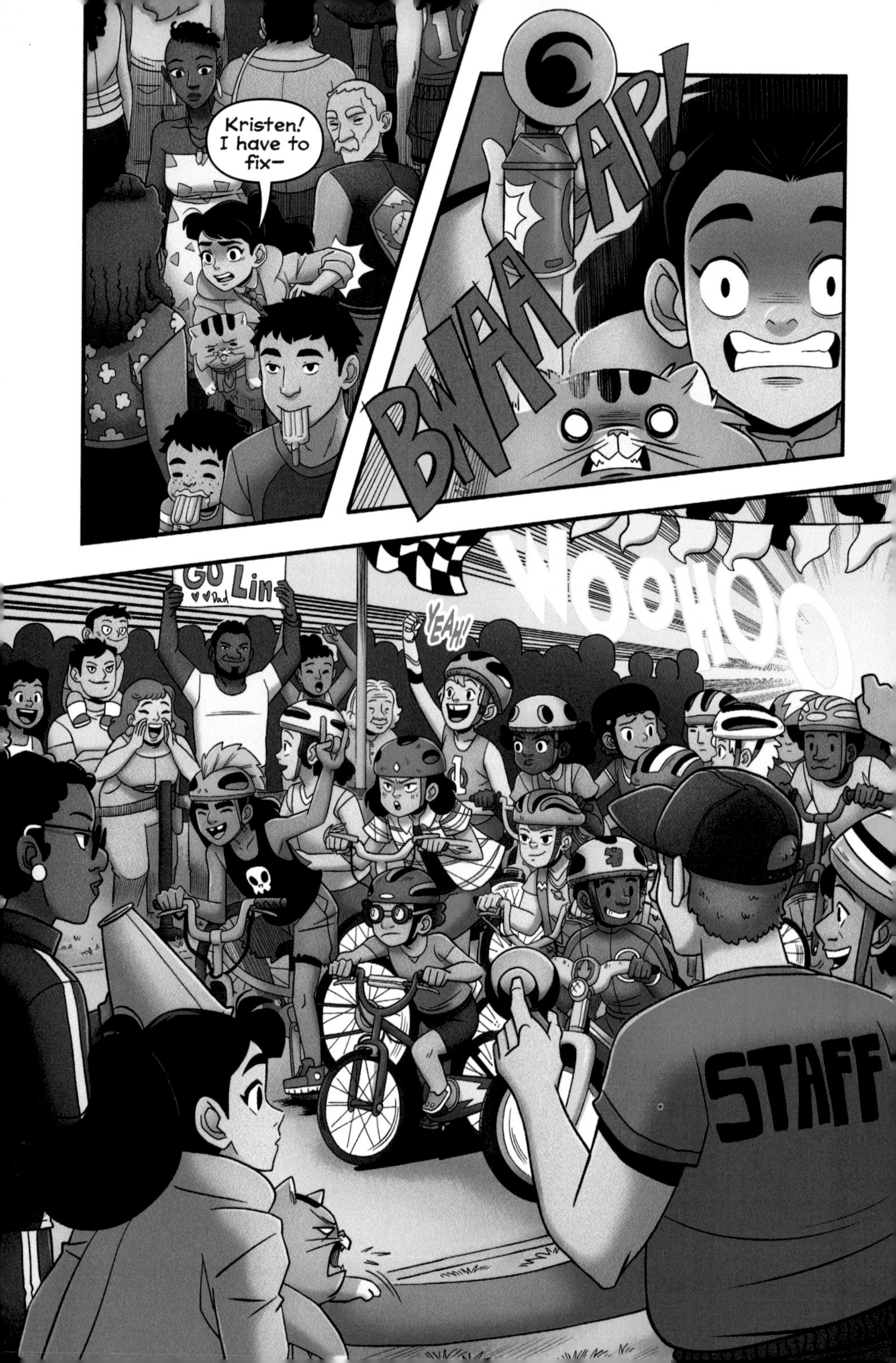

Kristen! I have to fix–
BWAAAP!
GO Lin
♥ Dad
YEAH!
WOOHOO
STAFF

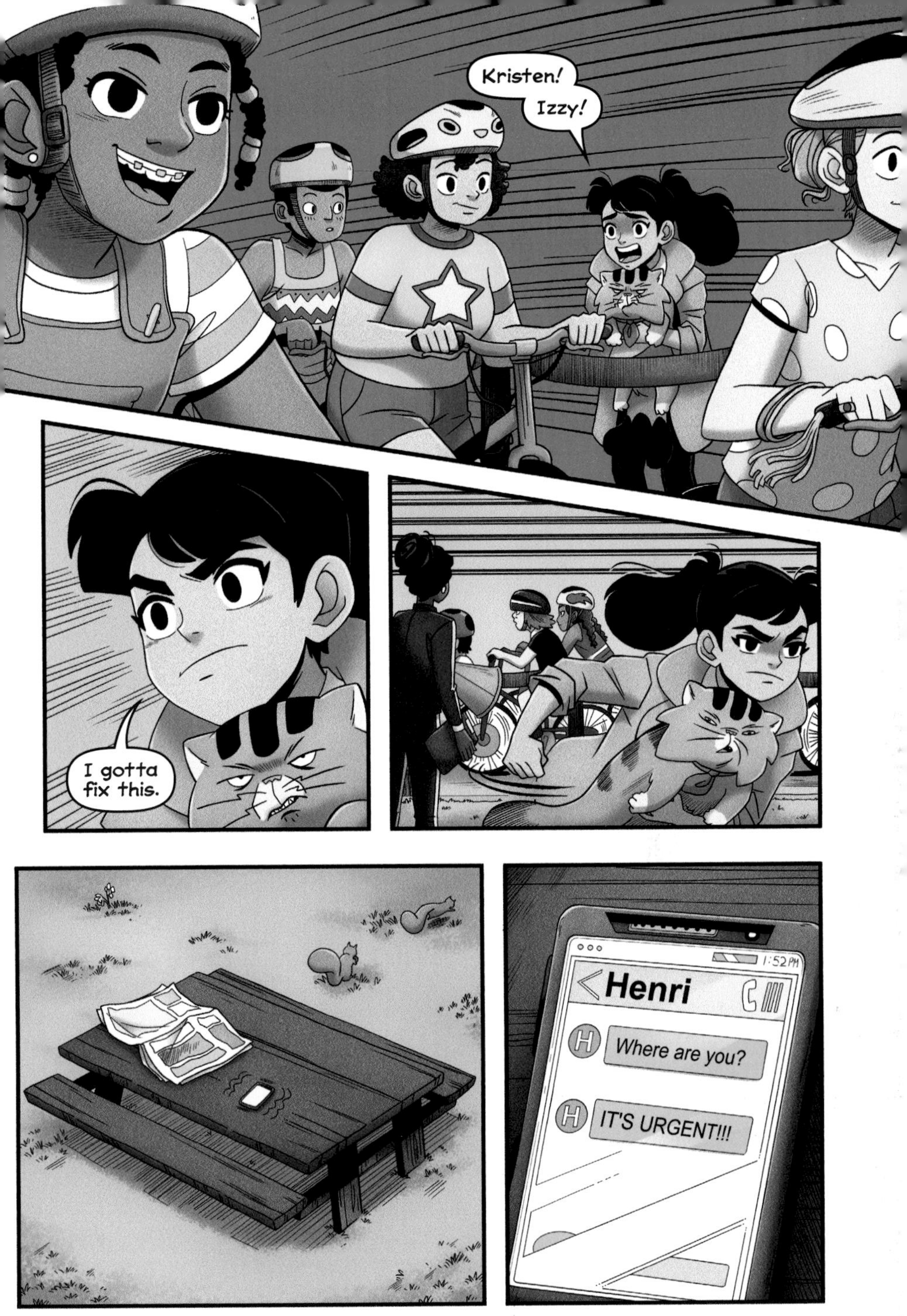
Kristen!
Izzy!
I gotta fix this.
Henri
1:52 PM
Where are you?
IT'S URGENT!!!

CHAPTER 5

*all's well that
friends well*

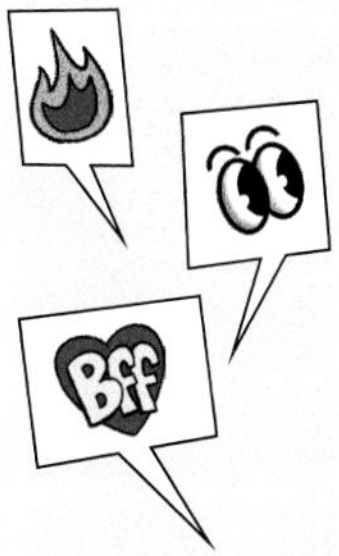
Bff

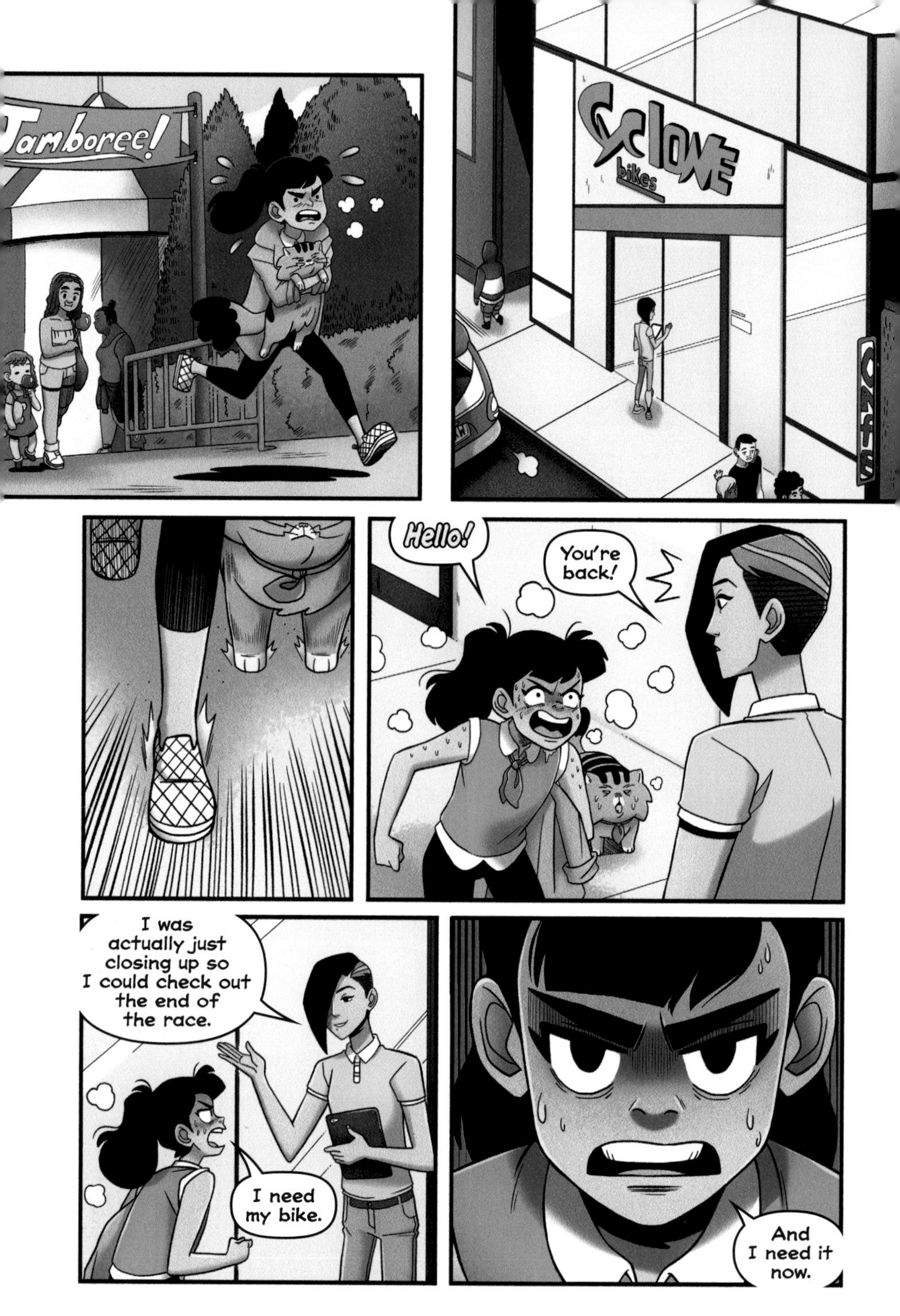
Jamboree!
Cyclone bikes
Hello!
You're back!
I was actually just closing up so I could check out the end of the race.
I need my bike.
And I need it now.

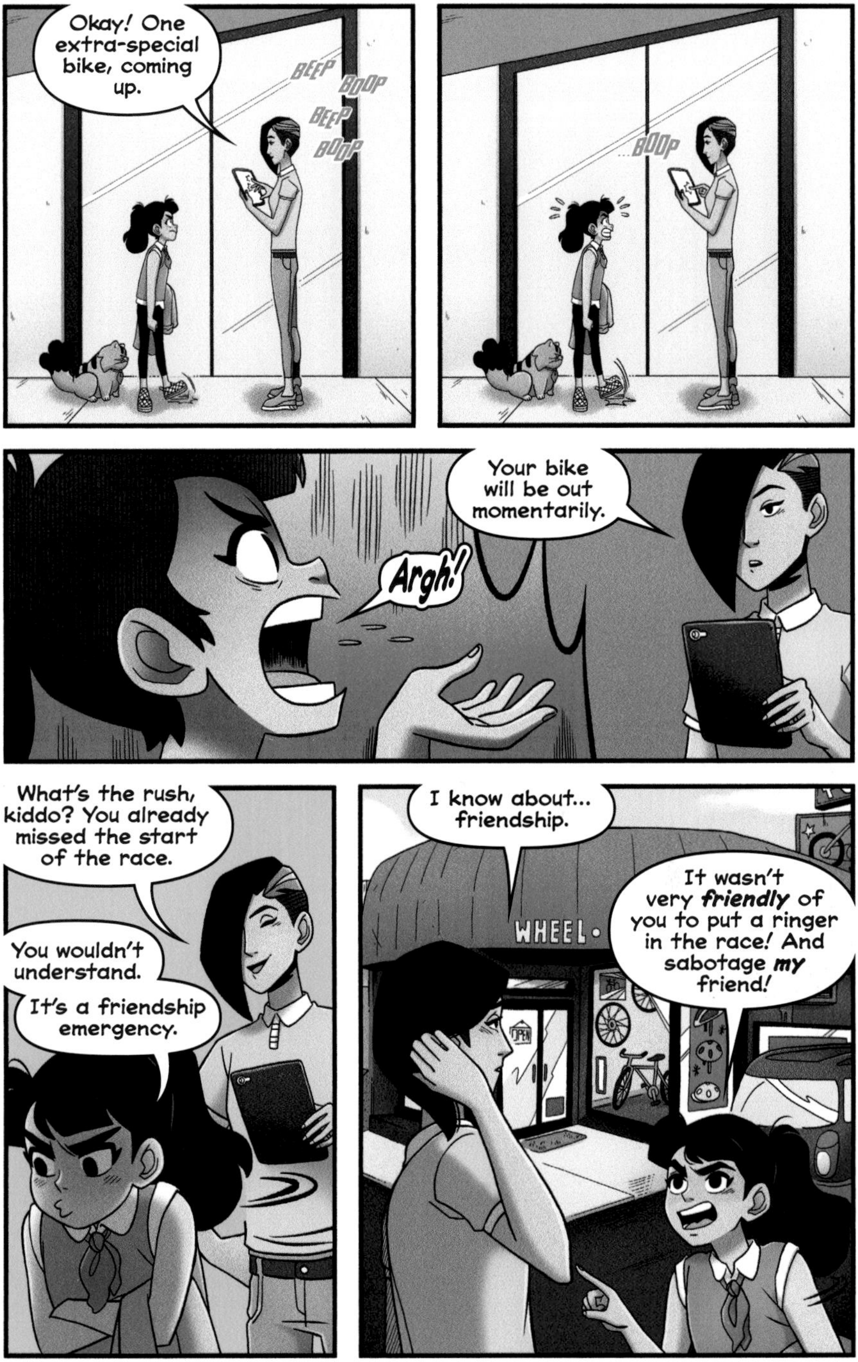
Okay! One extra-special bike, coming up.
BEEP BOOP BEEP BOOP
...BOOP
Your bike will be out momentarily.
Argh!
What's the rush, kiddo? You already missed the start of the race.
You wouldn't understand.
It's a friendship emergency.
I know about... friendship.
WHEEL
OPEN
It wasn't very ***friendly*** of you to put a ringer in the race! And sabotage ***my*** friend!

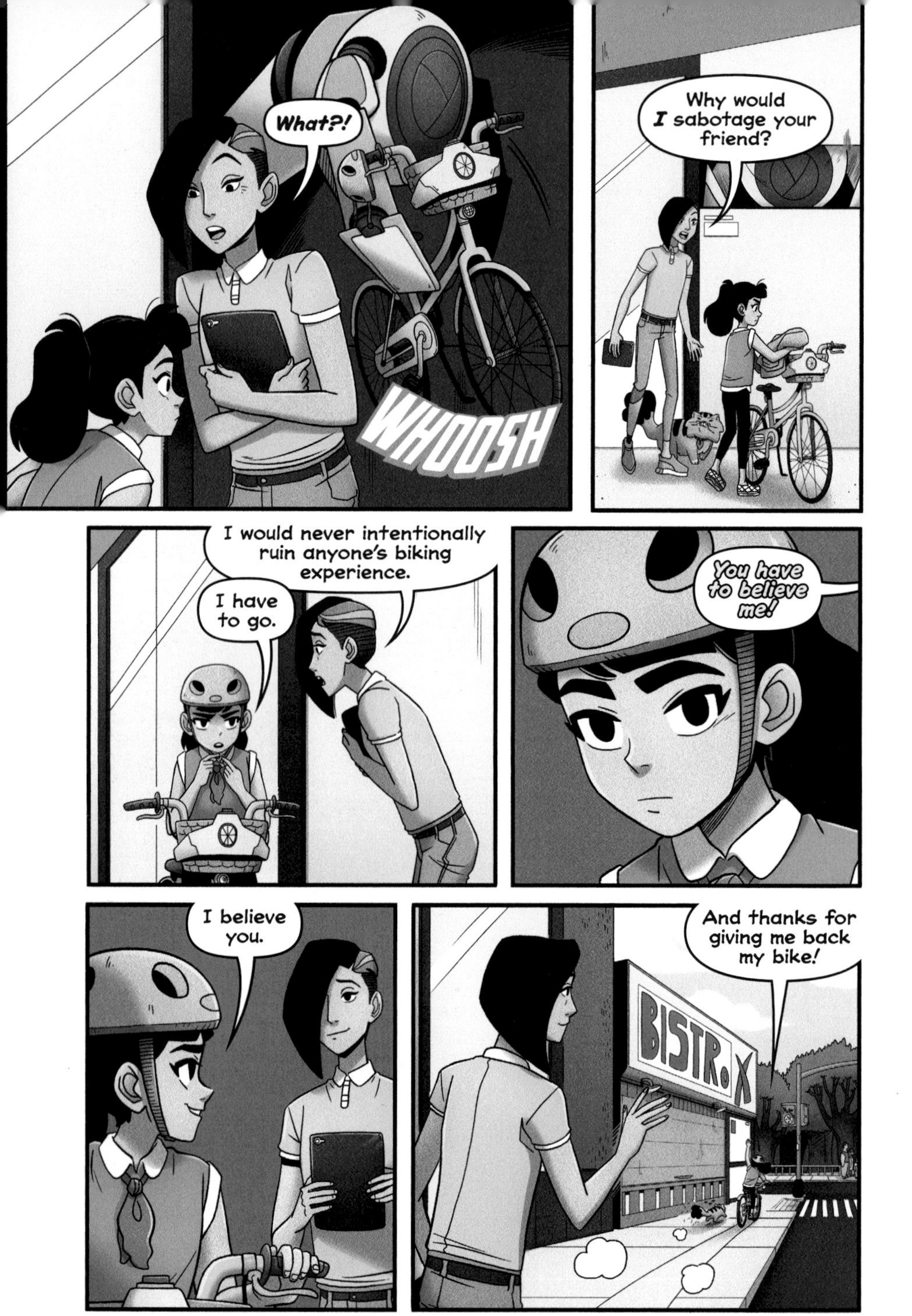

What?!
WHOOSH
Why would I sabotage your friend?
I would never intentionally ruin anyone's biking experience.
I have to go.
You have to believe me!
I believe you.
And thanks for giving me back my bike!
BISTRO X

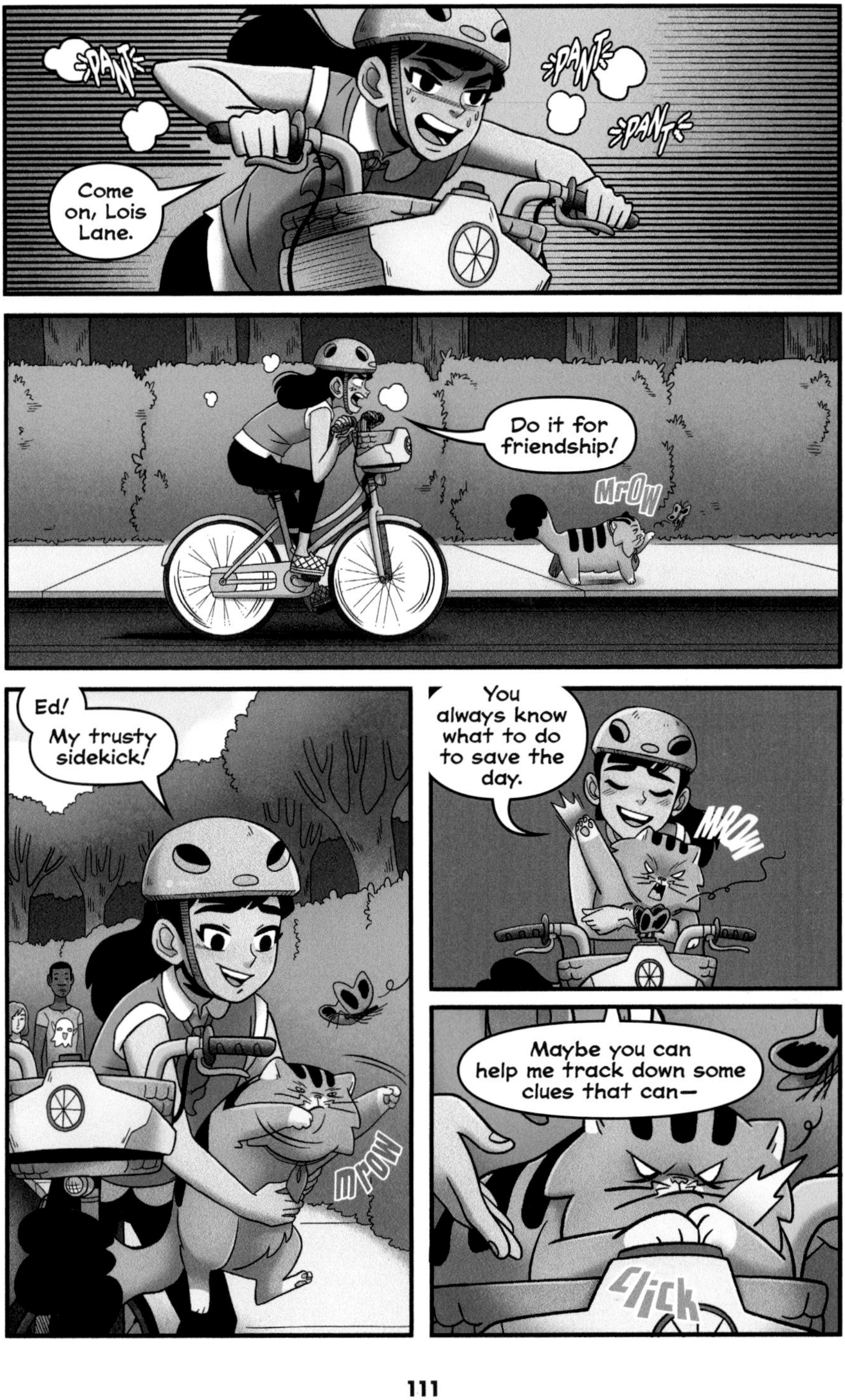
PANT
PANT
PANT
Come on, Lois Lane.
Do it for friendship!
MROW
Ed! My trusty sidekick!
MROW
You always know what to do to save the day.
MROW
Maybe you can help me track down some clues that can—
CLICK

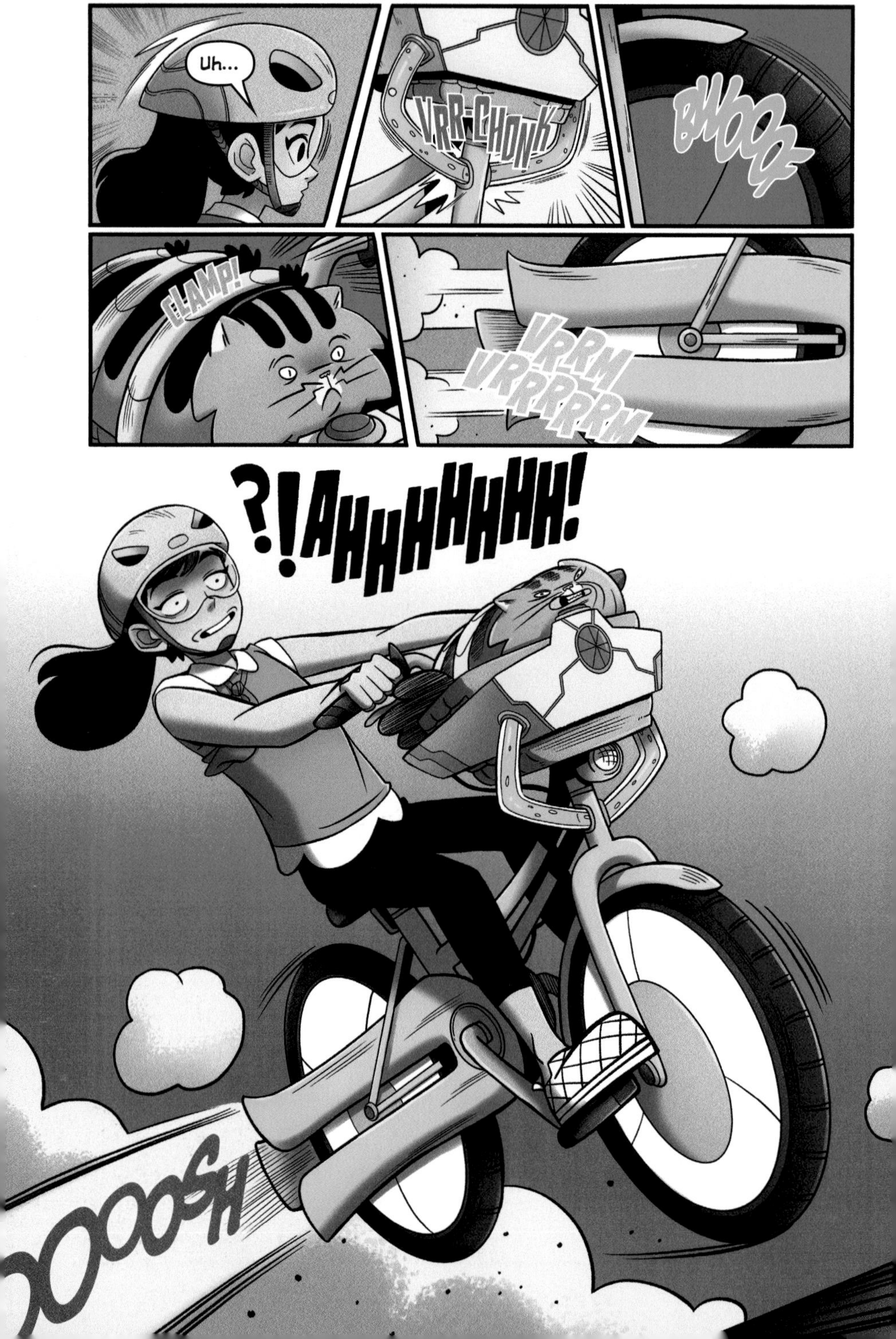
Uh...
VRR-CHONK
BWOOOF
CLAMP!
VRRM
VRRRRRM
?!AHHHHHHH!
OOOOSH

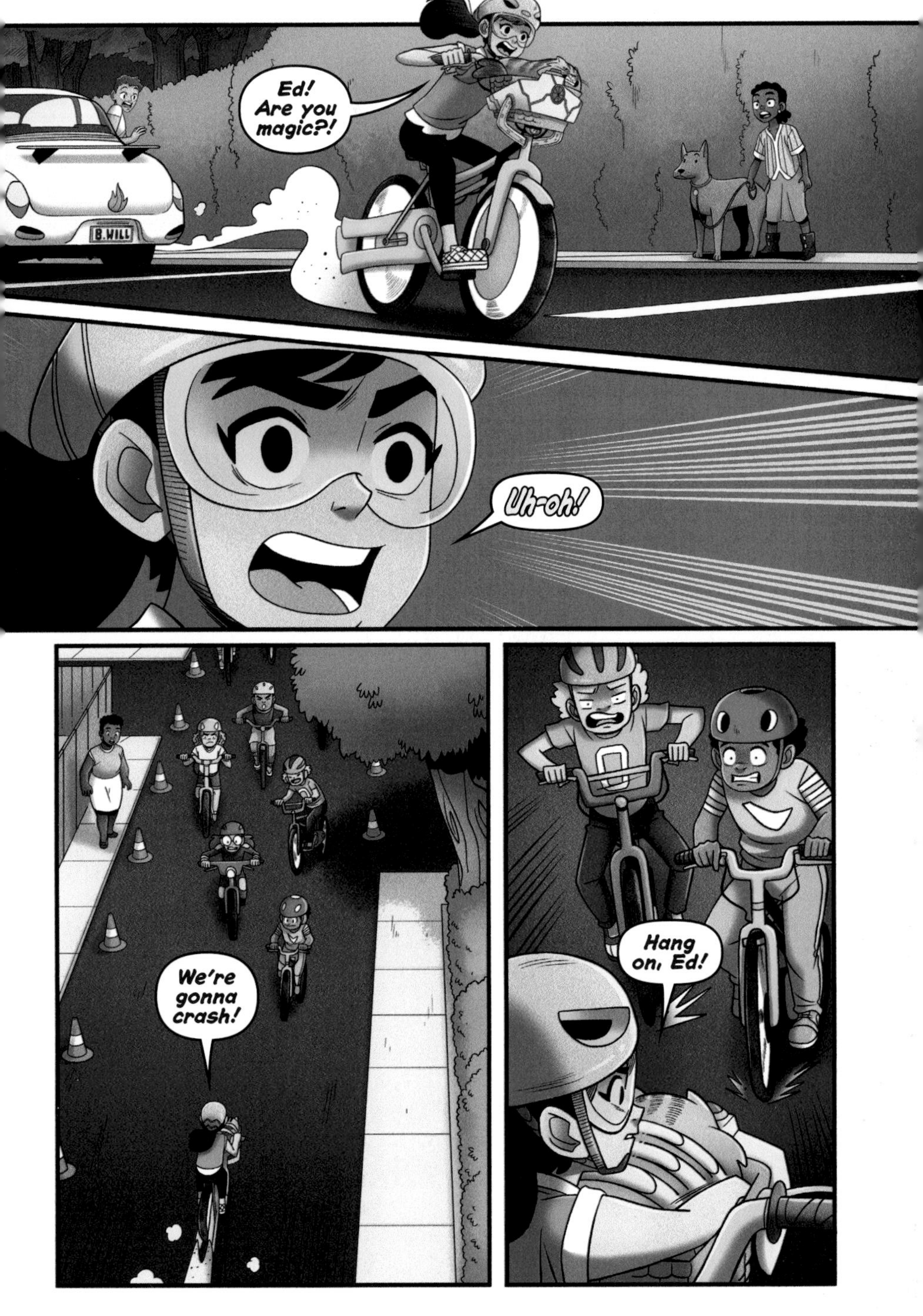
B.WILL
Ed! Are you magic?!
Uh-oh!
We're gonna crash!
Hang on, Ed!

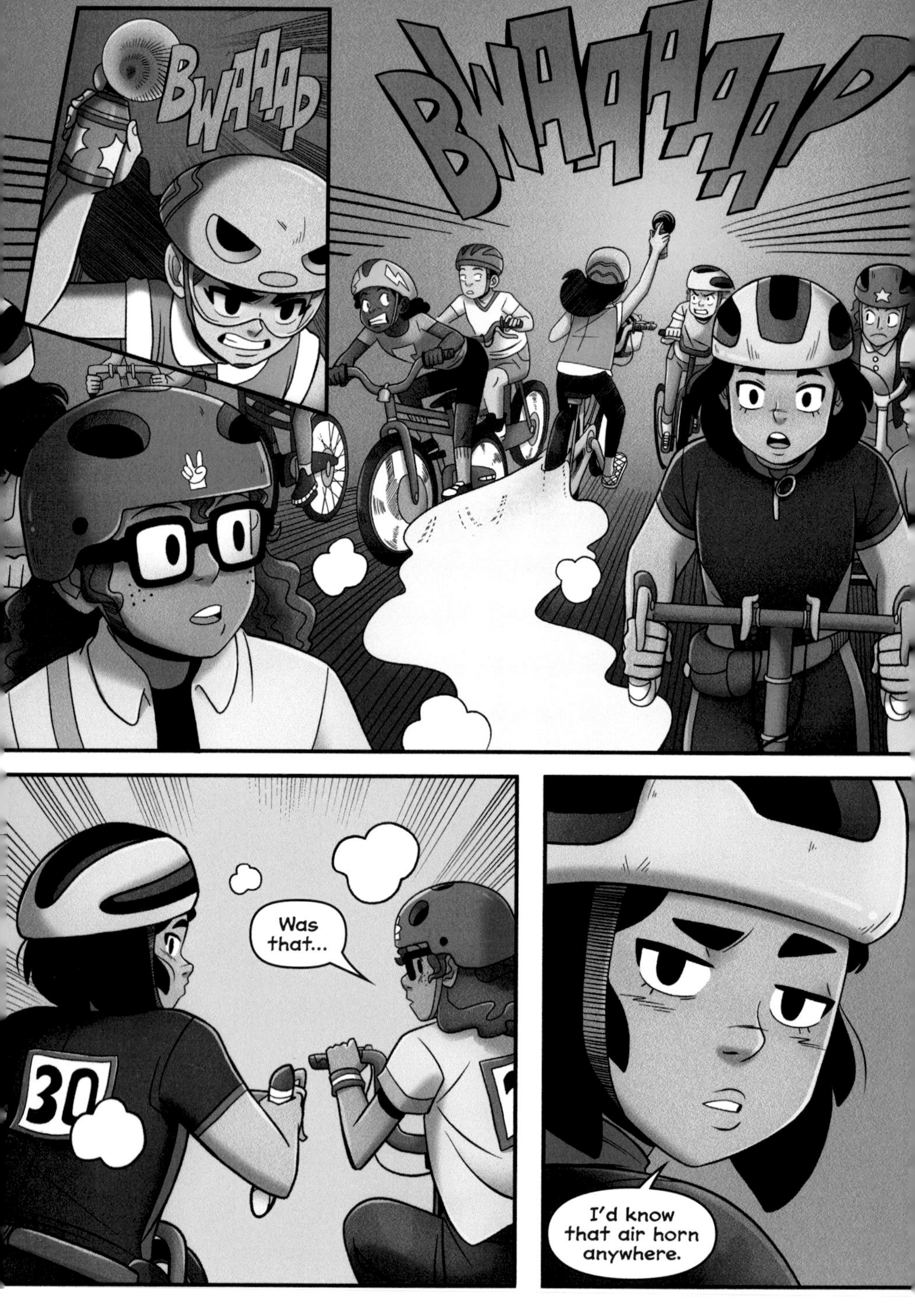
BWAAAP
BWAAAAAAP
Was that...
I'd know that air horn anywhere.

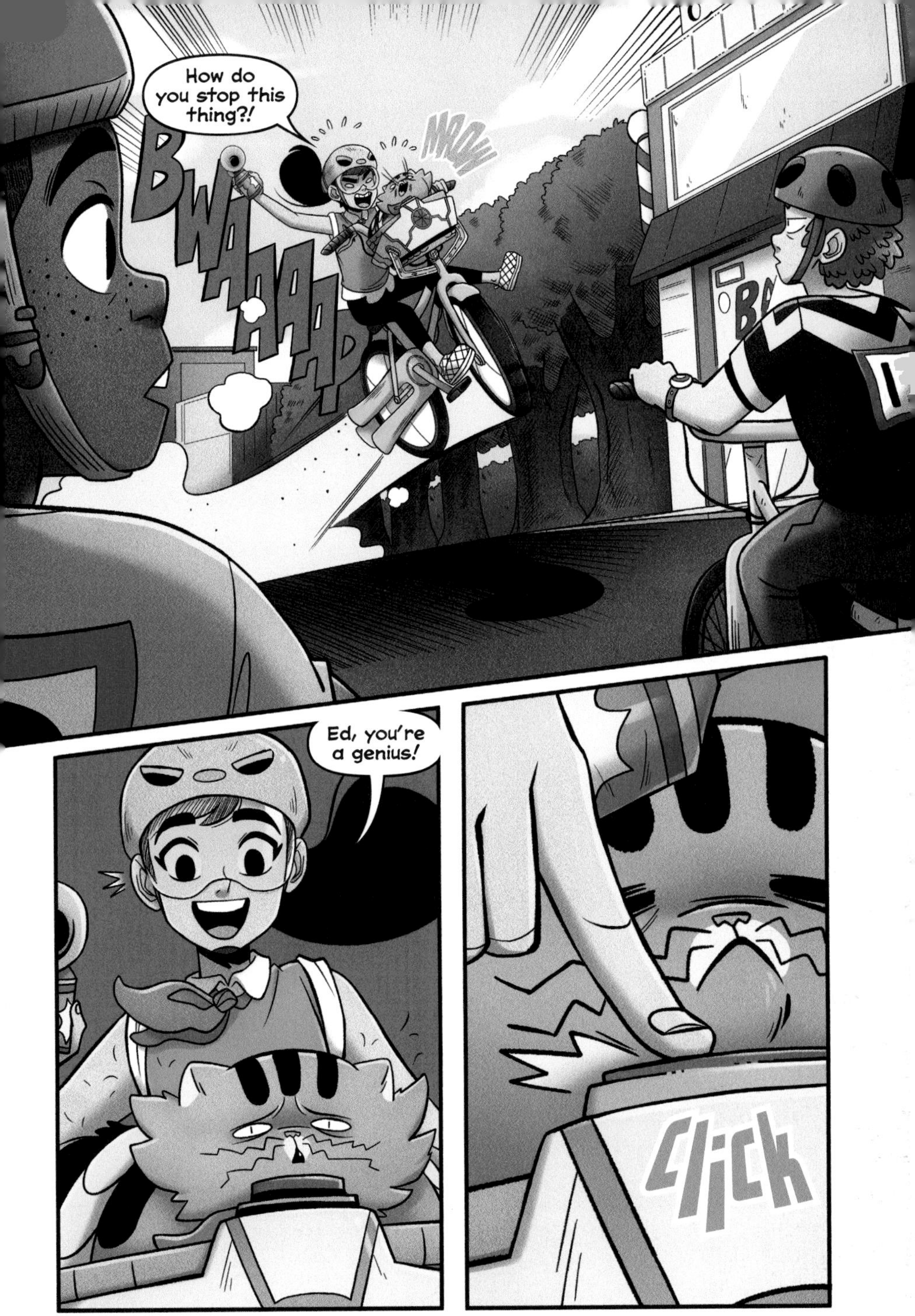
How do you stop this thing?!
BWAAAAAP
MROW
Ed, you're a genius!
Click

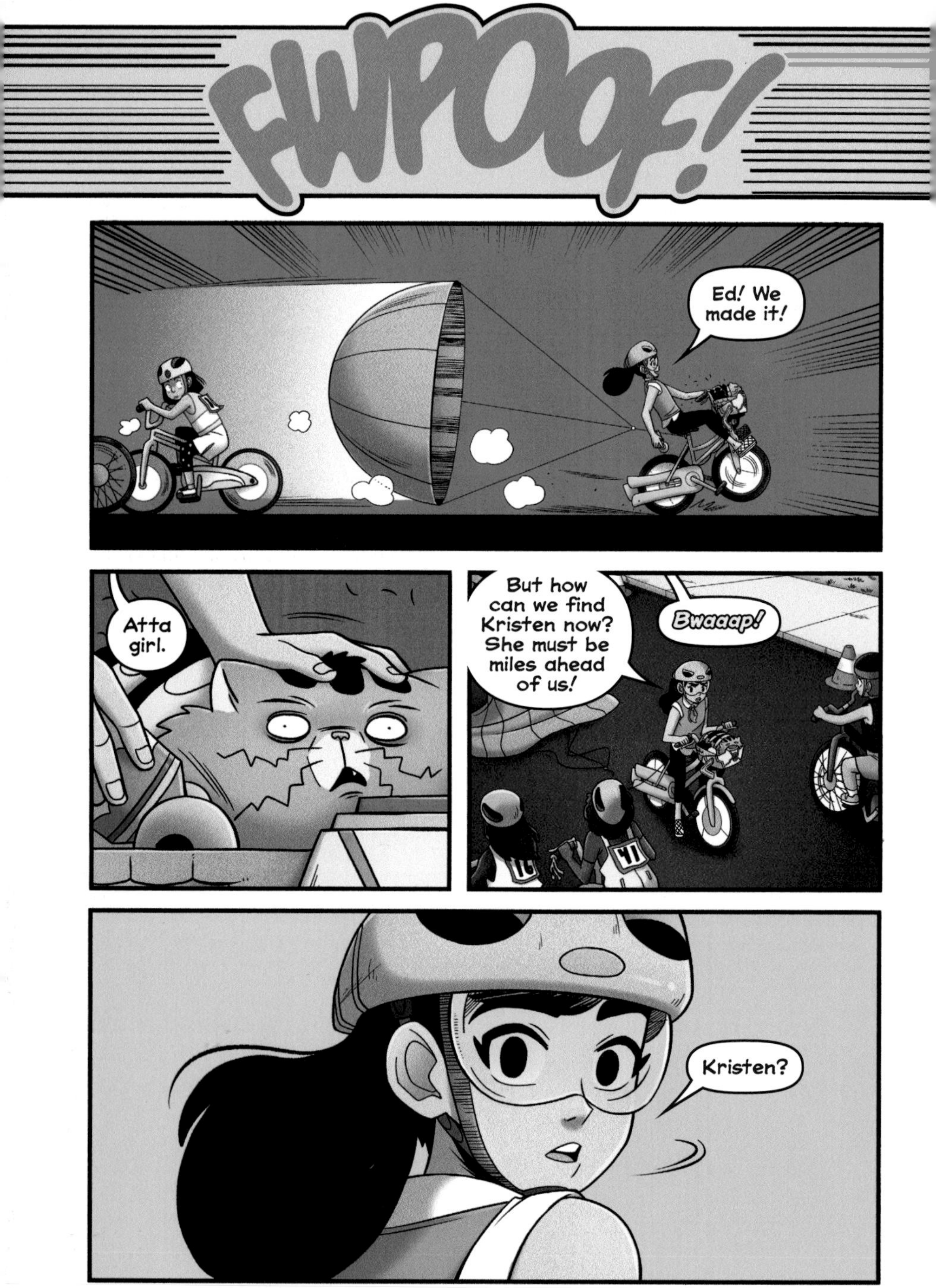
FWPOOF!
Ed! We made it!
Atta girl.
But how can we find Kristen now? She must be miles ahead of us!
Bwaaap!
Kristen?

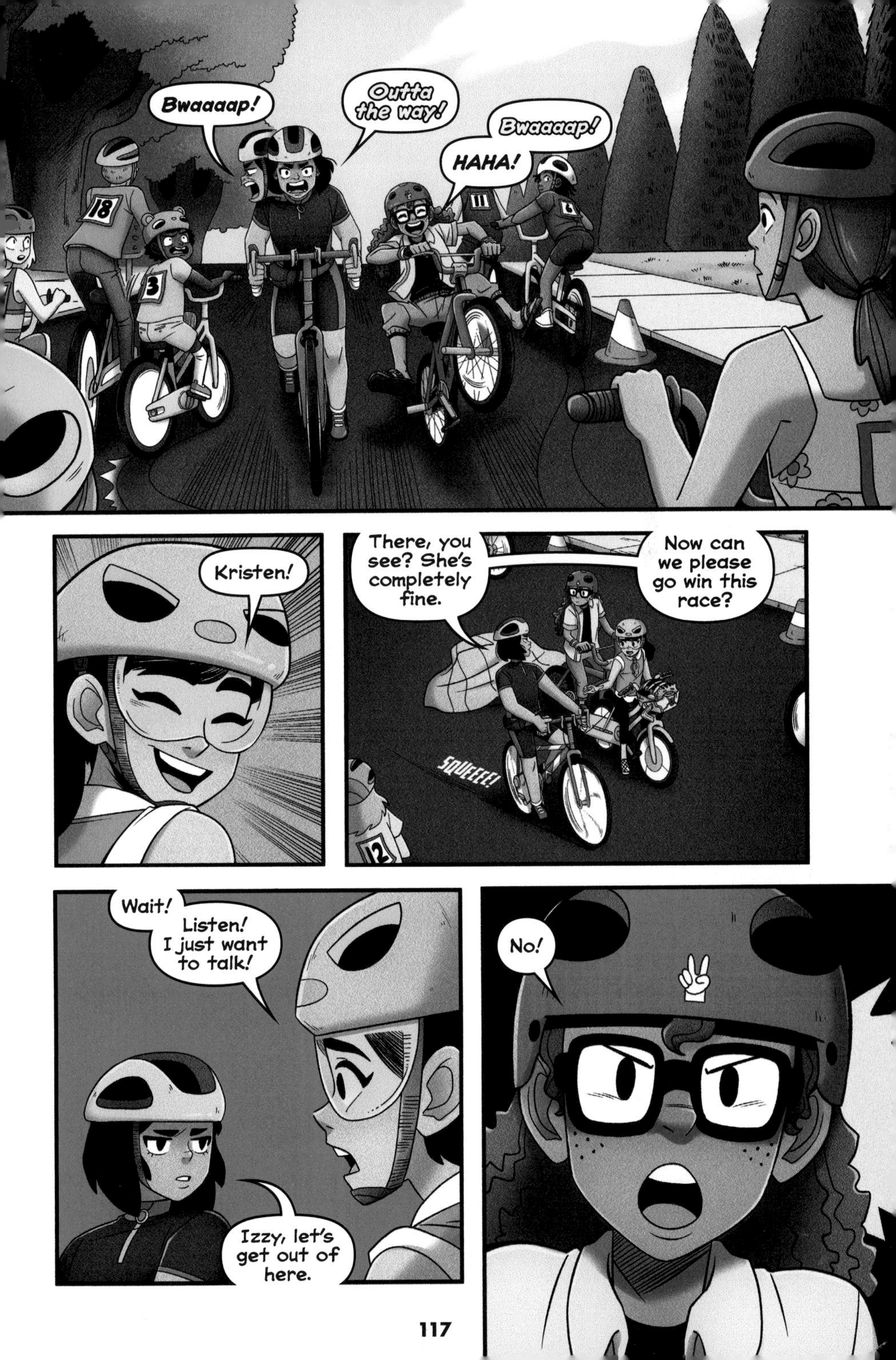
Bwaaaap!
Outta the way!
Bwaaaap!
HAHA!
18
3
11
6
Kristen!
There, you see? She's completely fine.
Now can we please go win this race?
SQUEEEE!
12
Wait!
Listen! I just want to talk!
Izzy, let's get out of here.
No!

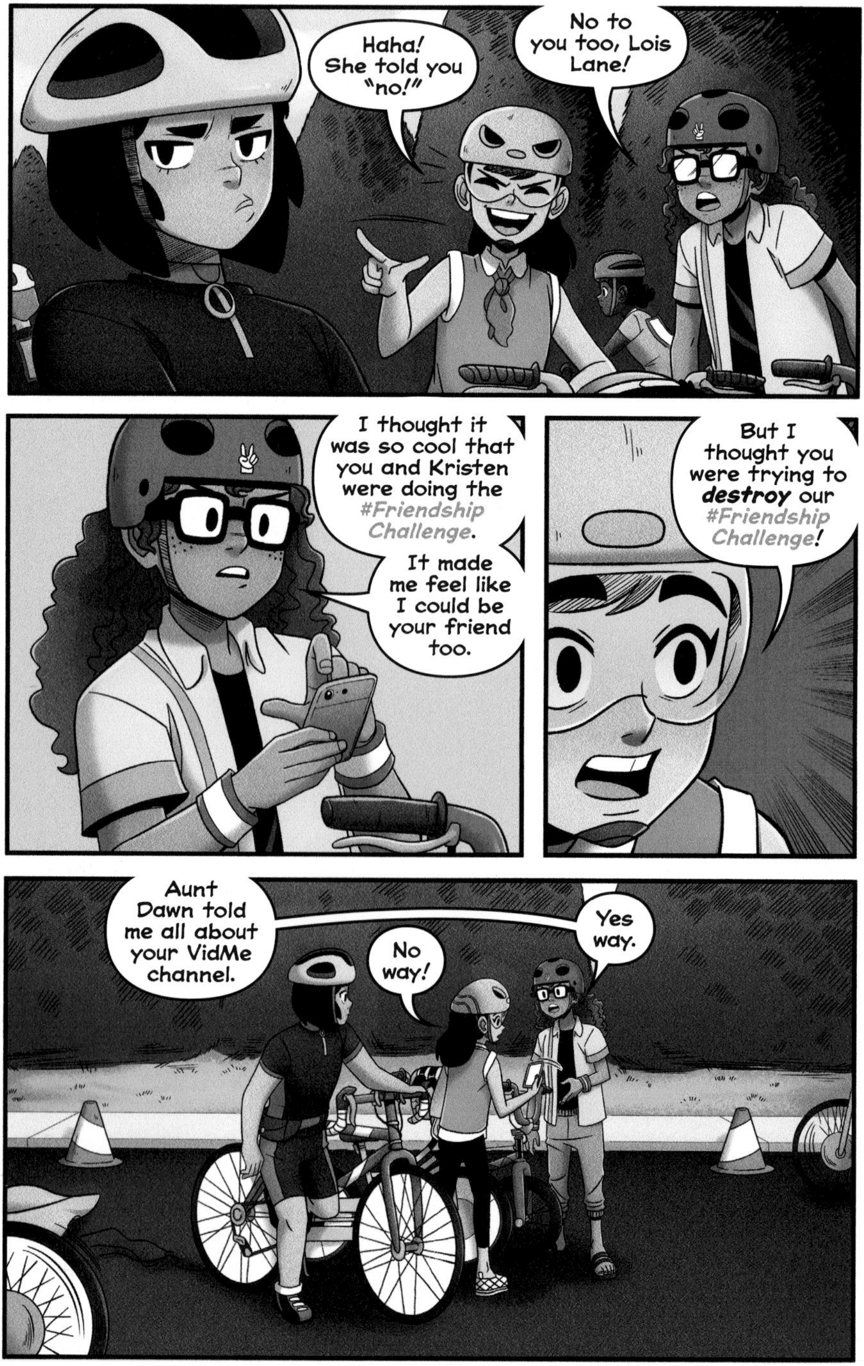
Haha! She told you "no!"
No to you too, Lois Lane!
I thought it was so cool that you and Kristen were doing the #Friendship Challenge.
It made me feel like I could be your friend too.
But I thought you were trying to **destroy** our #Friendship Challenge!
Aunt Dawn told me all about your VidMe channel.
No way!
Yes way.

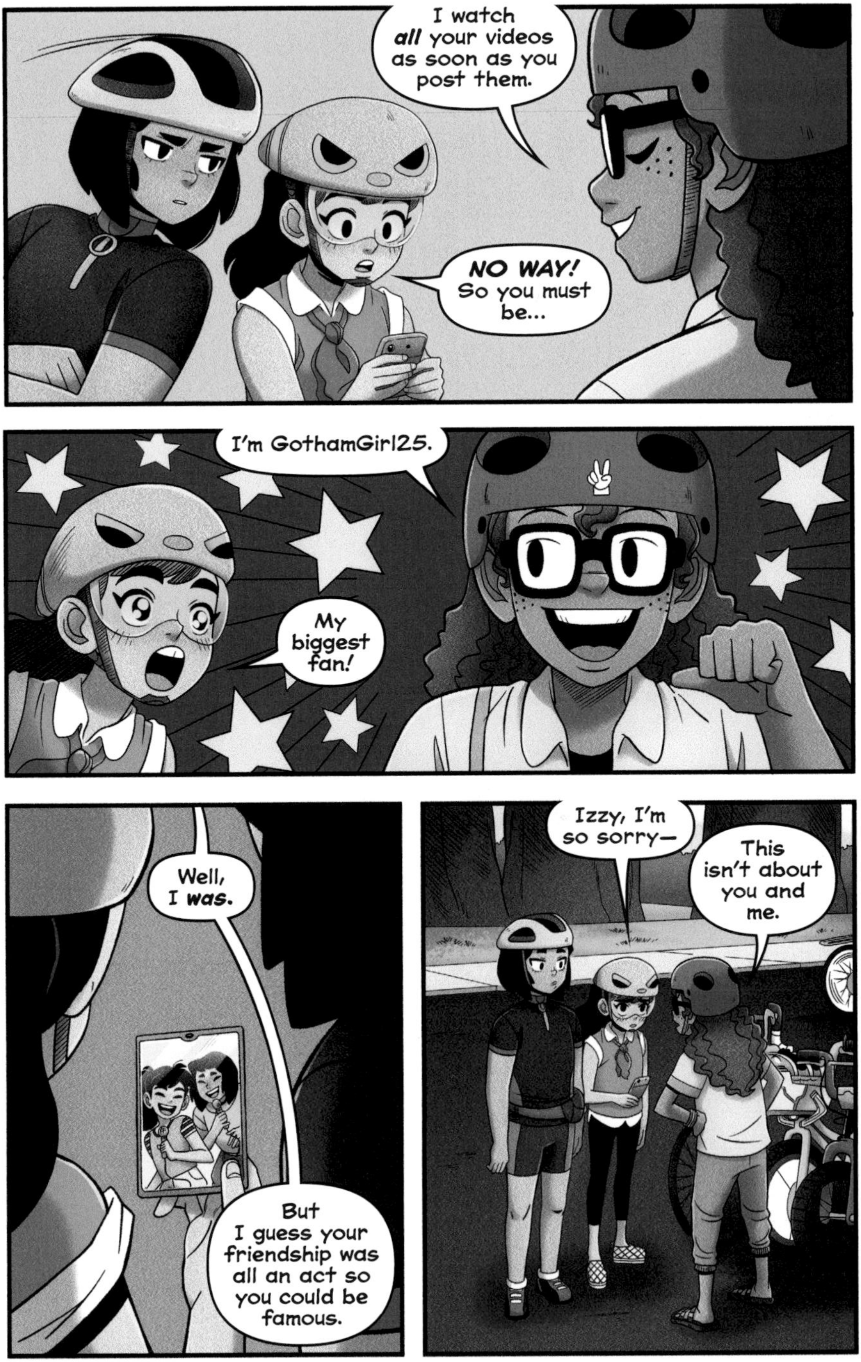
I watch *all* your videos as soon as you post them.
NO WAY! So you must be...
I'm GothamGirl25.
My biggest fan!
Well, I *was*.
But I guess your friendship was all an act so you could be famous.
Izzy, I'm so sorry—
This isn't about you and me.

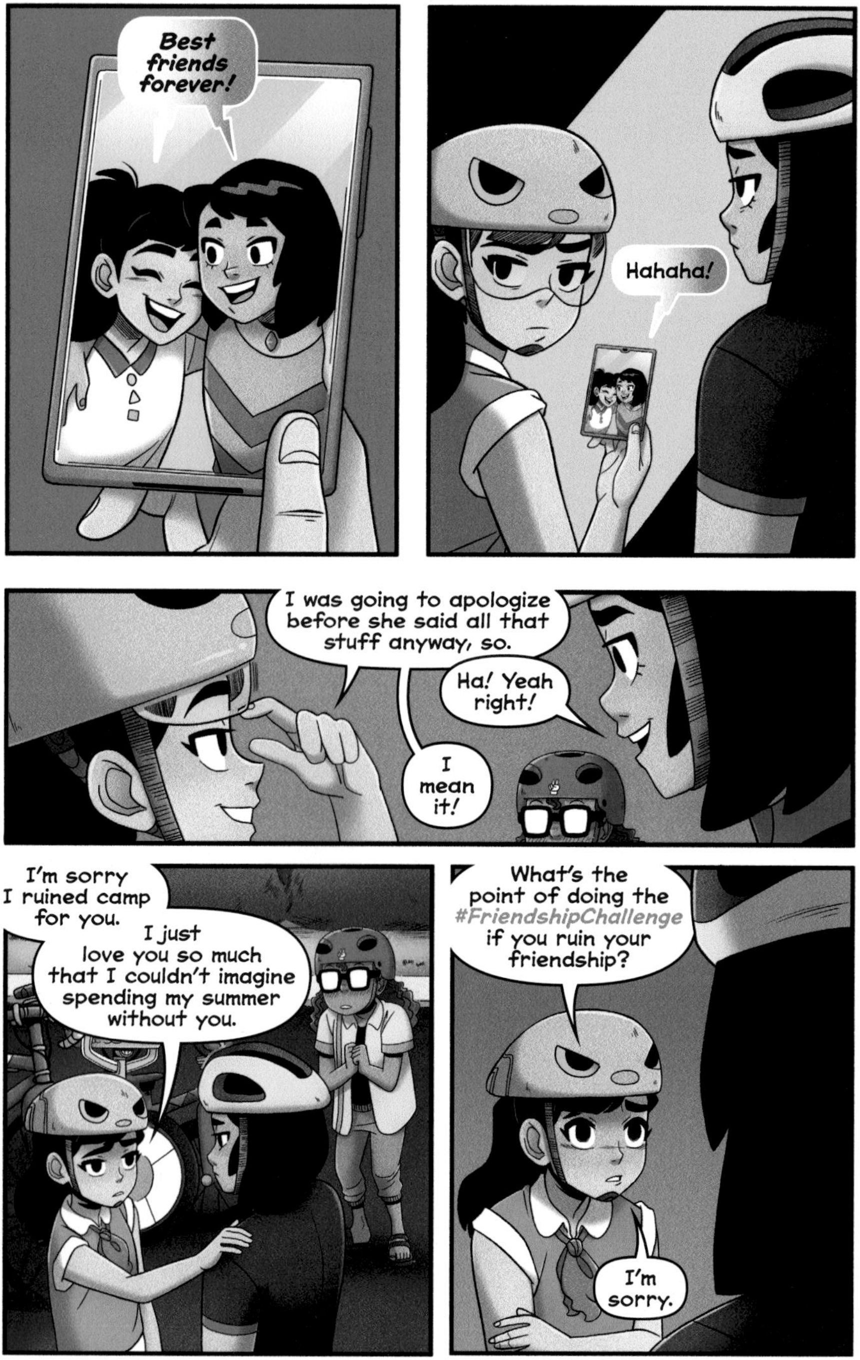
Best friends forever!
Hahaha!
I was going to apologize before she said all that stuff anyway, so.
Ha! Yeah right!
I mean it!
I'm sorry I ruined camp for you.
I just love you so much that I couldn't imagine spending my summer without you.
What's the point of doing the #FriendshipChallenge if you ruin your friendship?
I'm sorry.

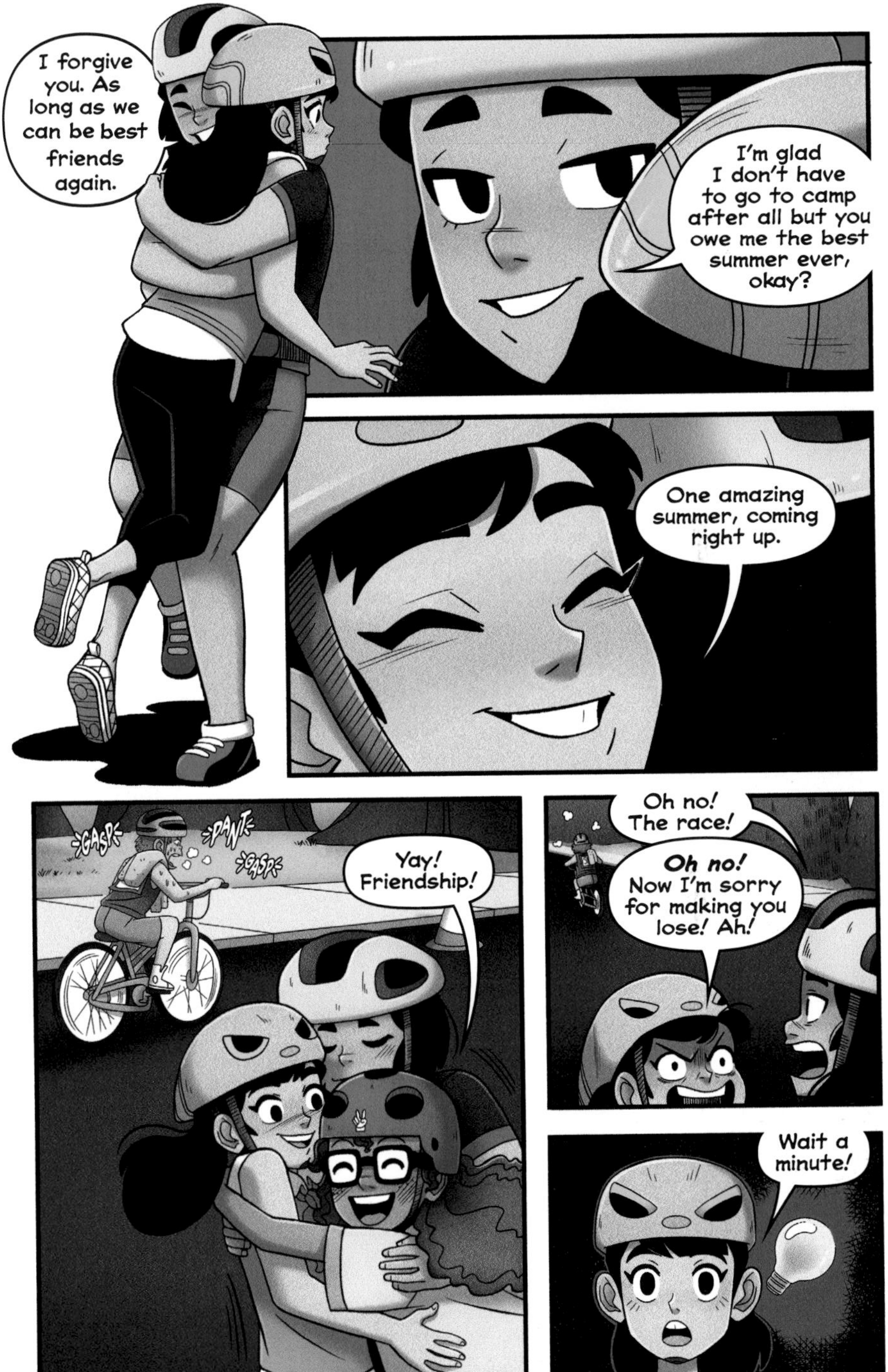
I forgive you. As long as we can be best friends again.
I'm glad I don't have to go to camp after all but you owe me the best summer ever, okay?
One amazing summer, coming right up.
GASP
PANT
GASP
Yay! Friendship!
Oh no! The race!
Oh no! Now I'm sorry for making you lose! Ah!
Wait a minute!

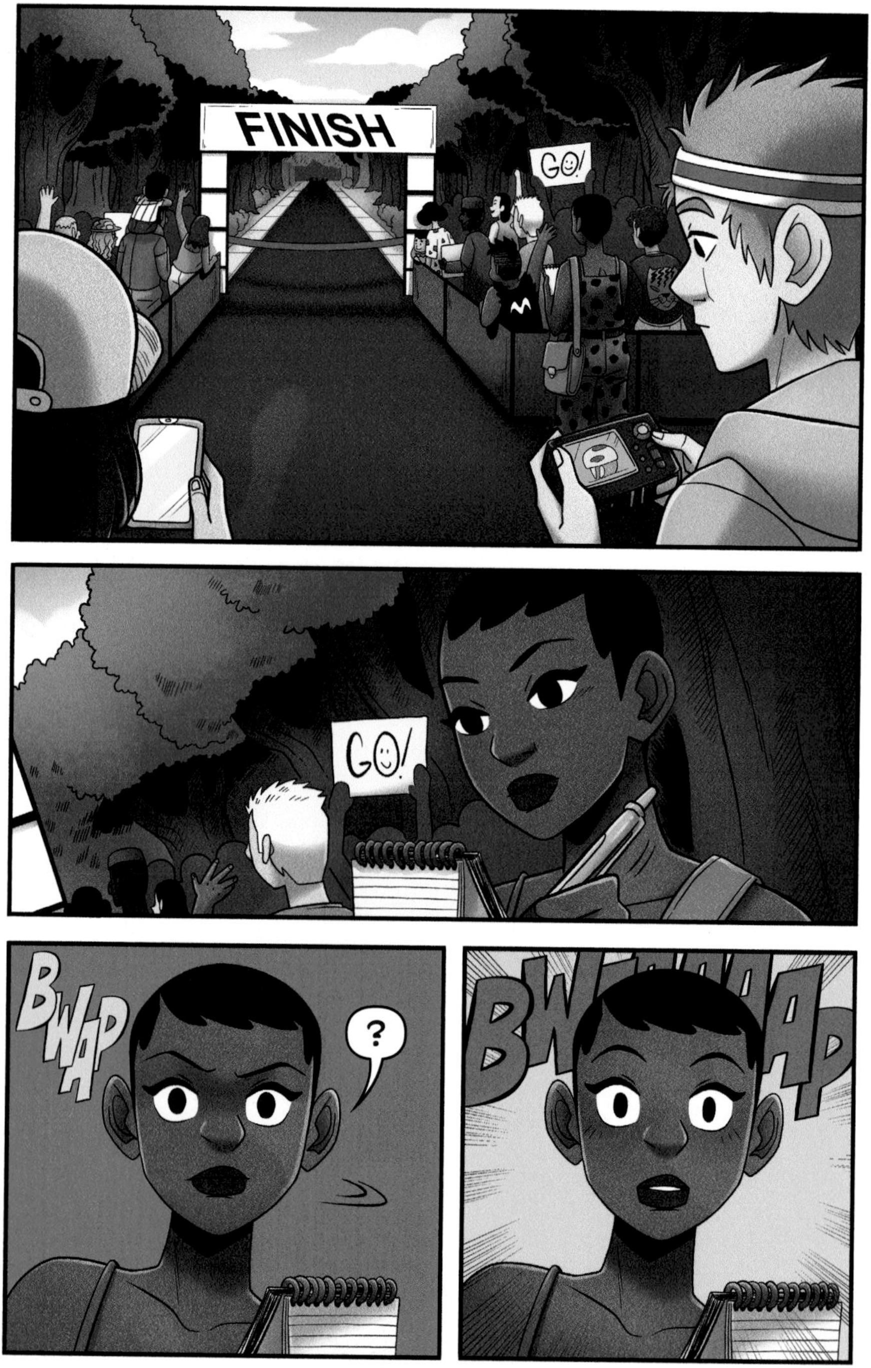
FINISH
GO!
GO!
BWAP
?
BWEEEAAAP

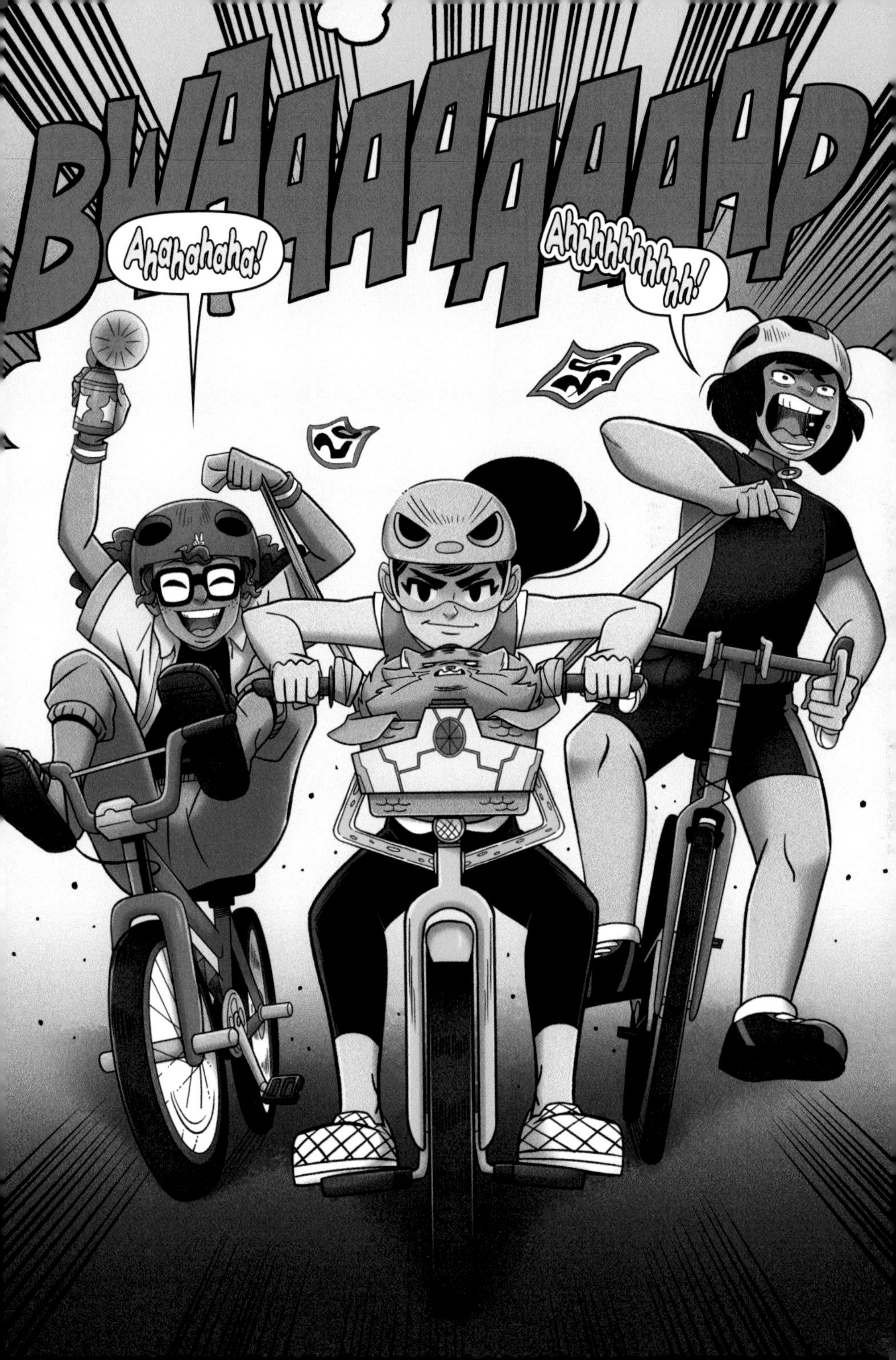
BWAAAAAAAAP
Ahahahaha!
Ahhhhhhhhhh!

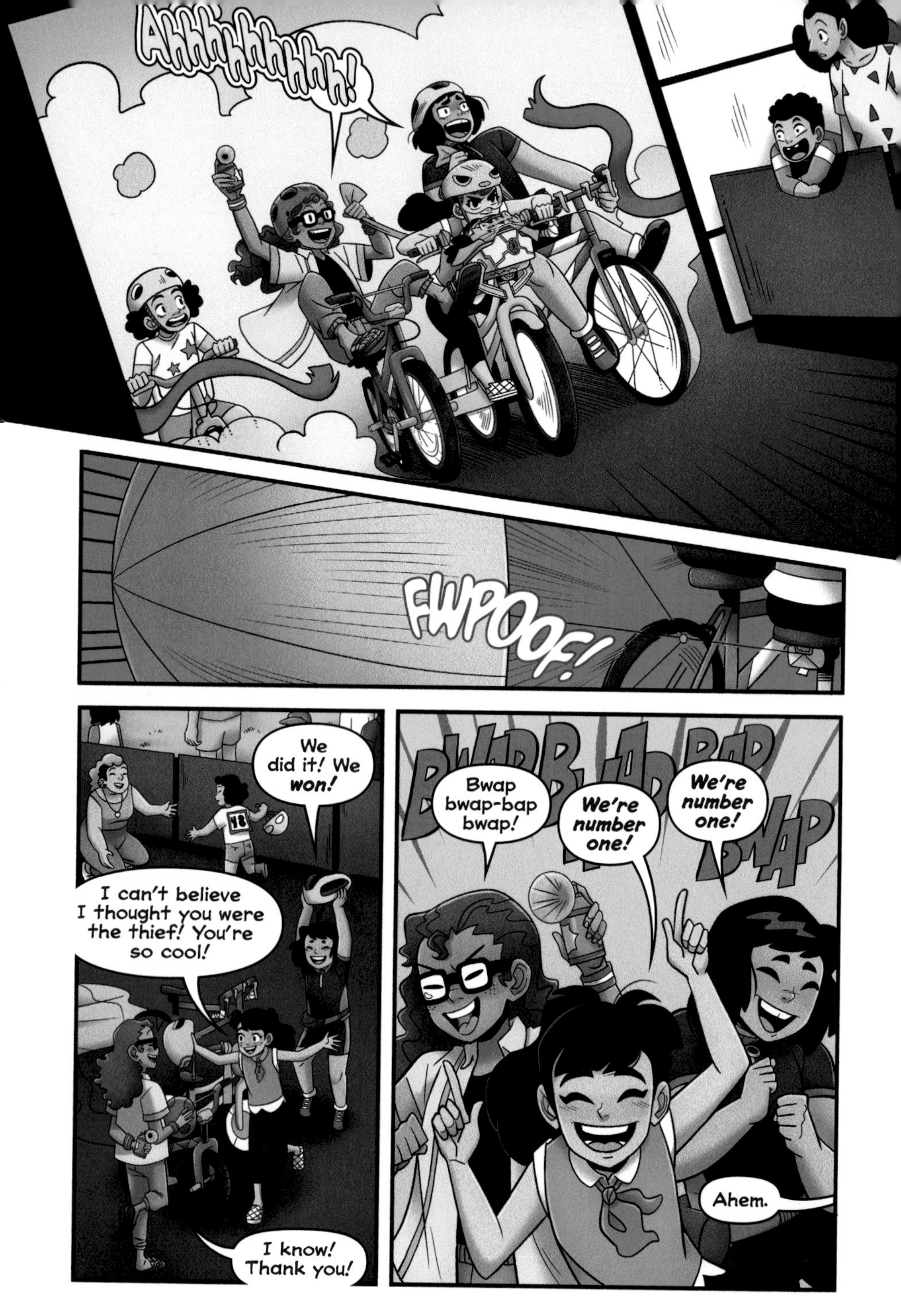
Ahhhhhhhhhh!
FWPOOF!
We did it! We won!
I can't believe I thought you were the thief! You're so cool!
I know! Thank you!
Bwap bwap-bap bwap!
We're number one!
We're number one!
Ahem.

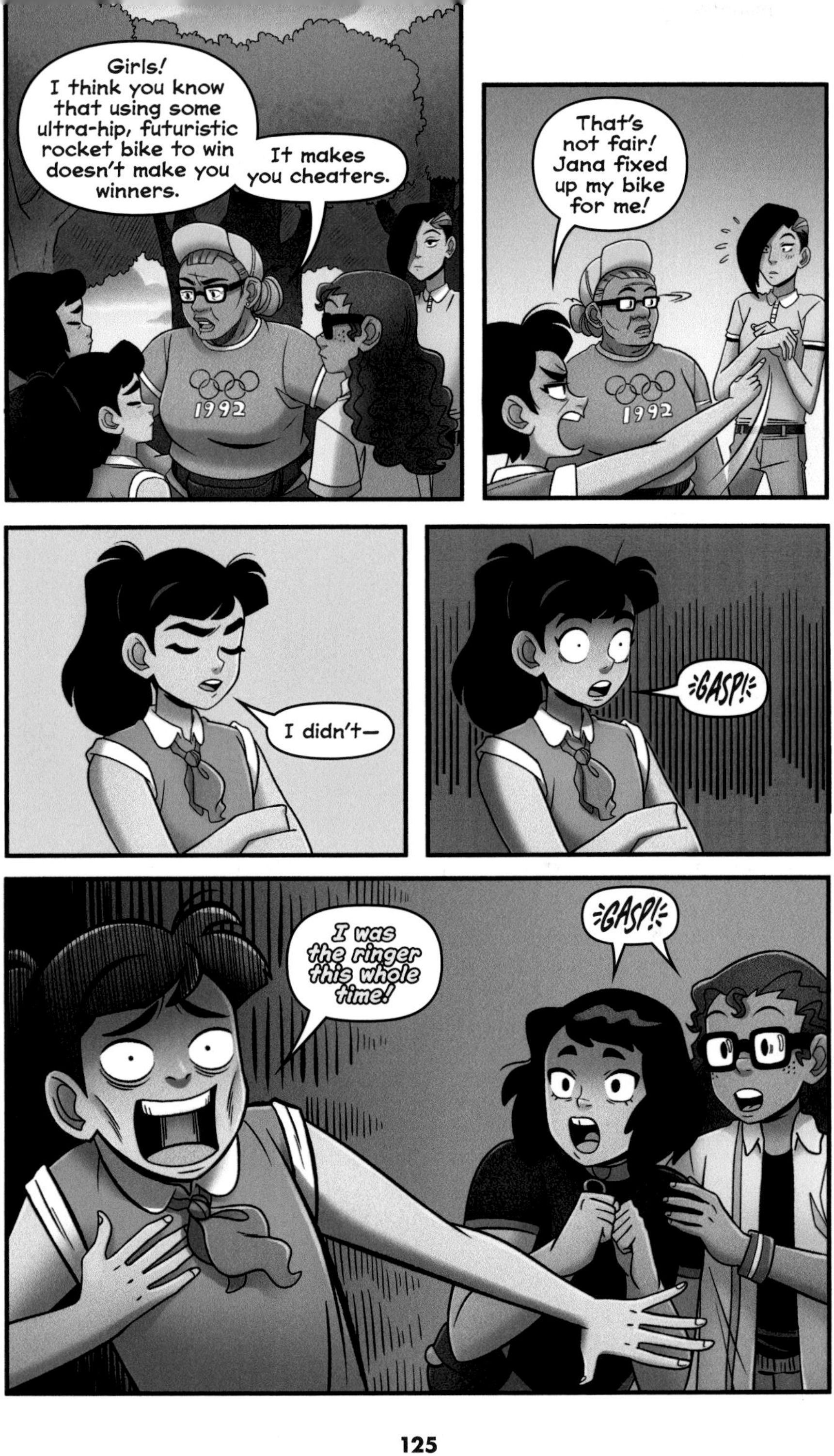
Girls! I think you know that using some ultra-hip, futuristic rocket bike to win doesn't make you winners.
It makes you cheaters.
That's not fair! Jana fixed up my bike for me!
I didn't—
GASP!
I was the ringer this whole time!
GASP!

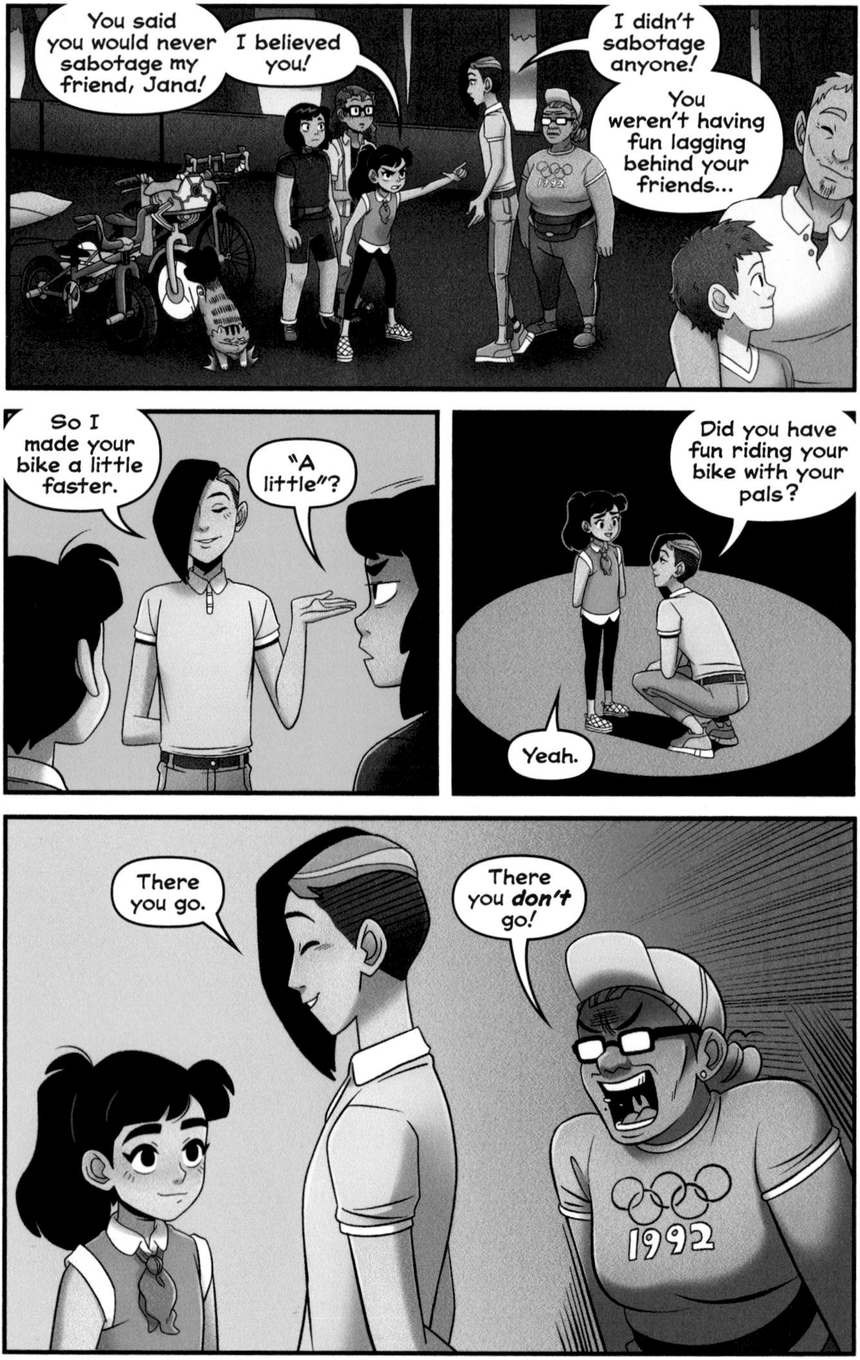
You said you would never sabotage my friend, Jana!
I believed you!
I didn't sabotage anyone!
You weren't having fun lagging behind your friends...
1992
So I made your bike a little faster.
"A little"?
Did you have fun riding your bike with your pals?
Yeah.
There you go.
There you ***don't*** go!
1992

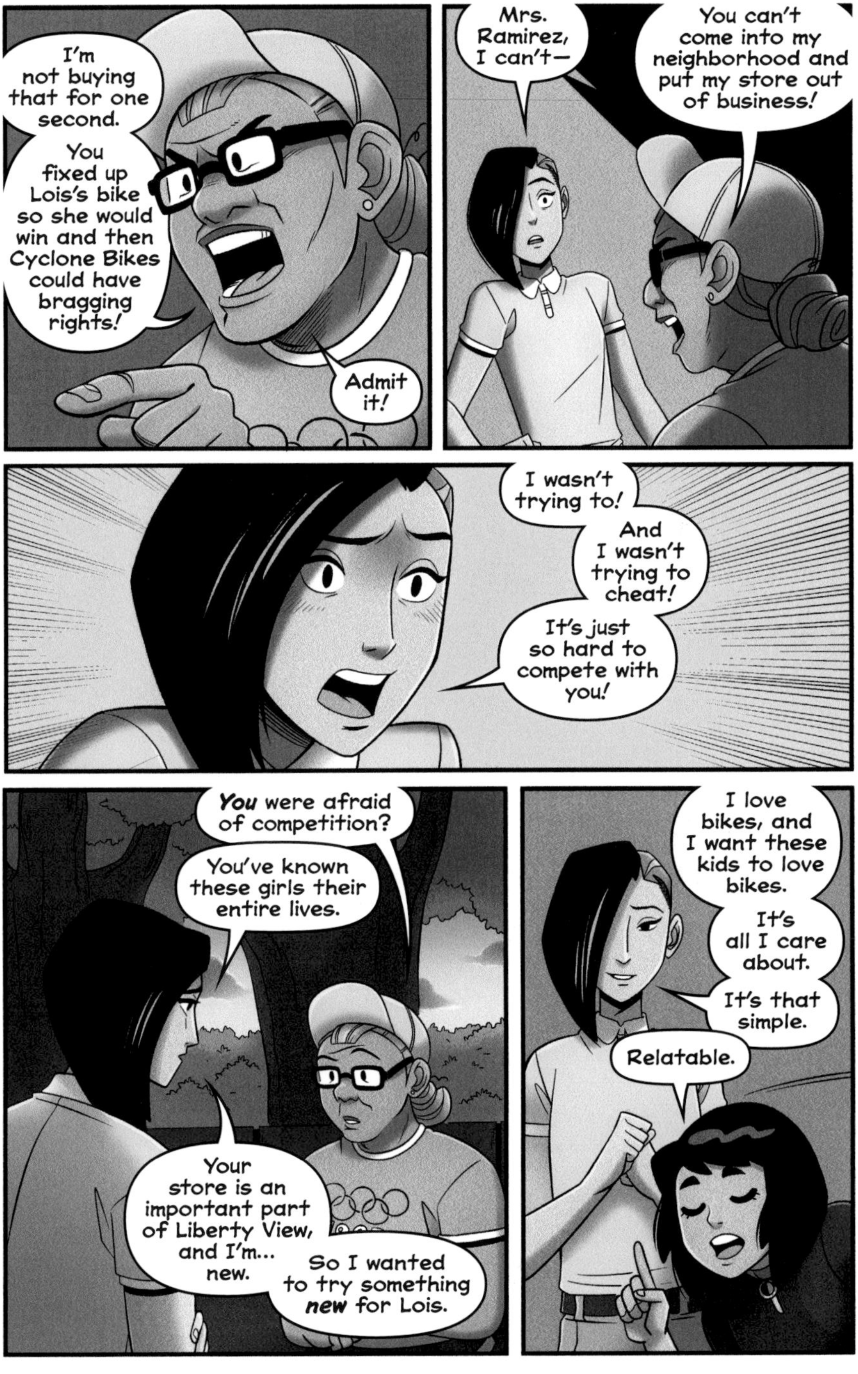
I'm not buying that for one second.
You fixed up Lois's bike so she would win and then Cyclone Bikes could have bragging rights!
Admit it!
Mrs. Ramirez, I can't—
You can't come into my neighborhood and put my store out of business!
I wasn't trying to!
And I wasn't trying to cheat!
It's just so hard to compete with you!
You were afraid of competition?
You've known these girls their entire lives.
Your store is an important part of Liberty View, and I'm... new.
So I wanted to try something *new* for Lois.
I love bikes, and I want these kids to love bikes.
It's all I care about.
It's that simple.
Relatable.

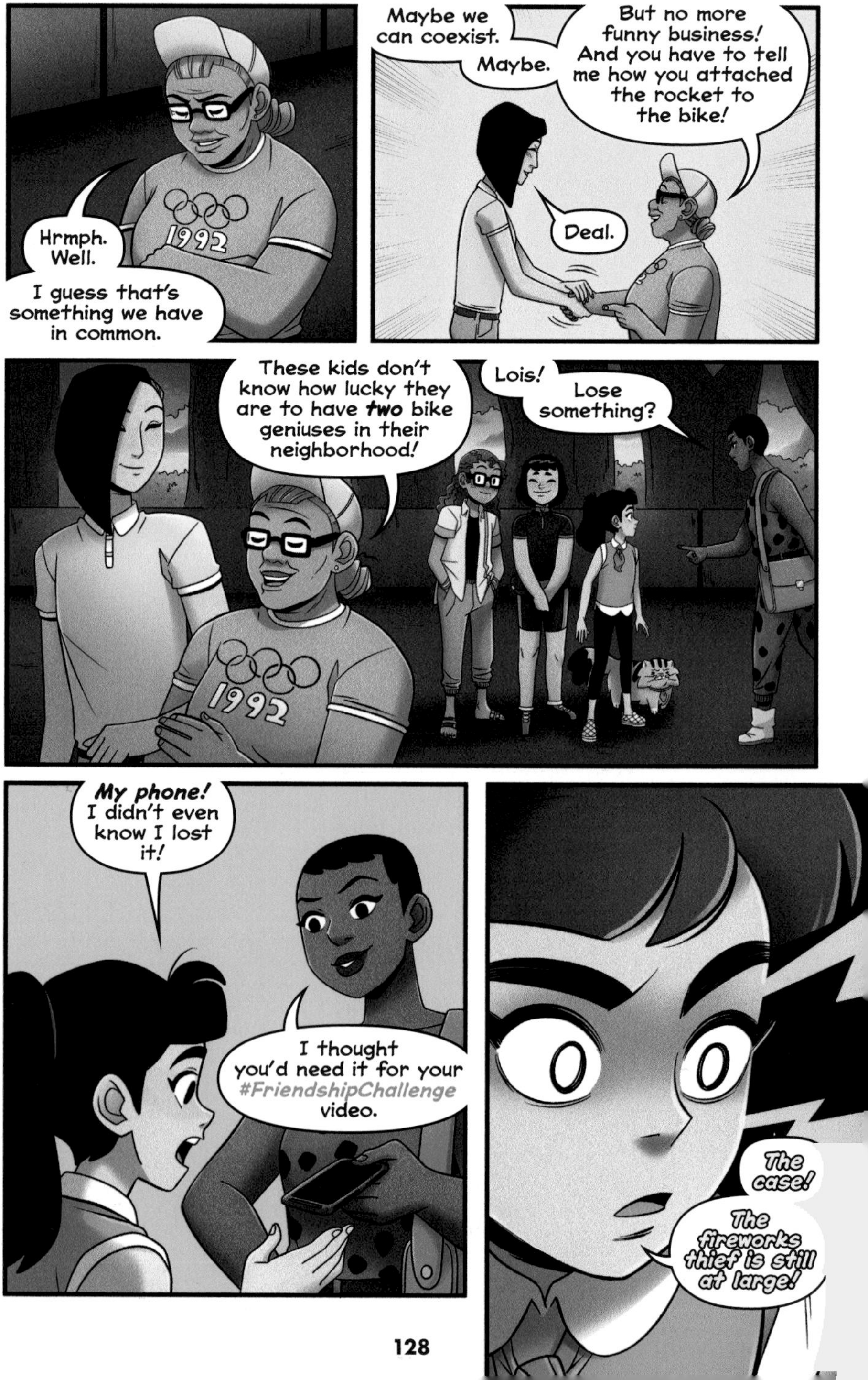
Hrmph. Well.
I guess that's something we have in common.
Maybe we can coexist.
Maybe.
But no more funny business! And you have to tell me how you attached the rocket to the bike!
Deal.
These kids don't know how lucky they are to have *two* bike geniuses in their neighborhood!
Lois!
Lose something?
My phone! I didn't even know I lost it!
I thought you'd need it for your #FriendshipChallenge video.
The case!
The fireworks thief is still at large!

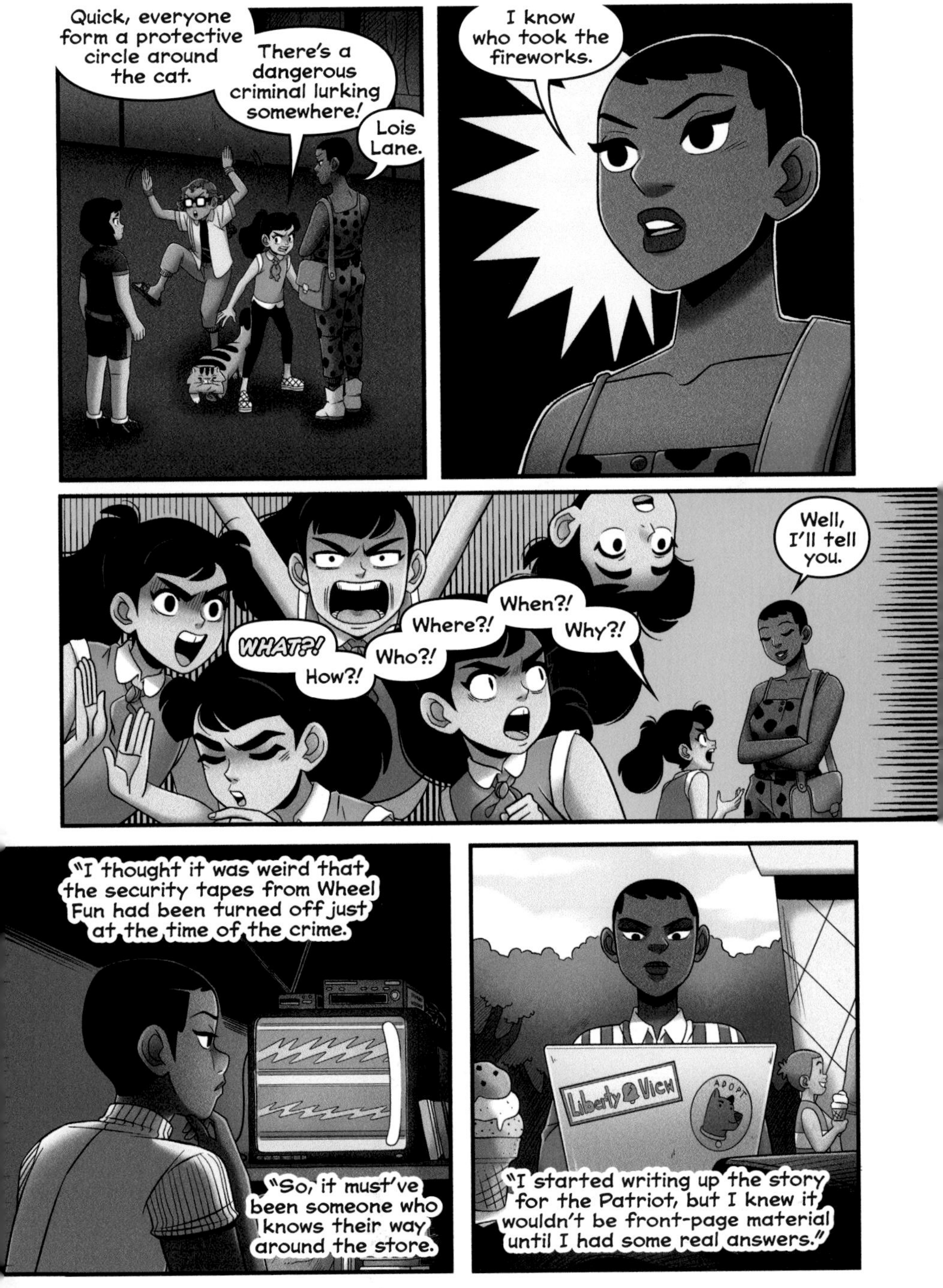

Quick, everyone form a protective circle around the cat.
There's a dangerous criminal lurking somewhere!
Lois Lane.
I know who took the fireworks.
WHAT?!
How?!
Who?!
Where?!
When?!
Why?!
Well, I'll tell you.
"I thought it was weird that the security tapes from Wheel Fun had been turned off just at the time of the crime.
"So, it must've been someone who knows their way around the store.
Liberty View
ADOPT
"I started writing up the story for the Patriot, but I knew it wouldn't be front-page material until I had some real answers."

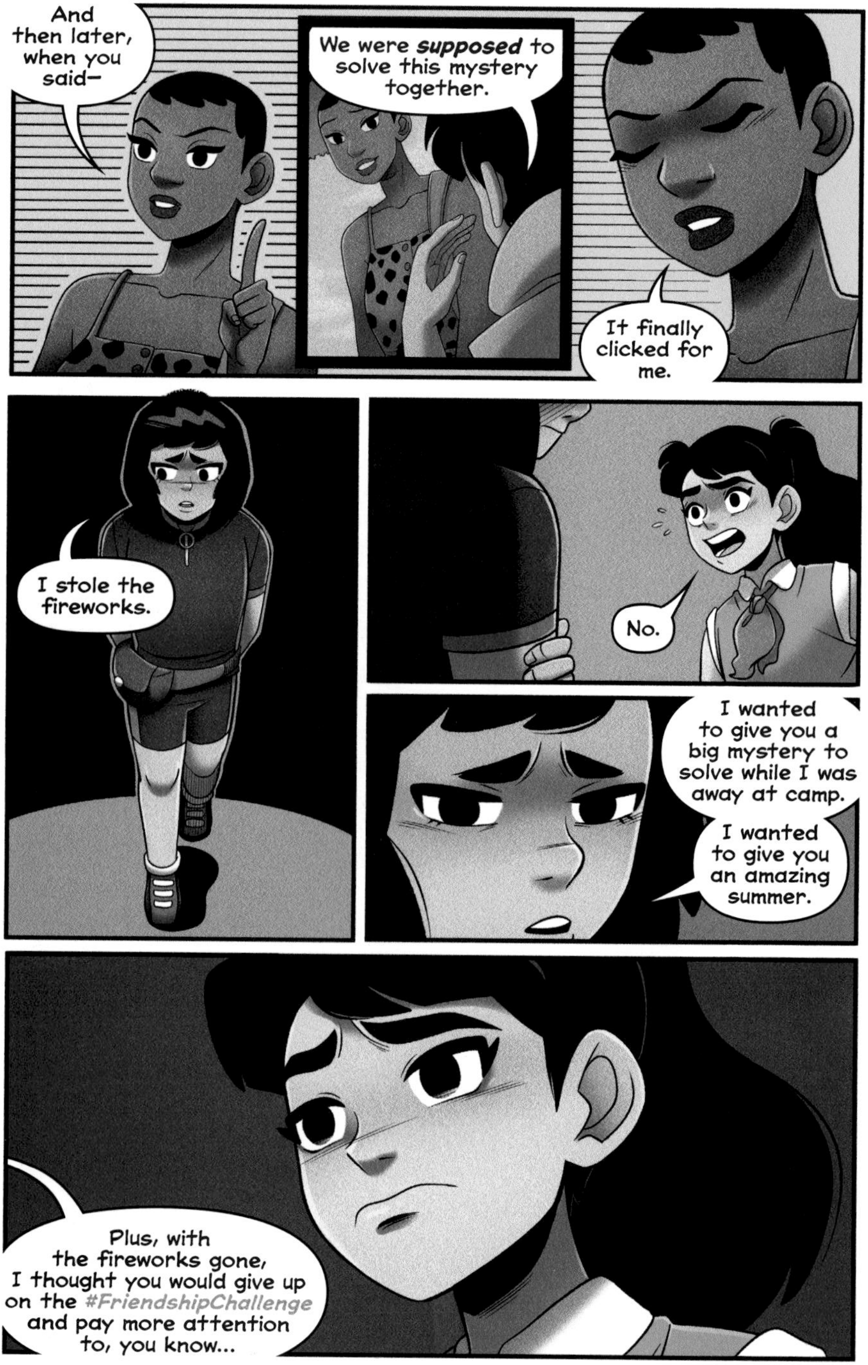
And then later, when you said–
We were *supposed* to solve this mystery together.
It finally clicked for me.
I stole the fireworks.
No.
I wanted to give you a big mystery to solve while I was away at camp.
I wanted to give you an amazing summer.
Plus, with the fireworks gone, I thought you would give up on the #FriendshipChallenge and pay more attention to, you know...

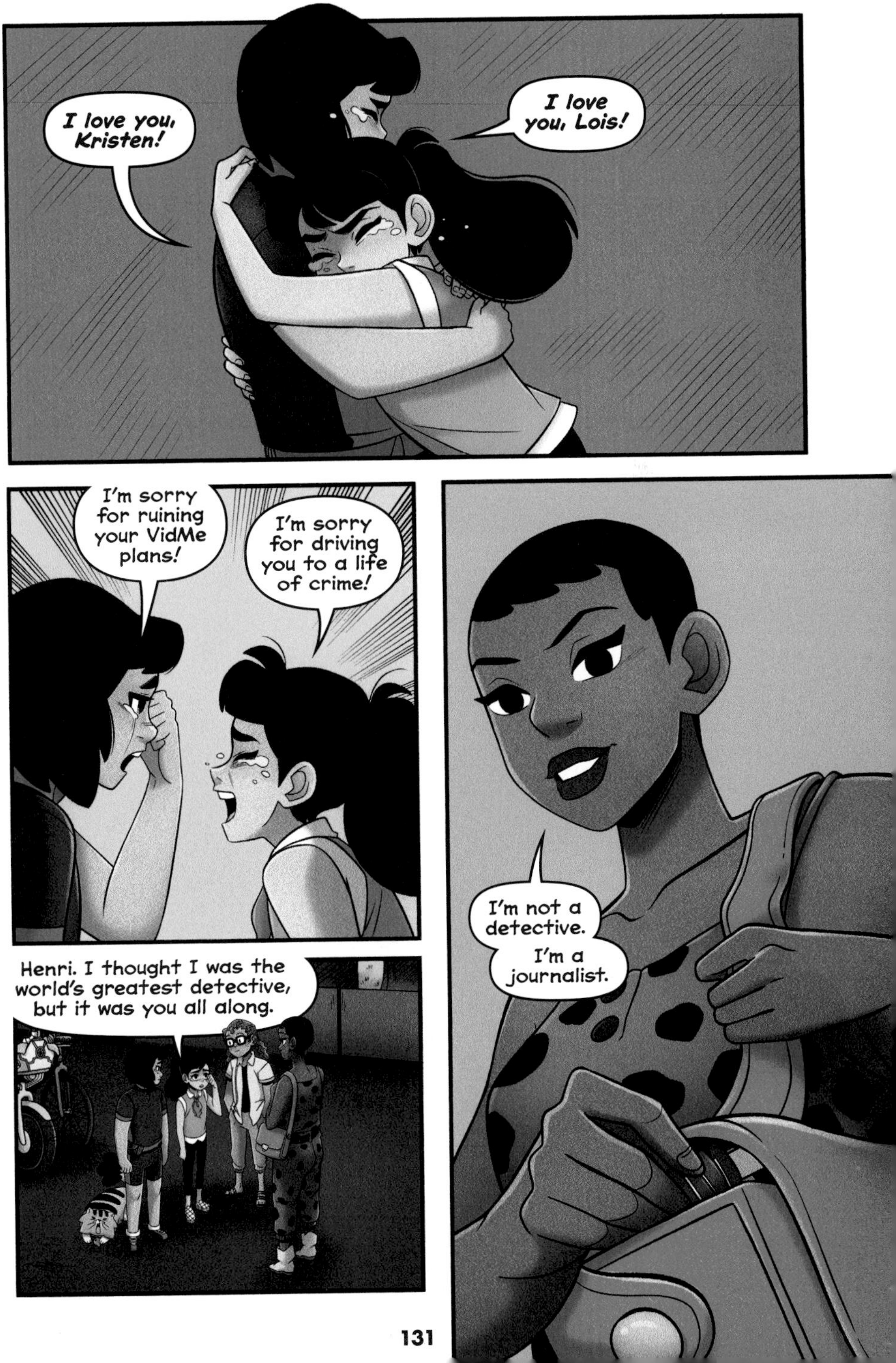
I love you, Kristen!
I love you, Lois!
I'm sorry for ruining your VidMe plans!
I'm sorry for driving you to a life of crime!
Henri. I thought I was the world's greatest detective, but it was you all along.
I'm not a detective.
I'm a journalist.

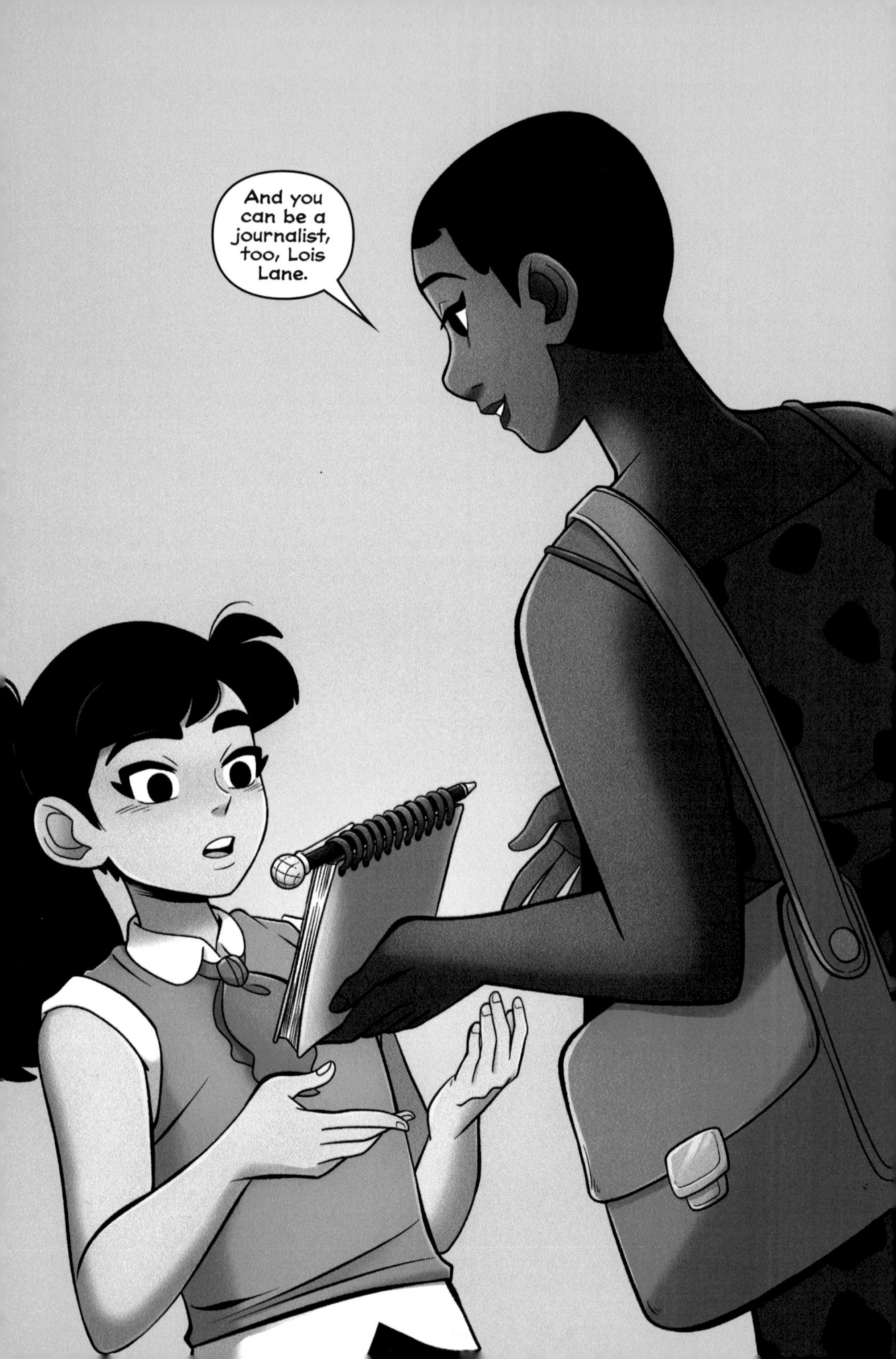
And you can be a journalist, too, Lois Lane.

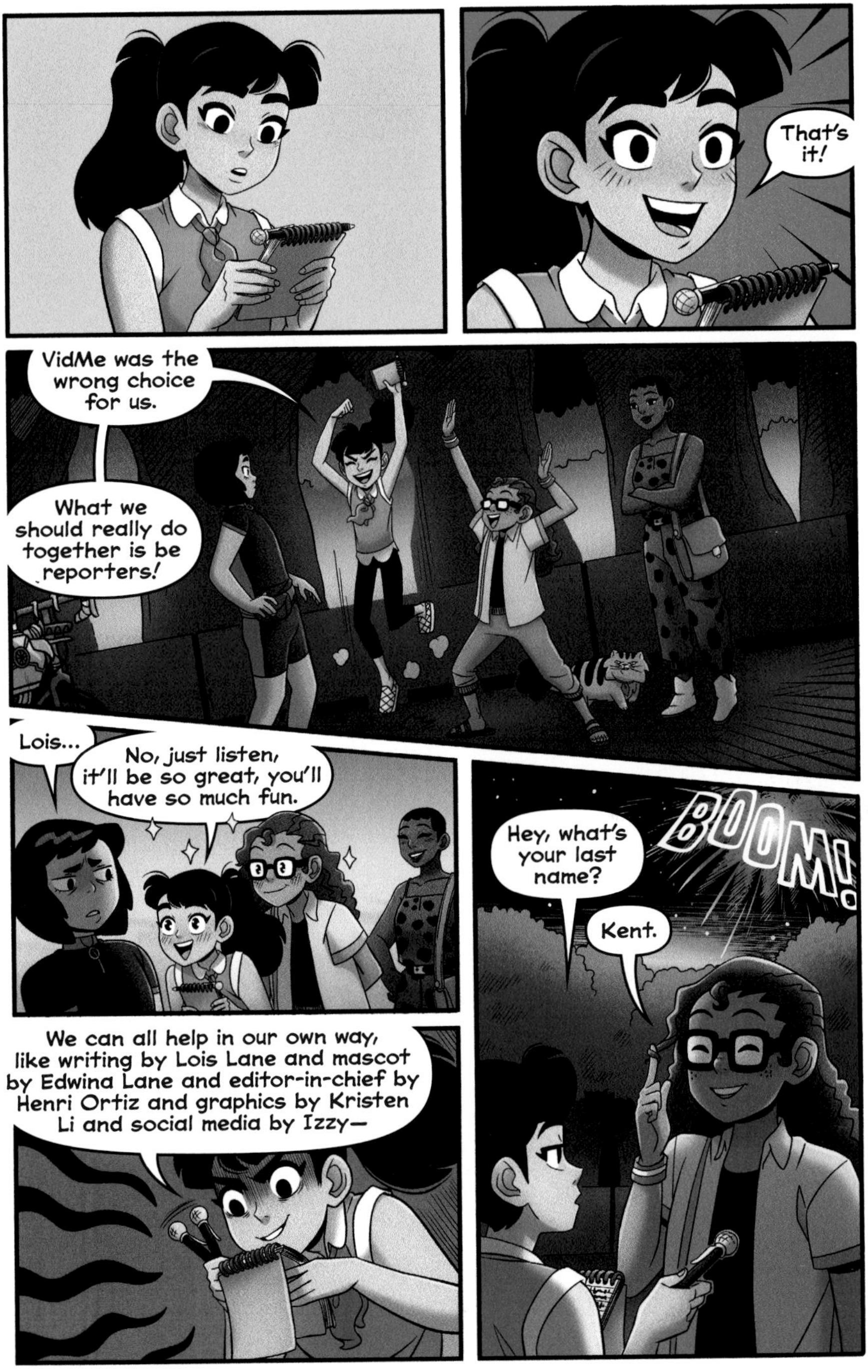
That's it!
VidMe was the wrong choice for us.
What we should really do together is be reporters!
Lois...
No, just listen, it'll be so great, you'll have so much fun.
We can all help in our own way, like writing by Lois Lane and mascot by Edwina Lane and editor-in-chief by Henri Ortiz and graphics by Kristen Li and social media by Izzy—
BOOM!
Hey, what's your last name?
Kent.

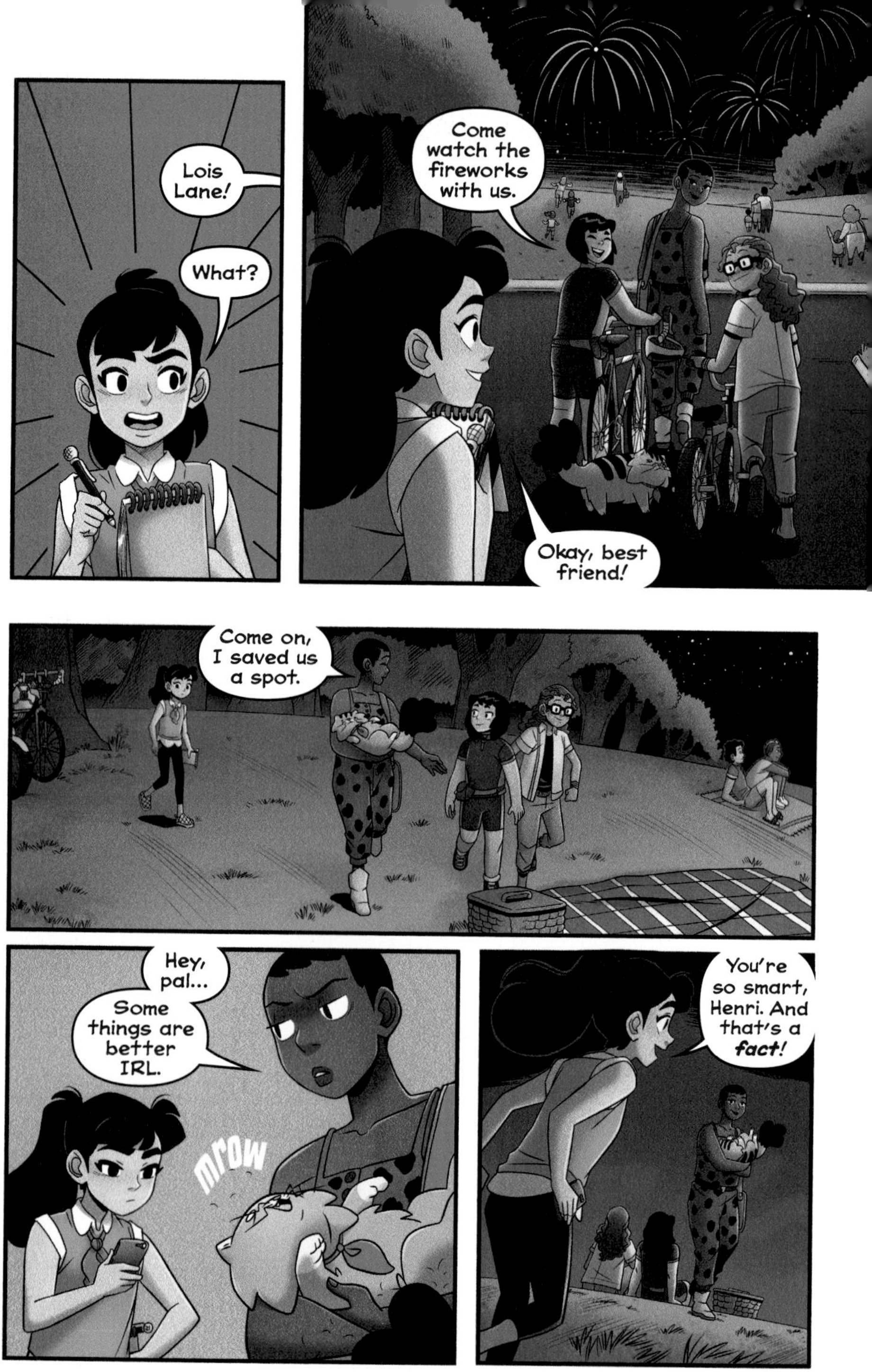
Lois Lane!
What?
Come watch the fireworks with us.
Okay, best friend!
Come on, I saved us a spot.
Hey, pal...
Some things are better IRL.
mrow
You're so smart, Henri. And that's a *fact*!

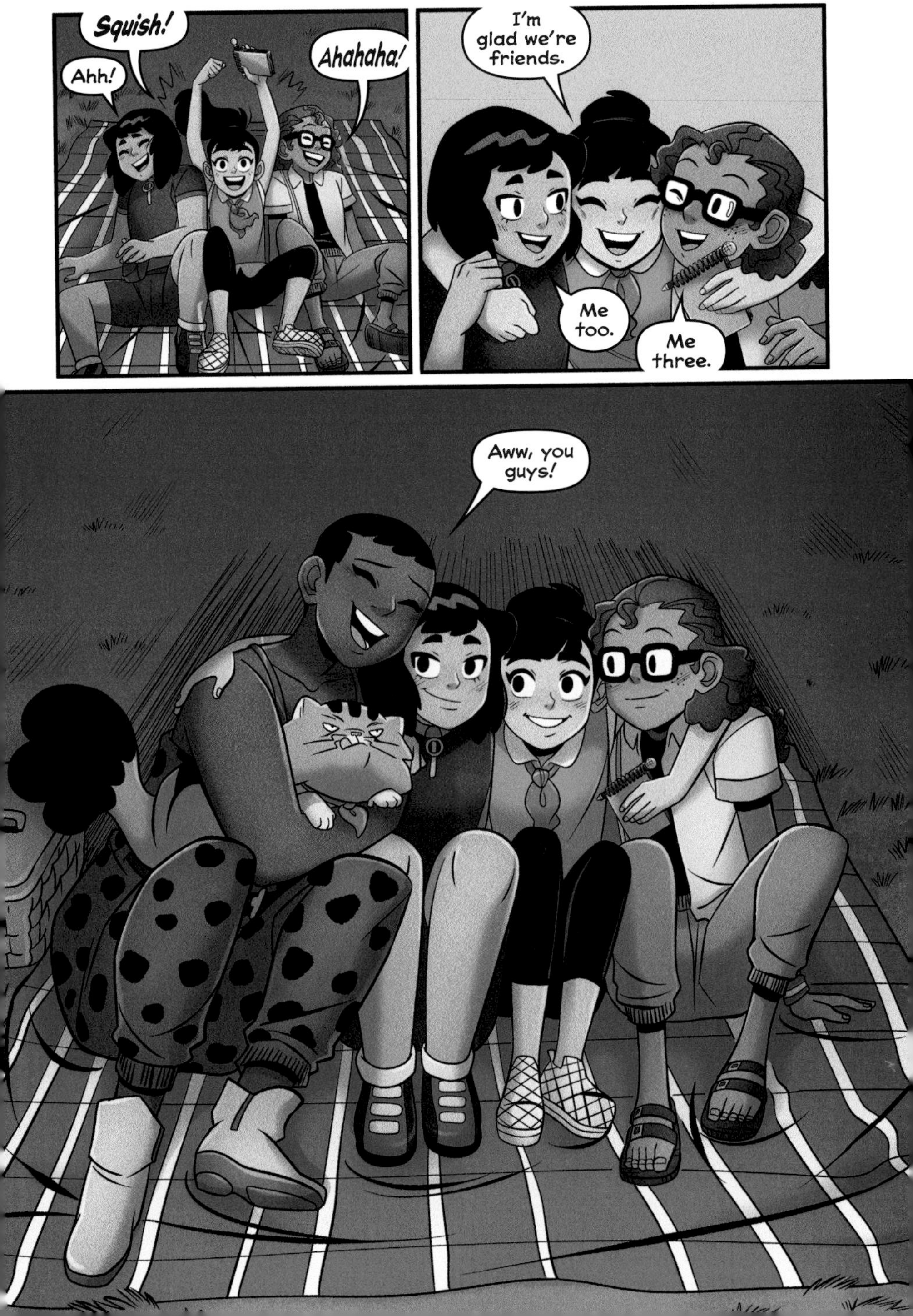
Squish!
Ahh!
Ahahaha!
I'm glad we're friends.
Me too.
Me three.
Aww, you guys!

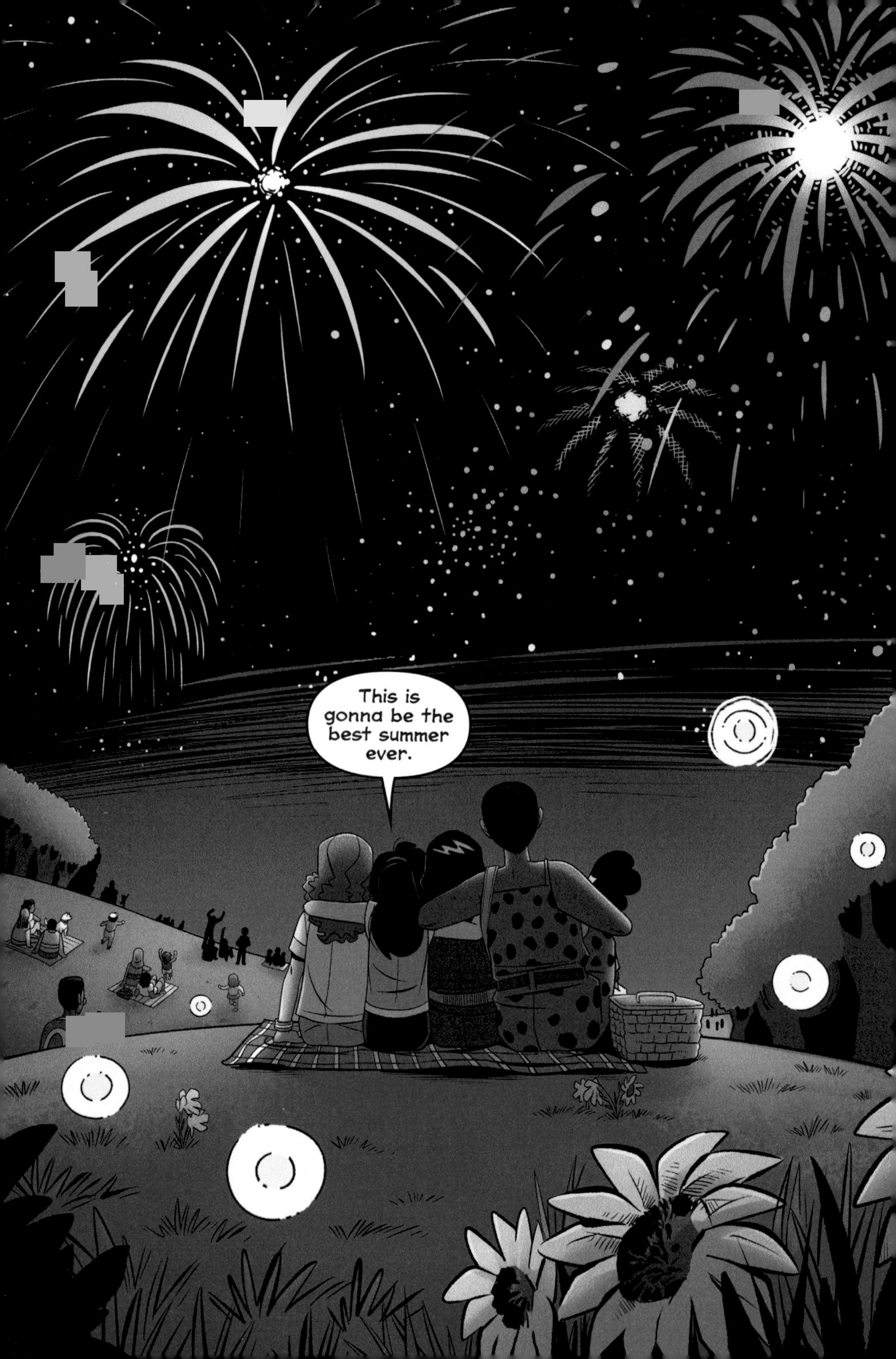
This is gonna be the best summer ever.

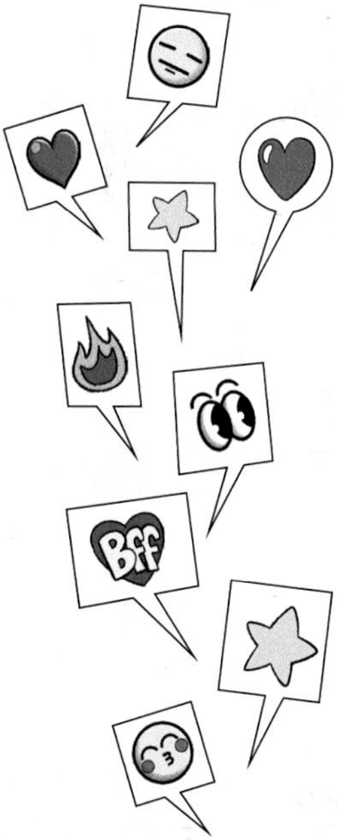
Bff

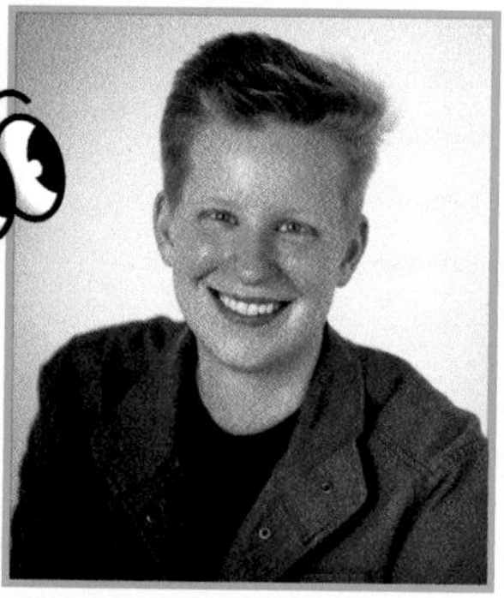

PHOTO BY EMMA PARKER

GRACE ELLIS is the *New York Times* bestselling and GLAAD Media Award-winning author of *Lumberjanes* (Boom! Studios), *Moonstruck* (Image), and the forthcoming Patricia Highsmith biography comic (Abrams Books). An Ohio native, Grace studied theater and journalism at Ohio State University. She enjoys reading the news and encourages you to support journalism however you can!

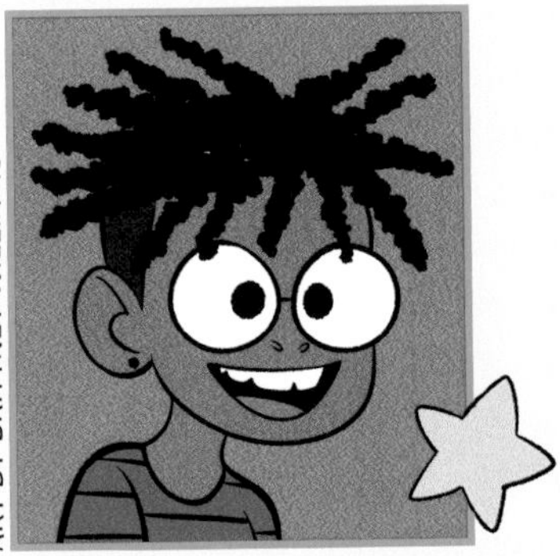

ART BY BRITTNEY WILLIAMS

BRITTNEY WILLIAMS is a storyboard and comic book artist who draws *a lot*. In 2012 she interned at Walt Disney Animation Studios as a storyboard artist. Since then, she's worked for a variety of animation studios and publishers including DC Comics, Cartoon Network, DreamWorksTV, Boom! Studios, and Marvel Comics. She's a two-time GLAAD Media Award nominee who exists to create things for kids and the queer community.

Artistry and super-heroics collide in this new superhero story!

"*Primer* is an action-packed, hilarious, and heartfelt debut. DC's newest superhero is totally unlike anything that's come before. *Primer* paints the town red...and blue and purple and double neon. Give me more, now!"
—Max Brallier, *New York Times* bestselling author of the *Last Kids on Earth* series

PRIMER

superhero
a graphic novel

Jennifer Muro & Thomas Krajewski
art by Gretel Lusky

Read on for a special sneak preview of this brand-new superhero from writers **Jennifer Muro** (Netflix's *The Last Kids on Earth*) and **Thomas Krajewski** (Netflix's *Buddy Thunderstruck*) and artist **Gretel Lusky**!

Available now!

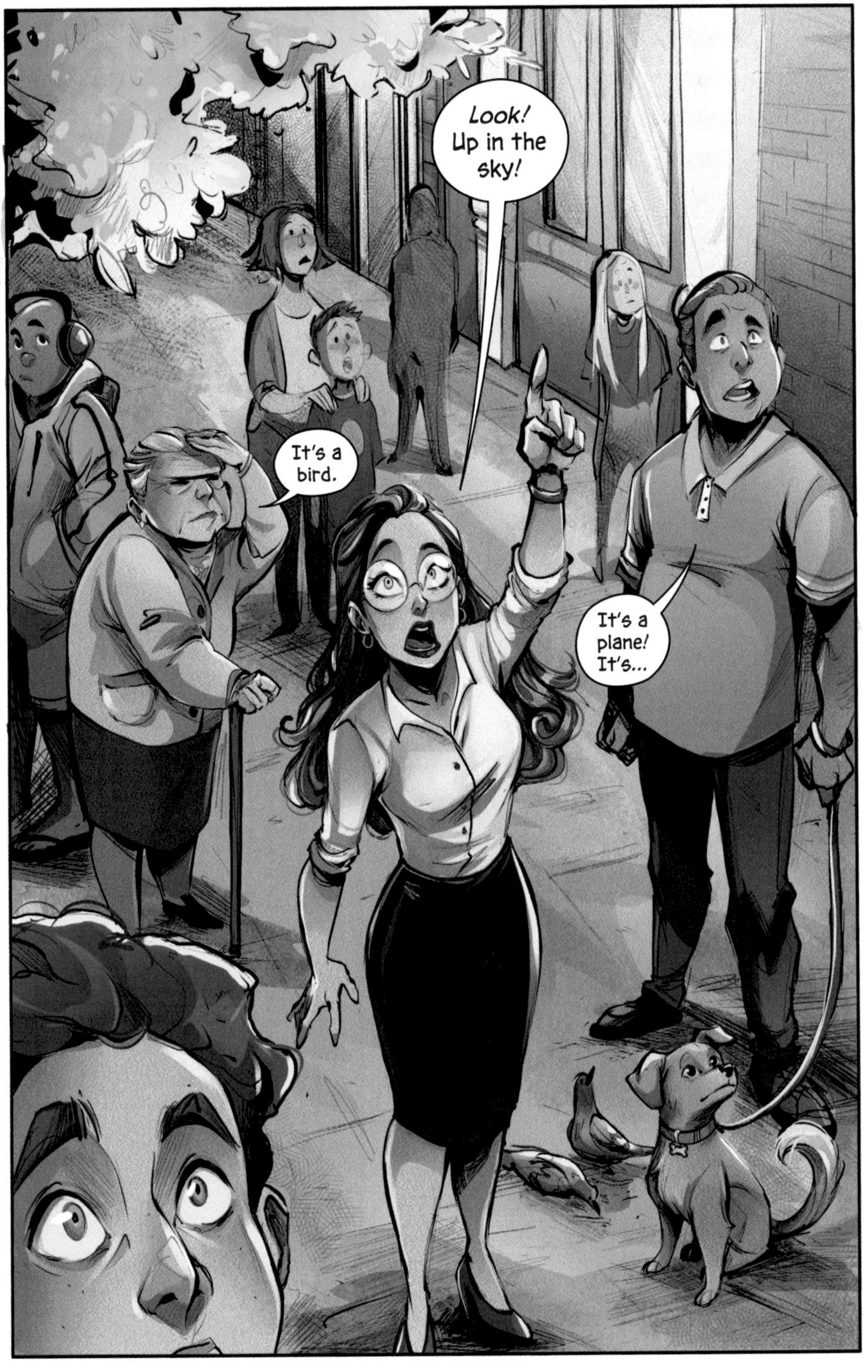
Look! Up in the sky!
It's a bird.
It's a plane! It's...

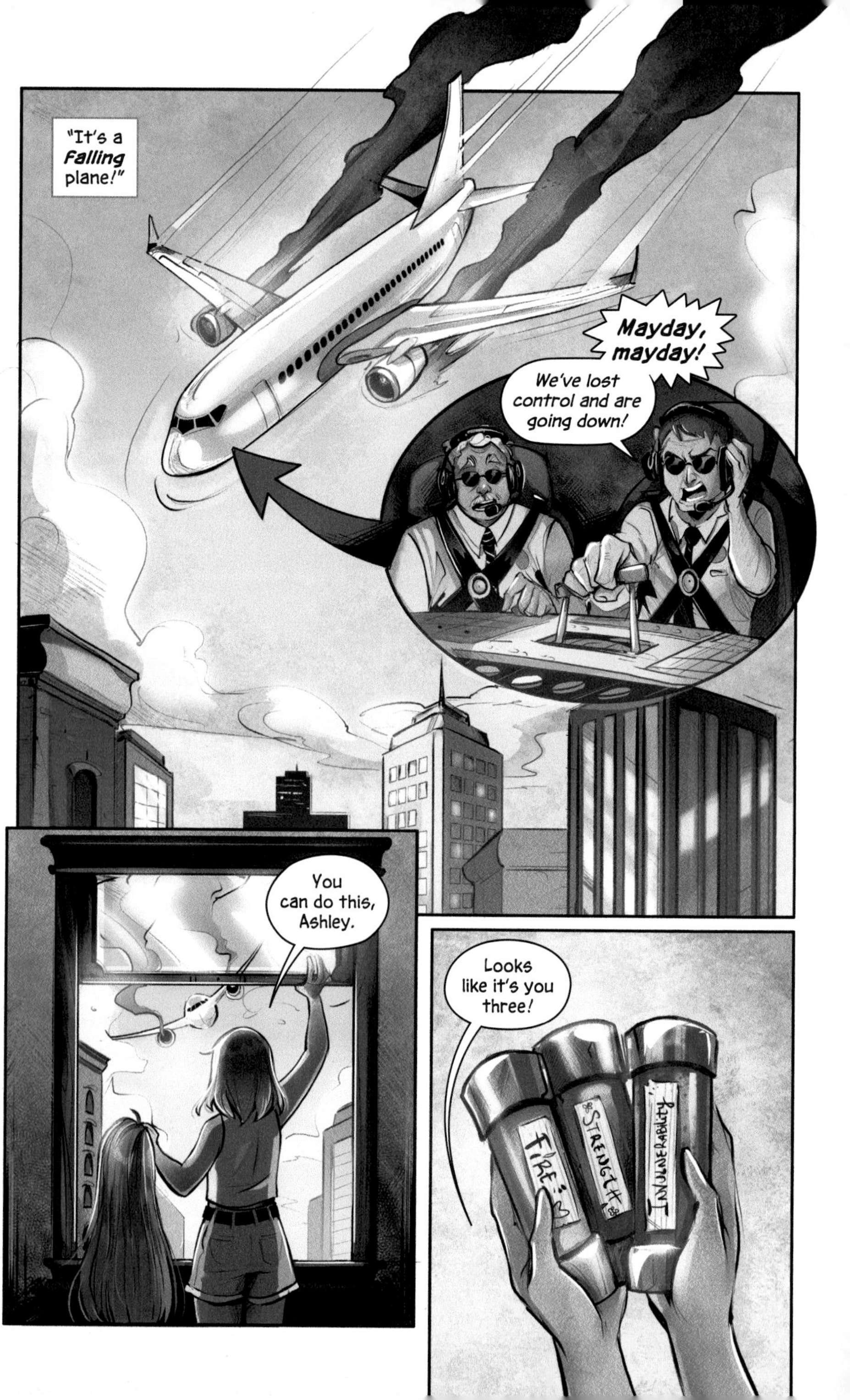
"It's a *falling* plane!"
Mayday, mayday!
We've lost control and are going down!
You can do this, Ashley.
Looks like it's you three!
FIRE
STRENGTH
INVULNERABILITY

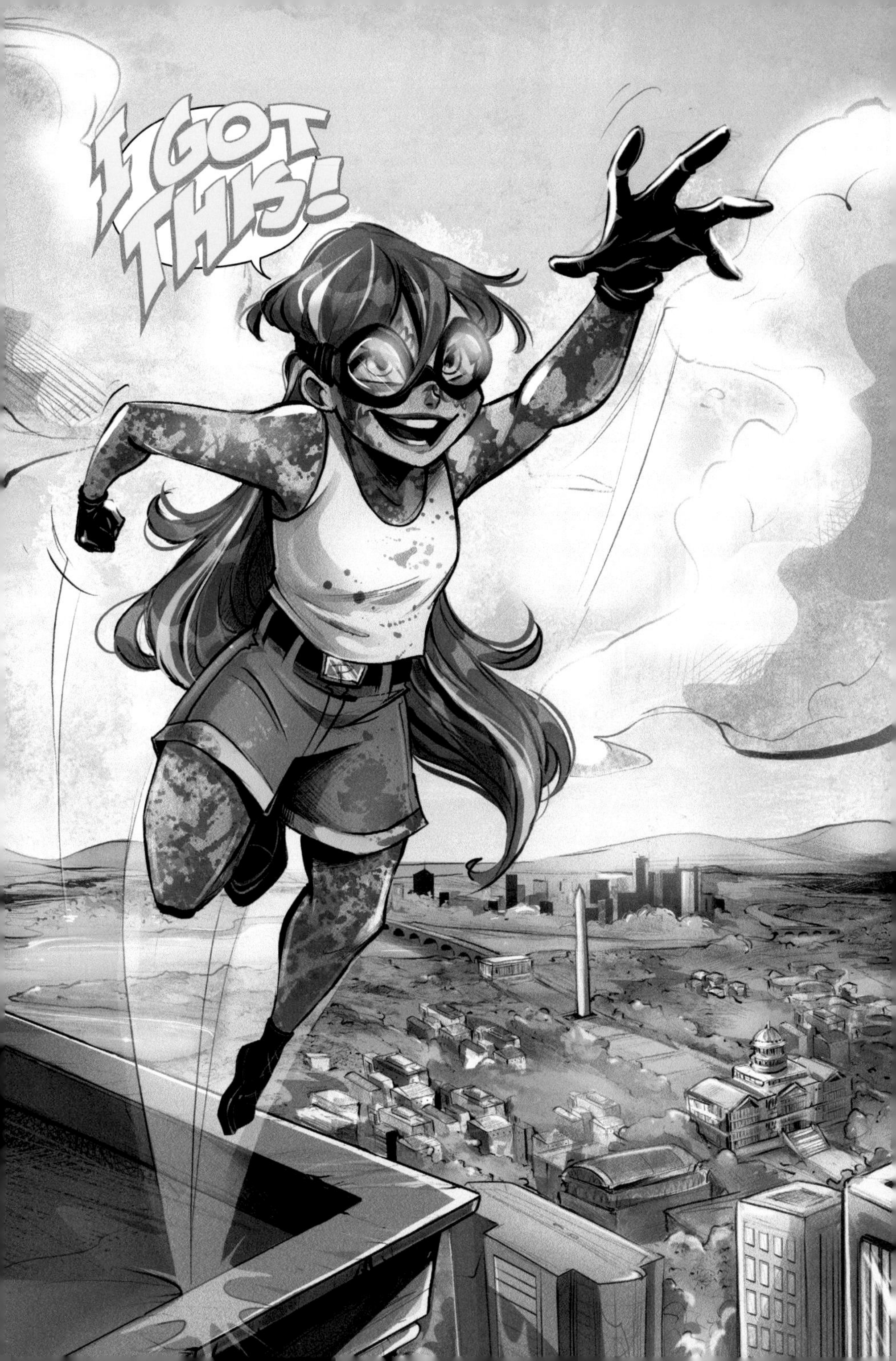
I GOT THIS!

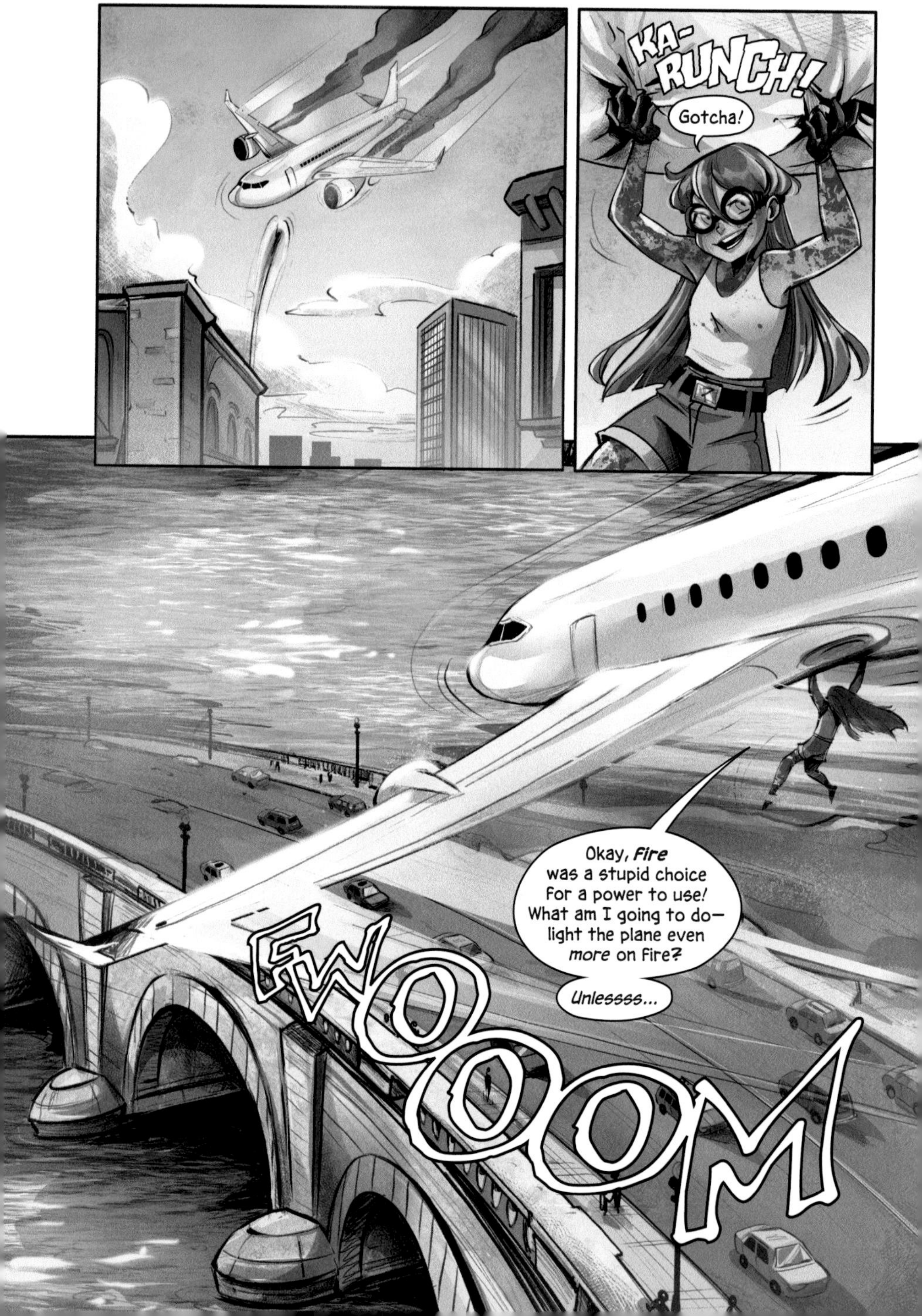
KA-RUNCH!
Gotcha!
Okay, *Fire* was a stupid choice for a power to use! What am I going to do— light the plane even *more* on fire?
Unlesss...
FWOOOOM

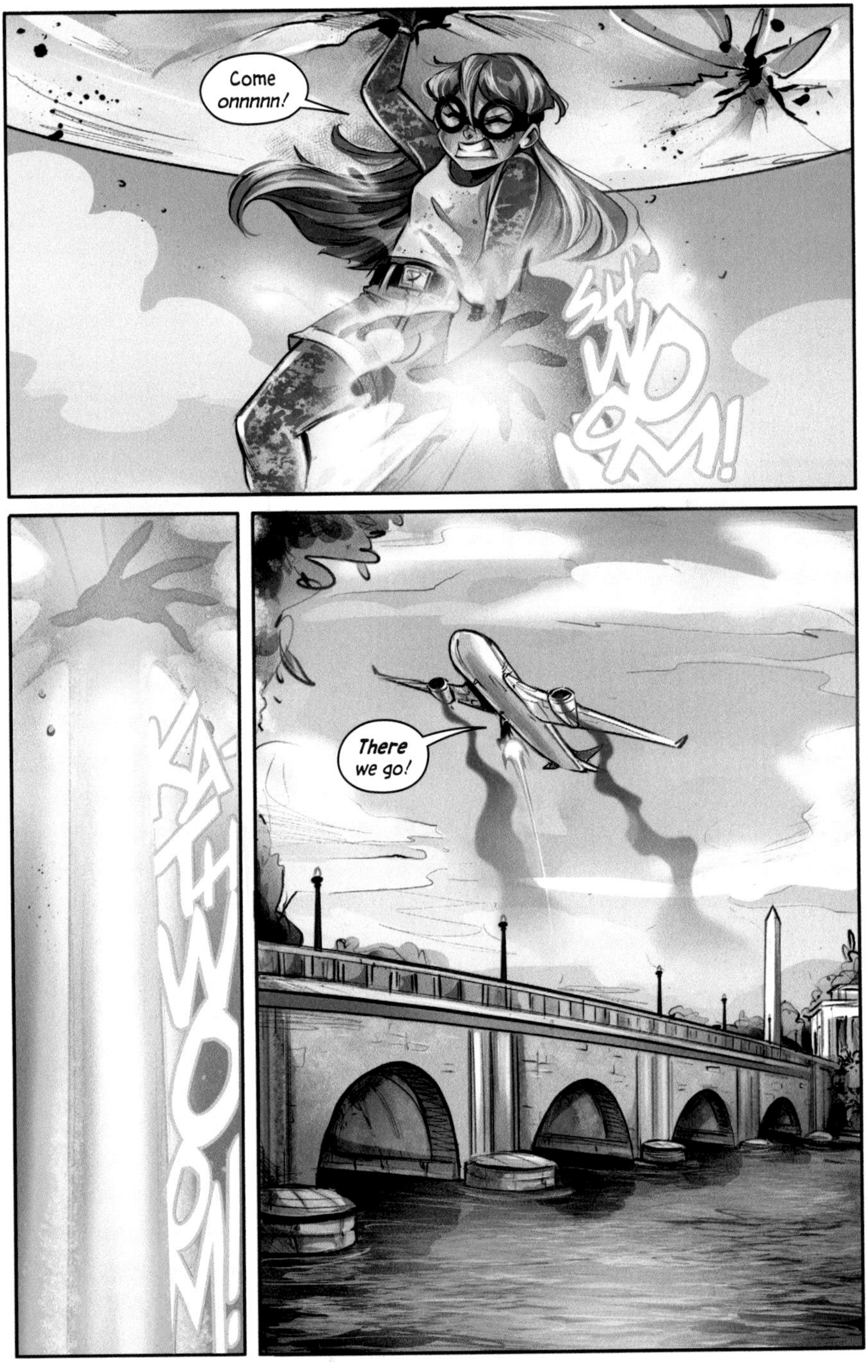
Come onnnnn!
SHWOOM!
KATHWOOM!
There we go!

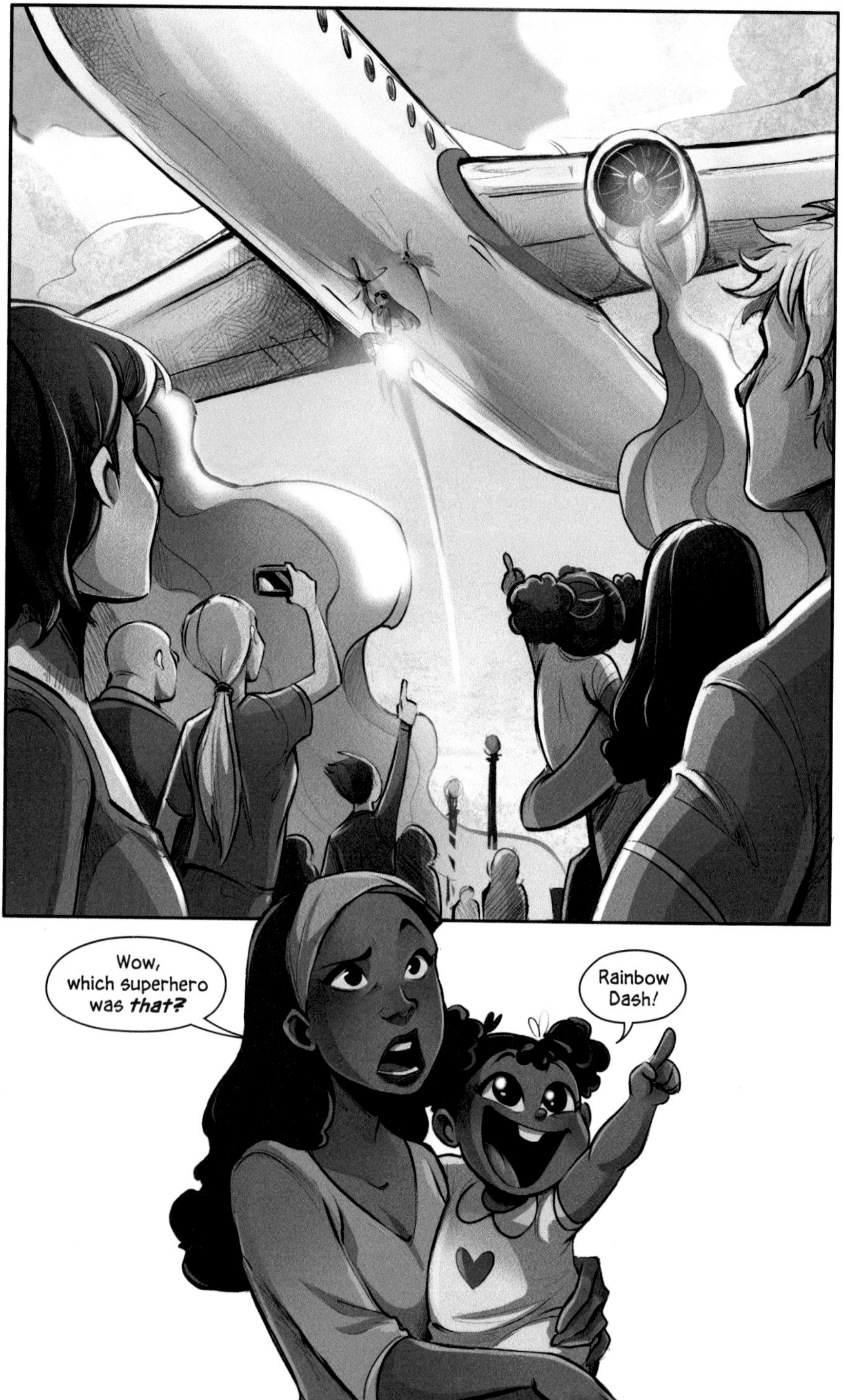
Wow, which superhero was *that?*
Rainbow Dash!

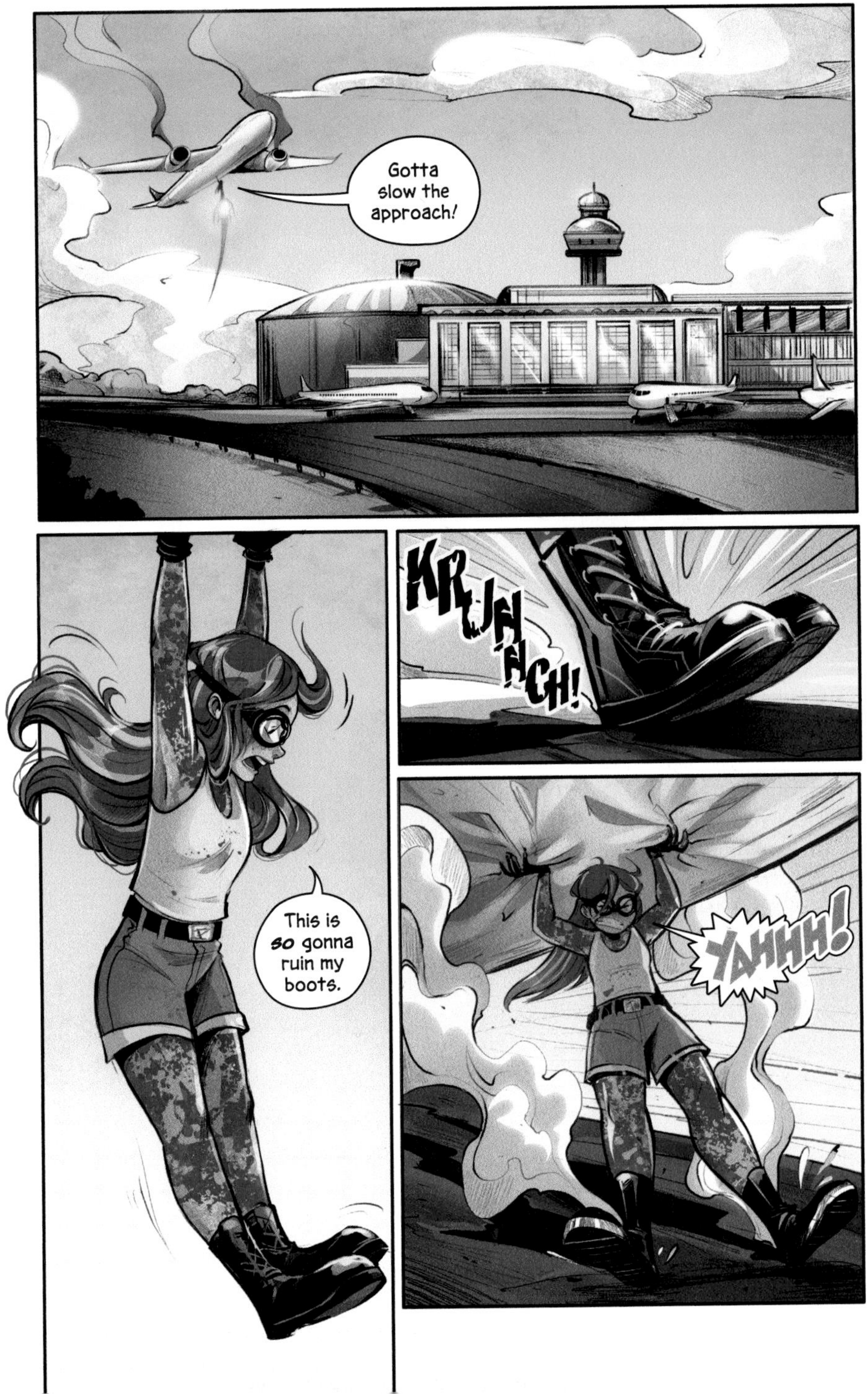

Gotta slow the approach!
This is *so* gonna ruin my boots.
KRUNCH!
YAHHH!

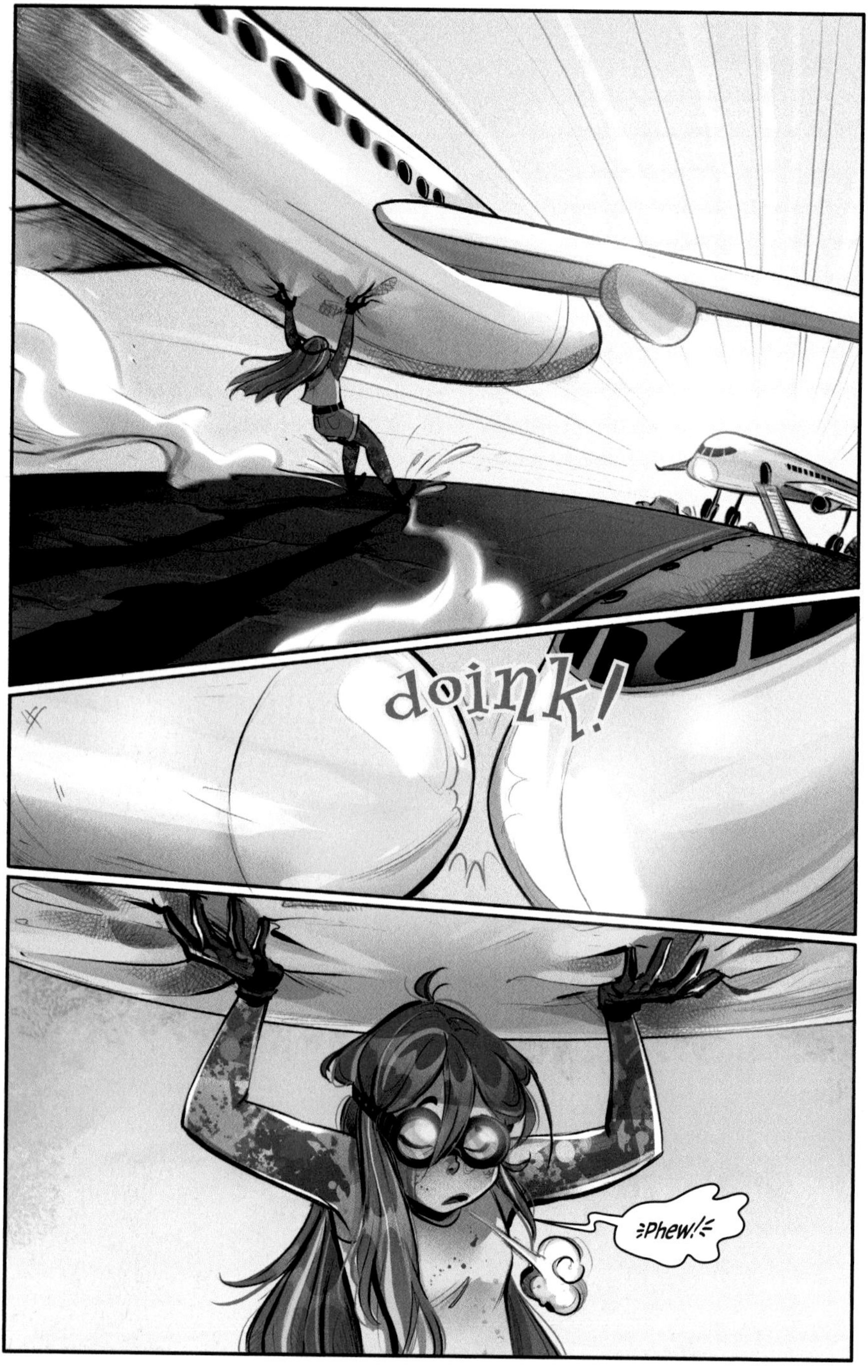
doink!
Phew!

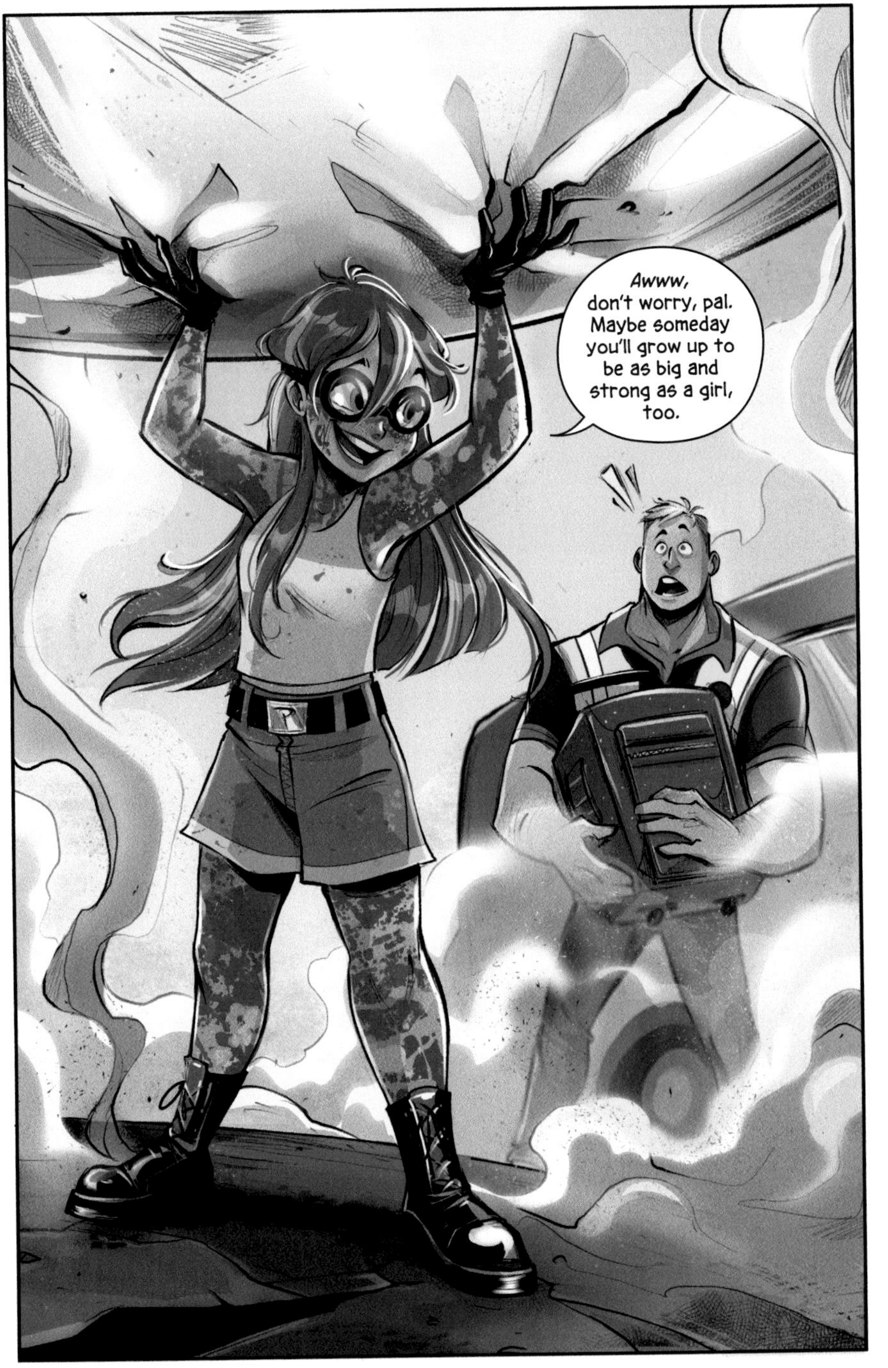
Awww, don't worry, pal. Maybe someday you'll grow up to be as big and strong as a girl, too.

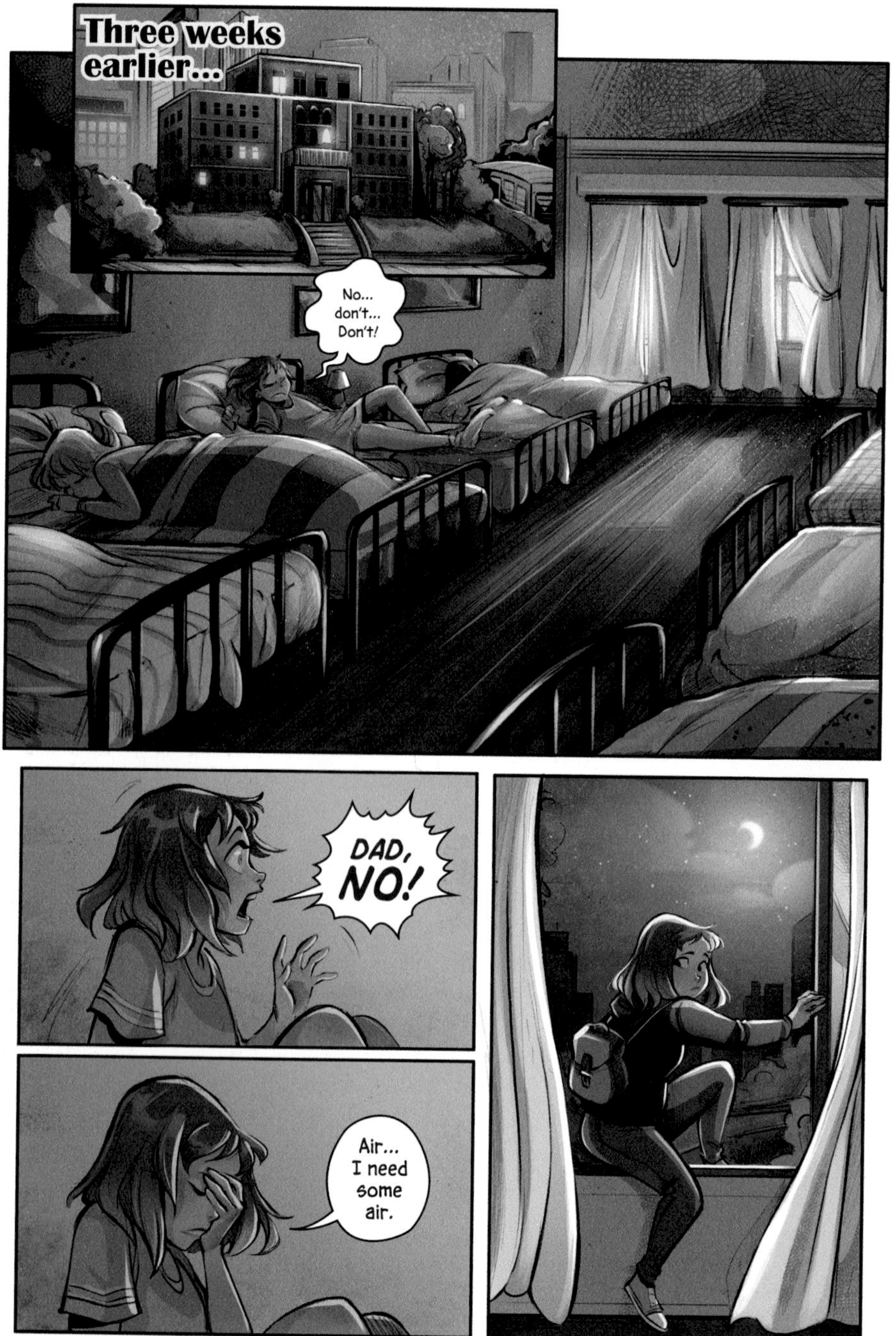

Three weeks earlier...
No... don't... Don't!
DAD, NO!
Air... I need some air.

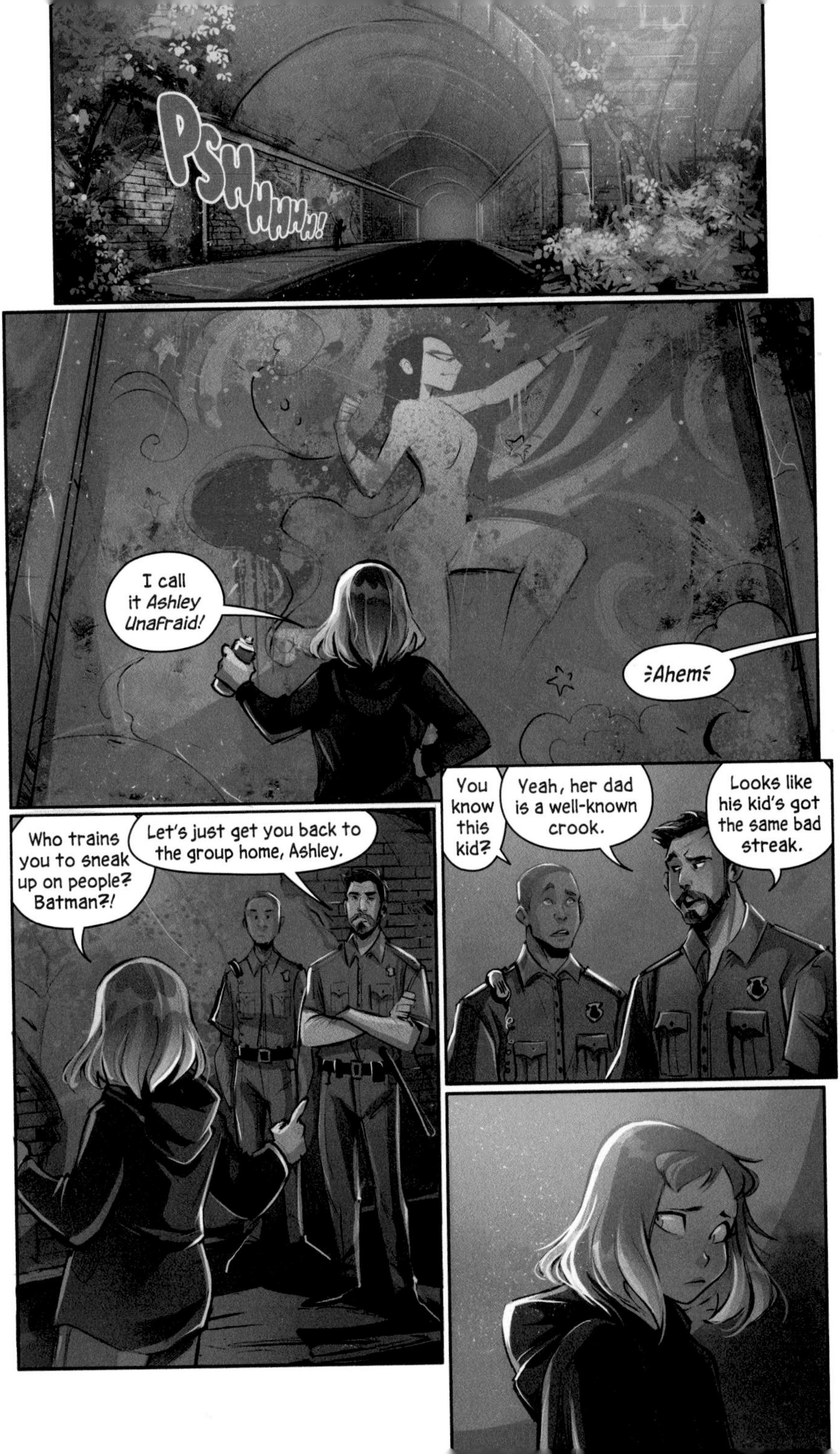
PSHHHHH!
I call it Ashley Unafraid!
Ahem
Who trains you to sneak up on people? Batman?!
Let's just get you back to the group home, Ashley.
You know this kid?
Yeah, her dad is a well-known crook.
Looks like his kid's got the same bad streak.

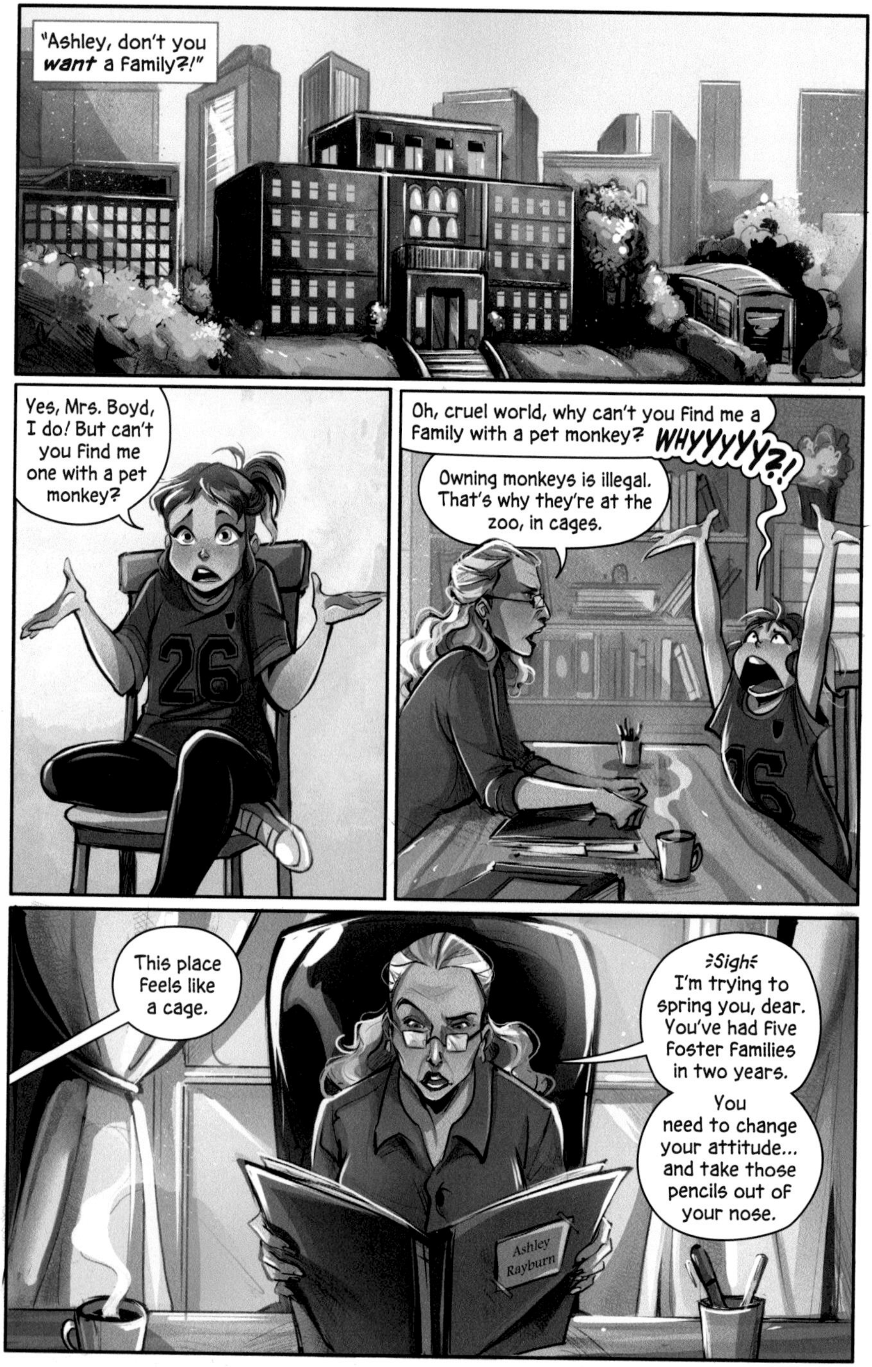
"Ashley, don't you *want* a family?!"
Yes, Mrs. Boyd, I do! But can't you find me one with a pet monkey?
Oh, cruel world, why can't you find me a family with a pet monkey?
WHYYYYY?!
Owning monkeys is illegal. That's why they're at the zoo, in cages.
This place feels like a cage.
Sigh
I'm trying to spring you, dear. You've had five foster families in two years.
You need to change your attitude... and take those pencils out of your nose.
Ashley Rayburn

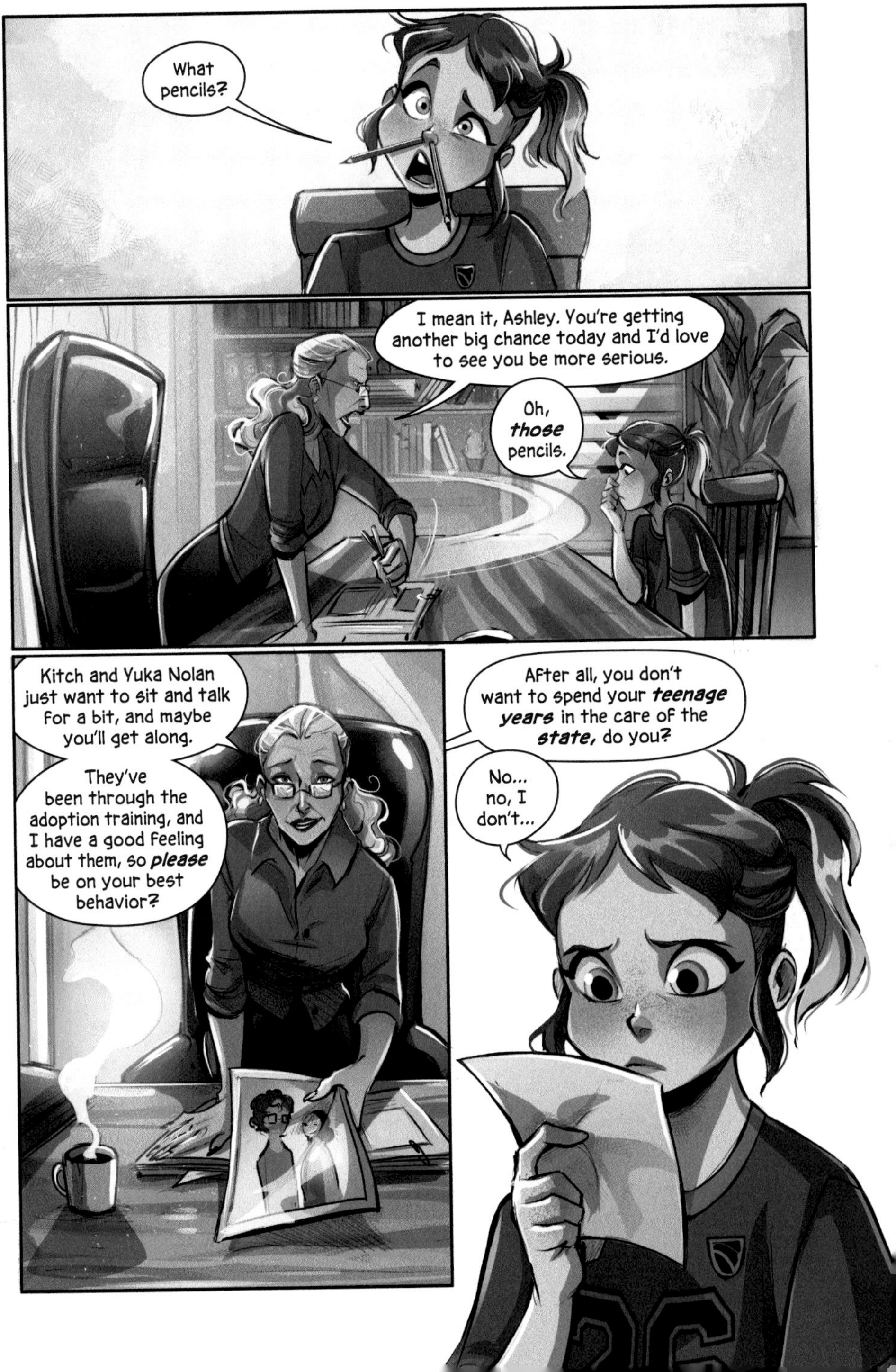
What pencils?
I mean it, Ashley. You're getting another big chance today and I'd love to see you be more serious.
Oh, *those* pencils.
Kitch and Yuka Nolan just want to sit and talk for a bit, and maybe you'll get along.
They've been through the adoption training, and I have a good feeling about them, so *please* be on your best behavior?
After all, you don't want to spend your *teenage years* in the care of the *state,* do you?
No... no, I don't...

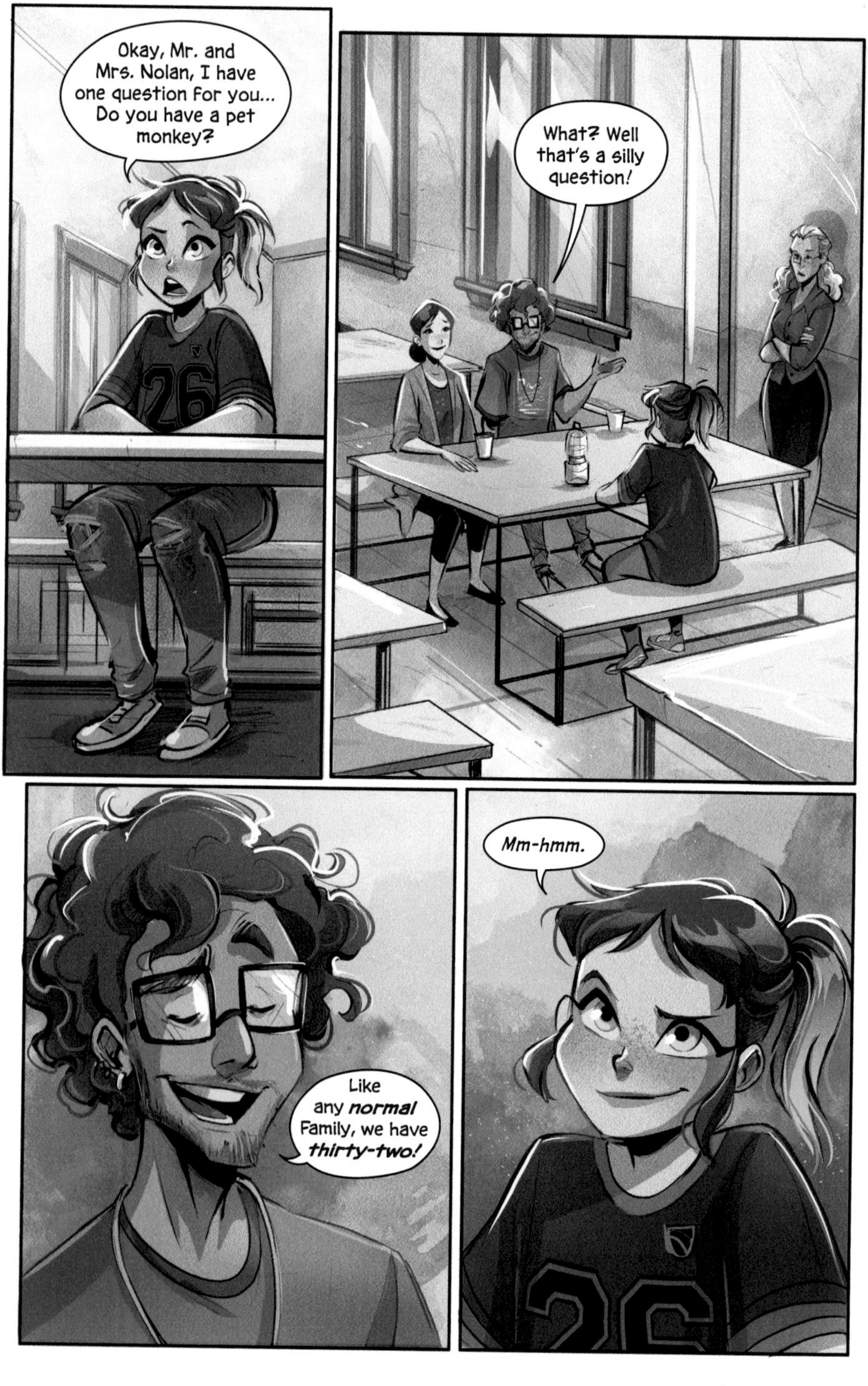
Okay, Mr. and Mrs. Nolan, I have one question for you... Do you have a pet monkey?
What? Well that's a silly question!
Like any **normal** family, we have ***thirty-two!***
Mm-hmm.

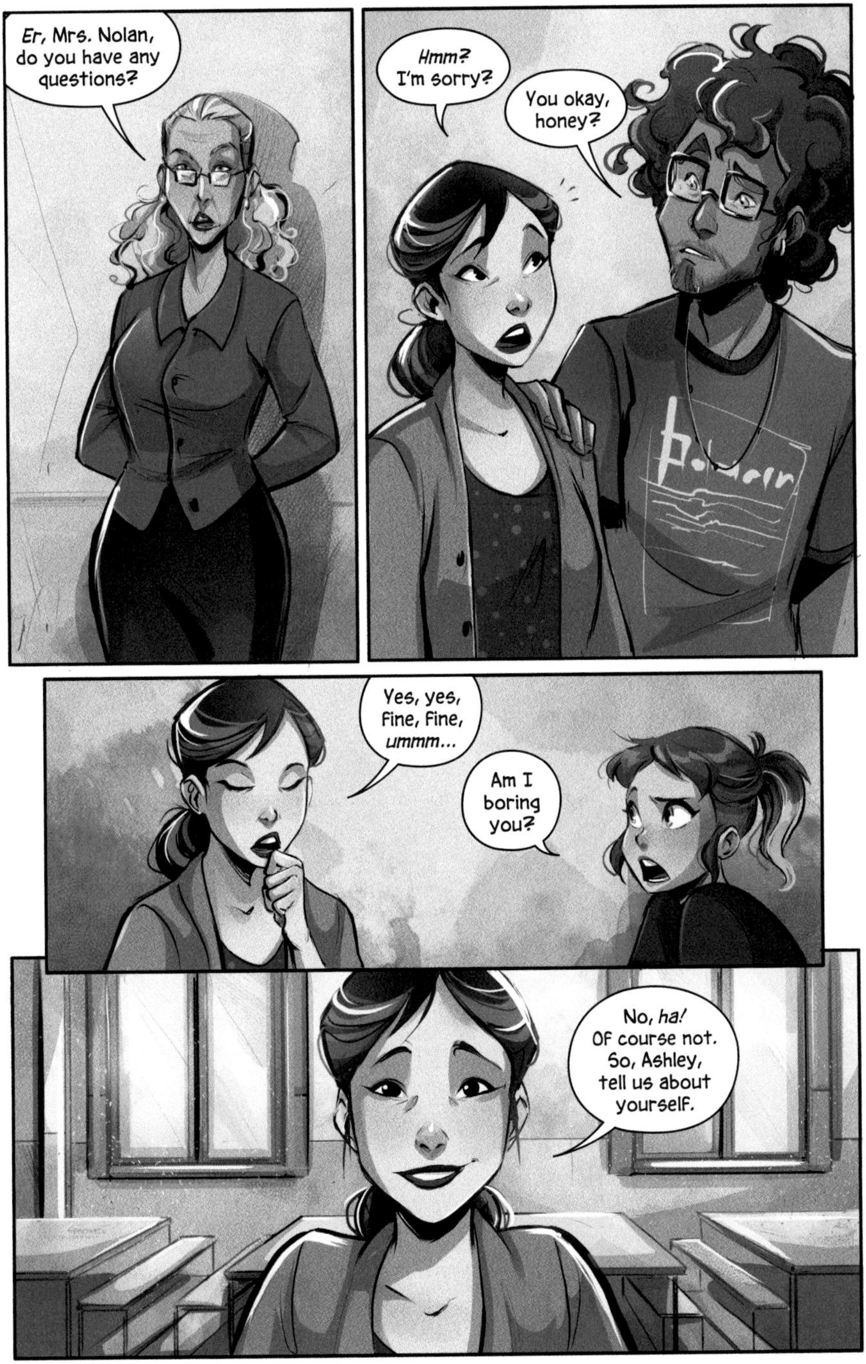
Er, Mrs. Nolan, do you have any questions?
Hmm? I'm sorry?
You okay, honey?
Yes, yes, fine, fine, *ummm*...
Am I boring you?
No, *ha!* Of course not. So, Ashley, tell us about yourself.

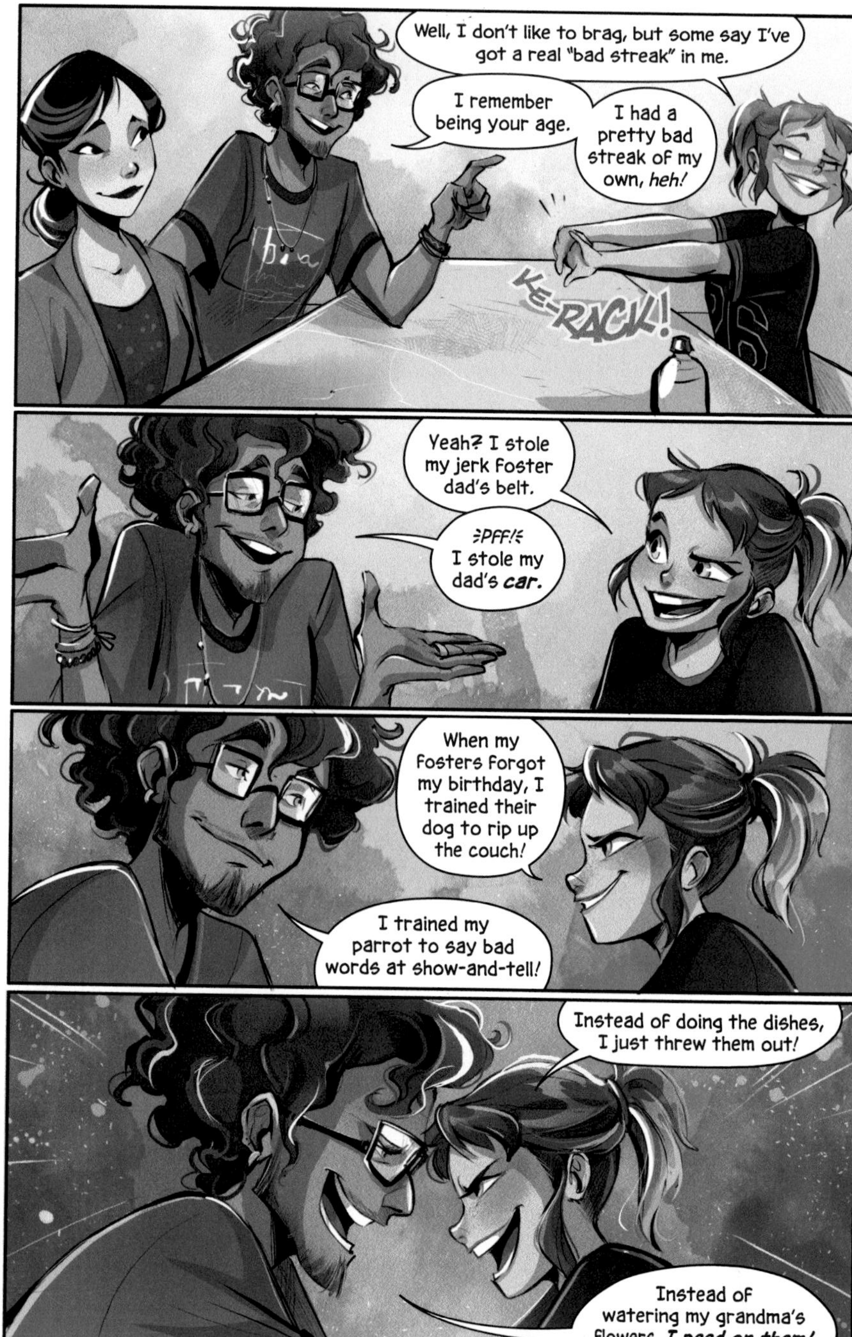
Well, I don't like to brag, but some say I've got a real "bad streak" in me.
I remember being your age.
I had a pretty bad streak of my own, *heh!*
KE-RACK!
Yeah? I stole my jerk foster dad's belt.
PFF!
I stole my dad's ***car.***
When my fosters forgot my birthday, I trained their dog to rip up the couch!
I trained my parrot to say bad words at show-and-tell!
Instead of doing the dishes, I just threw them out!
Instead of watering my grandma's flowers, ***I peed on them!***

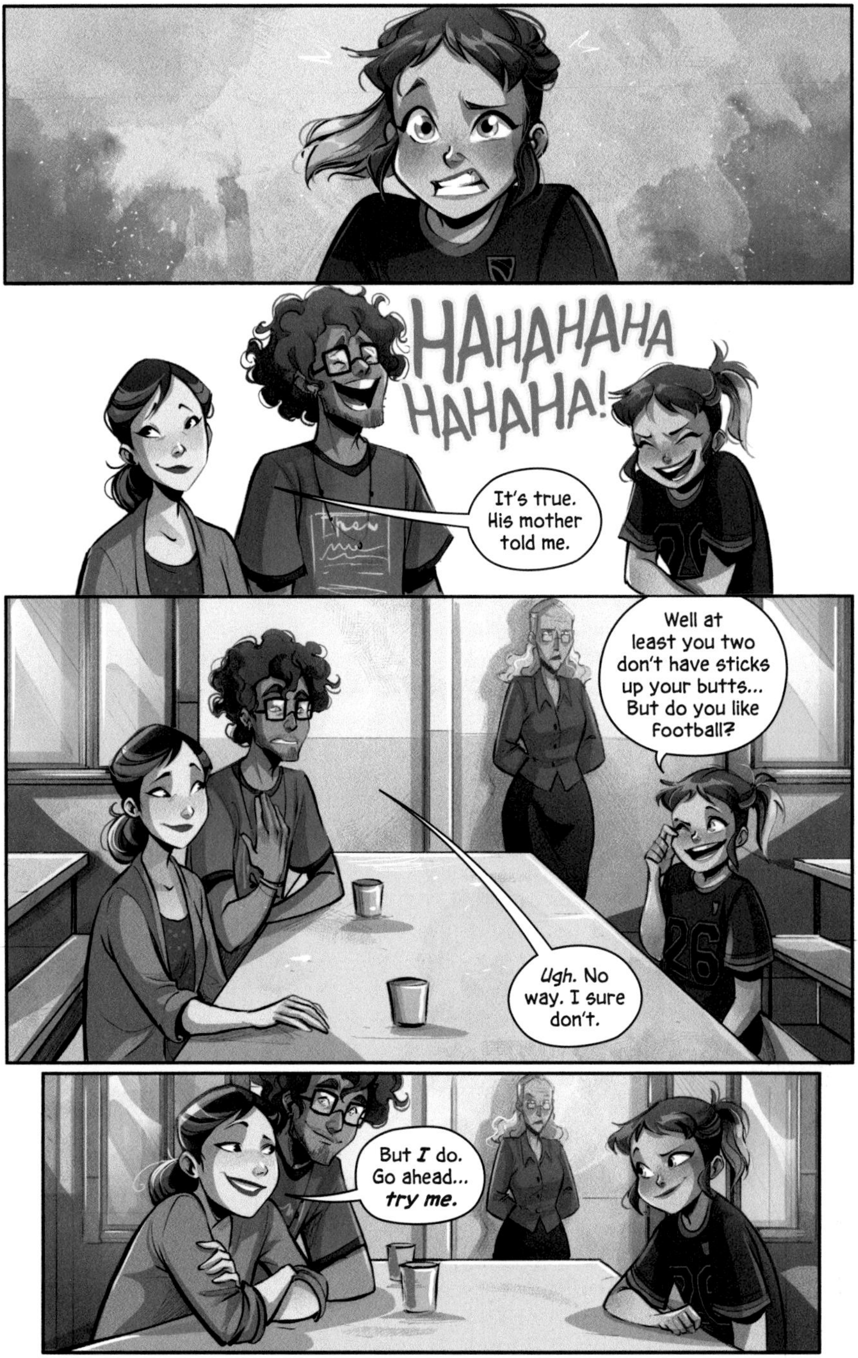
HAHAHAHA HAHAHA!
It's true. His mother told me.
Well at least you two don't have sticks up your butts... But do you like football?
Ugh. No way. I sure don't.
But *I* do. Go ahead... ***try me.***

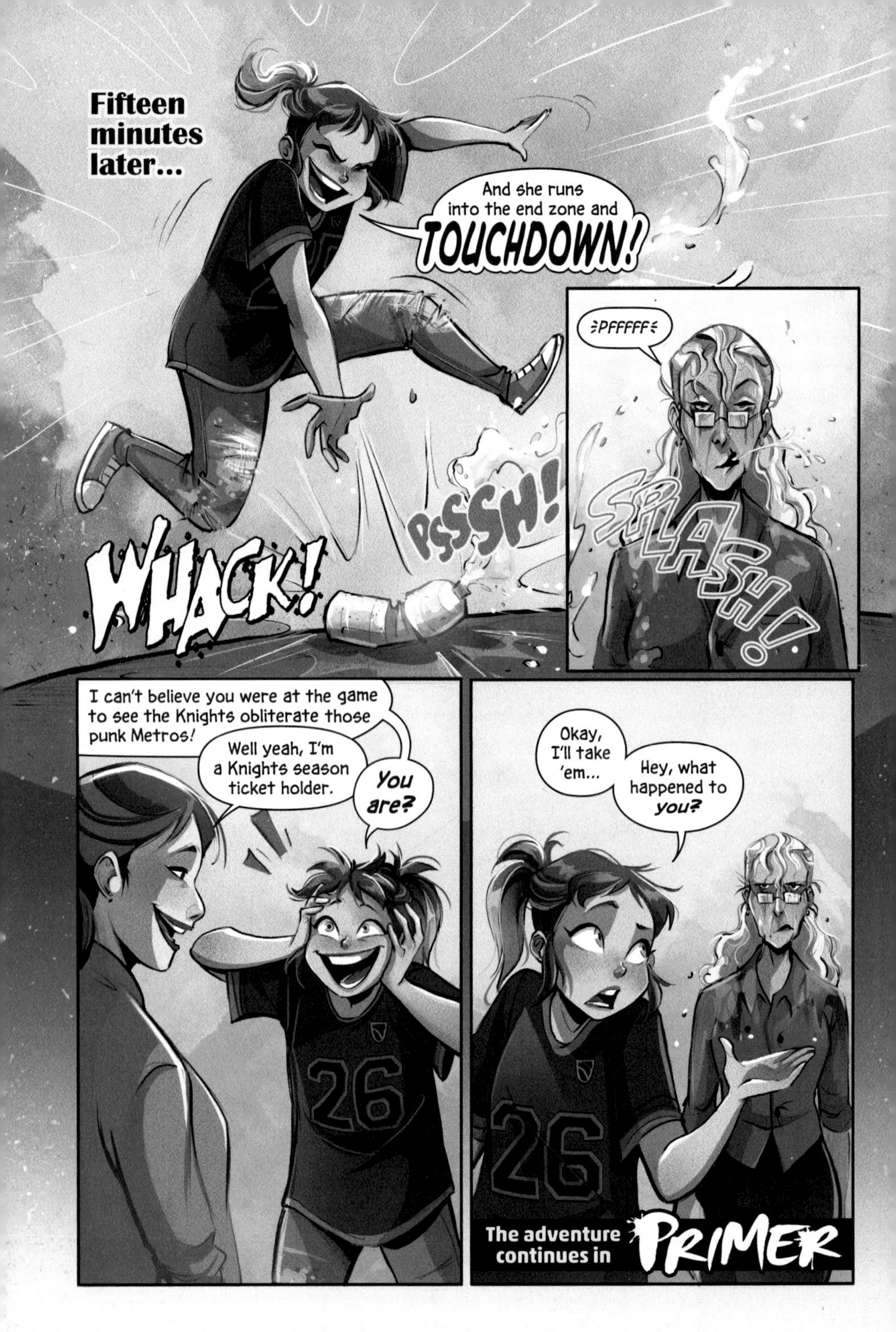
Fifteen minutes later...
And she runs into the end zone and TOUCHDOWN!
WHACK!
PSSSH!
PFFFFF
SPLASH!
I can't believe you were at the game to see the Knights obliterate those punk Metros!
Well yeah, I'm a Knights season ticket holder.
You are?
Okay, I'll take 'em...
Hey, what happened to you?
The adventure continues in PRIMER